Read or download *The Automation,* Vol. 1 of the Circo del
Herrero Series for free.

Learn more at: circodelherreroseries.com

Copyright © 2014
This edition copyright © 2016

This is a work of fiction. All places, events, and characters portrayed in this novel are fictitious
or used fictitiously (this includes BLA and GB GABBLER, who are characters in this novel,
based on no one). Further, the publisher does not claim any responsibility for author or third-
party website content, even if related to the novel at hand. Subtle variations may occur in the
manuscript depending on the format.

No animals were harmed in the making of this product. Except cats. We read aloud to them.
They didn't seem to like it.

CIP data pending.

Cover design by SOBpublishing. See end for credits.

All rights reserved, especially the one to call this book AWESOME.

Special thanks to Aeroplane Media and Julie Wallace for their help in the production of this
manuscript. The Automation, Vol 1. of the Circo del Herrero Series, copyright © 2010; print
edition published 2014.

Print:
ISBN-10: 0692157190
ISBN-13: 978-0-692-15719-0

Distributed by/through/from SOBpublishing.
Author's Dedication: "For the ones I lost like Bulfinch during the revisions of this novel."

[Circo del Herrero]

FAQ [Spoiler Edition]
Taken from work previously published at circodelherreroseries.com

What are your full names? Can't say, because it'd give away our genders. And that would give away several plot twists later in the series.

Why do the Editor and Narrator break the 4th wall so much? Because our work is a statement on the Author-as-God mindset (whether the Narrator realizes it or not). No one creates in a vacuum. There is no point to a story without an audience. Insert other excuses here.

Why have an Editor annotate the story? Because sometimes people need interpreters—not just on the language level, but on the reality level. Some say there are two sides to every story. We are living proof. Everything we do is a work in progress—we wanted you to KNOW more than one person has played their role in this. Stories overlap. There are different perspectives all saying the same thing.

Why do you guys use "s/he" or "he/she" at times when talking about each other? Why not use only gender-neutral pronouns such as "they/their"? That's a good point. The main reason was that the Narrator and I are cis-gendered. We didn't want to hijack a gender-neutral pronoun because, when we do finally reveal who we are, we didn't want it to seem like we were appropriating. It's not our pronoun and we wanted to respect those who do identify with they/their while still being vague enough to keep you guessing. But the use of they/their does that pretty well too. So, you may see us drop a few they/theirs in the series and newer editions. This was, originally, a plot decision. We were expressing that, on the gender spectrum, we do lean more heavily in a certain direction—unlike some of our future characters who *will* use a non-binary pronoun...

What is the REAL reason you guys collaborated on this series? Because we, like all couples, think each other are brilliant. That, and Gabbler doesn't want BLA to make a fool of themselves and therefore make Gabbler look bad by extension.

How'd the Narrator get the idea for this crap? Um, you clearly aren't paying attention here. BLA believes every word written.

Why is the story set in the U.S. — most of all, the SOUTH? Because natural gas? Subterranean fuel? F*ck if we know why Vulcan chose to stir sh*t up in the "melting pot." Probably because you have to scrape the bottom to keep it from sticking? IDK. I mean, who knows why he even has as statue in Alabama? There's no volcanoes around there, yet something is clearly attracting him...
[Because The Author of this series grew up in the Bible Belt and has a lot to say (sub-textually) in response to literature like *American Gods*, for instance.]

Why are there nine Automatons? Much like the nine Muses, it seems to work just fine.

But why doesn't this book mention Talos or any of the other automatons Hephaestus/Vulcan (may have) created? Why isn't there a greater use of pre-established mythology in this book? WHYYY? Slow down there, canon-hipster. Just because Talos isn't mentioned doesn't mean the story rejects that he or the others exist. This story just focuses on one batch Vulcan whipped up. If you wanted "old established myth," we suggest you go back to Hesiod and Homer. Or, gods forbid, maybe *Percy Jackson* is more your style. Have fun feeling smart about spotting the archetypes in *that* story.

Why does every chapter end in a slanty-name and a character list? Yes, we'll be upfront about the weirdness of it. Every chapter ends in a name and a list. Think it's a bit much? We wouldn't blame you. See (despite my best efforts to "free up" the chapters), our Narrator insisted. Our Narrator said (something to the effect of), "Like stanzas of a poem, the names create *form* for the novel." I, Gabbler, replied, "If poetry is your intent, then *why not write in verse*?" "Because I don't have f*cking time to write poetry! Is my writing not anal enough?" That's when I realized the Narrator's chapter "formula" was a great compromise. I'd kill myself if I had to edit iambic pentameter.

You said BLA is mute. How can they tell you ANYTHING? Like we said in Vol. I, the Narrator uses a computer to type to me. BLA is very good at typing. In fact, BLA typed most of this up and I, Gabbler, just edited it. And Annotated it. And censored it.

We already know Bulfinch is a male cat. And if the Narrator – BLA – is Bulfinch, then isn't it...safe to assume BLA is male? Well, if you *believe* our Narrator, then the gender question should be the least of your worries. I'd worry more about how a cat can turn into a human and write AN ENTIRE NOVEL. I know I, Gabbler, do.

[BLA and GB GABBLER are characters in this story.

This novel was written by one person, not two.

All other brackets are GABBLER's.]

[The Blacksmith's Circus]

Contents:

[The Blacksmith's Circus]

The Annotated Manuscript: The Pre-programming: BOOK TWO & THREE

Vol. 2 of the Blacksmith's Circus Series

By B.L.A., the Narrator, Storyteller, Feline

&

G.B. Gabbler, the Editor, Annotator, Enabler...

[The Blacksmith's Circus]

The Annotated Manuscript: The Pre-programming: BOOK TWO

Preface,

Freedom isn't free, but neither is slavery:

Is it OK if we put our prologue in the right place this time?[1]

So, the last book dealt with Freedom, if you care to remember (not that you should, because that's my job, *remembering*—I'm the one recounting *my* ~~history~~, after all). Gabbler will probably edit that part out, but I don't care.[2]

The Freedom therein implied—if you even picked up on it (and of course you did, because I wasn't too subtle)—was the lack thereof. Automatons have the least of it, don't they? Not that they really *know* to want it. They cannot want. Not for themselves. Their Masters might want freedom for them—might want them to want. But it doesn't work like that.

I could go on and on about how unjust, complex, and depressing the whole issue is—even for humans (poor humans, always mulling over such mortal-minded

---

[1] **Editor's foreword,**
Not that it will do much good:
How much is too much setup?

Dear Doubters and Believers,
All footnotes are the Editor's (I'm the Editor, G. B. Gabbler). This is to help the reader better grasp the Narrator (who is not me, because, once again, I am the Editor). Also, for the sake of prudence, some names, certain locations, and various details have been purposefully made as vague as I please (or perhaps haven't) to keep the story unbogged with "unimportant" details. This is volume two in our series. Enjoy the continued storyline, picking up right where it left off (so, yes, please read the first one). Also, hello again. Glad you're back.
-G. B. Gabbler
[2] No, I won't completely edit out our Narrator's madness. I won't hide it for our Narrator anymore. I *will* make my presence known. I would never leave you alone—wouldn't abandon you like that.

dilemmas as if it helps). However, I think you already get the point. Which leads me to my *next* point.

Slavery.

Freedom creates slaves. We are slaves to free will. We're all slaves to our choices. Just like I'm choosing to write this book, here, despite the fact Gabbler thinks I'm insane for *believing* in it—believing this book is my own ~~history~~.[3]

Speaking of books, where'd I leave off in my last one? Gabbler pried it from this dilettante's grasp before I could put any real finishing touches to it. Gabbler's always in such a hurry. Mortals usually are. But back to that ending, here. You may wonder how a person like me—a person who claims to be not only divine but a cat—can be typing this out now? I've been getting many questioning letters from readers, trying to make sense of it all. The smarter of you will guess that maybe Bulfinch was—will be—given an Automaton; that this is how I, Bulfinch, am able to type out these memories and interact on such a human level. Perhaps this is even, say, why I am mute? Like Mecca, it could be that my "language" is a bit off...

But I tell you it is much weirder than that. Though, what fanfiction could be done with it! I'd terribly love to read it—how it *could* have happened. I do think Vulcan Himself would have enjoyed such a twist. Perhaps He even entertained the idea once and that's how I ended up here? For sure, you see, He lost control over His story. It stopped clicking and chiming and ticking so well. His shiny toys caught the attention of other gods. He had to share. They tarnished a few things, including His intentions.

I do not have an Automaton. Not in that sense. A cat soul is different.

Though I doubt it had been properly tested, the only soul-key to fit into an Automaton is a human one. That's the only way they were wound. Can you imagine the design flaw in that—if any an inanimate had been dropped on the floor and a stray cat or dog's paw happened to grace over it—kick it?[4] Well, I do wonder.

---

[3] Like I've said before, this is a work of fiction. I believe this fantastic *story* is actually helping our Narrator work out some issues. Beyond that, I think it is a brilliant piece of literature (and of course I would, after I've helped make it what it is).

[4] Or squirrel or raccoon or...

Perhaps I'm a novelist after all, Gabbler? How creative I'm being now—branching out from the truth like this.

No, my reader, no.

You try too hard to make sense of chaos. You must let the primordial soup sprout its fungus on its own terms according to what rotten ingredients were brewed...

Gabbler, more than most, tries too hard also. Gabbler does not know that, no matter how hard we try, the gods have already decided to make use of this work—of what happened. I could type out a single word over and over again—*shit, shit, shit, shit*—and He would still find SOME way to use it.

He, of course, being The Blacksmith—our patron god *Hephaestus*.

Chapter the first,

Split personality:

Who are you when you're more than one?[5]

Way back in book one, Odys had synced with his Automaton Maud. It went a little something like this:[6] (see the footnote I'm having Gabbler insert).

---

[5] "[The Novelist] does not write books to confound philosophers, perhaps because she is able to write books that delight them. In conversation she is the least formidable of women, because she understands you, without wanting to make you aware that you *can't* understand her." —George Eliot, "Silly Novels by Lady Novelists."

[6] From book one (edited out in case you don't need the refresher):

'Odys had stepped toward Maud—he was going to do it—he was going to let go.
But wanting it wasn't enough.
Wanting wasn't working.
Otherwise, it'd be done.
Maybe it was a limitation on his mental ability, but he found hands-on so much more effective.

He came at her, snatching her up by the arm and bringing her in front of the store-front window. He wanted to *be* her—be able to find Rosemund and stop this fucking madness—so he *took* her. Had anyone been watching, they would have thought Maud should look afraid—as if she'd just angered some jealous lover who was about to beat the living shit out of her. But her subtle grin said otherwise.

See, Odys was nothing to fear. Not only because he didn't intend to hurt her, but because he toppled over at her feet. "You really needed that running start huh? You should

OK. Well, I think all that is enough of me doing the whole "Previously on the *Circo del Herrero* series" thing. We're all caught up. Let's get to it.

Stanza: "This one was not one working to have anything come out of him..."[7]

Maud had dragged Odys to the nearest gas station. After flirting with the high school kid behind the counter to distract from Odys's disgusting sick-face, they were out in no time with some painkillers, energy drinks, and food. Oh, and let's not forget cigarettes.

"These are for you," Maud said, handing him the pills. "And this is for me." She popped the tab of a too-hardcore energy drink. "I'm NOT going to sneeze out because of you." But she didn't chug it. Instead, she shoved the can into his face. "Drink up."

"I'll throw up!" He shoved her hand away, spitting out the drink. More dribbled down his front as she tried again.

"No, you won't. Not if you eat these."

"How much shit did you buy?" He'd been too dizzy to notice. The fluorescent lights messed with his eyes. Walking, he did as she prescribed. Having trouble opening the pill bottle, he hardly noticed they were walking to a parked car. The next thing he knew Maud was shoving him into the driver's seat, hissing at him to "Scoot the fuck over" before someone noticed them.

Odys had just let her steal a car, yes. Upon realizing what he'd just let her do, well...it was a very frightening moment. It came so naturally. He hadn't thought twice about it this time.

"Fuck, Odys, you can't reconsider something after you've already *done* it." Maud barked as they sped down the street.

---

have seen yourself. You looked ridiculous." *It looked like you were going to kill me. Maybe even kiss me.*

And that was how it was done.

That is how cloned personalities become one again.

...

Odys threw up.'

Also, in case you've forgotten, Odys is on a mission for Mother to stop Rosemund from giving the inanimate Automaton, Madus, to Leeland.

[7] Gertrude Stein. From her work "Picasso."

Driving driving driving.

He stared out the windshield as if viewing a photograph that seemed hauntingly familiar. This street was familiar to Maud. He recognized it from her memory. He rubbed at the goosebumps it gave him—who had put that memory in her head?

After some silence, and after Odys had finished off all his goodies, he wanted to fill the quiet. He wanted to distract himself from how stupid he had been not to sync with her before—how it felt like he had just taken a giant shit after being constipated for days. His stomach hurt but he was *better*. He wanted to admit it, but his lips would not move. Look, his lips try.

"You *can* still talk to me, you know," Maud said. She had just obeyed his unspoken command. She spoke. Because he'd wanted her to. "After all, it's nice to talk. Even if you don't need to anymore..."

"I feel like crap. But it's a different crap than before."

"Like the crap feeling you get after you just ran a marathon? The kind of crap that's good for you?" (Odys didn't want her to talk about "the constipation," so she chose a different comparison).

"I wouldn't know. I refuse to exercise." Talking to her was easy now—a joke with yourself. "But yeah, just like that."

The cell phone rang—they jumped at the unfamiliar jingle. Odys dug it out of his pocket, handling it as if he were a natural with them—even though he'd hardly ever used one (he's a grandpa, remember?). Maud was making him do things he wouldn't have before. "Hel-hello?"

"Odys!" Mecca's voice shouted from the other line. "Mecca's just calling to tell you that everything will be fine, and that Bullybird is fine too."

"You mean Bulfinch?" He was starting to catch on to Mecca's thought process.

"If you say so. Anyway, Odys, Mecca also wants your CD collection."

"What?"

"Mecca stole it from your apartment before Mecca blew it up. Because Mecca wanted it. Mecca doesn't just let things go to waste."

"Excuse me?"

"Mecca means, when you die, can Mecca have the CD collection?"

"When I *die?*"

"Well, it's not a matter of when. Mecca's really asking if he can have them now. Because Mecca already knows when you're going to die."

"What?"

"Rosemund's gonna to kill you. She may be an old lady, but she's still one crazy bitch, and Mecca's *pretty sure* he's the only kid in the world that's still willing to listen to CDs."

Maud grabbed the phone from Odys, "Listen here, you little shit. You can have the damn CDs, but if you so much as hurt a hair on Bulfinch, I'll fuck you up. I know where you keep your first edition Batman comics and I'm not afraid to use them as coffee filters!"

She hung up the phone and her tone softened: "He's only trying to scare you. Take it as a compliment. This means he's paying attention to what we're doing. And he's worried about us."

"Worried Rosemund won't finish the job."

Stanza: Let's speed this process up.

Drive, drive, drive, and: "Odys, we're here. I think." She slowed down the car. "This looks like what Mother said."

He woke up. Her hand was on his shoulder. Now it was shaking him awake. "You sure?"

They came to a stop outside a gated community. One of those fancy gates that blocks off an entire ritzy neighborhood—the kind that normally employ a security guard to push a button. But there was no one in the little attendant booth. The gate opened on its own.

"Well, I heard that people in Canada don't lock their doors..."

"Yeah, but this is a gate. Someone should be in there. What if she killed the security guard that's supposed to be in that box? What if we drive over and set off some signal and then we both explode?"

"That's not how she works, and you know that."

No, he didn't know that. Rosemund was supposed to be a good guy. The others thought they'd known her before. But they clearly didn't know shit. To top it all off, all the things she was capable of were worse now that she was, well, *rogue*. For example: Odys (drawing on Maud's memory, here) recalled the time Rosemund had almost (accidentally) killed Mecca with her "improved" Tesla coils (though Mecca had volunteered to hold "this," so it could have been prevented) and then blew up one of Mother's motor homes (also on accident). The authorities blamed the power outage on a lightning storm.

That's what they were dealing with now.

"Look, there's a hiring sign in the widow of the box. Maybe she didn't kill them. They just don't have anyone working it. Set to automatic or something."

"Is that part of the appeal of meeting here? No security guard? That's ridiculous. I just don't get it."

"She didn't necessarily pick this spot. This is just where Mother's tracked her. Her cell phone usage is from this area. So is her internet history."

"Yeah, but we could kill someone! The houses are so close together."

"That's the point. It keeps you from pulling out the big guns, doesn't it?"

They drove through the gate.

"Why don't they have street lights on in this place? For a fancier part of town they sure don't splurge," Maud muttered. Canada was weird. Their headlights showed a few cars parked on the curb and in driveways, but other than that the place looked like bedtime. Maud tried to spot lighted windows as she drove. "Maybe there was a power outage..."

11

"With Rosemund, that's a possibility. Wonder what she blew up this time—Maud, slow down!"

"What the—" She slammed on the breaks. "The hell?"

As they turned the corner into a cul-de-sac, the car's headlights flickered over something circling around.

Upon hitting the breaks, the circling thing in the distance noticed the lights...and had stopped.

Right in the middle of the cul-de-sac's loop.

It was no deer in the headlights look. The headlights flashed over her white windbreaker, her red hair sticking up in untamed, frizzy curls—as if she'd just stuck her finger in a light socket. The big granny glasses flickered like a nocturnal eyes, making Odys stiffen. She looked like some caged animal that had been pacing—pacing, pacing, pacing—her cage. Waiting to be fed.

Except this cul-de-sac wasn't a cage. It was an open range.

"Oh—oh God! She's got the electric powerchair!!!" Odys gasped (with just the right amount of exclamation). "You know what she keeps in that thing—"

Yes, Dear Reader, he's afraid of a lady in a pimped up wheelchair. Or, excuse me, powerchair.

"Shush!" Maud observed Rosemund.

Rosemund looked like she *could* have been attractive—outside of that windbreaker, wannabe afro, and scarred epidermis. Well, at the very least, most would call women her size and stature "cute" or "petite." But don't let the cuteness manipulate you. Seriously. Be prepared. Save yourself. That sort of shit.

"Stay calm, Odys. I've got the brights on. She—she can't tell who we are."

Hopefully.

Indeed, Rosemund scrunched up her tiny face.

"Yes, but Caffar can!" he hissed, looking about for Rosemund's other half.

Maud put the car in park. "She might think we're just normal people. If she wanted to kill us, we'd—we'd already be dead. After all, it's not like she's expecting *us,* of all people. That's *why* they sent us." Maud was trying to rationalize it, her body held tense and tight—ready to run—to fight if need be.

"Then why is she out rollin' around tonight? She's expecting something!" His voice was a bit too panicked. There were over a billion reasons why Rosemund Rosemary would be *rolling*. And those reasons ranged anywhere from *expecting something* to *wanting to burn battery power*. They watched Rosemund jerk her head like a wolf sniffing the air for scent.

"Maybe she's keeping guard?"

"For what? Another one of her experiments? For Leeland?"

"There's no way he's here—is there?"

"It's like she can hear us!"

"We look suspicious."

That was fucking obvious.

"Should we back up?"

"I don't know!"

They watched Rosemund for a few more seconds. And she watched them. She stared into the headlights like a mesmerized moth—her face whited out by the contrasting light.

"Honk the horn," Odys said. "Honk it loud. Get the whole neighborhood's attention. So she won't do anything stupid."

Maud did so, loud and obnoxiously. Over and over again.

Not unbuckling his seatbelt (because he didn't have it buckled) he shot out the passenger's side—Maud doing the same in symmetrical fashion. A handgun quickly formed into her hand.

With the headlights lighting their path, Odys scanned the houses as they walked toward the cul-de-sac. He told himself if he was noisy about this, the neighbors just might wake up. He needed the neighborhood to see this, if things grew violent.

Surely—surely!—Rosemund wouldn't cause too much trouble if people were watching. *Too many people to kill.*

Maud's high-heeled feet clicked like tap shoes upon the concrete. When Rosemund noticed Maud's figure, Odys could see a wicked smile spark in her eyes under those glowing granny glasses. She recognized *them.*

Pressing a button on her handlebars, the woman—who, up close, looked too young for a wheelchair—backed up. The loud beep-beep-beep unnecessarily alerted no one behind her.

Now facing them head-on, Rosemund moved forward a few wheel-turns. Odys wondered if those new lines in her face were finally wrinkles, or just her scars deepening. Maybe both. If Odissa could see her, she'd say this woman was too hip for this world. And then Odys remembered that, oh yeah, he's not concentrating. Back to the story!

But speaking of stories…

A story, as you know, can be delivered in many different formats. To properly introduce Rosemund, it might be best to shake things up a bit. We must do her justice. The meta is calling us to bring her out of the closet. Yes, yes this should add a bit of flavor to this baked fruitcake (if you don't get this joke then your gaydar is broken. Come back when it's fully functional)…

Mobility, A Play[8]

The Persons of the Play:

Odys Odelyn, a man who's just been connected

Maud, Odys's Automaton

Rosemund Rosemary, a woman who has something Odys needs

Caffar, Rosemund's Automaton

---

[8] A closet drama in four acts. Our Narrator is obviously bored with the story format and wants to try a hand at Goethe's medium (let's not mention how it falls short—we don't want to offend). Warning: This play involves Rosemund. You will notice she speaks very repetitively and tritely. She even maddens me. Our Narrator has said that "All characters have glitches. This one is hers."

Narrator, me, of course

Gabbler, shut the fuck up for once in your life, baby

Act I

[Setting: somewhere in Canada. In some strange neighborhood where the only light is only Odys's car headlights (well, it's not really his car, because Maud just stole it—but you know what I mean). Odys and Maud are approaching Rosemund.]

MAUD: [To Rosemund, a woman who looks older than Mother but isn't. Rosemund has slight hints of scars on her face and hands. The scars are burn marks. Rosemund is a tiny woman, barely taller than Mecca. She is wearing an AC/DC shirt (though she most likely isn't a fan of the band)[9] under her windbreaker jacket. Every time she moves she swooshes. Other notable attire is: the limp surgeon's mask dangling under her chin, the high-top shoes, and the too-big glasses.[10]] What's with the surgeon's mask?

ROSEMUND: [Pulls up the surgeon's mask before speaking] Masks are used to mask things, no? [Rosemund gives a slight shrug].

MAUD: No one thought otherwise.

ROSEMUND: They didn't? Well, how am I to knowknowknow what an Automaton thinks—if at all? [When she "glitches," she bobs her head to the side a little.] Thoughts are needed to think. [To Odys] AND YOU! You, young man! I've

---

[9] Before you think our Narrator cares less and less about subtly and is shooting straight for caricature, consider why these overt symbols trim the characters. My semiotics call them a clue to the truth—truth so piled on it reads as ridiculous and, therefore, lies. The fact the Narrator doesn't want to be taken seriously only drives my suspicions. There is a meaning in here. A meaning I want the Narrator to see once I find it.

[10] Which she probably needs because she's damaged her sight so many times from overexposure to bright light.

been expecting you, Odys Odelyn. You are looking well, as someone who is well should look.

ODYS: [Eyes narrowing] How is it that you knew we were coming? Do you know why we're here?

ROSEMUND: But of course I do. Mother *told* me. She tells me everyeveryeverything. I tell *her* everything. Just because we disagree doesn't mean we can't talk. That, and I *do* know how to track a phone. [She looks at her watch.] But you're here earlier than expected. I was surprised how quick your signal jumped around. How did you get here sososo fast? Did you catch a different flight? A flight *without* a plane?

MAUD: You could say that. Vulcan airlines.

ODYS: So you know what we're here for. [It wasn't a question.]

ROSEMUND: But of course, of course. She wants the coin. She wants Madus. She sent you like some ASPCA commercial—to beg me to save your poor sister from the pound. So gogogo on. Give us your thirty-second spiel. Sell me your sell!

MAUD: Tell us where the Automaton is, Rosemund.

ROSEMUND: [She puts her hands up slightly] It's simply not so simple.

ODYS: You haven't touched him, have you?

ROSEMUND: [Pushing up her full-moon glasses and observing him] Why would I want to touch Madus? Mother'd not likely like that. I need Mother to like me, in the end. I have no need for *two* Automatons. I still wantwantwant peace. [Rosemund waves her hands as if to settle the situation. Her nails are long and fake and painted an outrageous color. On every one of her fingers she has rings.]

ODYS: If you want Mother to like you, you shouldn't have kept him in the first place. You can't give him to Leeland, Rose.

ROSEMUND: Rose? Just because you sync with Maud doesn't mean you get to call me that, boy. Don't be so familiarly familiar. [She shakes a finger at him] If you want to call me that, then show somesomesome manners. Don't come to me demanding—

MAUD: [Over the hum of their car engine] You can't give into him! Madus is needed elsewhere. A twin for a twin! The fate is too perfect, Rosemund. You *have* to see it, don't you? Hell, forget seeing it. I can smell it. You know this is meant to be! Odissa *will* have Madus.

ROSEMUND: Meant to be? [Rosemund leans back in her chair] Don't tell me what's meant to bebebe, boy. I was meant to die a long time ago and look at me! Still kicking. And what's one more Automaton to Leeland? It'll save us from watching him torture another poor soul. He'll get to you as well, you know. Eventually. Mother may think she'll weaken my heart by sending you—a boy she's threatened—but it won'twon'twon't work.

ODYS: You don't care that you're forcing Mother to play the part of Leeland in this? She'll kill my sister! Don't you love Mother more than that?

ROSEMUND: Oh, listen to you—pulling that card! But Mother forgivingly forgives. [As if talking to herself] She hasn't killed me yet, has she? After all, she only sent *you*. She'll come to terms with it. She'll forget what I've done with Madus—eventually. I break no laws bybyby giving Madus away. Leeland will do the breaking—he'll break them only by touching him. That sinful sin will be upon his head. Not mine. What is best is for the best.

NARRATOR: [A voice from the sky that the other characters do not react to. In fact, they pause, as if time itself has stopped so that I might contextualize] Rosemund's platitudes never say much more than what they say—ha, ha!

MAUD: I wouldn't be so sure, Rosemund. Even if Mother forgives you, we can't. We'll kill you if we have to. We want Odissa back. You know who Odys is—how he's connected to Leeland. Mother's told you, I'm sure. [Rosemund crosses her arms, her windbreaker crinkling] Pepin didn't hide Madus this long just to have you give him to Leeland. Don't ruin everything he's built up—you wouldn't betray him like that. You were always on his side. He was like a brother to you.

ROSEMUND: You just threatened to kill me. [Leaning forward on her electrical wheelchair and resting her head in her hand] But just how do you intend to find out where Madus is if I'm dead? The dead are dead! What's your planplanplan, anyway? I thought you were going to beg. I expected a good begging! You're bad at begging. [A light down the block turns on in an upstairs window, her eyes make theirs flicker to it. With urgency in her voice] I've made up my mind, boy. Go home. I have things to do.

MAUD: Things to do? [Maud steps forward as if to follow her as she starts to roll away] Like what? You seemed bored out of your wits seconds ago, going in circles. I say you've got too much time on your hands! [Rosemund stops in her act of turning around, blocked by Maud]

ROSEMUND: [Defensively] Well, if you must know, I got a call from a new customer who would like me to restore and rewire a sixteenth-century automaton[11] for a museum. They want me to fix it so they don't have to wind a key. Make a robot turn the robot. Ironic, right? Have I ever told you the story behind my interesting interest ininin automata? How I think that's why I caught Vulcan's eye in the first placeplaceplace?

NARRATOR: [The characters freeze-frame]. Time to interrupt, here. Rosemund is what we might call a *tinkerer*. She is very much interested in converting anything and everything into an *electrical* contraption. But of course Odys knew this. Because Maud knew this. [Characters unfreeze]

ODYS: Of course you haven't told me. You just *met* me.

ROSEMUND: Oh, that's rightrightright. But, Maud is you and you are Maud. If I've told her—or any other parts that *were* once her—then I've told you.

ODYS: [Smiling down at his feet in frustration] If that's the case, then I do know your story. And I also know this...*behavior* is not like you, Rosemund. What would make you betray Mother—who I thought you loved?

ROSEMUND: [In a low voice, resting a hand in one of her jacket pockets] What is one more Automaton in Leeland's possession? It's one less person to suffer. We

---

[11] That's right, not capitalized.

can't seem to kill him, so why not pacify him? It's less trouble for us all. No one will missmissmiss an Automaton they've never had. It is also one less Master to make Gwendolyn cry.

ODYS: But your actions will cause more harm than help. It is *you* who make Mother cry!

Act II

[Setting: The three houses at the end of the cul-de-sac are suddenly illuminated by porch lights, bringing them to the audience's attention]

ROSEMUND: [Pulling something out of her pocket, making Maud and Odys tense] Mother cries no matter the occasion. But this is the lesser of two evil evils. Now, because we are standing at a standstill and it is in my nature to make sparks, I will make a proposed proposition. If you can guess which house, out of the three at the endendend of this cul-de-sac [pointing]—one, two, three—that Madus is NOT hidden in, then you'll know where he is.

ODYS: What?

MAUD: He's—he's in one of these houses?

ROSEMUND: I didn't say that. I said you'll know where he is. Knowing is only knowing. [A light turns on in one of the houses]

ODYS: There's people inside those houses!

ROSEMUND: Houses are sometimes homes, yes. They are grand homes, aren't they? Very upper-middle class. Middle class is not so middle anymore these days. [With a sigh] I need to know how much you want Madus.

ODYS: Rosemund, this isn't like you. You don't kill innocent people.

MAUD: On a regular basis.

ROSEMUND: You can always turn around and go home, Odys. We don't have to play this game.

ODYS: But I can't. Mother has my sister. I can't have her back until I retrieve Madus. Don't you even care, woman?

ROSEMUND: Well then, I'd pick a house if I were you. Pick a house, any house—any house that's a house! What'll it be? [Odys gapes] One? Two? Three? I give you three seconds—no more than three. One...two...three! Ah. I guess I get to choose for you. [She presses a button on her remote, house number three explodes].

MAUD: [Screaming, trying to get the neighbors to hear] HELP! FIRE! [No one responds, but a few lights down the street come on]

ODYS: [Shouting at Rosemund, panicked, eyes wide, coming at her] STOP IT! This makes no sense! There are people in there! How do I know that wasn't the house Madus was in? How's this beneficial to anyone? [Rosemund backs up her scooter to get away from him]

ROSEMUND: [Matter-of-factly] Who said my game was to benefit anyone? Get back from me or I'll blow them all up! [She shoos them away as she continues to roll, holding up the remote] Which house is next?

ODYS: I'm not picking a number! Stop this! FUCK! [Running to the middle house, shaking its large gate, screaming when the gate is locked]. Wake up! You have to get out!

ROSEMUND: [Shouting over the crackling fire] Funny how people don't care their neighborhood's being blown upupup. [She shrugs and presses another button, house number one explodes].

ODYS: [When no one answers the door, he starts looking around the dark neighborhood. Slowly, he realizes...] They're empty [Quietly]. They're all empty! [He watches as Rosemund pushes more buttons and lights flicker on in various windows down the street]

ROSEMUND: [Turning her wheelchair around and noticing his expression] That's rightly right, Odys. [She raises her remote, making him jolt from the house. She pushes a button. Number two goes up in flames]. They're vacantly vacant. All of them. [She pushes another button and a speaker in the distance starts playing Eddy Grant's "Electric Avenue." The lights in the houses flicker in unison.]

NARRATOR: Rosemund wired this whole neighborhood up quite nicely, though. She bought out this neighborhood a while back, decorated it herself. Picked out the cars and everything. Soon they'll be donated to homeless urchins of her choosing. Except the ones she blew up.[12] "Burnt houses are burnt," as she would say.

ROSEMUND: Oh, don't look so shocked, Odys. [Odys studies the buildings around him, panting. He now notices how much like a ghost town it looks, with the fires and flickering lights illuminating everything]. That's right, I wired all these houses. I control their lights. Planned to scare the shit out of this whole 'hood come Halloween. Didn't really care for these three architectural atrocities, though. There's no one in them. Welcome to my light show! [She starts pushing buttons and the neighborhood houses' lights flicker madly—offbeat to "Electric Avenue"].

ODYS: [The heat and light make him squint] Fuck you, Rosemund! [He flips her off, with both hands and paces as if he wants to go].

ROSEMUND: [Laughing] Cruel tricks are so cruel. [She continues to laugh, then starts coughing, from the smoke]

MAUD: [Her fingertips forming a gun again] It's not funny, Rosemund! Tell us where Madus is. [She points the gun at her, stepping forward].

ROSEMUND: [Giving a deep sigh, turns off the music] Oh yes, about that. Now that the funfunfun is over I guess it's time you knew. I don't even have what Mother told you I had. Lies are lies. I never even had him to begin with. We still don't know where he is—what Pepin did with him. This was all just to test you. [She pulls out a phone from her pocket] Mother lied about her lie, see. She lied about a lie to get you to come here.

MAUD: What? [Maud takes the phone, scrolls] Are you fucking kidding—

---

12 The houses, not the urchins.

21

ROSEMUND: [As if she didn't hear her] Also, they now know that you've synced with her [She nods in Maud's direction]. Couldn't have asked for more. Mother's been listening to the course of this eventful event.

NARRATOR: More like uneventfully uneventful.

ROSEMUND: Not only has Gwendolyn been tuning into your progress, but I can see it right now. I can see you're *aware*, Odys Odelyn. [Going on quite proudly, rolling between them as if pacing in her electric scooter] This idea was all my idea, really. [She gestures to the houses, the setup] I suggested to Gwendolyn what we might do, to get you to show some realrealreal colors.

ODYS: I don't believe you—*how* can I believe you aren't lying to get us to leave?

ROSEMUND: If you don't believe me, then you should call Mother. For sure, we hoped you would react this way to the exploding houses. You're a good boy, Odys Odelyn. I sure didn't want to waste all my wired wiring. Now if *only* I could remember the buttons for the sprinklers. [Squinting at the remote, pressing odd button combinations]

ODYS: [In disbelief] Gwen had me believe— [the sprinklers come on—helping to exterminate the fires]

ROSEMUND: [Looking up from her remote and rolling forward] Yesyesyes, she had you believe what she wanted you to believe. But we had to. We had to know your loyalty. [Smoke is wafting around them. Odys's phone chimes.]

MAUD: [Checking Odys's phone] Mother sent us a text. It just says, "She's innocent. You're free." [Turning to Rosemund, her nostrils flaring] Are you trying to give us emotional whiplash?

ODYS: [Cursing under his breath and kicking the car] This is ridiculous! All this. For WHAT?

MAUD: I should kill you right now for this fucking trouble, woman!

ODYS: [Apologizing for Maud] Sorry, I didn't mean that. [He rubs his face]

ROSEMUND: [Not bothered by his outburst] We wanted to be sure you're innocent. Even saints cause a lot of troubling trouble—and scream just as loudly as they're being burned. We can't have screamers here—screaming away our secrets.

ODYS: So did I pass your goddamn test?

ROSEMUND: You did shout a lot. But you did it for Gwen. For Madus. You obeyed her, so we know where your priorities are.

ODYS: [Mockingly] I believe you when you threaten to harm my sister. What a discovery for you!

ROSEMUND: [Scolding him] You're not dumb enough to disobey us. Now we know. [More nicely] Now, if you don't mind, I've been staying at 1606 Ernest Street, which is where my bags are. You can give me a ride there, so I don't wearwearwear out my powerchair. [She stands up, preparing to collapse her chair] Walking takes a toll on my lungs—but you likely remember that. [She uses air quotes around the word "remember"]

ODYS: [Still in disbelief] I'm not taking you anywhere. Not until you tell me where Madus is.

MAUD: You know where he is, don't you? I can see it on your face! You might not have him, but you know something. Does Mother have him or not?

ROSEMUND: [Swooshing over to them. She has a slight hunch as she shuffles] I told you, boy, I don't have him! We don't know where Madus is. You can't have something you don't have *because you don't have it.* God only knows what Pepin intended for thatthatthat penny. You really think I'd give that damned Leeland another? No. [Mumbling] Just one more Automaton to have to find when we kill him.

NARRATOR: Damned Leeland is damned!

ROSEMUND: You know me. [Her eyes flash to Maud, then back at Odys] You knew it was odd for me to threaten such a thing. Reasonable, but oddoddodd. Of course I might do it, if circumstances were different but... [She shrugs with her round shoulders] But you know I would never make Gwendolyn cry. Never. Now be a gentlemanly gentleman and open the car door for me. [She holds up her long nails]

ODYS: [Still skeptical that this was so anti-climatic] I'm not doing anything until you show me where Caffar is.

ACT III

ROSEMUND: All right then, if you're that paranoid about it. [Digging through her pocket and pulling out a few batteries, a few fuses, and one teeny-tiny screw. She scrunches up her face as she looks at them. Picking out the screw with her nails and tossing it into the air—] Caffar, he wants to know you're not hiding in the bushes.

CAFFAR: [After falling to the ground and twisting upward into life, appears to be a very average-height, white-coded Automaton, with dark brown hair, the color of corroded alloys. Her skin parallels the off-white glint of metal in the sun. She is "wearing" a skin-tight body suit and has too many piercings to count. She crosses her arms, defensively, yet her face is expressionless.] ...Not hiding in the bushes [she repeats].[13]

NARRATOR: And now you are introduced to Rosemund's second tongue. Her Echo.

MAUD: Clearly. You're hiding behind all that jewelry. Since when did you become a freak show attraction, Caff?

ROSEMUND: Do you hear her, Caffar? As if she wasn't a circus show herself!

CAFFAR: [Serious, without expression] Circus show!

ODYS: [Huffing at first, gesturing once aggressively. Then, toning down what he was about to say, to be respectful] I come all the way out here, and all of a sudden you're the good guy again? [He goes to open the car door for her] I don't understand why it had to be so much trouble.

ROSEMUND: [A smile underneath her surgeon's mask] Good guy? Good guys are good, Odys. And if good guys are good, then why are you so upset?

---

[13] Caffar repeats. She always repeats.

ODYS: Does this mean I get my sister back?

NARRATOR: If Dorian lets him.

ROSEMUND: Does this mean you ever lost her? [Noticing his gruff face] I know, I know, Odys. We're liars. Liars are liars. But look, we're bad ones. [She gestures to the area, as if he should have seen through this ruse] Granted, it did make you piss yourself. [She laughs. Odys turns away, thinking, hands on hips] You know as well as I it was the only way to test you. You had to go through this hazing, if you're to be one of us.

ODYS: [Scoffs]

MAUD: [Turning her other hand into a gun] Fine. Get in the car. Both of you. [Caffar picks up her Master's chair with ease and unlocks the trunk with her mutating finger, stows the chair away. Then, climbs into the car].

ROSEMUND: [Stuffing the batteries and fuses back into her pocket, she accidently hits the remote. Suddenly, nearby sprinklers turn on, misting Odys, who had just come over to the driver's side to drive] Curse these curses! [Rosemund tries to turn them off. She quickly slams her door to avoid the water].

ODYS: [Taking off his coat] Jesus, Rosemund, who put up the sprinklers to water the fucking pavement? Honestly! [He dabs himself off]

ROSEMUND: Didn't know who'd be on firefirefire. [Using her sleeve to wipe off her glasses] Must you point that gun in my face, Maud? Not pointing one at you.

MAUD: [Who still has her gun pointed at them lazily, notices the letter she retrieved from the mail earlier. It's inside the breast pocket as Odys drops the wet coat over her lap] Best take this out, so it can dry. [She flicks it, as if to dry it] Might as well open it too, to make sure no ink is running. [She tries to hand it to him].

ROSEMUND: [She and Caffar looking over their shoulders to see what has caught their captor's attention, says to Caffar] And he thinks we're the ones with secrets!

ODYS: [Trying to dab off his own glasses, he says to Maud] What? Oh. [He grudgingly opens the letter, shaking it.]

ACT IV

ROSEMUND: [Peering over the back seat, her huge glasses sliding down her nose] I dare say, that letter is a letter. I know that stationary. I know that typeface! [She points]

MAUD: [glancing down] What's it say?

[They all start to read it]

CAFFAR: What's it say?

The End

Of the play, anyway.

Stanza: Mail Delivery.

The posthumous spam-letter from Pepin read thusly:

Dear Odys, I gave Maud to <u>you</u> for a reason, but I am sure you have figured that much out by now. If anyone asks, Madus is safe. I have a plan for him as well. Also, though it might not matter (depending on how you take to her), tell Maud I am sorry I had to make her forget. I know it sounds silly, because an Automaton does not have personal feelings, but I left a part of me in her that will understand why I erased so much of her—rather, <u>me</u>. At least, I hope part of me is still in her. I plan to leave myself there. I apologize to myself, then. Just in case.

The real reason I am sending this message is to tell you no one is safe. Leeland may think—may even tell you—that my actions speak for him, but they are entirely my own. Do not trust Leeland, and certainly don't trust Mother. I will not go into detail as to why but—

Well, why do you think I have avoided them both all this time? Hell, I should probably tell you to not even trust me, because I have played my part in this. I have known for a while what Leeland had done to you and your sister. I am just now getting around to doing something about it. I hope you will forgive me—though hope is of little help to you. What help is a dead man?

I am sending this letter—well, my <u>friend</u>[14] is sending this letter for me, <u>I</u> will be dead by the time it needs to be sent—in a way that will hopefully keep them from finding it in your mail—Vulcan willing. I know they will check everything on you until they "trust" you. And even then they will not give you peace. Only when you are dead can you rest. I have learned that the hard way.

    -Pepin J. Pound.

Odys threw the damp letter on the dashboard, the paper rustling and sticking. "Pointless!" he hissed at Maud. "Your Master was pointless!"

"Is there a P.S.?" Rosemund asked, leaning forward. Maud reminded her with the flick of a wrist that she still had a gun. *Don't be nosey.* Rosemund leaned back. "Well, there you have it. When Pepin hides something you're not going to find it. It has to let itself be found."

"Thank you for the obvious," Maud snapped.

Rosemund chuckled. "It's from his typewriter. That's his signature. It's really real."

Odys, "No one doubted that. Of course it's real. Far too real!"

"Real!" Caffar shouted back.

"Why would someone even fake a letter from Pepin, Rosemund?" Maud asked, narrowing her eyes.

Rosemund shrugged. "Weren't you just ranting about how you can't trust us anymore?"

"But Mother would hardly fake a letter to us warning us to distrust her. Why would she even do that?"

Rosemund shrugged and Caffar mimicked the gesture—just seconds off.

---

[14] Our Narrator did not seem to know who his "friend" was and said it was "likely a hotel clerk or someone else who could be paid to do such things on a specific date."

"Well," Rosemund said, "Are we going to mull over this worthless plot device or are we going to go and see your sister?"

Maud shoved her gun in their direction. "You want to talk pointless? Everything with *you people* is pointless! At least Pepin had the decency to mail his pointlessness. You make us go all the way to fucking Canada."

"If being pointless is the point then it's not pointless." Rosemund tapped her forehead with her knuckles, telling them to think about it—as if it made sense. Her skull echoed from its metal plate (put in after one too many explosions). "Now, let's go get my things in that house, there, 1606. We can't be late for our plane. It leaves in two hours."

"You were so sure we were coming with you, weren't you?" Odys grumbled.

Stanza: This would not be the last of her beautiful creations that were beautiful.

"The house there, 1606," Rosemund pointed out for the hundredth time. The car stopped. She led them inside a very spacious house and up the stairs. Caffar helped Rosemund like Vulcan's own female automata walking sticks.

"Don't touch anything. It's probably booby trapped," Maud whispered to Odys.

"No, not booby trapped," Rosemund said as she climbed her way up the stairs. Her rings and nails clicked against the wooden rail every other second. She paused for a breather and looked down at them as if in a trappy music video. "Just a few cameras here and there if I wanted to check up on things." She pointed left, and right and sighed. "My lungs might not be able to kill me"—breath—"but they can sure remind me they're perfectly imperfect." She continued up the stairs, all but wheezing.[15]

They entered a room with a door decorated in cartoonish robot patterns. Rosemund flipped on the light and gestured as if she had brought them there just to see it. "This house is for a family with twins. Like you and Odissa, Odys. Because you're a twin. The boy of a twin pair."

---

[15] This may be a good time to remind you, Reader, that Automatons do not heal retroactively. They preserve and extend the life and function of the human body they inherit.

"A twin pair," Caffar repeated as she grabbed two suitcases from the corner. Apparently they'd slept in this room. Not the main bedroom.[16]

"Yeah, I know the definition of 'twin,'" Odys said, looking up as an electric train ran about their heads. He was very distracted with the busyness of the room—flickering string lights and spinning galaxy lamps, a bookshelf shaped like a robot with arms that moved every ten or so seconds and with a muted TV in its painted stomach, a child-sized merry-go-round with frozen-posed horses spinning about. It was a less like a *Blade Runner* toymaker scene and more like Willy Wonka—sans candy. "Where are you getting these families, anyway? Syrian refugees or something, Rosemund?"

Rosemund paused in her journey to the center of the room, avoiding a Roomba and panting. Her poor lungs had always been weak—weak from that original discovery of electricity and the fire it caused. She shrugged to him. She didn't want to elaborate.

"So you're putting up entire neighborhoods now, Rosemund?" Maud pushed her. "And decorating them on top of it?"

"I didn't build this neighborhood. I bought it out. Will give these houses to people I like. People of my choosing—the choicest people. I'll keep a few for myself, of course. Need places to store my things and things to store in my places." She shrugged, stuffing a laptop in a bag.

"You have some sort of list of people like Mother has for new Automaton Masters?" He didn't know why he was asking, for this did not surprise him.

"Yes, but my list is much more ininintricate than that."

"How so?" Maud laughed.

Rosemund's glasses flashed when she turned. Her surgeon's mask bobbed over her lips as she said, "Because I'm dealing with people who will never end upupup on

---

[16] That's not weird at all.

29

Mother's so-called list. These people are much more important, because their lives will go *unprolonged*." She zipped up her handbag and handed it to Caffar. Then, she began to straighten up the bed they had slept in. "Every detail countscountscounts."

"You've decorated to match your own interests, Rosemund." Maud avoided the robot's moving arm as she turned off the TV (to grace Odys's thought to save electricity).

"What? All the automata? Nah, automata are everywhere." Her red eyebrows were waving over the too-big glasses. "People just don't notice. But children, well. Children notice. They can be taught to notice." She gestured to the room's bells and whistles. Her eyes traced her designs. "Ceiling fans, spinning trays in microwaves, printers—all automata in some way, Maud. This room just givegivegives those concepts a more friendly interface. Some collectors say that electricity has no value in automata—that we should keep the windup keys and not have them run constantly. But energy is energy, no matter if sporadic or constant. So why not *automate* the automata? On and on and on."

"And on and on," Caffar said as she nodded for them to leave.

Before moving to the door, Rosemund picked up one last toy as if she couldn't resist a demonstration—a fuzzy rabbit. Rosemund wound the rabbit and put it on the ground. It hopped in its pre-programmed fashion until it missed its last leap, kicking on its side. "You tell me whether or not that rabbit would like to live and die constantly like this? Electricity is the cure."

"It has no brain," Odys said, entertaining her point—a point that might help him understand her if only he could get her to keep talking.

"But if it did?" Rosemund's eyes sparkled up at him.

"Electricity only works for stationary automatons," Maud said, picking up the rabbit and placing it on the shelf. "Wires would just hold him back."

"But batteries, my dear!" Rosemund pointed to the air. "That's what we humans are for you. *Batteries.*"

Maud laughed. "I'm sure museum curators would love for you to strap battery packs on the back of priceless antiques, Rosemund, but is it really worth your while?"

Rosemund tilted her head and huffed at Odys. "Exactly why I focus on this room instead. *Worth my while.* You're just jealous this wasn't your childhood room."

A shadow overtook his face, sucking him back to the reason he was here. "I had plenty of toys, thanks to you people. I never wanted for a damn thing." He pointed for her to get a move on.

But Rosemund didn't budge. "We would have given you a room like this, had we known about you, Odys. You do realize that, don't you?"

He noticed a tone of guilt in her words. "You wouldn't have given me back to my real parents? Or the orphanage?"

Rosemund narrowed her eyes and thought for a moment. "No," she said in that scratchy, high-pitched Eartha Kitt voice.[17] "Your real parents would have always died. That couldn't have been prevented. That's the only way we—" But she redirected. "If Leeland wanted you, we would've known you were worth something. We would have saved you from him, had we known."

"Rosemund, who do you think that he is?" Maud demanded, stepping forward as if trying to catch what Rosemund had just said. "Did Pepin tell you anything— mention anything—before he died? Did he know who Odys was—*really* was?"

As if Maud had shaken the floor with her divine weight and somehow jiggled the gears in the wooden rabbit to make its notches click, the toy kicked again, startling them all. Rosemund watched the rabbit tick to a complete stop—she, the seer who

---

[17] So Rosemund dresses like a black woman and even talks like one? Why not make her one? Couldn't seem to convince our Narrator of this because "Well, she wasn't black." Apparently she just wants to distract in any way possible from those scars? I'm also getting mobster wife vibes so I'll let it slide.

foresaw the rabbit's life winding down and the real reason it had jumped. Rosemund looked to Maud. "Vulcan says no. Not yet." She pointed to the cursed toy.

"Not yet, not yet," Caffar said to herself as she checked the time on the too-colorful clock above them.

"But you know *who I am*, don't you? You know. Tell me my real name. The others know too, but they pretend they don't—as if I mean their worst fears are true."

"Not *all* of them think it would be a badbadbad thing, Odys, if you really were Dorian's nephew."

"Who of them?"

Rosemund adjusted the threads of her mask. "I ever tell you the time I met Dorian?"

"You mean did you tell Pepin and do I remember for Odys?" Maud asked, rolling her eyes. Of course Odys didn't remember.

Rosemund didn't seem to hear her. She sat down on the bed with the spaceship sheets, crossed her legs. She flicked her fake nails as if adjusting her settings—fine-tuning the channel she was about to broadcast: "He was such an ugly little duckling. It was Bob who introduced us to him—when we were finally introduced to him. Bob and her husband had fallen in love with his charm. Never seen anything like him ever before because there was never anything like him before. You know whywhywhy we picked him? Because *he* knew *we* were different and so we had to pick him. You could see it in his eyes—his eyes could tell and you could see it there—there in his bulging, droopy eyes. The second we were in the same room we knew we couldn't live without this boy and this boy knew that we couldn't live without him. He knew we had chosen him—for whatever mysterious thing we had picked him for. Him, this rebellious college dropout who won us over with his bug-eyed stare. He had such huge eyes that were huge! And now he covers them."

Odys remembered those eyes—eyes that Maud remembered. It sent a shiver down his spine.

Rosemund clacked her nails together like a teacup dog on wood floors, added soundtrack to the story her words painted. "We wavered and debated over him, even though we had already made up ourourour minds and there was no need to waver and debate. There were others—more worthy and older—who we had wanted to give an Automaton to. Out of respect, that is why we wavered and debated. We at least wavered. That, and Dorian hadhadhad a family. Although a small one. Well, really he only had a sister. A step-sister. No blood relation whatsoever, but still. We knew he loved his step sister. We eventually settled on it *not being a big deal*. But you know this now, right? You know it was a *big deal*. You're synced with Maud. So you know *the deal*." It was almost a question.

Odys knew, but he wanted to hear her go on. "But Pepin wasn't there when you chose him."

She pointed with her long, sparkly nail. "He knew what we were doing, though. By then he had given us the finger and told Gwendolyn, 'Do whatever the fuck you like.' He didn't give a shit—though he hadn't left us completely. He was only *removed*—but still part of us. He was there, but wasn't. He wasn't there to choose Dorian, but Maud was there. Maud was watching for him because he wasn't there. But even though Maud was there, he had no opinion in the matter." She pointed at Maud. "But when Pepin saw him with Maud's eyes, he actually came outoutout of his shell. We were graced with few visits here and there. No one could make Pepin laugh like Dorian. Pepin had always been the clever one. But Dorian surpassed him in that cleverness. And then Leeland rose from his silence. His ears perked up with our laughter and he roused himself from exile and was no longer silent. It was then that his crusade hit a new height. When he went on the rampage, Pepin retreated for good. Twenty years later, here we are."

She stopped playing with her nails and fanned them out in presentation. She looked like a manicurist waiting for her client to take a seat with those claws and that mask—ready to inhale fumes.

"Pepin left you all to your own mistakes," Odys said, watching the toy train coming back around.

"We're all apart. Every single oneoneone of us. I've been held up here, staying away from it all."

"But you talk to Mother every day. She can't help but cry to you. You and Bob," Maud scoffed. "She calls and demands you help her do this or that, and you just do it."

Rosemund's eyes smiled up at them as she re-tucked the comforter into the bed corners. "What can I say? I can't refuse her."

"Just like you couldn't refuse her when she got arrested on suspicion of kidnapping and you had to take out three cops just to bail her ass out of jail?" Maud had meant it to sting.

Bail is not meant in the literal sense here.[18]

"I admit she should have lied better about who Anselm was to her."

"She could have gotten out on her own! And you people wonder why Pepin avoided you."

"If I hadn't helped her, many more would have died. They had Anselm. Cameras on him! What did you want him to do? Kill everyone who would have seen him break Mother out of jail? She needed back up. Someone to turn the lights out and help her leave unnoticed…" She went on smoothing out the bed—as if it didn't look tidy enough.

"You people never care about who you hurt to keep on living," Odys muttered.

Rosemund stood with a groan. "Be careful, there, Odys, you sound just like your father."

"He wasn't my father. And Dorian isn't my uncle."

Rosemund's head turned to him. "You can't blame Dorian for what happened. Hasn't he been punished enough?"

---

[18] Maybe all of Rosemund's Habitat for Humanity projects were her way of making up for her sins—sins Mother made her commit.

"Blindness isn't a punishment if he has a second pair of eyes in Fletcher. But don't worry, I don't blame him. I blame *all* of you."

"I know you don't trust anyone, but your want for control won't get you control. I'm on your side, Odys. Just why do you thinkthinkthink I contrived all this, if not to finally meet you? Don't punish us for the past."

"You people let Leeland live because you agree with him," Odys growled to the air. "Deep down, you *agree* with him. You think he might have the right idea. You're so unsure and afraid that he *may* be right that you passively let this—this *chaos* churn."

"No. We passively let the chaos *settle*. And for Christ's sake, put Maud's gun away, Odys. You know you don't scare me."

Maud's eyes narrowed. "Only if you tell me what's with the surgeon's mask. Why do you need it? I know it's not to breathe—"

Rosemund unhooked one of the thin strings from behind her ear. Grinning, she flashed them her braces. "Didn't want to lead with them is all."

"Why the fuck do you have braces?" Maud asked, knowing Rosemund never needed them before. But these didn't look quite right. More bolts and wires than what you typically see.

"Either I, one, got into an accident restoring a carnival carousel or two, wanted to be a better electrical conductor."

"Why do I feel like it's both and that you injured yourself accidentally on purpose?" Odys screwed up his face, cocked his head.

Rosemund shrugged, taking her mask completely off. "They were so worried about me suing them that they didn't notice I stole somesomesome original parts."

"Why hide it from us?"

"Because who can take an adult seriously serious when they have braces?"

"You think *that's* why we can't take you seriously?" Maud clapped for them to get a move on.

She already talked like Gertrude Stein, but now, with those bolts and wires in her mouth, she was a Frankenstein.

Stanza: Pepin left them to assemble them.

Now, let's see what Odissa's been up to, shall we? In the last book she had just been given a heavy dose of mega sleepy-time in the theater and was about to be driven to an undisclosed location…

Odissa woke up in a bed. A very comfy bed.

But that's not what surprised her. Neither was Dorian lying next to her surprising. And neither was his nakedness. What *did* surprise her, however, was the fact *she* was still fully clothed—shocked he hadn't taken *the liberty.*

"Where are we?" Her voice cracked.

"Oh, you're awake? You've been out for a while. But so have I. It took hours to get here. We did need sleep, didn't we?" He adjusted the sheets which covered both of them. "We're in the cabin—our cabin. I can't tell you where, though. But it's a cabin."

"That little boy—Mecca. Where's he?" (A bit concerned and paranoid).

"In his room. With Bulfinch too. Bul will stay in Mecca's bathroom." He fingered her hair—hair fanned out on her pillow—hair he had placed there. "With the litter box. Cat litter makes Fletcher sneeze, you see—makes him not function well. Sensitive nose, sometimes, and I hate to push his snivels when things are tense right now. Otherwise I wouldn't mind. I wouldn't let that come between us. Bulfinch got a saucer of warm milk and a whole can of tuna. Which he did not eat."

"He doesn't like tuna. Only canned food. He'll only lick the juices."

"We've made a store run, don't worry."

"Can I see him? Why isn't he with us?" She saw multiple doors. One must be a bathroom. Why couldn't Bulfinch be held in theirs?

"Gottah give Mecca *something* to do. Otherwise we'll not be left alone." He stroked her arm lightly, as if wanting to tickle her. It didn't. It only made her more afraid. *They're holding Bulfinch hostage.*

"Where's Fletcher?" Her cloudy eyes searched for him, though she hadn't lifted her head.

"He's over there—the table. Are you done filling in the gaps now?"

She yawned, noticing her cheek had crusty drool stuck to it. She blotted the rest away with the back of her hand. She saw the rusty paperclip was next to a pile of books no one had likely ever opened. Fletcher was too well angled to spring up and block her. She wouldn't be looking out without his permission. She noticed the little lock-button was pressed in. No one (especially Mecca) would be getting in.

"Can we go outside?" She wanted to judge how trapped she should feel.

"We're still on our date." *You're stuck with me until I say so.*

Rubbing her eyes, "Why are we here?"

"Because this is where Mother wanted us to meet. It was all arranged. She likes to make us feel like family every once in a while. She probably has something important to drop on us too. Probably something about your brother. That's what these family *vacations* are usually for."

"You mean you don't know why we're here? You came because you were told?" One minute he was kidnapping her from a kidnapping and the next he was bringing her back.

"I know *some* reasons why I'm here. Your brother is coming too. Don't worry."

"I wasn't. I wasn't worrying about that part."

"You should. I'm still wondering whether or not I will even let you see him—if I should let you out of this room at all. I have mixed feelings, now, about your relationship. I don't want to *promote* anything."

37

It was like Dorian didn't have control over the words slipping from his mouth—but that he didn't mind they weren't his. Love was making him do such crazy things.

"I would never—we would never—not here..." She rubbed her forehead.

"Even so. I'm mad at your brother."

"Reasons?" She closed her eyes as she waited for his answer.

"He knew damn well you were married and never told us. It changes a lot of things. It changes everything—how I view it all. It changes the motives of everything."

"I don't know what you're talking about, but I know he didn't do it to anger you. You know he hates Augury."

"Leeland. That's his real name."

"Whoever. It doesn't matter. It's not *real*."

"It *is* real, Odissa." *Even if Leeland destroyed the documents to prove it.* "And there's a reason Leeland did it. There's a reason he married you. There's even a reason he'd be willing to fuck you, despite everything we know about him."

"You're making me feel ugly. He didn't mind me *that* much."

"I'm sorry. That's not what I meant."

"What *did* you mean?"

He paused, running his fingers over her skin in thought. "You may not understand it all, but you *must* understand that Odys should've told us. That was part of his—his *duty*. To help us stop what's going on."

She closed her eyes again like someone about to admit things to their therapist—why did she feel like she could speak to him? "He pretends I'm not married," she said simply.

"I'm not stupid, Odissa. He may pretend to himself that you aren't married so he can forget about his father. He may pretend to himself that you aren't his sister so he can fuck you. But he's not going to be able to pretend that I'm out of the picture now, you understand? I lost you once—I lost everything once." He said it so casually—an announcement of no more importance than favorite color or food (which was grey and pizza, by the way). "Though Odys is important to me too, I can't protect him if he lies to me. I can't protect him if he treats me like an enemy. You understand?"

"No. I don't understand anything." There was a tremble in her voice. Her hand near his arm threatened to pull back. She wanted to sleep and forget this was happening. To sleep alone.

"Don't be so afraid of me." His voice almost begged her. "You have to realize, Odissa, I only say these things because I'm not the one in control, here. Everything depends—so much—on you." He sunk lower on the bed and pouted. "Don't make me go to extremes."

Her eyes darted across him, calculating what response he wanted. "You're a manipulative little cunt."

He took off his sunglasses. Set them aside. "Manipulative? Yes. Cunt? Yes. Little? No." He stroked his dick over the covers.

She studied him and his size for a moment. "Then get it over with." She was quite irritated now. Not only did he have the opportunity to molest her while she was out cold, but he hadn't even taken her clothes off. He really *did* make her do all the work here.

He scratched his bare chest, as if considering it. "You know that's not my style."

Leaning toward him, she nodded. "It might be mine, though."

"Already got you pussy whipped." He flicked his wrist as if he had the world's smallest whip and went back to caressing his groin.

She laughed and brushed back his hair—testing what it was like to touch him. "You might be able to keep me from my brother, but I wonder how you intend to keep him from me."

"He's outnumbered here. Plus, he wouldn't want to jeopardize everything he's just earned with us. We own him."

"And who owns you?"

"You do, Odissa. Or are you just making sure?" His brows came together. "I'd do anything—anything, Odissa—to make you love me." He made sure every word came out clearly.

Frowning, she looked around the lodge-style room. At the moose-patterned curtains. Slowly, she removed her cat ears and studied them, thinking. "And even if I never fuck you, you'll still love me?"

"I have no choice in the matter." The tips of his fingers tried to find her skin under her clothes.

She let him explore, pretending to be lost in thought. "That's a very disappointing answer. Feels fake. Like I've given you a love potion to make you like me." Or, rather, shot CUPID'S ARROW.[19]

"All biology is a love potion. We never *really* get to choose what we're attracted to. It's in our genes. Our DNA. We never have a choice."

"Don't know if I believe that." She felt the obligation to draw him from his new isolated expression. In a whisper, "I will tell you something, Dorian. Listen to me, all right?" She put an inartful hand on his hairless chest and grabbed at his searching fingers with her other.

"Yes?"

"You can let me see him. Nothing bad will happen."

"He'll want to take you from me. The others might let him."

"Where? Where will he take me?" She whispered back to him. "You've killed me off. You have my cat. I've nothing to go back to. Plus, you all are so interesting here. Why would I leave?"

He laughed at her attempt to soothe him. "But he still might take you away. I can't let him do that. I'll have to stop him if he tries. He won't get far. They may not stop him but they won't stop me either. You understand? I see you do."

His laughter and threats sent a chill across her skin. She didn't know which to believe—his expression or his words. She was starting to believe both. "I won't go

---

[19] Talk about insta-love, am I right?

with him. If he needs to stay here, he'll stay here. Wherever here is. I won't let you hurt him. I can handle him."

"...Handle him?" He smiled at the thought. "You're yet to convince me of your *abilities*."

"If I recall, I'm not the one who stopped the sex last time."

"You should stop flirting with me, Odissa. Take it if you want it." He tipped his chin up, making himself easy to kiss.

But she wouldn't fall into him so readily.

She pushed the covers off of her legs, prepared to do as he wanted. "You *are* going to let me see my brother," she hissed at him.

"That all depends on you." He picked at the sheet's hem.

"And I'm telling you, Dorian, that *you* need to let it depend on me, then. You're *going* to let me see him. You're going to trust me." She grabbed his chin. "And that will be all. I will only *see* him." He tried to move his chin away from her but she grabbed it again. "No. Dorian, if you want me to like you—to *love* you—you have to let me see my brother. You have to let me keep him calm. The minute he thinks you have me is the minute he causes trouble. The minute he causes trouble is the minute I have to choose sides. Let me make this easy for us, Dorian."

She could see the wheels in his head turning. She had never felt so influential before—so powerful.

"That's all I needed to hear," he said, putting a hand on her wrist. "Now are you going to fuck me or not?"

But as the smile faded from her face, she realized he was too serious to be funny. She knew this person before her was the perfect excuse to save her brother from himself—to save her from herself. Odys and Odissa could never go back to what they once were. Not after this—not after having your whole life ripped open and examined, the festering let open to breathe.

41

She studied Dorian, watched his chest move up and down. She could almost hear the blood in his ears.

Better to kill the past quickly than to draw death out with suffering, she thought to herself.

She started undressing. Fletcher must have been on screen-saver mode, because Dorian had a confused expression on his face, wondering if his ears were deceiving him. He put his arms behind his head, very pleased. He waited for her to come to him.

His smile was too wide for her liking. "Hard and slow, baby," he said as she helped him ease into her, "make it last."

"You'll get what I give you," she said through her teeth as she arranged herself.

And just like that, she had turned her back on the past in order to preserve what it once had been.

She jumped when he actually touched her face—making her pause and open her eyes. The act was a little off, but he still found her cheek.

"Look at me," he said through his breaths. "Look at me."

She looked at Fletcher, who was clearly paying attention now.

"No, at *me*," Dorian said. She looked at him for a half-second, his own eyes closed.

She covered his mouth as she kissed his forehead. She didn't need his help. She knew what she was doing. She buried her face in his neck—in the pillow.

Shall we give them some privacy now? Do we really need to know that Odissa hadn't expected to come, but, when she did, it fueled Dorian to use her crumpled body above him to latch onto her? Do we? No, we don't. We don't need to know that when he finished he groaned into her with such strength she felt she had stolen his ability to breathe. We don't need to know.

She needed a cigarette.

He rested his cheek on her chest. She stared down her nose at him with a frown, but let him anyway. "Are we really at this point? Cuddling?"

"Well, you aren't at a good angle to spoon…"

She heard the hurt in his voice. "Not here, but here." She pushed back his head to shoulder. "You're just heavier than you look. I can't breathe."

She realized she should probably show him affection, and so put her hand in his hair.

"You're so beautiful when naked." He cupped her breast and kissed it. "You should be this way more often."

"The one-liners need to stop. You're smart and funny and I know it already."

"Then what will it take to get you to smile?" He ran his hand between her legs— so eager to please.

She tried not to react. "How do you know I'm not smiling?" She glared over at Fletcher. *You don't have to show him everything, you know.*

Dorian laughed at her—laughed at how well she, a common human, understood him. But when his laughter died, he couldn't let the silence settle. "Why didn't you tell me you were *married*? I mean, from the get-go? All that flirting and you didn't mention it until the very last moment."

She rolled her eyes. "Because I liked you flirting with me." She pulled his chin up to kiss him.

He accepted her answer. His fingers—as his eyes—brushed her features. "If you break my heart, I will break him."

"You think he won't do the same when he finds out what I've done with you?"

"Don't even look at him."

She latched onto his chin. "Then poke out my eyes so I can't see him, you dick. You promised I could see him if I fucked you."

He licked his lips, slightly angry. "Did I?" He pulled away from her.

"You know that's what this was."

"Yeah, but don't phrase it like *that*."

43

She held back. "Look, I'm sorry. But you shouldn't say things like that either. You can't flip flop like that—"

"Just because I say something dramatic doesn't mean I actually mean it." He swallowed back the darkness in his voice.

"Well, I don't know that."

"Now you do." He sat up from her. "You want to take a bath?"

She thought about it for a moment. "I don't like having sex in the bathtub."

"Who said anything about having sex? I just want to give you a bath." He pulled the covers off and away from her.

"You saying I smell?"

"Your attitude does." He stood up.

Stanza: Mind your Mother.

Odys, Maud, Rosemund and Caffar got on the plane. They had boarded with the tickets Rosemund had already purchased. The already-purchased tickets were yet another sure sign Rosemund hadn't been *lying about the lie*—all this was planned out too well.

They sat together, despite being able to sit apart. There were so many open seats around them that Odys assumed Rosemund had bought out half the plane just so they wouldn't have to sit next to anyone. And that meant they could talk more freely. Rosemund wanted to talk. She was proving with her every gesture she had something to say—and in multiple ways.

As they drifted over America, Rosemund used Caffar to pick her nails. Screw-Caffar proved to be a bit less effective than a metal nail file, so she pulled one out of her hair.

Odys quickly snatched it away. "The fuck are you thinking? That's a weapon!"

The TSA agent clearly hadn't thought to pat down that massive mane of hair.[20] When Rosemund walked through the metal detector, her "medical papers" proved all the beeping was from the metal plate in her head. Never mind the nail file in her hair.

---

[20] Simpler times, man.

Rosemund didn't even demand her file back to hide, merely went on picking her bejeweled nails with Caffar as Odys hid it in his pocket.

How does she wipe her ass with those nails? Odys found himself thinking to Maud.

Probably has Caffar do it for her.

Rosemund flicked her nails and kept on picking.

A flight attendant walked by. Her eyes lingered on Rosemund's hands too long for comfort.

"Would you put her away? You're making people stare."

He wasn't sure if screws were on the no-fly list.

"Calm down—don't be so uptight. You almost gave us away back theretherethere in customs—with you needing to calm down. You really look suspicious when you are so uptight and need to calm down."

"I'm not the one that people are staring at!"

"With a face like mine, how can they not stare? My face is a giant scar and they would stare regardless. At least I give them something worthwhile to look at besides the scar which they can't help but stare atatat." She admired her nails and kept watching the silent in-flight sitcom.

At least she had stopped picking for a few seconds.

As Odys stared at the screw, he realized he thought Caffar was the most characterless Automaton. All else was kitschy paper doll dress-up. Her "characterless character" was most likely because Rosemund didn't need an Automaton to have a *character*. She was fine on her own. Caffar was so bland because Rosemund was *true*. True to her own soul.[21]

---

[21] Plane Jane. That's how Rosemund liked her women.

"You should sleep, Odys, while you have a chance," Rosemund told him. She turned off the overhead light. She studied it in its off state, as if she could see past the plastic and into the wiring.

"I'd like to, but I don't think I should sleep with you around. I might wake up to find I'm in some electric chair." Or find Maud naked on top of him—which would be much worse.

Rosemund turned back on the overhead light and cleaned her glasses, using the light to spot the smudges. Her scars around her eye wrinkled more as she squinted through the winged eyeliner. "So, about that letter. Why do you think Pepin doesn't want you to trust Mother? Besides the obvious fact that Mother likes to give a small fib here and there. But we all do that." *Mmhmm.* "Why just mistrust her and her alone? That's the question, isn't it?" She put her bottle rims back on.

Odys's lip twitched. "It's not so much a question as a fact. She's the biggest liar in the whole lot."

Rosemund laughed, rubbing her tongue against her braces. The peanuts on the plane always got stuck in them. "Did I ever tell you about the time I realized Mother killed her entire family?"

"What do you mean?" Odys ran through Maud's memories, not landing on anything.

"She killed them." Rosemund shrugged, digging out a toothpick from her wild hair. "Killed them dead when theytheythey started questioning her. That's how she got free from her past. A clean break is always clean."

She put the toothpick back in her hair. That's why she didn't carry a purse. Her hair held everything she needed.

Her voice grew softer as she said, "At first I thought I could never do what she did—kill my own family! Most of my family was dead or distant by the time I got Caffar. But then I realized I was a hypocritical hypocrite, Odys Odelyn. I realized that I've done many things to keep my Automaton, to keep my Caffar—even if I wasn't the one to finish offoffoff my own family. Leeland did that for me. But don't worry. They were just a few second cousins and a few great-great aunts. No one I liked. Most were dead by the time Leeland arrived anyway. But the thing is, I let them die. I let them die to keep this."

She held up Caffar between her witchy nails. Someone across the aisle narrowed their eyes. Rosemund looked strange enough, without waving screws about on a plane. She flicked off the overhead light once more, as if to take the spotlight off them.

She lowered her voice, leaning too close for comfort—those braces chomped at him. "There's a lesser of two evils always, but there is never a good to choose. That's my point. For example, I have a strange fascination with electricity"—her eyes darted to the overhead light—"But is electricity good in and of itself? Nonono. Electricity can be used for good. But it can also be used for evil. Electricity itself is neutrally neutral. It isn't ever a 'good' choice. There are no good choices. Choices are just choices." She adjusted a writing pen falling out of her hair.

Odys frowned, not wanting to argue with her comparison. "Part of me thinks that her family deserved it, from what I know about them."

"Yet you disagree with killing?"

He wanted to be clear: "I rejected Maud because I won't live for her—as all of you live for yours. I won't choose that. I think that's why."

Rosemund pushed up her bug-glasses. "You might not want others to diediedie for her, but *you* just might. There is chance for you to slip and give us cause to kill you still. You've been given a gift. You've finally unwrapped it, Odys. But will you get to keep it?"

"Since she's attached to my lifeline, I'd rather not exchange it," he replied.

"Pepin exchanged it," she told him gravely. "He returned her to the universe that gave her to him. He never asked for her, you never asked for her. Samesamesame thing. It's only strange because we don't know the reasons he gave her up. You, though, Odys, you have reasons you might give her up. To protect Odissa, for instance. But back to my story about Gwendolyn."

She wasn't done?

"My point is, Odys, is that justjustjust because Pepin doesn't want you to believe Mother's tears doesn't mean they aren't real ones."

"You want me to trust her, then?'

As if she couldn't see his expression, she turned on the overhead light *once again.* "I want you to trust that she doesn't want to hurt you. After all, she's gone to suchsuchsuch great lengths to keep your ass around despite it being easier just to kill you. Yes, real tears are real, even if she does make a mistake. We all make mistakes. Pepin made mistakes too."

Am I one of those mistakes?

Rosemund leaned over and tapped Odys's pant pocket, where he had tucked away Maud. "You want to know what Pepin sent me for my birthday?"

"He sent you something?" Odys asked, moving away from her—not liking her that close to his junk.

"Of course he sent me something. Every year. I was his favfavfavorite. Just because he wouldn't speak to me didn't mean he didn't love me." She hovered over his pants again. "Don't you want to know, Maud?"

A stewardess walking by the parallel lane made a face at Rosemund, catching Odys's red face.

It's not what you think! Odys shot her a nervous smile as he pushed Rosemund away from his crotch. "Yes, yes, she wants to know," he hissed at her.

Rosemund sat back up, turning off the overhead light as she dug in her hair. When her fingers came back she turned on the light once again, for dramatic effect. She opened her hand and revealed: "Nothing," she said. "He sent me nothing. Nothing but an empty box. An empty box with a card that said, *'Keep him safe.'*"

Odys recoiled, eyes wide. Something inside him knew that was right—as if Maud remembered. "He did send you Madus? He tried to? Someone took him?"

"No," Rosemund flashed her braces. "He sent me you."

Odys narrowed his eyes. Her face was too smiley.

She leaned back in her chair and reached for her light once more with a long claw—but Odys beat her to it, blocked her button. "Let's just stay in the dark from now on, why don't we?"

Stanza: Who are you when there's more than one of you?

"Seriously," Dorian said, giving a good stretch. "You need to check out this bathtub. It's got jets. It might as well be a hot tub. Get your cigarettes, there, in your purse and let's go."

Already naked, Odissa simply got in with Dorian. Because he left Fletcher in the bedroom, she actually had to help Dorian up the steps to the giant bath and run it herself. He accepted her assistance willingly. "Help me, darling. I can't see," he had said, grabbing at her despite remembering exactly where everything was. Nothing about the cabin ever changed. There was nervousness in his voice that she simply couldn't refuse.

"Don't you just love baths?" He said across from her. They sat apart, rippling the water between them. "I do. I do my best thinking in the tub."

She did not answer, merely sunk lower in the too-hot water. She was sure she was flushed from its heat but didn't care. The man was blind.

He ran his toes against her leg, reminding her he was still there. "I was always going to let you see your brother, you know."

"Yeah, you say that now." She flicked her cigarette ashes in the water. She loved to hear them fizzle out as they hit the surface.

"You make the most interesting sounds," he smiled, just before sinking his head under. He came up, smoothing back his black hair. It made him look like a greaser. It made her snort.

"Marco?" He splashed, almost snuffing her cigarette.

"Fuck you," she laughed as he floated toward her. He took a dip and spit out the water. He spread her legs and rested on his knees in front of her, holding on to hers as if he might sink into the tub. He just hovered there, probably because he couldn't see where her face was and also because he didn't want to brush his face against her cigarette. She jabbed it out on the side of the tub. Making herself at home.

She studied him, floating there. He was listening to her every movement. She touched his face and wetted her hands. She watched water drip around his cloudy grey eyes—eyes with scarred sockets—eyes with little white bumps and webs covering whatever color they used to be. And then that smile—that scary smile she wanted to wipe off his triumphant face. She hoped he didn't realize he was more spectacular than his perfect Automaton—that she valued imperfection.

It was her brother who wanted everything nice and tidy and perfect.

Dorian, as if he knew her expression through her touch, said, "What is it?" She was being too gentle toward him. Too kind.

"Why did you call me Dorothy?" She seized the sides of his face, as if she had him trapped now.

"Why? Do you not like this yellow brick road I'm escorting you down?" He sunk lower into the tub, angling her grip on him. Her fingers slid a little on his wet skin. His hair touched the water and fanned out like an aura. He wanted to make sure her hands were still playing nicely.

"That's not a real answer, Dorian." She leaned into him.

He floated away from her. He spread out his arms along the tub. His grey eyes closed, readying himself. "I suppose you have a right to know. Odys will tell you eventually, I'm sure. Can't keep his mouth shut."

"About what?"

He rubbed a finger over his pink upper lip at a false itch. "I knew your real parents, Odissa. At least, I think I did. But I won't tell you more than that."

"Why not?"

"Not only would your brother hate me for it, but…" He trailed off.

"Since when do you care what my brother wants? I think he'll be too distracted about the other stuff we've done to care if you tell me. And does this mean he knows? Why does he know but I don't? It isn't fair."

"Your brother knows as much as I do. And believe me, that means he's not sure of anything."

"Not sure of what, Dorian?"

He huffed out his nose. "I'm going to make the others adore you, Odissa. Just you wait. I need to warn you that when they start arriving they might be a little suspicious about what we've been up to. They might not understand. Don't worry. I'll handle it. They'll love you. They'll let me save you."

"Save me?"

"When we find Madus, he'll be perfect for you. A twin for a twin."

She had no idea what he was talking about.

"Then Leeland will never get to you. No one will ever take you away from me again." He was smiling to himself once more, his finger back at that lip.

"Exactly how many times have I been taken away before?"

"Once, in the past. But an Automaton will keep you here with me forever. You understand? Maybe then—once you have one—you'll understand what happened to your parents, why I did what I had to. The Automaton will explain everything."

"What did you do to my parents, Dorian?" Her heart was making the water ripple despite her body remaining still. "I don't want an Automaton."

"Your brother wants you to have one too." To himself, "That's why he went so willingly to Rosemund."

Not sure what he meant, "He won't give me one if I do not want one."

"None of us were really given a *choice*, Odissa. You think you will be? And the others will want to make *me* happy. I will win them over. I will gain their votes. Why wouldn't you want an Automaton? You either become one of us or we get rid of you eventually. Why not finalize the deal? You have no life to go back to."

"You've made sure of that, haven't you?"

He chewed his lip, wondering why she was so obstinate. Could she not see what he meant? Surely—for she could see everything else.

"Why you won't tell me? Why can't you tell me why I'm Dorothy?"

His jaw clenched. He did not like her persistence. "You would hate me, that's why."

"What if I promised I wouldn't? Why would it change so much between us? Aren't we *destined* to be in love with each other?"

"No. *I'm* destined to be in love with you. The gods promised us nothing about *your* love."

"You were angry with me when I didn't say I was married. Now you're the one hiding the truth."

The water rippled as he huffed. "Leeland has leverage—family members, pets, friends. He uses leverage to try and get our Automatons. He *had* leverage on me, but...I still have an Automaton, Odissa. You understand what I'm saying?"

He heard her try to swallow.

"Do you understand, Odissa?"

"I—I think so."

"And do you hate me? Do you fear me?"

She was taking her time to answer when—

Fletcher opened the door. Dorian saved himself from her answer. Odissa sunk lower in the tub, self-conscious for a moment.

"They're here. In the drive." Fletcher cocked his head. He noticed her sinking in the tub and stared at her. He hadn't needed to barge in here, but his Master had wanted him to. He needed an excuse to look at Odissa. And he kept looking. Even when he said, "And you got a text from Rosie. She says he's very angry. He'll expect to see her..." he kept looking.

"Hand me a towel, Fletcher." Dorian stood up, water rippling off him.

Fletcher did so, never taking his eyes off Odissa. He loomed over the tub, a wicked smile on his tight lips. Dorian left her. But Fletcher told her to stay in the tub, as if guarding her.

"Who's here?" Odissa asked him.

He sat down on the edge of the tub, crossed his long legs. "Don't play stupid."

"Is he earlier than expected?"

Fletcher raised an eyebrow. "You're still ours for a little longer if you're indecent, now, aren't you?" He stuck his hand in the water, smiling when she didn't recoil from it.

"You think Odys hasn't seen me like this?"

Fletcher stopped smiling. "Don't be mean."

He swung his feet into the tub, the cloth of his pant legs not absorbing moisture. He hadn't cared to add that detail.

Stanza: Time zones and pinecones.

Odys barged into the cabin after Caffar and Rosemund. Maud was in his pocket, hidden from his sister. Rosemund had heard the good news that Odissa would be there—and had kindly shared it with Odys. And though his eyes searched for her, the first thing he noticed in the quaint-but-plush cabin was Dorian...in nothing but a towel. And some glasses. He was holding a steaming hot cup of cocoa.

"Ah, Odys!" he said, gently blowing on his drink. "Congratulations on your A plus plus. And your fully-functioning second brain."

Odys said nothing as he took in the surroundings, trying to find his sister in the cramped walls lined with doors. Dorian set his cup down, smoothing back his still-wet hair. "Rosie! Damn, look at those nails. "

They kissed on the cheek.

"Caffar's certainly looking gothic. What have you been reading lately? No, let me guess...*Girl with the Dragon Tattoo?*" (It had just become a best seller).

"I wear my heart on my Automaton's sleeve, what can I say?" Rosemund rummaged in the fridge, puffing up her hair as if it were an afro.

"Nice headgear, by the way," Dorian added. "You've got more metal than Caffie, here."

Rosemund gave him the finger. The scarred finger.

"Speaking of metal, you should have seen the junk Fletch sneezed out the other day. A fancy microchip of some sort. Wonder where that came from."

"I don't know what you're talktalktalking about."

"Mhmm. Sure you don't."

Odys's eyes landed on Mecca asleep on the couch—tongue slightly out. He was on top of Q—who was, quite clearly, nude under that scanty blanket someone had been kind enough to drape over them.

"He drove us all the way here," Dorian informed in a whisper (trying not to wake them),[22] itching his bare chest. "Wore him out, but thankfully we only had to steal one car."

Odys didn't care. "Where's Odissa? Is she here or isn't she?" He looked to Rosemund as if she'd been lying.

"I wondered when you were going to ask. She's getting dressed. In there." He pointed to *their* room—a room Odys knew Dorian always used when at this cabin. "I'll also let you know, Odys, that she knows everything, basically. Except where she is. We knocked her out so it wouldn't complicate things."

"But you didn't knock *me* out."

"No need, really. Leeland himself knows about this place." Dorian shrugged his bare shoulders and ran a finger over a dusty shelf, feeling the grime. *Cestus was supposed to clean.*

"Then why the hell did you knock her out?"

"Mostly for her own safety. The less she knows, the less she has to worry about."

"But I thought you said you told her everything."

"*Basically.*" He turned back to his hot cocoa.

---

[22] Please don't wake them! I don't want to have to *read* them.

"Why would you do that?" Odys's voice was low, trying to remain in control. "You know I didn't want her to know."

"Yeah, well, Mother didn't want her to know either, so I've not only disappointed you." He stuffed his face with a cookie. "Mother will be here soon. She's about twenty minutes away. Texted just before you came in."

"And Bob?" Rosemund asked as she rummaged through drawers.

Oh, yeah, Bob. Bob, if you care to remember, had just killed herself for mysterious reasons. Reasons I'm yet to properly illuminate.

"We can't seem to get in touch. She's likely passed out somewhere. Mother sent Ansi to go and check up on things. Mec said that she came to him right before we headed here. She had been looking for me."

Rosemund made a face at him. "I wonder why."

Odys narrowed his eyes at the conversation flow. "Yes, why?"

"Honestly," Dorian moaned, "Bob freaks out when you break the rules just a little. Could be that."

"Well, your little excursions have caused us trouble in the past" Rosemund nodded to Caffar in answer to some unspoken question about the luggage.

"Excursions?" Odys repeated. But everyone ignored him.

Dorian shrugged it off. "But anyway, Rosie, to answer your question, Gwen's traveling alone. No Ansi until we find out where Bob's at. She probably forgot what day it is."

"It's not safe for Gwen to travel alone," Rosemund commented, concerned for her. She was already investigating the toaster, probably wondering how she could make it explode. "Why wouldn't she send one of us? She's the bigbigbiggest target."

"Mother can handle herself." Dorian assured (himself more than anyone else). He unplugged the toaster before Rosemund could push down the lever.

"I still don't like what you've done, Dorian," Odys lectured. "What—what did you do? How did you just—just tell her? Why would you even do that?"

Dorian frowned. "Vulcan complicated things."

Odys's brows merged. "How so?"

"I think what made things *most* complicated was that you didn't bother to tell us your sister was *married* to Leeland." Dorian was hissing now. "That was a major plot point you overlooked."

"Is that why you did it?" Odys brimmed, choking back volume. "Because I lied to you? It—it doesn't mean anything! I didn't even realize the full implications of *knowing* that fact until I synced with Maud."

"Yes, but you knew enough about Mother—sans Maud—to know your facts were valuable." His voice so low, Odys inched forward to hear: "It means he was willing to fuck her, doesn't it? Which is strange, since he killed *your* parents to get to *me* because *he* wants to fuck *Mother*."

"You don't know if they were my parents! It's too much of a stretch." Odys felt defensive—defensive although he was the victim. "That's just what Leeland wants us to think."

"Good to know you haven't completely turned against our side of things." Dorian put another cookie in his mouth angrily. Chewing, "Look, be mad at me all you want. But you and I both know my punishment from Gwen'll be worse than any shit you can dish out."

Odys hesitated in place, wondering if he should be grateful that part was over. "And she knows what Maud is?"

"She's not stupid."

"You had no right to do that—to tell her," Odys huffed, looking at their door—the door Odissa was behind. He could feel her.

"That's not all he did to her," Rosemund said, sticking a knife in the toaster slots.

Dorian snapped at her, "Honestly, does Mother have to tell you everything? I miss the days when she didn't know how to text—"

"Wait," Odys said too loudly (making Mecca stir). "What does she mean?"

"You should tell him, Dori," Rosemund said, plugging the toaster back in—sure that it would work to her satisfaction within the tested outlet. She then began to look for the switches in the kitchen—the ones to the lights and the garbage disposal. This was her routine, to inspect for booby traps of others as well as test her own. "That's the only reason Mother lets us keep her anyway. It's not because Odys is actually oneoneone of us. Odys might even find a way to be grateful for it."

She turned on the garbage disposal and listened to it gurgle; they cringed and looked at Mecca—still asleep. Whew.

"For what, Dorian?" Odys said over the noise as it died.

"Vulcan, like I said." Dorian pushed up his glasses. "His wife got involved."

"You fucking with me now? Why do you speak in vague warnings?"

"Just go talk to your sister, Odys." Dorian waved him off and blew on his cocoa.

Odys scoffed, uneasy with the invitation to enter Dorian's room. But she was already standing there, in the doorframe when he turned around. Fletcher had just left the room. She had clearly tried to listen to this entire conversation.

Fletcher gave a mocking bow to Odys as they passed each other—a guard stepping aside for the peasant.

Odys fought back tears when he grabbed her. When Odys saw that the others were going to let them have a moment—a private moment—he jumped at the opportunity. He closed the door behind them, locking it, and not letting Odissa go. He was surprised they didn't shout at him to leave it open. "Fuck, I'm so sorry."

He pulled back to study her expression.

"Where the hell have you been?" She found his eyes too interested and too needy, so she looked away—at the messy bed that, thank God, had the sheets covering any proof of what she'd done.

"Why is your hair wet?"

Her skin prickled when he walked past her to inspect the room and Dorian's bathroom—how did he know it was the bathroom? Had he been here before?

"I haven't blow dried it yet," she answered quietly. It was the truth.

He paced back to her. "They told me you know what's going on. What I am. What I have." He expected her confirmation.

"Yes. An…an Automaton." She stuttered it out and beamed. She'd finally gotten it right.

"You know why you're here then?" He sat down on Dorian's bed—that unmade bed.

"It's OK, Odys." She touched his sleeved arm and sat down. "We'll be fine."

He just sat there, tired and wanting to sleep. Yet he also didn't want to take his eyes away from her. His voice dropping, "You know they *know*, right? About us." *What we've done.*

She swallowed and turned her head. "Of course they do. Half the people we know eventually let it cross their minds."

"At least we don't have to hide it, I guess." He tried to laugh, but the sound caught in his throat. It was muffled by his hands. "They know everything about us, Odissa. They've ruined us."

She didn't want to stay on that subject. "Where's Maud?" The name was foreign on her tongue.

Surprised by her question, he touched his coat pocket. Reluctantly, he took her out and placed her in Odissa's hand. It felt very exalting, to let Odissa hold his soul. He could feel her fingers tracing Maud's ridges—holding her until Maud warmed like flesh. He wanted to like it, but wasn't sure he should.

"I know what she is to you, Odys." She said it as if he'd better not deny it. "They talk about her enough. Can you make her form?"

He cringed at the use of her new vocabulary—how did she know to use these terms? *"Form."*

He took Maud from her hand and set her on the bed. Maud appeared before them, between them. Odissa stood up, as if to get away from her. Maud smiled—because

Odys made her. It was a smile that said "Sorry." Sorry that she existed. Sorry in general.

"She looks different than when we first met. Not just what she's wearing—not just her skin."

He didn't like how Odissa talked about Maud as if she was an inanimate doll—normal humans shouldn't be able to tell. It was hard for *him* to remember she wasn't human, yet his sister regarded her with perfect skepticism. "It's because I'm controlling her now. I've finally—what's the word?—I've finally accepted her and we're...meshed together. She's me. I'm her."

"Like an avatar?" She was fascinated and horrified in her subject.

"Want me to make her go away?"

"No, let her be. And let her be herself."

"She doesn't have a self."

"Fletcher has a self."

"What do you mean?" *And why are you even mentioning Fletcher?*

"Even though he's Dorian's soul, right, Dorian still lets him be. She's you, right? That, there, is not acting like you. You're inhibiting her—inhibiting yourself. Aren't you?" She was staring at Maud as if watching a friendly ghost—recognizing the dead.

"How else would I act if I were an Automaton showing myself to my sister for the first time—the *real* first time?" He was sort of impressed by how he was handling her questions.

"I don't know. But she seems afraid of me. Are you afraid of me?" *I'm not judging you.*

He made Maud turn back to a coin and took her up—not only because he was embarrassed. He could no longer stand the smell Maud smelled—the scent of gods and secrets. "I don't know how you want me to make her act. I wish I didn't have her at all. Then I wouldn't have to act."

Odissa knew then that she would never see her brother again. Not as himself. He had to reestablish an identity—it was all still so up in the air. *He's a girl now too.*

She rifled for words to soothe him. "If Vulcan lets you keep her, you must be meant to have her, right?"

"What do you know of Vulcan? He lets even your goddamned *husband* keep one, doesn't he?" *She shouldn't know these words—these connotations! Vulcan, Automaton, Masters.* "What do you know about any of this, Odissa? You can't understand. I don't even understand!" He jabbed his chest with a finger, blood pressure rising.

She looked alarmed at his shaking but nodded. "I didn't mean—"

"I know you didn't." He brooded away from her. "Where did you sleep last night?"

"I'm not even sure how long I was asleep. But it wasn't just night. I woke up here."

"They gave you a room to sleep in?"

"Yes, this one." *That's what I meant by here.*

He looked around the room, seeing Dorian's suitcases scattered about. "Do you have a change of clothes? Where did you get those?"

"Dorian gave me these." She laughed, pulling at a blouse he had stolen.

Why was she laughing? Odys rubbed his face, knowing something was not right. But what? That smell burned into Maud's nostrils.

"Odys," her voice was low, "what else I should know?"

"Like what?" He found a smile—as if she were conspiring with him.

"The man who committed suicide? Who was he really?"

"Pepin? Pepin, gave me Maud. That's why I touched her, right after he killed himself. The first person to touch an inanimate Automaton is their Master." He went on.

"And this 'mother'—what is her name again?"

"Gwen. Gwendolyn. 'Mother' is her nickname. She's the one who had Dorian kidnap you."

"*Why* did they take me, by the way? Where were you?"

He didn't want to frighten her. "They wanted to make sure I got a job done. And they needed you out of the apartment. They destroyed it; you know that, right?"

She nodded. "Bulfinch is here too. I saw them destroy my dental records, Odys. We're 'dead.'" She used bunny ears.

"Dorian didn't do anything...bad to get you out of the apartment, did he?" He was trying to pull it out of her like a con artist. When had he gotten so clever?

She could tell Odys knew more than he could ever speak. It expressed itself outwardly. He couldn't look at Odissa the same—couldn't even see so much as a speck of dust without recalling an unfamiliar memory. He was FULL of memories. Memories that weren't his. He had to constantly remind himself that he wasn't dreaming—watching some home video—becoming someone else. And that mental reaction affected his expression. Maud affected everything. Odissa studied it.

"Dorian can be very frightening at times," Odissa assured him as she stood up. "But he didn't hurt me, if that's what you're thinking. I'm hungry. Is it OK to come out?" she asked as if he might know the rules. "Isn't there someone else out there? I heard her voice..."

Before he let her open the door, his hand still upon it: "Things will be different, now that I'm here—now that they trust me. But I don't know how different."

"No, you don't." She put a hand on his arm, telling him it was all right to open the door. "Honestly, Odys, I'm surprised they let you alone with me. Even if they can hear us. I think you have more sway than you realize." She looked at the door and gave a disappointed sigh. "This all should be more fun."

Her words sent a chill down his spine. "Fun?"

"Mythical Automatons and gods and shit. Odys I think I saw *Venus*. A fucking goddess lifted the door like in a—a hallucination or something! She was huge and yet not really there. I mean, am I making Her up?"

He frowned, not understanding and not wanting to—but *that* was the smell Maud had twitched at. "Should you blow dry your hair first?" He didn't want her out there yet.

She blushed, remembering her wet hair. And how it had *become* so wet. She touched it. She caught on. "Yeah, that's a good idea. There's one of those attached ones, on the bathroom wall. This place is a rental cabin or something, isn't it?"

"Or something." He didn't want to tell her.

She gave him a dutiful kiss on the cheek then backed away to the bathroom. "I'll be right out, then."

"And collect your things—if you have any. You'll...you'll stay with me."

She bit her lip. "I don't think I should, Odys." He could see her grow pale, could see her heart pounding in her chest. "They—they said this was my room. I don't know why. I don't want you to get in trouble." She was talking too fast.

She did know why.

"I'll talk to them. You'll at least get your own room, if I have a say."

She nodded obediently. *Oh fuck, he knows he knows he knows.*

Odys came out of the room into mid-conversation between Dorian and Rosemund, plowing over Fletcher who had been eavesdropping. They stopped their word-flow as he stood there, glaring at Dorian and flipping over a barstool.

They went quiet.

"What's the matter?" Dorian's long fingers set his cocoa mug down by the brim. He only reacted because Odys risked waking Mecca.

Odys's fist slid over the island counter, wavering between punching or breaking something. "Having Maud's memories, Dorian, lets me know a lot about you. Like how you always get the room with the best bathtub. I even seem to know the smell of your favorite cologne and soaps and lotions."

"As everyone should. What's your point?"

Odys had him against the fridge in an instant. Fletcher merely munched some cookies from a bag, continuing the conversation with Rosemund where his Master had left off. Caffar was busy staring at the ceiling bulbs. The lights had dimmed since Odissa started pulling wattage with the antique hairdryer.

"I thought you liked boys, Dorian." Odys growled. "But here she is, smelling like you and in the room with the tub. At first I thought, nah, this is just you wanting to be the gay BFF. Wanting to study up for when you finally get the nerve to chop that dick off. But that's not Odissa's style. She doesn't do sleepovers. She *has no* friends. You better fucking tell me I'm wrong, Dorian. What are you playing at? You better fucking tell me this is just you wanting a fag hag, so help me—"

"I'm—I'm in love with her, Odys," Dorian replied, very honestly, very respectfully. He didn't even protest the arm choking him.

"What?"

Dorian shivered. "Vulcan told me to. Made me. Changed my—my very nature." He raised his hands to Odys's face, to his own nose. "There, you can still *smell* the gods on me. I don't want this either!"

Odys dodged his hands in repulsion.

"Perfumed ash—that's what it is." Dorian sniffed his hands as if he couldn't decide if he liked the scent, a dog fascinated with trash. "And I have no intention of chopping my dick off. I'm a femme he and always will be!"

"They have gender-neutral pronouns now, though," Rosemund mumbled, walking past them as if she could care less if Dorian lived or died.[23]

"We *transcend* gender," Fletcher snapped back, unable to resist defending how Dorian could still embrace his *he* at a time like this.

---

[23] I inserted this to acknowledge Dorian's decision to not use a they/them pronoun, but want to voice that historical accuracy is what we were shooting for. At the time, they were not as prevalent in our culture.

Odys shook his head, nostrils gaping like a bull's. "Do you know how sick this is? What if she *is* Dorothy, huh? What if she is?"

Dorian's face melted in sorrow. "You think I don't know how this looks? You think I wanted this to happen? It's not my fucking fault!" He jerked, rattling the fridge.

"Such an Eve!" Odys spat at him, hating how that shamed face made him feel—a face Odys made in the mirror far too often when looking at himself. "To blame someone else."

"Eve? Nah. He likes to think he's more like Paris claiming Helen because Aphrodite said he could have her," Fletcher said, licking his fingers. "Granted, both had apples involved."

Odys re-slammed Dorian into the fridge. A few magnets fell off. "What have you done?"

"I'm not the only one involved here, Odys," he warned quietly behind his wet hair. *Odissa played her part.* "And if you want to continue to be a welcomed guest, I suggest you recognize that."

Odys leaned in threateningly close. "I will not forgive you for this."

"I never asked for your forgiveness. Not in this." He breathed in deep when Odys let him go, controlling himself. "It's His Wife. The gods let His Wife to do this."

"*Why* would They do this? To what purpose?"

"Maybe He *really* wants to see you fuck Maud?" Dorian offered up.

Odys smacked the glasses off Dorian's face. They cracked on the floor. Odys chased Dorian's retreating visage. "Though you all fuck yours doesn't mean I'm going to. Why's He so concerned with us now, then? He's been silent all these years. How do I know you're not lying?"

Dorian uncurled. "Because, like you said, Odys. I used to fuck guys. Just look at my dick right now!" He chuckled. "I think it's proof enough when it does the same thing for her."

Odys looked down at Dorian's towel and cringed in disgust. He turned to Rosemund for input, but she was too busy taking apart the coffee maker now.

"You can join us in a threesome, if you want," Dorian gave a mad laugh—a laugh at the fact he couldn't believe what he was saying. "Might as well make sure we're incesty enough."

Odys pursued him around the kitchen island to kill him. Just as Odys was about to catch him, he jumped—the front door opened and Mother came in shouting. In Spanish, she asked Dorian *what the fucking hell was going on and why had he upset Odys? Better yet, why was he letting Odys beat him up?* Odys, because Maud was fluent in more than one language (do I even need to stress this point?), understood them. Picking his battles, he gave one more shove onto the ground and left Dorian.

Mother, who had just been bringing in some heavy grocery sacks, set them down and began removing her black leather gloves by each finger. Staring at her naughty children, her nostrils flared. "Odys, remember whose home you are in." She unbuttoned her black pea coat and removed her black cap. Her thick black hair was braided and re-braided down her back in one, lone mass. Her blackness distracted the puffy redness in her eyes. She looked like she'd just gotten back from a funeral.

"If I'm one of you now why can't you let us go?" *Why are we here?*

She smoothed down her skinny black dress, her hands trembling in fear that he would not forgive her. "Please, Odys, let's sit down. All of us. Let me explain."

It was like some galling "family meeting" invitation.

But Odys didn't move. "What more is there to explain? None of us are worthy of knowing what the fuck is going on in your world, Gwen. Not until it's over."

"But it *is* over, Odys," her eyes danced with happy tears. She came up to him, reaching out with that slender brown hand as if she might cup his cheek. "Don't you see? You're one of us now."

He backed away from her—from them all—in disgust.

"I'm not one of you. You didn't pick me."

Then, turning, he picked a random room (that he hoped was vacant) and locked himself in. He vowed to himself that if they tore down the door, he'd set Maud on them. *If I'm a captive, I'm a captive.*

He accepted his fate.

"No, let him go," he heard Mother say. "Give him some space. He's earned it."

Though he couldn't see it, and didn't care, Mother went back to her grocery sacks and took out some contents. "I got these for Cestus. He'll want to bake at a time like this."

"And where is Bob? Any news?" Dorian asked, rubbing his red throat.

Dead, of course, but that cover story hadn't broken the news just yet.

So let's get back to Odys:

He tossed Maud onto the queen-sized bed. "Let's talk this through, Odys." Maud's words were steely-but-faint whispers, so no one would hear though the walls—if they even cared to.

"Yes. Let's do," he almost growled the agreement, reaching out and expecting a pack of cigarettes. Maud pulled one out of her "bra," keeping a cigarette for herself. She had a whole carton in there, tucked away. They got it at their last pit stop. They may or may not have paid for it. "She was embarrassed. She couldn't look at me. She's always like that, when she…"

"Has sex with someone other than us." She snapped in front of his cigarette, making it catch fire.

He leaned forward, fingers in his hair, cigarette trembling in his lips. "This makes my skin crawl."[24]

"I know, that's why you made me say it." "At least if Dorian likes her then—" "She's twice as protected." "They can't threaten to kill her anymore. Dorian won't let them." "Maybe this is a good thing, Maud. The only reason she—she even…"

---

[24] OK, so all this talk about Odys's face and hair yet there's no mention of his glasses lately? I find this strange but somehow forgivable. Maybe Maud makes him more confident that he doesn't need them, like Dorian?

"Perhaps it's necessary to give her a chance." "A chance to choose." "She's never had one of those." "Is that her?"

They stopped to listen to Odissa's genial voice through the door. She'd come out. And where was her brother?

They waited for her to come to the door—to ask to see him—to demand it—to bang on the door—to shout for him. But she didn't.

They lit up another round of cigarettes.

Stanza: Dry hair.

"You think I don't know that?" Dorian was saying to Gwen in Spanish. "Don't you see I couldn't help it?"

"There's always a choice, Dorian," Gwen admonished. "And now he'll be out of control."

Odissa's eyes flickered over the familiar and unfamiliar. Mother stood up to greet her, dabbing her eyes. They would never be dry. She glared at Dorian. *We'll finish this later.*

"I'm Gwen," Mother took her hand in both of hers, brought them to her chest. "I am very glad you're here and safe with us now. You don't know what danger you have been in. And this is Rosemund, and her Automaton, Caffar."

Rosemund waved from the table, but she didn't look up. She was too busy searching for a lost part to the dissected blender (the coffee maker had checked out).

Odissa found it hard not to stare at Rosemund's scars. And the blazing red hair, the brace-face, that goth-punk next to her.

"Rosie," Fletcher said, "Make Caffar change, you're scaring Odissa. First impressions and all."

The countless piercings disappeared back into the Automaton's head. Rosemund grumbled under her breath.

The introductions continued. "My Automaton should be here later," Mother said. "He went to pick up Bob and Cestus, who were supposed to beat me here." She looked at her watch, one last time. "Did you at least get some rest? I'm so sorry for the way we did this. Do you need anything? Has Dorian taken good care of you?"

Odissa looked to Dorian and nodded. She quite liked how calming Mother was. Even though it looked like she'd been crying, she made the room feel orderly—like she could control everything like an axis. "I'm afraid your brother was tired, so he went to bed." She leaned in to whisper, "Let's not disturb him."

Odissa's stomach tightened. Why had he abandoned her? What had she missed? Dorian sensed her questions and shook his head. *Don't ask questions, Odissa, it won't go well for anyone.*

"The long flight was long," Rosemund said—the first to come up with an excuse. "Jet lag."

"The food will be here soon, too. Pizza," Gwen said, quickly changing the subject. "Hope that's all right? What kind do you like?"

Odissa couldn't remember what she said. It was probably "Any."—anything to get them to stop looking at her so that she could look at them.

As if Rosemund could tell Odissa wanted free from this alien probing, she cleared her throat. Taking a deck of cards out of her pocket, Rosemund shuffled them all the way to the couch. Most were surprised she didn't take them out of her hair. "Who wants to play poker?"

Mecca sat up from his seat beside her and rubbed his eyes, fully awake now but refusing to look at them like a lazy cat considering another nap. "Poker lost its fun when Mecca lost his favorite machine gun to Dorian last time."

"Which you stole back anyway," Dorian mumbled.

"You weren't using it!" Q shouted, as if Dorian were wasteful.

Caffar, her body hardly moving as she picked something out of her Master's back pockets, unrolled two tickets as her Master said, "But money can't buy the sold-out [BIG CITY] Anime Con tickets, can it?" Rosemund sat smugly.

Mecca and Q were moving the coffee table toward them in an instant (Q wearing a fancy black-jack dealer costume and shuffling some self-formed cards that disappeared back into her palms). ANTE UP.

"You play?" Mother asked Odissa as she dabbed her nose with a handkerchief. She chose a chair in the living room, moving it forward. Caffar brought the wooden dining room chairs in, considered dragging in the actual table, left the rustic benches.

Odissa found it hard to answer Mother's question when she had so many of her own. "Not really," was the kindest response she could muster under her current frustration.

"We need a diversion, believe me. I will encourage you to wake up your brother when he's had rest. Come, you'll like it." Mother put a hand on her arm and tugged her in—a perfect hostess.

"Odissa is my partner," Dorian declared, just as Mecca had opened his mouth to. No one dared question him. Odissa found it odd that Rosemund was dealing out to Automatons as well.

"I can have my own hand," Odissa said, thinking this was awkward enough as it was.

"Yeah!" Mecca said, still moving chairs. "Give her a hand."

"No, no," Rosemund shook her head. "Mortals never have anything we want. We play for real tonight!"

Mecca grumbled, making Odissa wonder what he could possibly want from her losing hand. A boob squeeze?

Everyone settled in except Odissa, unsure where she might sit—no vacant chairs—no real space on the floor. They all looked up to her, waiting for her to sit.

But Dorian patted his towel-covered lap from the love seat beside Fletcher. "No thanks," Odissa declined, wanting to slap him.[25]

"Don't worry, my love. If you haven't caught on, they already know I'm fucking you." He said it in his toneless manner, waving his fingers just how Odissa thought Oscar Wilde might.

Mother tsked at him for saying it that way. "Your manners, boy."

Odissa turned bright red—more at the fact they hadn't ignored him.

"Here," Rosemund made Caffar give up her tight seat beside her. The Automaton could sit on the arm. But Dorian snapped his fingers.

"No, she already has a seat." He waved for Caffar to keep her ass planted.

And Caffar sat back down, glaring. *The fuck are you doing, Dorian?*

"Best show them that you like me, Odissa." The bright smile on his face did not match his dark words.

"Don't be silly, Dorian—" Gwen lifted her hand—there was a stool just there.

But Dorian cut her off. "Do I have to make you sit, Odissa? Your brother's not making you act up now, is he?" He took some gum Fletcher offered him. He chewed it under those new glasses Fletcher had supplied as well.

She looked to Mother and Rosemund. Would they say nothing about *that* comment? No, they would not. She saw where they drew the line. He showed her clearly: she was there only because she made Dorian happy. *And she best keep him happy.*

"I'm not a child, Dorian. I want a chair."

The silence deepened. Fletcher moved half an inch, daring her to sit between them. It was enough for a leg.

When she hesitantly sat down across Dorian's lap (leaning away from him toward the arm as if they shared two heads to one body), Mecca made it a point to switch places with Q. So he could sit closer to her in a wooden dining chair.

It was not normal to see a woman on Dorian's lap. It did not suit him. Even he knew this, but he carried on with the performance. The others watched the show with

---

[25] Thankfully this wasn't strip poker, or we'd ALL see Dorian.

all the curiosity of an anthropologist interpreting a new cultural artifact they could not make sense of. Odissa wasn't being infantilized, she was being enthroned; they, her Hephaestus chair.

"You get to be my eyes, love," Dorian said kissing the back of her tense neck. It prickled her skin. "Now, let's keep Mecca from going to that con, shall we?" Dorian adjusted his towel under her.

"I will burn those tickets, if I keep them," Rosemund stated, fanning out her cards. Her glasses flashed as she studied them.

"Even though you spent money on them?" Mother asked, taking account of her own, reordering them.

"Who said anything about money? Stole them off a prick teenager."

"Sure you did," Fletcher rolled his eyes, adjusting his cards (playing with Automata increased the odds of winning, apparently, and switching out cards between a Master and Automata pair was freely done since "they know each other's cards anyway," as Gwen would say, despite her odds being currently halved).

And so Odissa watched them play poker—Texas Hold 'Em, Five Card Draw, or some variation she'd never heard of. She would put Dorian's cards down for him, for she could reach the table better, but Fletcher always double-checked her play—not because he didn't trust her, but because they had too much to lose.

And so it went.

Fletcher lost Dorian's David Bowie vinyl collection he kept in climate-controlled storage in Nebraska (to Mecca); Rosemund, not only the convention tickets, but her right to plug anything in for a week (to Mecca); Mother lost a kiss on the cheek to Mecca (which she would have given him anyway); and Dorian lost Fletcher's right to eat ice cream (which didn't bother Fletcher because he'd already eaten all of it) (to Q, and therefore Mecca).

71

Are they letting him win? Odissa wondered. *Or are these things worthless to them?*

"Mecca cheats," Dorian whispered to her. Which seemed true enough to Odissa, who caught all of them attempting to at one point or another. But faking cards and sleight of hand only got Automata so far when someone else was also cheating.

Still the games continued.

Their IOUs were written on scraps of paper from the notes section of Rosemund's pocket calendar. Those that didn't require a rain check seemed more like the results of Truth or Dare.

Suggestions for what the others should bet were unwelcomed, but offered and sometimes obliged. When it wasn't equal to the other raises, some refused to play a round. "No one cares about your passwords to the bank accounts, Rosemund. We can hack those anyway," Q announced. "I want to know what you did to our undeveloped Judy Garland negatives."

"You mean *my* Judy Garland negatives," Dorian grumbled.

"I won them fair and square last year!"

"Yeah, fair," Gwen snorted.

The pizza came and they kept on playing.

Mecca was most pleased with his winnings and had only once lost the right to take pictures all night (which they knew he wouldn't stick to) and had even gotten Rosemund to ante-up an experiment demonstration:

Caffar (though she had to plug her finger in the light socket, which was against their recent losses) demonstrated Rosemund's latest technological advance (for their Automaton world). "It only works if your Automaton has enveloped a rechargeable power supply inside them—car battery or something else they can hook their inner parts up to."

"She has a car battery inside her right now?" Fletcher raised and eyebrow and crossed his arms.

"She has two," Rosemund corrected. "And some...other stuff. Now, Caffar, if you will..." And she did. The lights in the house dimmed. "Look how easily the energy increases the pull of her skin," Rosemund had said as Caffar's head had split into two sparking masses like an amoeba. Apparently, with the right focus, Caffar could *almost* split. It wasn't exactly the most pleasant thing to watch (and Rosemund discouraged other Automatons from doing it) but Rosemund claimed, "It's the start to replicating an Automaton. Like asexual creatures, it's possibly possible. But it takes too much out of mymymy concentration." Her scarred lips frowned as she remembered something, making Caffar fizzle out of her hydra state. "Though it's not as if one could *actually* become two different beings. It's cloning." She looked at Q. "Not unless the Alchemy and electricity combined seamlessly, which I haven't figured outoutout how to do. I don't know enough Alchemy. Admund might know what to look for but the Words don't come to Caffar…"

Caffar wobbled in place, holding her nose as if it might bleed. But Automatons do not bleed. They sneeze out. Rosemund reached for her other hand to recharge, her own nose bleeding.

Fletcher cringed and grabbed them a hand towel.

"Is this you asking me to look into it?" Q wondered, taking out a lollipop she'd been working on for some time. What she lacked in knowledge she made up for in connections.

"If you're interested," Rosemund shrugged. "But that doesn't mean I'll give you the inner secrets to how Caffar does it."

"Another game, perhaps?"

This is how they govern themselves, Odissa observed. *This is their legislation. This is their justice.*

"Why are you trying to create a second Automaton anyway, Rose?" Dorian asked. "Not like we need more of them around."

Rosemund was not one to share reasons; that would take another card game.

But Mother checked her watch. They were running out of good material. "Odissa, maybe you should see if your brother's doing OK? I know he needs his sleep, but..." Her eyes darted to Dorian. "He also needs his supper."

Odissa jumped at the chance to get off Dorian's lap—well, it had really morphed into a position that was between his legs, the towel threatening to untuck itself at any moment.

Odissa could smell the smoke behind the closed door and the humid air of a shower. She knocked. Softly called his name. No answer. She tried the knob, just for grins and giggles. He hadn't locked it. The others weren't paying attention. Fletcher was watching from the corner of his eye, but otherwise they didn't seem to care she had been able to open it.

"No, Mecca," Fletcher squabbled, "We won't gamble our hair products on the next round. Out of the question."

Odissa let in a crack of light in the dark, smoky room. Odys really was in bed. With Maud. Fast asleep. They had used a candle as an ashtray and it barely held the butts.

At first it took her breath away—that he would even fall asleep when she was here, when he hadn't seen her for so long, when she had worried so much about him. *How dare he. He really had been sleeping.*

She knew her brother well enough. She knew this hadn't meant to hurt her, this accidental sight. Even though the naked woman in his bed—so beautiful and sweet—shocked her at first, she reasoned it out. Even her brother, there, holding the naked woman could be reasoned out.

Maud's eyes flickered open, startled. But Odys didn't stir. At first Maud's reaction was sad. Then shocked. Odissa saw her brother in Maud's eyes. A flash of anger—an anger directed at Odissa—and then a pleading apology. Odys woke up when he sensed Maud's emotions. He almost said her name but stopped.

The only thing frightening about this situation was that Odys didn't try to cover Maud's half-exposed body—the body touching him. There suddenly was no shame or grace to this intimate scene. He was letting his sister see what he had become. He *wanted* this chintzy image to impair her—as she had impaired him.

Backing out, she closed the door and pretended she hadn't been thrown off. She smoothed down her hair as if patting thoughts back down.

"He's asleep still," she told them as she came back to Dorian. But no one seemed to care. They were all too distracted by Mother, who was holding back a sob, crumpled over in a living room seat, everyone asking her what was wrong. They had noticed her get up from the table—listening to the voice in her head like someone answering a phone call—watching the images inside. Anselm, like a ghost, was speaking to her—from such a great distance—from such a horrific scene—from such an unwanted moment:

"Oh my god," Mother answered them. "He's just..." Tears welled up in her vacant eyes, as if watching something they couldn't see. "They're there."

"Who? Bob?" Rosemund pressed.

"Oh god," Mother gasped. "I see them. They're there."

Rosemund limped to her and grabbed her hand. "Who, dear?"

"He got to them!" Mother screamed, looking up as if she, too, could see Bob dangling from the ceiling. "Leeland got to them!"

Odissa recoiled at the painful sounds. She wasn't sure she should continue to enter the room. She was caught between two private worlds—caught where she didn't fit.

"What?" Fletcher pressed, his voice strained. His Master, on the other hand, had no words at all.

Rosemund pat Gwen's back—tried to get her to speak. "What does he see, my dove? What does he see?"

Mother clutched Rosemund's arm. "She—she did it, Rose. She finally did it. She killed herself."

Yes, Mother could see Bob. Anselm was standing below her in the hotel room, looking up with tears in his eyes at her swaying body.

Mother's eyes closed. Anselm's eyes closed.

Gwen did not want to see this site.

Odissa noticed a hush fall over the room. She watched it with unwilling eyes, not knowing what this really meant.

"Can Ansi find Cestus?" Mecca asked, almost panicked.

Mother looked about her, as if searching the hotel room. "No," Mother sobbed. "He's gone. Cestus is gone. He's not there. She wouldn't have hidden him, would she? She would have made it obvious—"

Rosemund turned to Caffar. "Go find Ansi. Help him."

"No!" Mother shouted. "Don't leave me. Don't leave me. All of you must stay here, Rosemund. Don't go." She pleaded with Rosemund, clutching her face. "I can't lose another one of you."

"Yes, Gwen. I'm right here. I won't leave. All of me isisis here."

"Has she texted anyone?" Fletcher asked the room, as if accusing them of hiding something. *Who did she tell?*

No one answered.

"Mecca saw her last," Mecca said, guilt rising in his throat.

Gwen rushed to him, leaving Rosemund behind. She picked him up in her arms and they wept together. "Hush now, it's not your fault. It wasn't you." She stroked his head.

"Can Ansi handle the cleanup?" Dorian asked, a bit too controlled.

Mother nodded, taking Q's hand as the Automaton tried to soothe her. Silver tears trickled down Q's pretty cheeks…

I'll admit this scene is melodramatic.

"I can't believe she did it." Fletcher pushed at his mouth. "She actually gave in."

"That's three he has now," Rosemund whispered. "That's *three*."

"Maybe even four if we count Madus," Dorian said.

In Spanish, Mother wept, begging God to forgive her for leaving Bob alone. Of course it would be Bob who Leeland would target next. She was the most vulnerable.

"But what did he have on her that he didn't before?" Odys said from the door frame. He had gotten up when he heard the crying.

Everyone stopped to consider, even though it wasn't pleasant. Finally Rosemund said, "Nothing." And maybe there really was nothing. No reason Bob had finally let Leeland have Cestus. Maybe *no* reason was the *best* reason, if it would make their guessing stop.

"She told Mecca that Vulcan came to her," Mecca said.

"What?" Fletcher growled. "And you're just telling us this now?"

"Vulcan came to you too," Q said, drying her eyes on the hem of Mecca's shirt. "Why would V coming to Bob be a big deal?"

"Because Vulcan *told* her something," Dorian said—growled at the Master-Automaton pair. "He told her something, and we should have known about it, Mec. Why didn't you *tell* us she knew something?" His fingers twitched to strangle the boy's neck.

"She was trying to find you. She could have told you herself," Q defended her Master. "But she didn't find you, did she?"

"You found me, though. *You* could have said."

"Long after we thought Bob had found you and gone on with her business!"

"You didn't think *to ask* why Bob wanted to find me?"

"Don't you yell at him!" Mother scolded Dorian. "It's not his fault. If Bob wanted to find you, she could have. But it...it must have been too late. She must have arranged it—" Her voice cracked. *There had been a timeline.*

And the tears started up again.

Rosemund held Gwen tighter, kissed her hair, hushed her.

They sat for some hours around the fire. Just thinking. Just waiting for Ansi. Just waiting for Ansi. Just waiting for Ansi. That's all they could do.

When Mother finally said, "He's here," they began to move again—to remember they were still alive. Odissa woke up with her head on the arm of the couch. Dorian had let Odys sit beside her, apparently. He had not fallen asleep. He had pretended to, though.

Dorian was suddenly wearing clothes.

Their eyes watched the door. Q rushed to the window. When Ansi walked in, Odys stood up from Odissa. Maud had been in his pocket since he'd left his room. That was probably for the best. It was very crowded in the house as it was.

As the Automaton walked in, Odissa guessed who it was—this small being with his head hanging low and doll-sized hand wringing the doorknob—and didn't expect a proper introduction.

They watched Ansi and Mother, expecting closure: Ansi moved his lips as if he weren't used to talking. "It's taken care of." The sound hit their ears only after he stopped speaking.

"What did you find?" Rosemund asked him—as if he might know something Gwen did not—knew things Gwen might suppress.

"I couldn't find any *reason*." His eyes flickered over the group, defeated in his study of their faces—hoping they might have a guess. "No reason."

"We knew she would break eventually," Dorian said, his voice barely audible. He uncrossed his legs and leaned forward. *We knew she was suicidal.*

"How dare you," Ansi scolded him, letting the door slam behind him.

"But we didn't know she would break for Leeland. He'd never brokebrokebroken her before," Rosemund said, her hand squeezing the fancy hook of a metal cane.

Dorian shook his head. "She knew Odissa would be his next target to get to us. She didn't want to live through it all again."

"She didn't even know Odissa!" Odys barked.

"You think we know half the people who've died because of us?" Dorian laughed.

"Shush now." Rosemund shook a long nail at him. *Not in front of Gwen.*

"She was the only one with guts to do it," Mecca said to himself—a lonely little ball on the loveseat. Q put a hand over his mouth, realizing he had spoken it aloud. They both blushed and withdrew like an armadillo with two heads.

"I think the time is time for bed," Rosemund took over the leadership position, since Mother was avoiding eyes. She poofed up her hair nervously, waiting for obedience.

"Don't leave me, Rose," Mother sobbed, reaching out to her. Rosemund followed Mother to her bedroom. Anselm's phone dinged inside him—a muted sound and vibration. He reached for it but thought better of it. There was only one person it could be—he who was not here—and he could wait.

Everyone trickled out except Fletcher, Dorian, Odissa (who didn't know where to go), and Odys. They glared at each other's feet, unwilling to meet eyes. Odissa watched Caffar close the door behind her and her Master, those blank bead-eyes *knew* why the others lingered. Caffar never blinked. Never. Odissa's eyes blinked and begged for them not to go—don't leave her in the middle of this.

But there was a reason Rosemund wanted Mother alone.

"Odissa," Dorian spoke, crossing his arms over his sweatered chest. "Sit down." She sat back down. "Odys," Dorian addressed him, "this is a very difficult time for us. For you too, I'm sure. Maud hasn't forgotten Bob; you've lost someone as well. However, until we figure out what exactly is going on, I'm going accompany your sister. Do you understand? Let's not beat around the bush any longer. She's safer with me. Leeland won't guess that I have her. You're the more obvious choice. ¿Lo entiendes?"

"I do," Odys answered, crossing his own arms. His jaw clenched as he took a step toward Dorian. "I do understand. But I want *you* to understand I'm only comfortable with it because I know there's very little dirt Leeland *has* on you.

Because you've already gotten rid of the dirt yourself, right? What little grime is left is now *part of the family*." He looked at Odissa as he said it. To be clear. To scare her. "And I'm weaker than you are. Leeland knows I'll break for her. If he comes looking for me, I don't want Odissa to be there."

"I'm going to ignore the fact you're correct but also give you my promise that—"

"Save it." Odys held up a hand. "However, I wanted to share this with you." Odys handed him the water-rippled letter from Pepin. *So you don't bitch at me like you did Mecca.*

Fletcher read it over Dorian's shoulder for him. Odissa didn't like the fact she had NO FUCKING CLUE what was going on.

"When did you get this?" Dorian whispered up at him.

"Before I left on Mother's wild goose chase, I stopped by my apartment to see the damage. Something inside me—inside Maud—told us to. Pepin meant for us to check the mail."

Dorian handed it to Fletcher, who calmly examined it—smelled it—tasted it. And then threw it in the fire.

Odissa expected Odys to react, but he didn't.

The orange fire light glowed over Dorian's body as if a demon.

"Mother already knows. Rosemund sent a text to her. Mother forwarded it to us. Secrets drift like ash. It's nothing surprising, Odys. But I do thank you for sharing it with me. I see you trust me, despite everything."

Odys wasn't surprised by Dorian's reaction. He leaned in closer, as if Caffar might be spying. "Vulcan also visited me."

Odissa's ears perked up.

"And?" Fletcher asked, tense with questions.

Odys shrugged. "And I'll see you in the morning." He kissed Odissa's head before leaving—his body pausing too long before tearing itself away. He didn't care if Dorian saw. "You know where I am if you need me. But tell him where you're going first. Don't want to *upset* him."

She glared at him—at both of them. She didn't like feeling like the placeholder.

Dorian led Odissa to their rooms. Once inside: "My brother's not as angry as I thought he would be."

"Why? You want him to be jealous?" Dorian asked, going into the bathroom to brush his teeth.

"I just don't understand."

"Well, if it makes you feel any better he did try to kill me earlier when you weren't looking. Come and brush your teeth." She watched him brush as she squeezed out toothpaste on her new tooth brush.

"Who just died?"

He did not answer immediately. "Someone named Bob. She was older than me. I was friends with her husband. She's the reason I have an Automaton, really. Her Automaton was named Cestus."

Those were the only facts that came to mind.

"Why aren't you more upset?" She began to do her own nightly ritual.

Dorian spat out the rest of his toothpaste and rinsed off his toothbrush. "Who says that I am not?"

Toothbrush impairing her speech, "I can't tell what you're feeling right now."

He was stoic once more. He waited for her to finish and then said, "I can't see. Help me find a cup. I know one's here somewhere. Fletcher's already asleep."

When they got to the bed, "Get in the middle, please."

"Between you both? But that's weird."

"Not only is it safer that way, but you'll be warmer."

"No."

"I know it's weird, but you'll get over it. Do it before I *make* you do it."

Obeying him, "So bossy."

He made her inch up close to Fletcher (who scooted in to sandwich her) and he put his arms over her in the blanket, his fingers brushing Fletcher's arm. Odissa kept on her back, hoping she might take up more room that way (which would allow her to turn sideways later and not have to touch both of them).

"I have to touch him," Dorian said as he snuggled against her. "I haven't in a while. We get sick if we don't."

"...Is he naked?"

"Why? You want me to be too?" He tried to say it jokingly, but it didn't lighten the mood. He buried his face in her neck. She felt something wet hit her skin. Dorian was crying.

So she let them have their Odissa-sandwich. She held his head grudgingly.

"Do you believe in hell, Odissa?" he whispered after choking down a sob.

"Why are you asking?" she responded quietly—as if she might wake Fletcher.

"Despite that you know there are gods walking around, do you still believe in hell—after everything you've seen?"

"Why wouldn't I believe in an afterlife?"

"No, *hell.* A place of torture."

"Why not, then?"

"Because how can so many versions of religion co-exist? Hell has little to do with the Greco-Roman gods, right? How can a normal person like you still believe in heaven?"

"I don't know what you mean. But if you think I'm so stupid, why don't you tell me what to believe?"

"There *is* hell, Odissa." He sniffed—though it was an emotionless sound. "If there's a hell then there's a heaven."

"Are you sure?" He didn't sound sure.

"No."

Fletcher started snoring softly. Something told her that the Automaton was sleeping for Dorian. He could force his Automaton to sleep but his own body was harder.

"Some say the absence of God is hell," she suggested.

"But there's nowhere God can't be. God is existence—the *gods* are everywhere. That means the condemned stop existing."

"So you think Bob stopped existing? You think she went to hell—to non-existence?"

"This isn't about Bob's fate. She sinned less than me." He reached from the covers to rub his eyes. "Even if I believed suicide was a sin, she wouldn't be damned. Where's her forgiveness? She sinned against no one. She did her gods-given job till then end."

"Then why are we talking about hell, Dorian?"

"Because I'm going there, Odissa."

"Who says? Why would you say that?"

"Because I left Bob. I've abandoned them all for you. Vulcan only makes sense to the person He directly speaks to, but Bob was going to warn me. That's why she was hunting me down. I know it. You've changed everything, Odissa."

"What's changed?"

"Who I am. I'm revenge. Leeland is the gods' leverage. I'll kill him because They allow him to live. I'll take vengeance into my own hands, because the gods owe *me*. The gods will damn me for this, Odissa. It's not justice. There's no justice from the gods."

She shrank away from his cruel face, back into Fletcher. "They won't damn you Dorian. You have every right to kill him. I wouldn't mind him dead myself."

"But your wants are nothing, Odissa—not to Them. You don't have the right to say who lives and dies. I've killed many people, Odissa. To protect my Automaton. I have let many people live as well to protect Fletcher. One of them is Leeland. The gods gave Fletcher to me and I've given my life to him. But the gods need to be punished now. And They will punish me in return. I can smell it."

She didn't know what he meant by that, but knew better than to correct a grieving man. "You've already been punished. You won't be punished more."

"How would you know?"

She held his face—thumbs too close to his blank eyes. "You're my Dorian Gray. Fletcher's your painting in the attic. You won't die. You're too beautiful. They've too much stock in you to take everything away."

He kissed her neck, lips trembling against her skin. He knew she hadn't understood his tangent. "To think I let you die once..." He sobbed.

The words sent a chill down her spine, but she found herself holding him anyway.

Stanza: Fairness and squareness.

Odys didn't brush his teeth before going to bed. He actually didn't have a tooth brush. If he'd rummaged through the cabinets, he would have found a fresh one, but he was never one to snoop. He sat on the edge of the bed, counting the cash left over from Mecca's generous donation. His feet were very cold. But he didn't want to wear his dirty socks. Tomorrow he'd ask if he could drive into town and buy new clothes. *Fucking permission.*

"It's not like the old days," Maud said sitting down beside him, crossing her legs and leaning in like a devil on his shoulder, "when you could just trade gold for anything. Now you have to have paper. Plastic."

"We should ask Dorian. He owes us. And he knows it."

"At least we have him wrapped around our finger." Maud studied hers.

"I just wish it could have been a with string less precious." Odys stared up at the ceiling, continuing his plan—his long-term plan and short-term plan—to kill Leeland.

It seemed so doable and worthwhile now.

"She likes him."

"How can you tell?"

He wanted to hear himself say it. "Never seen her have so much *fun.*"

There was a silence just long enough to feel endless. "It's not Dorian's fault—"

"Never mind, I don't want to hear you say it, Maud."

Maud fell back on the bed, curls tossed about. Odys found himself lying parallel. They watched the ceiling. Maud turned to him, his impatience expressed through her. "You always knew your paradise would be lost eventually. Nothing stays the same."

"It was never Eden," he huffed. "In a way, I always knew what we were doing was selfish. Lazy. Like we were characters in a novel written in to defend masturbation—fucking yourself.[26] Loving her was loving me." He turned his head to the side, to look at her. He was reaching a point—a turning point—he'd never considered reaching before. "Funny," he mumbled, his eyes studied her face, as if seeing it differently. "Funny how much she's like..." he paused. "How much you're like her."

"You're making me act like her, that's why." Maud rolled over on her side, intent. "Get it out of the way, Odys. Let her go. She can be a part of you *apart* from you. Has she ever really been yours? She's not even fully Dorian's right now. Stop splitting her so many ways." Maud reached out and tapped Odys's ring-finger band. "Leeland could make her run to him. You never had that power."

Odys shook out that thought. "Am I trying to make myself hate her right now?"

"Leeland could make her run to him," Maud repeated, leaning into his face.

"But only because she thought we were dependent upon him."

"But were you?"

"She could always find excuses. She needed breathing room from me."

"Venus and the gods are a pretty good excuse this time, though."

"Leeland was always available as a backup plan for her. That's how she sees it."

"And we're her new backup plan?"

"I don't want to be backup."

---

[26] I'm not going to psychoanalyze this.

85

"I don't think she wants you to be, either." Her lips pulled down. "I think by fucking her you were prolonging the inevitable, Odys. You were always meant to be alone. You've always felt that way. That's what made it so easy. You were alone with her. She was you—a version of you. You were two. But you're still two." She pointed. "One, two."

He nodded and rubbed his face. "I can see the signs, same as you."

"This is what the universe wants so there's not a lot of use fighting what you are."

Alone.

Odys, as he rammed his face into her to kiss her in a disaster of teeth and skin, accepted the fact that he'd always been cut off from Odissa, no matter how much they were from the same thread. The thread had been cut. Long ago. Only knots kept bringing them back together. And that's just what this entire life was. A Gordian knot.

Maud took his face in his hands and he kissed her mouth hard, carelessly. As he found himself on top of her—and yes, let's not pretend this wasn't going to happen eventually—he delighted in the fact how easy it was—how easy it was to fuck her, himself. She could disband her clothes in an instant. He had no need to please her. He enjoyed, however, her pretend reactions—though he didn't make her do many. Why make such an effort? Her noises expressed his own delight. When he closed his eyes, her soundless responses made it feel real—though he liked that it wasn't. It wasn't real. Somehow the falsity of the act made it all the more acceptable.

With only one party, there was less shame.

He opened his eyes at the ironic thought. He stared down at her in her warmth as their rhythms became faster. Or, as he thought about it, *his* rhythms became faster. Maud grinned up at him—an expression he willed for her. It made her easier to fuck, if her expression provoked. As he pressed against her, he got even with his sister. He never fully had her and now she'd never fully have him. He was as self-reliant as he had always wanted to be. He let Odissa go, freed her from his over-bearing, lonely nature.

When done (so efficiently too), he made Maud lay next to him in her exposed state. "That gets rid of some of the frustration, at least…"

"…Did we just jerk off on the night of Bob's death?" He remembered. He felt no shame for what he'd just done.

"But we were quiet about it."

Odys's eyes reddened, fighting back tears at his pathetic lot in in this story. Maud held him.

Odys choked into her hair. "This is why we didn't sync, isn't it? Not because of what I was repressing. But because I knew it would come to this."

"There's nothing wrong with this." With masturbating. "It's not like you did anything weird with me."

Automatons can do some weird sex stuff, believe me.

Stanza: Wash your hands after Petting the Dog.

Rosemund had finally gotten Mother to sleep and decided to take a shower before bed. Caffar sat at the bottom of the tub, bony and angled, looking up, rememorizing her Master's scars. Rosemund scrubbed and absent-mindedly thought aloud. "Bob wanted to see Odissa. That's why she was hunting down Dorian. That's what I think."

Caffar squinted past the water sprays. "I think."

Rosemund stopped scrubbing her pits and listened for a moment, as if she could hear something between the walls. No—she *did* hear something.

Maybe it was the fried wires in her brain picking up the radio-omen signals; maybe it was Caffar with her sound-magnetic ears—the only Automaton not asleep or preoccupied; maybe it was both of these beings who noticed the intruder. "Company is company—even if it's unwanted company."

"Unwanted company."

Stanza: A stranger visits strangely.

Maud and Odys had been lying on the bed for some time—hours. Dozing in and out. Not sleeping. Unable to rest. "I want a cigarette."

"Me too."

They sat up, Maud assuming a new outfit and shorter hair—the strands retracting from her face so they wouldn't disturb the future said cigarette.

"Next time I will be kinder," he told her, zipping up his pants.

"I know." He didn't have to apologize. Not to himself.

There was a soft knock on the door. Well, it wasn't even a knock. It was more like a brush on the wood before the doorknob fell off. Odys and Maud stood to their feet...as Coraza walked in.

The gun in Maud's hand wasn't matched with another's. Coraza paid no mind to it. "Answers won't be given from dead lips, Odys," Coraza warned them with a frown. "We'll make this worth your time."

Odys recognized her, of course. Maud knew who she was. Seeing her, now, he remembered her face in his own memories—not just from Pepin. Faces are easily forgotten over the years; but the fact he now realized she'd been there through part of his life, well, it sent chills down his spine. A babysitter here, a maid there.

Her face was expressionless—robotically void of awareness. She held the door opened for two others. First came in Leeland. The man who had married his sister. Following his Master was the other Automaton—the once-father.

"Hello, Odys," Leeland said—he looked about like a dad entering his son's room for "a talk." "How Maud has changed you. Aren't you going to frown at me like you used to?"

He didn't even care that there was a gun in his face, merely studied Odys for a second—searching for a reflection of himself in the boy he had made his own.

Keep staring. You made me what I am, old man.

He was clean-shaven. He wore a mid-length coat with a dark scarf bulging out of the collar. He looked so refined, especially in his unsoiled boots (Odys was sure there was mud outside, with the snow—yet he always managed to stay so *clean*).

Leeland kept his bare hands in his pockets, relaxed and unworried. He'd not need to use them.

The wrinkles of his face did not age him. They added to the intensity of his look—the large nose—the ambivalent eyes—the wide-lipped mouth. But his voice was the most interesting—like crisp book pages scratching against your hand.

Maud was torn between shooting him there and now and wanting to know why he would offer himself up like this.

"I was hoping this was the right room. Rosemund usually takes the one to the right"—he pointed—"and Gwen, the one behind. I could hear Mecca snoring, and Dorian always picks the room with the biggest tub, so I figured this *must* be your room. Bob usually takes this room. But she's dead."

"Is that why you're here? To pay your respects?" Odys wasn't afraid for his life. He knew Leeland didn't kill. The only thing Odys feared was letting this asshole get away.

Maud's copper eyes flickered between the two Automatons. They stood as god-like pillars beside their Master. Today, Coraza had a slight inch of hair with shaved sides. Had Odys cared to study her, he would have noticed the designs cut into the hair—little waves like wires from machinery. Leeland had given her intricate details. Even Admund had them. Admund—Odi Odelyn—was never so fancy in his pretend life. Perhaps this was because he had always been so distant from his Master when playing the role of "the father." It took too much out of them.

"I'm sure you're wondering, Odys, if I have Cestus on me." Leeland turned out his pockets. "I don't. But of course that doesn't mean you'll believe me."

"I'm more interested in why you're here."

"I was about to ask the same of you, Odys. Why haven't you just run off—run away while you still have the chance? You really think you're safe here?"

Odys said nothing for a few seconds, staring at each part of Leeland in turn. *Is this really happening?*

Leeland chose the chair by the closet door, his Automatons framing him. "Here I am, Odys. In your grasp. My time is almost up. Take this last chance for closure, son. Go on."

Odys boiled, Maud's hand restraining itself from firing. "There's one thing I can't quite sort out in all of this, Leeland. Why make the Automaton the father instead of doing the job yourself?"

"Isn't that part obvious, Odys? No, that's not the question you really want to ask me, is it? But fine. For one, he can make himself look more like you than I can. Also, it was *always* in the books the father would die. And it would be very hard for *me* to fake death. I can't hold my breath very long, you see."

"But why? Why did you make him"—he pointed to his once-father—"die?"

"Because you needed freedom. And I needed space. It was hard, with him being away from me for long periods of time. And I was getting so tired. Over nineteen years I acted! That, and it was very important I marry your sister. That was the most important part of all. I needed a *reason* to get her to marry me. His death was the very thing. Ah, look, you are still so angry about it. Believe me, I never did it to hurt you, Odys. I did it to hurt others."

"Who, exactly? You think Mother gives a fuck about who you sleep with?"

"Shh. Keep your voice down," Leeland soothed. "Believe me, Mother cares. I freed two birds with one key by fucking your sister."

"Why did you?" Maud asked. "Why *marry* her?"

"Yes, yes, get everything off your chest, boy. But look at me, not him. He's not your father. I was." He tapped at his chest. "You really want me to tell you why, Odys? Look at me. I'd be an old virgin without her. There were passions within me needing to be released. I am a pathetic man and I chose pathetic, convenient means."

"You love Gwen. If you wanted to hurt her you could have had anyone else—"

"But like Dante to his Beatrice, I could not have *her*. Having the idea of her is so much more...poetic. So I chose your sister. Like prose, it was easier to read. Isn't that what you *want* me to say, Odys?" He gripped the knobs of the chair, his face snarling in some sort of pain. He composed himself. "No, you *know*. Maud lets you know. Without being married, I wouldn't fuck her otherwise. I'm a devout man—a *good* man. I gave her a choice. It worked well for all of us. I thought it might even save you both from yourselves but it did not. That, and a marriage really is the ball and chain. Keeps the participants in place. I couldn't have her moving around—and I *knew* Odissa wouldn't move around because divorce is messy. Makes people afraid of losing everything. Especially if they think they've signed prenups. Especially if they think it will bring to light all their darkness." He frowned, not proud of what he'd done. "The marriage made for a cleaner tie between us. It made the situation ideal; you couldn't stand the thought, so you would stay away. My marriage to Odissa put the perfect distance between us, Odys. Not too close and not too far. She agreed because she loved money. It made her feel secure. She can't make gold on her own. She needed me."

"Because she wanted to take care of *me*. Don't forget that. Everything she did was because of *me*." Odys glared at him over Maud's shoulder.

"Yes, *you you you*. It was always about you, wasn't it?" Leeland nodded. "I don't understand it. I suppose it comes from some form of guilt, why she attached herself to you. It wasn't my intention to torture you, Odys. You were just in the wrong place at the right time. I do love you as a son, Odys—as much as I can. It may seem untruthful, but I—I never expected to have a family. Not in this way. It all fell in my lap. I do not hate you.

"You see," Leeland leaned forward in his chair, "Dorian wasn't alone when he became one of us. They're supposed to be, though. He had a sister. Well, a *step*sister. She was married, too. They tried to get them to safety when I, as they will call it, 'went rogue'"—he used air quotation marks—"Dorian had invited them to his 'new place'—a diversion to get them out of their current location. The Dimitris were

91

living in [redacted] at the time. I tracked them down quite easily. Put the bomb on the taxi. Admund was in the car, to make sure I knew what happened. Do you remember how it played out?"[27]

His question seemed to be asking something more than what was in Maud's storage space. Leeland waited for an answer, running the back of his finger over his lip. He pointed up with that finger. "I'm sorry it was all too easy. All too like fate. See, Dorian hadn't talked to his sister, or his best friend—whom she'd married—for quite some time. They'd lost touch. He avoided them because, as you know, being a Master means you have a lot of secrets. It is best to avoid people in general, to keep stories straight. And, because they wanted to surprise Dorian, they had kept a secret of their own. Dorian's stepsister had had twins. I even called Mother, to tell them the good news—to tell Dorian he was an uncle!"

Leeland spread his arms, eyes growing red. "I had hoped it would make him change his mind. But he didn't believe me. Do you know why? Because his sister was declared infertile many years before this. I found the letters of her confessing and complaining about it to him. The twins were completely unexpected. Didn't seem like they'd even been *trying*. Dorian's sister had been tested because her own mother had trouble conceiving, back in the day. A genetic thing that runs in the family, as you well know. They hadn't expected to have kids. Maybe adopt. That's what they'd told Dorian. So, as you can see, Dorian didn't believe me. He also thought his sister would have told him. But she didn't. Wanted to surprise him. I was sad to spoil it. I told him when he had about, oh, thirty minutes before the bomb was set to go off. I thought that would be enough time for them to figure out if I was

---

[27] Something that comes to mind—and sorry if this actually conflicts with what is known—is that perhaps Leeland uses bombs on non-Masters is because, if he were to use bombs on a Master, they might not work? If Masters can only kill Masters, I wonder if delayed bombs would still count? If slow poisonings would count? If intention counts? There's definitely a time delay that gives opportunity for the murderer to change his mind about what he wants the outcome for the victim to be (death or survival). And *this* leads me to wonder if that's why he could put distance between himself and the act of murder in scenarios with mortals like above? I also wonder if part of the reason why he didn't try these bombs on Masters was actually because he didn't want anyone to die, so his bombs would never work on them (thus he wants them to kill themselves)?

lying about the children or not. But it wasn't. And so Dorian started to panic. He didn't expect children. Children changed everything. Dorian had cut off ties with a lot of friends. They refused to speak with him or he couldn't reach them any longer. He had run out of ways to know the truth, you see. That's what Automatons do. They cut you off from everyone."

Leeland pulled his coat around himself, remembering. In a lowered, tearful tone, "So I said Admund could take the long way around with the taxi for a price—that Admund could get lost and slow the bomb down. I really thought Dorian would find more information about the twins in that time. Back then, though, there wasn't texting or the internet—not a lot to verify if I was lying. And even then there was the possibility I had faked their existence. I am good at faking, as you know. But as I was saying, Dorian ran out of time. Coraza watched it all—all the others helping Dorian as he suffered through the pain of burning out his eyes. I still remember it. It wasn't like a normal human wounding themselves. He healed so *gracefully*. That's what made it so...unworthy."

He rubbed his own eye as if the memory made it hurt.

"You know what he used to take out his eyes? Fletcher. Fletcher touched his eyes so exactly. They bled and then healed white. White. Not red or some other unfortunate color but pure *white*. Then Fletcher and the others tried to make phone calls in Dorian's place but they had no luck. They had some leads but it was too inconvenient to follow through. Dorian begged Coraza—begged me. But I think we all know what he let happen. He didn't buy enough time with his eyes."

He shook his head, blinking back tears that Odys wanted to crush out of his face. Leeland wouldn't be held responsible for their deaths. He would, however, have taken responsibility for saving them if Dorian had done what he wanted. *If only Dorian had done the selfless thing and killed himself.*

"Dorian wouldn't let me save them. He *refused* to do the right thing." Leeland frowned. "I sometimes think Dorian had already forsaken them and giving up his eyes was his penance for such abandonment. Not that there was much hope anyway. I destroyed the records of the twins after, you see. I also knew extra minutes wouldn't solve his problems—Masters have so many. However, before the bomb blew up, I saw something that made me reconsider my Trolley Problem. I was given an idea." Leeland paused, smiling and biting his trembling lip. He was censoring something. "Before it went off, I stole the children from their parents. At gunpoint, sadly. Well, Admund did. Your mother was screaming. I want you to know she cared about you, Odys. She didn't deserve what Dorian did to her. Admund was able to shield you both as the car exploded. But Dorian thought you were dead too. Later on, they were able to track down the loose ends and verify that his sister had, yes, had twins. He connected what dots I hadn't destroyed. He realized what he'd done."

Odys shoved aside his own personal ethics to Leeland's *Trolley Problem*. "Do you swear I *am* one of those twins?" It seemed like the more important issue.

His eyes lit up with an eagerness that scared Odys. "I can see how you'd think I might lie about that. But yes, you are. I really have no reason to lie. In fact, I've been wanting to tell you for some time. Just look at your sister, for example. Has she gotten pregnant? Even though we've been fucking her? No. She's just like her mother. I really hope you'll forgive me—forgive me for doing what had to be done with her."

"I won't forgive you," Odys laughed. "Perhaps Dorian didn't believe you'd do it. Perhaps he thought you had the wrong couple. Still does, really."

"Even so, he let them die. Here, look at these pictures I have of them, your parents." He pulled two photos from his pocket. "Look at how you resemble your father. Your mother was Cherokee. Enrolled citizen. Did Pepin let Maud remember? Your father's name was Dominic Dimitri. Your mother—her name was Doris. They called her Dory. At least, Dorian did." He noticed Odys wasn't entirely interested in the photos, so he put them on the nightstand. "They called their twins Dorothy and *Doric.*"

MAUD: Automaton of Doric Dimitri

MONEY: It changes you. She'll change you. She's change.

CHANGE: She's not the same Automaton Pepin once had.

TWIN: Your two cents is worth something. Be careful how you spend it.

Chapter the second,

It was always so simple:

But does that make it less complex?

Leeland raised a brow. "But you knew that, didn't you? You knew. I know you can't forgive me. I don't expect you to. I can't forgive myself, either. I hate that I have them, these Automatons. No one should have them, Odys. No one."

But Leeland will be their willing burden. A martyr. A saint.

"Someone will always have them," Odys said, straightening up. His mouth twisted to keep from matching Leeland's frown.

Leeland's old eyes danced over Odys's face, searching for interpretation to the words. "So you know it can't be helped. That's why someone—and only *one* someone—needs to have them all. So that no one else suffers. Someone needs the burden all to themselves."

Odys stepped forward from his half-crouch by the bed, threatening as best he could. But he could not bring himself closer. "You created the burden, though, Leeland. You did. It would be easier to bear if you didn't kill everyone."

"Would it?" He scratched his graying hair, oiled back and parted with precision. Odys noticed the wedding ring on his left hand. It made the fury boil up inside him. "Are you so sure that everyone agrees with you? After all, Bob saw the light, didn't she?"

Maud raised her gun, ready to get this over with. Her eyes burned like fiery coals.

But something deep inside Odys told him to stop—a ghost's voice saying *No—not yet. We must know.* "What did you have on her? What did you threaten her with?"

Leeland's eyes reddened with tears. He covered the bottom half of his face to hide his weakness. "The funny thing is, Odys, I didn't. I didn't threaten her with anything. She had nothing I wanted—except for Cestus. She had nothing *anyone* wanted." No leverage. No life. "It was her time to go. She wasn't happy. It's not suicide, you see, when it's the only way out. It's only reversing immortality—our curse. Our souls are damned if we stay. Vulcan, our devil."

Maud, the only part of Odys that could push through the rage caused by this pathetic display, demanded: "Why did Pepin give me to Odys? Do you know where Madus is?"

Leeland pursed his lips and calmed his face. "I think Pepin thought I wouldn't harm you. I think he knows how fond I am of you and your sister. Perhaps that. Or perhaps he knows I've nothing to threaten you with, since your sister is something I'm using to threaten someone *else* with." He watched Odys's expression, wondering if he believed him. "But Madus? No. I'm not the one who has him."

"Just like you don't have Cestus."

Leeland smiled at that, a laugh sounding through closed lips like a muted cicada. "You've never spoken like this before. It's strange, to have you *aware* of what's going on. Your sister was always better at it than you."

"What do you mean you can't threaten me with my sister?"

Leeland averted his gaze, his Automatons becoming uneasy. He lifted a hand the way you lift your shoulders to shrug, searching for words. "Gwendolyn, of course, boy. How could I kill my wife when she's doing exactly what I meant for her to?" He stood, eyes daring Odys to shoot him—go ahead. He did not care.

Why didn't he care?

"I have been trying to show Gwen her selfish ways. The most I got were penitent tears. But now? Now that she knows she is finally listening to me. And Bob overheard, it seems."

"The fuck do you mean?"

Leeland turned to leave—as if he were allowed—but stopped. He remembered something worth saying. "I tried to get her pregnant, your sister. I really tried. Admund's sciences failed. It might have made things a lot easier for all of us—given us more time. Things would have been different. You wouldn't have had to be involved for so long. But, thankfully, I can work with what I have. Good bye, my boy."

Wait, wait, wait.

Something needed to happen. And that something was Leeland's death, for sure. As the Automatons escorted Leeland out like human shields, Odys briskly followed. And Maud was even faster. "Stop!" Maud shot at him, aiming to miss. "Don't move." She needed to know where Madus and Cestus were first, before she finished him.

The funny thing is, though, that Coraza and Admund didn't try and protect their Master. In fact, they didn't need to. He was protected by Anselm—who had come out of nowhere.

"Do not!" Anselm ordered Maud. Once and only once. Odys, through his focus, realized that everyone was watching—out of their rooms. They had been listening. Mecca from Q's arms, Rosemund and Caffar from bath towels, Mother from the center of the room.[28] Dorian was just opening his door. Fletcher and Odissa popped out their heads. Odys noticed Odissa's eyes growing wide. Fletcher was shielding Odissa—telling her to get back.

Rosemund was a good, welcoming hostess: Caffar assumed a nice cattle gun. "Nice of you to stop by, Lee. And I mean that sarcastically."

---

[28] Why is Caffar in a bath towel???????

"As if I couldn't tell," Leeland laughed at her. He walked around the coffee table, taking them all in like a proud grandparent. He jerked when Maud went for him again.

Maud glared at Mother as Anselm's hands caught hers from the floor, causing her to spark. Anslem had gotten to her in a matter of seconds. His long white hair twisted like snakes around him. His hand was alight with radiating soul—it clicked with a scraping, ratcheting sound. Maud's own skin continued to glow where Anslem touched her, yet the two would not submit. Admund and Coraza seemed well at ease.

Leeland's eyes landed on Mother. His eyes lit up at the sight of her. Just as he had wanted.

"Don't, Odys," Mother said, raising a hand as he took a step forward.

"What the fuck?" Q shouted at Mother, her gun ready to shoot. Mecca's brows knit together as he peered from behind her.

"Put the gun down." There was a strain in Gwen's voice. She didn't look well. It threw them all off, upon considering it. It was Maud who was finally able to look past it—able to do the math.

Maud shot at Leeland again, but Anslem blocked it with his shoulder, shoving into her. His skin boiled back into flesh, ringing and popping their ears. The wall where Maud's "bullet" hit did not catch fire, but it smoked behind Admund, his face blank and unbothered.

"Why?" Maud demanded, not relenting so easily. Leeland was so close—right *there.* She tried to push past Anselm, but Caffar jumped forward to hold her back.

"We need what he knows."

She sizzled and rang: "If he does have the Automatons, then he's not telling. Killing him wouldn't be any less than the leads we have now!"

Mother stumbled over to the back of the nearby couch. "You will do what I say or we will have reason to disown you, Odys."

"I won't let him walk away from this. I don't care where Cestus is—"

"Don't let anger from what he's done to you and your sister dictate your reaction, Odys. I need him alive. We all do. He's not going anywhere." She was staring down Leeland now.

Maud thrashed against Caffar one more time and Anselm stepped back. They stood in silence as Leeland observed Mother. When he finally spoke, it was: "You are not well, Gwendolyn."

"You've seen what you came to see, Leeland. Don't make this more complicated. I can't control their hate for you. This wasn't what we agreed on!" Her words caught their attention—the tension snapped through the room.

"You look beautiful, though. Despite that he's draining you."

She flinched as if his words had made her heart stop. *Don't say it where they can hear.*

"But it's easier, the second time, isn't it? The soul's already been split once. The body has been through it before and knows how to cope—it remembers."

The Automatons drew to their Masters, recoiling from a traitorous Gwen and Anselm. Dorian stepped back to his door, where Fletcher was making sure there was something between Leeland and Odissa. Guns formed in the hands of the Automatons. Caffar's fingertips buzzed with soul-light.

"How dare you—in front of them!" Mother spat. She could barely keep her eyes open from the pain. "You've betrayed me."

"No, my love. I've given you a reason to actually carry out what you promised me." The others were too caught on his tangled words to kill him yet. "I had to make sure you weren't lying to me. But I see that you weren't." His eyes gestured to her form. She looked as if she might pass out any moment—just as Odys had looked only nights ago.

"Forgive me," Leeland continued to Gwen, reaching into his coat. "It felt too good to be real. But at least I'm sure you have enemies now. A picture over text isn't proof enough. Images are faked—your hand, holding him." He looked around the room, noting their reactions. "These reactions are not faked. And apparently neither was Bob's when I sent her the screenshots of our conversations—even though she accused them of being fake; she *reacted* against her words. At least I'm sure you'll be worth it now."

"Worth what now?" Gwen hissed through her red, wetting face. "You have ruined everything—" *This wasn't how I was going to tell them.*

"Don't blame me for this, Gwen." *This is for your own good.* "I love you, Gwen. Don't worry, I'll keep my end."

He'll stop toying with them now. He'll stop fantasizing about eternity with her. He'll stop.

Her body buckled over, his words shaking her. Her fists turned white. "I know. I'm sorry. I'm so sorry." *I'm sorry I don't love you.*

But the others could not see her face; was she acting? Was this really happening?

He stopped looking at her—at them. "Don't be sorry. What's wrong has been ·made right." He checked his handgun they hadn't seen him pull out, cocking it. His hand was shaking but his flow was steady. Everyone's eyes grew wide. "I know we didn't plan it for tonight, Gwen, but I'm ready now. I've been ready, you see, for a very long time. I don't want to die by an Automaton either," he said, exhibiting the gun. "I wasn't born by them and I won't die by them." He pointed it to his head— just like Pepin had done. "May we finish what He started."

The blood rippled through the room. His Automatons fell down, inanimate.

They let the guts settle before breathing again.

"Jesus fucking Christ," Dorian cursed, turning back around. The blood had sprinkled even in their direction.

Rosemund's eyes darted to Odys. She took off her glasses, to wipe the blood on the clean side of her bath towel. "Well, I think we're owed an explanation, Gwen."

Mother, whose legs sagged a little at the knees, left her perch and found a blood-splattered chair. Anselm helped her into it. She was not crying now. Her eyes were wide with shock—with fear. She looked at Dorian—at Odys. She noticed Odys still had Maud's gun at the ready. She shook her head, "I didn't mean for him to do this."

She waved a trembling hand over the mess.

"How did you get him to do it?" Dorian pressed, though the deep sound in his voice let everyone know he already guessed the answer.

"I—I lied to him," she looked at her clenched fists, splattered with small dots of his blood. She wiped them on her knees, smearing and staining more. She looked once to the corpse but focused on the dripping ceiling instead. "It was the only way to get him to do it—to get him here." *On the floor.*

"But what was the lie you lied?" Rosemund asked, using her towel corner to smear the blood off her arms.

"I—I had him all along. Madus," she looked at Odys—but not at his face. Never his face. "Even before Pepin killed himself."

A lie of a lie of a lie of a lie!

"You knew about this?" Dorian snapped at Rosemund.

"I know about things *about* it." Rosemund used Caffar's towel corner on Mecca's pouting face. He backed away from her—no longer sure who to trust.

"But don't think I know why Pepin killed himself," Mother begged. "I don't know why Pepin chose—of all people—Odys. I know it was wrong to lie to you—all of you—all this time. But I saw an opportunity. I took it. Just now. I took it. Oh, Dios mío, I took it."

"And where is he then? Where's Madus?" Dorian pressed, stalking her. Gwen could see the effects of her betrayal on his face. "How did you get him?"[29]

---

[29] At this point, I flipped backward and reread Pepin's letter. I'll copy and paste it here for you as well:
Dear Odys,
I gave Maud to you for a reason, but I am sure you have figured that much out by now. If anyone asks, Madus is safe. I have a plan for him as well. Also, though it might not matter

"How should I know why Pepin finally gave him back?" she snapped. She rocked slightly in place. "I don't know anything about that damn circus man! But I used him. I used Madus, Dorian. I knew Leeland would have so much on us now that Odissa and Odys were here, and so I took him. I took Madus. I *lied* and said I would give myself up, Dorian. I lied to Leeland and said I saw the goodness in his plight and Leeland believed me! He gave himself up instead. He told me to take over his role. Because he loved *me*." Her face contorted, disgusted with herself. "He believed me too," she gestured to the floor, where the blood was pooling around the headless body. "You know he wouldn't have stopped. I finally stopped him, Dorian. Lo hice parecer *real*."

"Too real," Rosemund said gently. "Too real is too real, Gwendolyn."

But Gwen did not need to beg for Rosemund's clemency. Rosemund would love Gwen no matter what.

"How the fuck was this the best way to stop him, Gwen?" Maud shouted at her—at them all—her mad eyes demanded the others agree with her.

(depending on how you take to her), tell Maud I am sorry I had to make her forget. I know it sounds silly, because an Automaton does not have personal feelings, but I left a part of me in her that will understand why I erased so much of her—rather, me. At least, I hope part of me is still in her. I plan to leave myself there. I apologize to myself, then. Just in case.

The real reason I am sending this message is to tell you no one is safe. Leeland may think— may even tell you—that my actions speak for him, but they are entirely my own. Do not trust Leeland, and certainly don't trust Mother. I will not go into detail as to why but—

Well, why do you think I have avoided them both all this time? Hell, I should probably tell you to not even trust me, because I have played my part in this. I have known for a while what Leeland had done to you and your sister. I am just now getting around to doing something about it. I hope you will forgive me—though hope is of little help to you. What help is a dead man?

I am sending this letter—well, my friend is sending this letter for me, I will be dead by the time it needs to be sent—in a way that will hopefully keep them from finding it in your mail— Vulcan willing. I know they will check everything on you until they "trust" you. And even then they will not give you peace. Only when you are dead can you rest. I have learned that the hard way.
-Pepin J. Pound.

"I had to make him believe me, Dorian," Mother tried to explain herself to him, as if he held her fate. She held out her fist—and whatever was in it. "I don't know why Pepin killed himself but I know he wanted to keep Leeland away from Madus." Her fingers opened to show Madus—that modern-day penny.

"He didn't send him to you," Odys said, realizing that his first guess about Pepin's birthday gift to Rosemund had been correct. "You stole him from Rosemund's mail."

"And even if I did?" Gwen tried to shrug—too weak for forcefulness. "Rosemund didn't care. She didn't stop me. Tell them, Rosie! Dígales..."

Rosemund sighed, her eyes closing for a half-second. "This is me telling you, Dorian." She came to Gwendolyn and cupped her head. "Shh, shh, now. I know."

"If Pepin didn't want me to have Madus he wouldn't have been so stupid as to send him in the mail!" Gwen cried up to Rosemund, her voice reaching hysterics. All her gasping made her start to heave. She leaned over the arm of the chair and vomited, not caring where.

"Now, nownownow," Rosemund grimaced. She kneeled down and threatened to flash everyone with what was under her bath towel.

Anselm glared at them all, studying their reactions. He noted Odys's own glare.

"I broke the rules to fix the rules," Gwen confessed, gripping the sides of her nightgown. She was pleading to Rosemund for forgiveness. Forgiveness was easy to come by, but not easy for her to accept. "I didn't think it would be so simple. But it was. I don't know if this is what Pepin expected me to do, but when Bob died, I knew Leeland was in action. I touched Madus tonight."

"No shit," Odys said, waving an arm at the floor—her vomit.

"And where does Bob fit into this? Do you know where Cestus is?" Dorian demanded, gesturing to the untouched Automatons on the floor.

"I don't know." Gwen shook her head. "But I had wanted to find out. That's why I had to touch Madus. I knew Leeland was skeptical. I knew it! He was testing my reaction to her death. I don't know why she gave into him. He was there, ready to take Cestus—like he knew she was going to do it. Maybe Leeland told Robyn my lie and she believed my lie? She believed I was taking over Leeland's plight? She died thinking *this* was what I wanted…"

And Mother began to weep into her hands.

"No," Odys shook his head, his face falling. "Vulcan let her believe it too." *He didn't stop it.*

They watched Mother weep.

"He wanted us to hate Mother?" Mecca squealed, wiping his tears away on the back of his sleeve. "He wanted Bob to die?"

Dorian rubbed his face, trying to hide his own tears. He had never hated Vulcan so much.

"We don't know where Cestus is," Anselm told them, his own eyes were cloudy and weary. Mother could talk no more, so he would. "This wasn't part of the plan. We thought Leeland would tell us if we did this. We know we broke the rules. We wait your judgment accordingly."

"There is no judgment," Dorian whispered down to Mother. "Not tonight."

"Are you kidding me?" Odys growled, every inch of him objecting.

Dorian's voice deepened, as if to match Odys: "We know what Leeland would have done if he hadn't been stopped. He would have…" Fletcher's eyes flickered to Odissa, who was lingering in the doorway. "She saved us from him. We are too tired to make decisions tonight."

"To bed, then," Rosemund said. "Clean yourselves up. Fletcher, you'll tidy this mess. You too, Odys, Maud. You helphelphelp me." By mess, she meant body. Caffar glared at everyone until they started moving—especially Mecca who had eyes that asked to stay. But Mecca was too upset for such work. He never worked well when upset. Rosemund sent him to shower and bed—one of them needed full rest, at least.

Dorian told Odissa to go back to sleep. She wanted to obey him, but she would find she could not sleep. Even though her life was no longer seemingly in danger (*That's what this meant, right?*), this greyness bleeding into what was once black and white made rest unthinkable. She would spy on them through the door; she would filter out the contrasts.

Fletcher was already putting on Dorian's leather gloves (strange for an Automaton to do) and placing the inanimate Coraza and Admund on the coffee table. Maud pulled off some bed sheets and used them to wrap up the body after they had stripped it. They'd turned out his pockets—to make sure Cestus wasn't in there.

"I don't want to say Mother is lying to us, but I think Gwen is lying to us," Maud whispered, hands on her hips. Or perhaps her arms were crossed. Whatever sounds best, so long as you know she was skeptical.

Dorian brushed off the comment. "Even if she is, she has good reason to. I'm sure."

"Are you *fucking* kidding me? You're going to side with that psycho in there? She got Bob killed!" Odys hissed at him. "And now what Automaton is Odissa gonna get?"

"I guess we already know your vote then, huh?"

"Oh, I *get* a vote, do I? Is this why Gwen made us come here? So she could break this news to us like some mom telling us she has cancer? She *is* cancer!"

"Less yapping more cleaning," Rosemund barked, tossing a paper towel roll at them.

"Should I make a store run?" Dorian offered. They were going to have to do a lot of cleaning.

"No. We'll just burn the place in the morning." Her eyes looked up at the brain-decorated ceiling. Those eyes were sad behind the magnifying lenses. "We won't want to vacation here again. Vacations are to escape the past, not be haunted byby by it. Just clean what we want to keep."

Odys studied her little body, the bath towel engulfing it. He could make out her scars so easily now—a whole map covering her. Caffar held the door open as the other Automatons took out the body to the garages. "Whose car are we taking?" Fletcher asked as they exited.

"I'm done for tonight," Dorian said and he went to his rooms. Part of him should try and get some sleep.

Before the door was shut, Odys glanced into those rooms, the rooms with his sister trapped inside. She was sitting on the bed—and then the door closed.

"If you don't mind me saying so," Rosemund said, "I think Leeland wantwantwanted this."

"What do you mean?" Odys asked, wadding up a paper towel. *Of course he wanted chaos.*

"He wanted to say goodbye to you. He wanted a way out. Could you live with yourself, Odys, if you were him? He'd tried so hard these past decades to break us. He finally thought he had. But he wasn't willing to carry out the work after he broke us, was he? Even though Mother made him believe he was always right, he didn't actually want to be the oneoneone to carry out his justice. As long as he had—in his mind—been proven right, then he did not care to live. He had life figured out. He didn't want to be the only one with all the Automatons. He'd let Mother do that."

"He loved her."

"Yes, but he loved the thought that she'd given into his logic all thethethe more," Rosemund frowned. Her damp curls made her look all the sadder.

Fletcher came back in, "Forgot a lighter," he explained, eyeing them. He waited for Odys to fork one over.

Rosemund called after him. "Don't forget to mark the spot. It will look different when the snow is gone. We need to be able to find it come spring. Forgotten grave sites are forgotten." Fletcher saluted Rosemund sloppily and went on with his business.

"You going to decorate that bastard's grave?" Odys frowned at her.

"Odissa might. She has before, I hear. Come have some milk with me, Odys."

Realizing she wanted to talk to him way from doors, he didn't protest.

"I won't leave you alone with your lonely thoughts just yet. Being alone is lonely." She sat down the carton of milk in front of him as she found two glasses. She poured him a drink and downed the rest from the carton. Such a strange woman.

She noticed his eyes looking out the window over her shoulder. The sun was rising, making the winter sky an off-orange pink. Through the trees and across the street she could see the neighbors. "That van of theirs, in the driveway. It would fit all of us nicely. I'm going to steal it in the morning. If I can. I would call a taxi, but wewewe need to keep people from coming here. Can't have people knocking on doors and seeing blood splattered everywhere. And it's too much trouble to gogogo and rent one. They always want to see identification. I'd rather not go through that if we can work around a taxi. That van's always there. Begging to be taken. Room is room and we'll need more of it."

"Are we going someplace?"

"That depends on how many stick around after the vote."

The vote to keep Gwen alive.

Not drinking yet, "You knew all along that Mother had Madus."

"I am her oldest friend. Of course I knew."

"She didn't care if you knew or not?"

"She knew I wouldn't do anything about it. Because she knowknowknows I trust her. It's that very trust which makes me valuable, Odys Odelyn."

He scoffed, not only at the statement but at how she always glitched *in threes*. He mumbled "Know" one more time for her to make it an even number and pressed, "Don't you get tired of the—the lies?"

"If lies protect us, then why would I tire of them?"

"They didn't protect Pepin. They didn't protect Leeland."

"That's because they knew the truth, Odys. They knew too much of it." She picked up her unused glass. "They *believed* in too much of it. Do you want to know why it was so easy for Leeland to believe Mother's lies? Because her heart was in it. She believes herherher own lie. Only partially, but she still believes in it. You know as well as I that she's always thought Automatons shouldn't exist. She may not want them all under one Master, but she doesn't want any human to suffer with them. Part of the lie is only part of it, but she still believes that part."

"Bob was willing to die for her even if she was planning to take them all." Odys downed his milk as if it were alcohol. Anything to get the taste of those words out of his mouth.

"Bob had been willing to die for a long time. If she thought Mother had plans of her own, why's it so hard to think she believed Mother might do good?"

She's trying to sway my vote, Odys thought. "Because Mother's 'good' isn't any *more good* than Leeland's." He looked over her shoulder, out the window. The sky was brightening now—he could see it. The Automatons had better hurry.

"You think it's not, but how is it not? Your sister's life isn't in danger anyanyanymore. Neither is anyone else's."

"We don't know where Cestus is, do we? What good does that do us?"

Rosemund didn't say anything for a moment. Just looked at the wall behind him. "Funny, isn't it, that Anselm showed up after Mother last night? She was running late herself." He eyed her suspiciously. She picked up her unused glass and turned it over and used the concave bottom to better examine her bright nails. "Bob wanted out. She found something that justified her outing—just as Leeland found something to justify his."

"After all these years, why did Mother *just now* decide to lie to Leeland?"

"I think we all know the answer to that question, Odys, that question that we're asking. *You're* in the picture now. We were making up forforfor sins. All of us let you die once before. Now you are free to live your life. We all are."

"What life?"

"You have a goose that lays golden eggs, and you're acting like there's something that inhibits you? The world is youryouryours, Odys, because you already have it. You have something everyone wants and that the world revolves around—gold."

"It can't buy my old life back, can it?"

Rosemund licked her braces in thought. "No, but you could always kill Dorian. Then she'd have no choice but to come back to you."

"I wouldn't."

"I'm glad to hear it. We just got rid of one Leeland. We don't need another."

"Mother's the new Leeland, Rose," he said without inflection.

"Then tell them so. Don't vote for her. Leave us. We have a new Leeland and we need a new Pepin. That seems to be the onlyonlyonly way this damn lot can function."

"You call this functioning?"

"I meant when we had two of them—when we had a Leeland and a Pepin—we were fine, fine, fine"—she gave herself a tick, noticing him counting and rounding her up under his breath. He restrained himself this time and she smiled a scarred, knowing smile. "Now we're all astir."

"Not Dorian. Dorian's happy."

"You think he's happy, do you?" She pulled out a pen from her drying hair. "No. Love does not equal happiness. Odissa will make him happily miserable. I can already seeseesee it. Not only is she free to reject him, but you're still in the picture, Odys. It's not veryveryvery fair on him to constantly fret on whether or not she still loves you and could come back to you." She finally stopped waving the pen around and wrote something on her hand.

Is there anything to come back to? He sighed and brooded.

She finished writing *STEAL VAN* on the back of her hand and said, "Come now. There must be *something* to live for besides Odissa, because you haven't diediedied yet, have you?"

He nodded, agreeing. "Vulcan. He's using us, and I will find out how and why and kill every damn thing He plans."

"You think that's possible?" she laughed. "He probably means for you to say such a thing as what you've just said!"

"If I can't dictate my own purpose in life, then I'll accept it blindly. Vulcan means for me to hate Him, so I will." He leaned forward on his elbows, as if threatening *her*.

"You really want to accept your fate that you think you want to accept, Odys?" Rosemund leaned in to match him. "Then take this advice." She paused for effect. "Become Pepin. Leave us. Pepin gave you Maud. The gods let him do it. You're his replacement in this game. Like I said, we were doing just fine with a Pepin and a Leeland. Now look at us. At each other's throatthroatthroats."

Stanza: After the deleted scenes there's still a story.

The three Automatons who had just "gotten rid of" Leeland came in from the cold, their job done. They stomped the snow off their feet-boots. The blood-splattered living room could wait until tomorrow. It was time to recharge with their Masters.

But before doing so, the three Automata bent over the two inanimate Automata. They would begin the second debate for their Masters:

"How will we keep these safe?" Maud asked. "Who will watch them?"

"Caffar and I will each take one," Fletcher said. He gestured to them in their new plastic bags.

"How's that fair? Rose knew Mother had Madus. We can't trust her. No offense, Caffar."

"No offense, no offense."

"We have seniority. End of discussion," Fletcher said, reaching down to pick the bags up.

But Caffar caught his hand. She shook her head. Rosemund didn't want this to be decided tonight. Leave them there. She pushed them away from the coffee table where the inanimate Automata slept and went to her Master's room.

Stanza: The author's Hand Wave.

That morning at brunch (everyone slept in late), Dorian pulled out a chair for Odissa so that she might sit next to her brother. Between them. Maud and Odys were both drinking coffee, Odys smoking his last available cigarette, Maud holding a frazzled ~~me~~ Bulfinch. Maud passed ~~me~~ Bulfinch to an overeager Odissa, who squeezed ~~me~~ him in her arms.[30] *Thanks so much for your concern up until now, Odissa.*

"I have more if you want them—in my purse," Odissa told Odys quietly, about the cigarettes. She seemed nervous—embarrassed, even—to see him. She used Bulfinch as a distraction, trying to feed him toast crust Maud had just offered.

"I'll be just fine, Odissa," he replied. *Don't make them notice me.*

She ran her fingers into Bulfinch's scruff, keeping herself from doing something stupid. ~~I just wanted to go back to my bathroom. It was safer there and less stuffed with weirdos.~~

"We're out of milk," Fletcher informed. "That means only orange juice or coffee." He stood up, going to get the coffee. Odissa didn't even have to place her order. He presented her a full mug.

Dorian turned to Odys. "Yes, Mecca was very upset about the lack of milk. He bought that specifically for Bulfinch. Some must have been *spilt* last night."

When Odys didn't bite, Fletcher added. "Must have some giant babies in this house. They should apologize to Bulfinch."

---

[30] I leave these edits in there to remind you what I have to deal with on a daily basis—I have to deal with someone who thinks they are a cat! Or, excuse me, someone who thinks they *were* a cat.

Odissa was about to forgive all and announce milk usually made him throw up when—

"Not giant babies. Giant liars." Odys stuffed his face with some bread, as if more words might come out if he didn't stopper them.

"That's your final vote, huh? Mec's already said he's in if we're in. Rosemund's in of course. That leaves our vote," Dorian said. *And we already know how I'll vote.*

"I swear to God, Dorian," Odys snarled at him, "You worship the ground that bitch walks on."

"If it weren't for 'that bitch,' we'd still be at a stalemate with Leeland."

"She used the one Automaton we had that would keep Odissa safe."

The raised voices made Bulfinch hide under the table in Odissa's lap (this conversation was beneath me and I was afraid to be associated with it, you see).

"She—we were never going to be safe with him. I'll not kill Mother over this."

Odys glared at Dorian. "Fine. Vote to keep Mother in. Fuck your democracy. You vote on rules just to break them anyway. But think on this, Dorian, she could have admitted to us—all along—what her plans were. God only knows how Rosemund figured them out. Maybe we would've *let* her touch Madus then. But no. She has you—and everyone else—believe from the beginning that *I* know something about Madus's whereabouts and that *I* know where Pepin hid him. Fuck you and your Mother." He stood up and plopped his cigarette butt into Fletcher's glass of half-drunk orange juice. Stormed off to his room.

Crickets.

"That's how you decide if someone lives or dies?" Odissa asked, horrified. "You vote on it over breakfast?"

This was why Bulfinch preferred the bathroom.

Stanza: Mother knows best.

A few minutes later...

Rosemund peeped her head in the kitchen. "I told Gwen."

"Are you packed yet?" Dorian asked her.

"Yes and no. Caffar went for a gas run for the living room a fewfewfew hours ago, but she's back now. She's packing for me. I'm going to go hijack the neighbor's van. Spacious vans are spacious, you know. We'll all fit in it."

"Don't bother, I'll do it," Fletcher said as if it was ridiculous for a human to go to the trouble of stealing vans.

"No, no. I need out of this place. And don't insult me. I know how to wirewirewire a van."

She loved a challenge.

"All right then," Dorian waved her off. "But if you get caught don't expect me to come bail you out."

To Odissa, "Don't let him fool you. I've saved his ass from needing saving more than he's ever saved mine." Rosemund shuffled out of the room, her windbreaker swooshing.

Odissa leaned in, "I want to like her, but she's a bit insane, isn't she?"

"No more than you or I."

Fletcher got up for a new glass to replace the one Odys had tainted. He took his time in the fridge, debating on what drink he wanted. As he straightened up to pour, his eyes looked out the kitchen window. Fletcher paused. "Oh my God..."

Odissa noticed Dorian pause as well, as if inclining his head to the radio. He was watching what Fletcher was seeing through the window. Fletcher dropped his juice and ran to the living room.

Odissa stood up to see what he was looking at—Odys driving with Maud— away—driving away! I struggled in her grip, not caring what they saw.

They chased after Fletcher to the living room.

"He took them." Fletcher picked up the note Odys had left in their place. "'You know I will not touch what he has touched,'" Fletcher read for their/our benefit.

113

"'And I won't let you give one of *his* to Odissa. Call me when you want to discuss how they're used.'"

They stood there for a while.

Mecca and Q came running into the house from the back (where they had been wiring the house, readying it for explosion). "We saw one of the cars was gone— who left?" And then Q saw the bare coffee table. "Where are they?"

"Odys. He took them," Dorian barked at her.

Bulfinch tried to leap from Odissa's arms, scratching her.

"You want Mecca to go after him?" Mecca asked, already headed to the door.

"No," Gwen said, coming out of her room with her bags. She still looked sickly and unbalanced. She had yet to show them Madus fully formed, as if she was ashamed of her new face. "He is one of us now. He is the safest place for them. I think this is a fair trade, all things considered."

At that moment, Rosemund walked in through the back door. "Why is everyone standing around and just standing? Are we leaving or not? It won't be long before thethethe neighbors realize their van's gone. We need to hurry—"

"Odys took the Automatons, Rosemund." Fletcher said.

"He took both, right?" She squinted and wheezed at the coffee table.

"You knew he was going to?" Mecca's brows lowered.

"He had every right," Gwen said. "Now, let's stop talking about this and get going."

Dorian recoiled. "We're not going with you."

Anselm narrowed his eyes. "Why not?"

"If Odys has a right to steal the inanimates, then I have a right to solitude!" Dorian proclaimed.

"Fine," Mother said, tears welling up. "We go our separate ways." Family vacay was over. "But we go them together. Mecca, you'll go with them."

"What? No!" Dorian protested.

"*Why* does Mecca have to go with him?" Mecca crossed his arms.

"Because Vulcan is planning something—killing off Bob and making Dorian fall in love—it is safer for us to be together. He's tweaking the gears. Adjustments have been made and we must make our own counter adjustments. That's why Mecca goes with you. Buddy system."

"And who goes with Odys, then?" Dorian buttressed his argument. "Who keeps him in line?"

Gwen looked at Odissa. "I think he has a direct *line* at all times. A direct reason to behave."

"If you haven't noticed, he just fucking left her, Mother." Fletcher pointed to the direction he supposed Odys to be going.

"He's going to come back, Dorian," Gwen said, putting a hand on Anselm to steady herself. "He's going to want to make contact. What's more, he's going to want to know where Cestus is when we find him. Cestus is perhaps the only Automaton he'd let Odissa have. The only one you'd let her touch, too. Isn't that right, Dorian?"

"And just where is Cestus, Gwen?" His accusatory tone shifted even their footing.

Rosemund laughed. "You don't care that she has broken the rules for Madus but you care that she might be lying about Cestus? You do have a funny way of loving your Mother, the lot ofofof you."

Dorian put a hand on his hip and huffed. "I don't care if you have Cestus or not, Gwen. I trust you with my life. But I need to know why you suddenly trust Odys more than me. I could have kept them safe. It's like you *wanted* him to take them."

Mother sighed. "Dorian, I love you. But Mecca will go with you, and that's final."

"We don't get a say?" Q asked, glaring at Dorian and Fletcher's shared expression.

115

Dorian denied them an answer from Mother: "Fine. But if Odys so much as hints where he is, I'm tracking him down and taking them back."

"Why bother?" Rosemund asked.

"You know why." *In case we never find Cestus.*

"Dorian, you wouldn't," Gwen begged him. "Have you even asked her about this?" She gestured to Odissa.

Odissa was surprised they remembered she was still there.

Oh yes, she was there. Because Odys had left her. He'd never left *her* before. She cocked her head as the fact flooded her, filling her up to her eyes.

Mother studied Odissa's reaction, pitying her as they spoke about her.

"I would give her Coraza," Dorian said, speaking theoretically—as if it to justify what he meant. "I don't want her to have *him*, though," Dorian said. "She shouldn't have to deal with *him*."

"And you think Coraza wouldn't have those same memories? I understand you, Dorian, I do. But—" Gwen paused, barely able to say it—"it would be unnatural."

"As if they aren't already!" Fletcher laughed in mockery for his Master. Dorian was unable to control himself, so consumed by his need for Odissa's lifespan to match his own.

"We are all unnaturally unnatural." Rosemund picked up her bags as if to remind them to *get a move on.*

Mother walked over to Dorian and patted his cheek. "She will have all you want for her and more, I swear. I'll make sure of it."

Dorian pulled away from her. *I wanted Madus for her.* "Is this another lie, Gwen?" Dorian said to her in Spanish.

Mother tightened her lips, unable to come up with more assurances and left them.

"Another reason to split up, Dorian," Rosemund stated as she went to the door. "We're not going to have you huffhuffhuffing all the time—breathing down our necks, thinking we know more than we do about Cestus."

"But tell me why I get stuck with the kid again? I would rather have you babysit them."

Rosemund and Caffar snorted. "You're not the one babysitting this time." In a whisper only Dorian could hear, "And because, Dorian, we all know what Mecca does when he doesn't have job to do—what he does when he can't handle something—**who** he runs to." She squeezed his arm as he inched closer to listen. "If you don't want to deal with that *who* then let him keepkeepkeep an eye on you." She let go of his arm and smiled at Mecca, who was queuing up his bomb with a tablet, making sure he had not heard. At little louder, "And besides, if we asked him who he'd want to go with—"

"Mecca wants to go with Odissa," Mecca said, ears perking up. Mecca didn't get a fresh audience every day and he wasn't about to waste it.

Rosemund's eyebrows raised—*There you have it*—matching the opposite arch of her frowning lips. Mecca grinned wickedly, though there was a twitch in the grin.

As the door closed behind Caffar and Rosemund, Dorian went to collect their bags. Fletcher followed, pushing Odissa along. "Call a cab, Mecca," Dorian shouted over his shoulder, "for the house down at the neighborhood entrance. Tell them your car broke down. Anything. Take your bags. We'll catch up to you there. Just go."

"But that's so far away!" he cried, gesturing to his heavy bags Q would have to carry.

"Then don't take as much shit next time you travel!" Dorian countered.

Dorian's shout made Bulfinch scratch free from Odissa. Q quickly scooped him up (fast as a cat), gesturing to Odissa, *It's OK. He's safe. Don't piss Dorian off. Go.*

Q and Mecca lingered in the living room, standing still, comforting Bulfinch. They'd call the cab in just one minute. Just one minute. Just one minute after they figured out why Dorian had hurried Odissa away from them:

"Tell me something," Dorian asked Odissa as he moved a bag to get his footing.

"Yes?" she whispered back, stopping as she went for a different bag.

"Do you think your brother will come back for you?"

Odissa straightened. "He just left me. Why would he come back just for me?"

"But would you go with him if he came for you?"

Her mouth twisted.

Fletcher was staring at her—watching her every reaction. She avoided looking back, lest she give too much away. She was so preoccupied with avoiding Fletcher's eyes that she didn't notice Dorian coming at her. When she finally realized his exact location, he had pushed her against the wall—too harshly to be playing. "Do you sympathize with him?"

"I don't sympathize with any of you. You all seem like such *great* people." She tried to cross her arms but he inched too close to let her. "You trying to be intimidating, Dorian? That what this is?"

"Hard to control a girlfriend that big, huh?" Fletcher mumbled as he picked up a few bags.

"I think enough is going on without your commentary, Fletcher," Odissa said over Dorian's shoulder—a shoulder too tense. She didn't know if Dorian was about to beat her or kiss her. "Stop making jokes, Dorian." She lowered her tone, "I can't read you.'"

He caged her against the wall with his arms on either side of her. "If I gave you the chance to run, would you?" He pushed back her hair with his hand so his face could better press against her skin. "Would you just leave me if I gave you the choice?"

"Why would anyone leave you?" She grit her teeth, grabbed onto his arm—his shirt. "How could I leave someone the gods speak to? You're too interesting. I don't seem to have a choice. It's what They want for me."

"They speak to your brother, too." He paused in his invasion of her What if he's in the right? What if They like him *más que yo?*"

She pushed her face into his, so that he could feel her words as her lips formed them. "I'm not interested in the gods' favorites. I can't stop them from talking to Odys. But I can stop Odys from disobeying you."

He gave her face a centimeter.

"You think I want him to obey me? No. I want him to not exist. There's a part of me so jealous of him—"

"Odys loves me because he sees himself in me. You love me because you have no choice." She had taken the sides of his face, ran a thumb over his lips. "You can't even control what you're doing now. I see it. You don't like what you're doing. But I do." He leaned into her fingers. "You think I would give that up? Give up someone so devoted to me?"

Fletcher noticed Mecca and Q out in the living room attempting to get in a glance. "Didn't we give you something to do? Go do it!" He shooed them away, going to slam the door. As they turned, he noticed a fear in their eyes. A fear for Odissa.

"Let me go, Dorian."

"I can't let you go." He pushed his whole bodyweight into her like a koala bear to a tree. He pressed his forehead to the wall, face in her neck.

"Am I fucking trying to run away? Am I struggling? I'm not going anywhere." She latched onto the back of his neck with a hand, gave it a squeeze the equivalent of shaking.

"That's all I wanted," Dorian said, releasing her and giving her a kiss.

"Fucking hell, Dorian," she said as she pushed him out of the way and smoothed down her hair. "Don't you ever do that again."

"Or what?" Dorian said, putting on his glasses. There was no humor in his voice. He wanted to hear her make a threat.

Her eyes were threatening enough and they fell into silence.

Fletcher began to hand Dorian some bags, too embarrassed to look at her.

Stanza: This is just another silly novel, I would like you to think.[31]

---

[31] "For all this, [the Heroine] as often as not marries the wrong person to begin with, and she suffers terribly from the plots and intrigues of the vicious baronet; but even death has a soft

"I hope it's a yellow cab," Dorian said, adjusting the strap of his backpack—the one with all his hair products. He wobbled in the snow-covered road, trying not to slip.

Fletcher watched over his shoulder as they heard the fire trucks—the fire trucks that were coming to put out the house that smoked above the trees in the background. They'd gone out the back door—into the woods—and rounded out to the road.

"Why wouldn't it be yellow?" Odissa asked softly, wondering if they looked suspicious coming out of the woods like well-dressed campers.

"Well, you'd think so. But it's not like it used to be. Lately I've seen many a variety of colors for the cabs."

"Rather," Fletcher added, his voice a subtitle, "*I've* seen them. Green. White. Maroon."

"I *mean*," Dorian continued, pinning back some black hair with his many-ringed fingers, "as long as there's those little box-signs that say 'Taxi' on them, then they think they can get away with it. And I don't think it's fair. If I pay for a taxi, then I want to pay for the original experience. I didn't order a town car or limousine, you see. Besides, I take my colors seriously, sí?"

As the snow crunched under their feet, they could see the taxi cab just at the corner. But only one face—the driver's face—in the window. Fletcher looked at Dorian, and Dorian sighed. "Fuck." He knew what this meant.

As they neared, the driver rolled down his window. "Are you Fletcher?" He directed the question to the one who had fit the description.

"Why, yes I am, sir," Fletcher said, leaning down. Way down. He had his hands in his faux-skinny jeans pockets, balancing luggage off his arms.

"The kid, man," the driver said. "He told me to give this to you."

It was a neatly folded piece of paper, which Fletcher took.

As Fletcher prepared to read said paper, his eyes squinting because of the too-white snow, Dorian asked the cabbie, "Which way did he go?"

---

place in his heart for such a paragon, and remedies all mistakes for her just at the right moment." —*Silly Novels by Lady Novelists*, by George Eliot.

"He had a car," the man shrugged. "Was that girl with him even old enough to drive?"

"I don't know who you're talking about, friend."

The money Mecca had given him was reason enough to not see the age.

Odissa noticed Bulfinch in the back seat, freaking out as usual (I associated cars with trips to the vet). She quickly opened the cab door to soothe him through the bars. Her fingers were no comfort to me.

Fletcher crumpled the paper and tossed it over his shoulder.

"Where'd he go, though?" Odissa asked, concerned. She was clutching her coat collar in motherly anxiety.

As Dorian slid in beside her—knowing what Fletcher had just read—he mumbled, "To fucking *Maurice*."

MAURICE MAKEPEACE: The undead.

WAS: Once a Master.

PURPOSE: Vulcan's.

LIKES: "Ethnic" women. That's how he got his "ethnic" baby.

Chapter the third,

Éclaircissement:[32]

Is the past making more sense?

Odys stood in line next to Maud. He liked how the other men around them eyed her body. She was the curtain he could hide behind. Like a puppet, he made her cut her eyes in targeted directions, flip her hair at certain times, smile here and there. Flirting with every man. He had made her change her nose a bit, and sink in her eyes, darken her skin. Just a tad. Didn't want her face to be recognized later, should later ever come.

---

[32] French word. Look it up. Too hard to explain à la English.

"How can I help you today?" inquired the frumpy Post Office lady. She didn't like the way Maud was dressed, clearly, or the fact that there were so many people in line. Busy day.

"I'd like to mail this package; first class, please."

She punched in the addresses, lowered her eyebrows. "Any liquids or perishables?"

"No."

Will that be all? Yes, it would.

Mailing back Mother's broken cell phone, cut up credit cards, and fake identifications was only the first step, but, yes, that was all for now. He even made the return address quite obvious for Gwen—inviting her to look for him *thereabouts*.

He didn't need her *things* anyway. Did he ever? He was free. He finally accepted the fact he DIDN'T need her help. No, not when he had Maud. After making her memorize every number in the cell phone and the details of the passports, he had methods of reduplicating anything he'd need.

The only things he didn't put in the package were the inanimates.

They were one thing he wouldn't give back.

When they left the Post Office, he had Maud drive. And scan for a new car to jack. His eyes barely saw out the foggy window.

"What about that piece of shit there? Easy alarm system to disable."

"Go for it."

And Maud went. [33]

Stanza: Of drug lords and landlords.

Dorian, Fletcher, Odissa, and Bulfinch got out of the cab. Paid the man. Unloaded their bags. And cat.

"A house," Odissa said—it was more of a question. She wasn't sure this was really their final stop.

---

[33] About stealing cars: I cut a piece in book one, I think, about how, when going through a toll with possible cameras, Automata sometimes stick a hand out the window and let their skin trail down the car like a film to cover the license plate or give it a fake number. Chameleon-like, if you will.

"Dorian, she's not as stupid as she looks," Fletcher commented, practically lugging everything but the cat for them (Odissa clutched his carrier like a swaddled baby).

"I don't like that you're mean to me through him, Dorian. It's cowardly."

"Get in the house, Odissa." Mecca left him in no mood to explain.

She followed Fletcher up the steps. Dorian took his time. He pulled up the mailboxes' flag. *Was there even mail in it?* Odissa wondered. No. It was a symbol. A signal.

The door was open. No key needed. It was a shabby place, on the outskirts of downtown. The houses squeezed together as if little monopoly pieces. No real lawns, just a patch of grass here and there—the road lined with cars because, back when these houses were built, garages weren't a big thing. Every other house seemed for sale for foreclosed...or like it should be. This neighborhood was so close to the highway it was a wonder anyone still lived here. The roaring of the cars echoed off the concrete.

Odissa stepped into the furniture-less house, the scuffed wood floors squeaking.

"We paid off the neighbor's drug debt if they'd keep out the squatters," Fletcher informed. He plopped the bags right down. "I'll see if they left the cot in the attic space. They seem to have sold everything else."

Dorian shut the door behind her. "We've property scattered here and there. This was the closest. Haven't been here since, well...since your parents died, Odissa."

"When you said the address to him, I thought—I thought we were just going to stop at a friend's house or something. We're staying here?"

"If you don't like it, we'll leave."

"No. It's not that." *Though why couldn't they just get a hotel?* "But you could have told me where we were going." She put Bulfinch's carrier down by the window. *Did you not trust me?*

"I'll turn the heat on."

Fletcher brought back a cot covered in dust—dust that danced about when he pulled it open. "I'll go to the store and bring back some necessities. Like sheets and sleeping bags. And cat litter."

"But you don't have a car," Odissa said. "You can't steal one in broad daylight!"

"The neighbors, clearly, hawked all our stuff—or *have* it. So, I think we'll be fine. Their car is as good as ours anyway."

He left.

"He's going to just take their car?" She watched him walk across the street. He barged in as if the door were unlocked.

"Oh, no," Dorian said. "He'll let them know he's doing it. They won't have a problem with it. And, well, if they do then he can explain why *he* has a problem with their problem."

Dorian sat down on the cot and invited her next to him. "I need to be honest with you, Odissa. I picked this house because it's also safest. Pepin didn't know about this house, and so neither will Odys. You understand? Maud doesn't know about this house." He fumbled to find her leg—to make sure she was there. "The fact Mecca bailed on me will also have Mother on my back. Mecca will be free to come here, though. He can, no doubt, find me."

She bit her lip, watching him. "I've never had a house before."

"Don't get too attached. We won't be here long."

"How long will we be?"

"We will be here until someone else makes a move. We all know something is about to happen, Odissa. The Automatons can smell it."

"You mean until a human makes a move—or a god?"

"That's what I don't know."

"Might as well let Bulfinch out until Fletcher brings back a litter box."

Bulfinch stayed in his carrier for a long while, rather than venture out. He had stopped meowing, settling on quiet judgment instead.

"This has traumatized him," Odissa commented, feeling guilty.

She had nooo idea.

She took out a cigarette to smoke. "I think it's colder in here than it is outside," she said, sitting back down on the squeaky cot.

"Give the heater time."

"How does this abandoned place have electricity anyway?"

"You don't know by now that we know how to wire and rewire things?"

"Sorry, I forget I'm not with normal human beings who are above the law."

"The neighbors pay for our usage. We steal from them. We've got a wire that runs from here to that house, there." He pointed at the houses, off a hair without Fletcher. "And one from there to there, if that one fails. Underground. That sort of thing. Rosemund taught us well. Has Bulfinch come out yet?"

"Yeah, but he went back in when he saw you."

"Smart cat. He knows when we need a moment alone." He smiled. Something in her was glad to see that smile.

She found herself reaching for his cold hand. She balled his into a fist and held it for a second until it was as warm as her own. Ran her fingers across it. Stuck her finger inside.

"You flirting with me now?" he asked.

She leaned back from him. "No. I'm trying to woo you. I'm trying to get that wrinkle, just there, off your face."

He blushed because he couldn't see where she was pointing.

"I've not run away yet, have I?" She touched his arm—she wasn't sure why.

He leaned back. "No, you haven't…"

To fill his silence she assumed the role of narrator. "Bul's not more than two feet away from the carrier now. He doesn't want to go back in there, though. He's about to have a panic attack. Doesn't know where to go—especially since there's no furniture to hide under."

"What was it like, being fucked by Leeland? Fucking him?"

"That had no lead-in."

"Doesn't need one."

"Haven't we talked about this?" She stared outside at the bright snow, visualizing kicking at it, crunching it beneath her shoe.

Bulfinch started to meow, nervous. Odissa calmed him, calling to him. But he settled for dashing under the cot, wide-eyed. He curled his tail around himself by her feet and waited.

When the wrinkle in Dorian's forehead grew deeper, Odissa leaned back on the cot and said, "I think you know what it was like having sex with Augury."

"Odissa, I need to tell you something. I know who your parents were."

Long story short, he explained it.

"...So, you really are my uncle?"

"Step-uncle." He wanted to be very clear. "Your brother knows, too."[34]

"I can't keep from fucking family members, it seems." She watched his expression, wondering how he'd react. She didn't know if she meant to be funny or not.

"Sometimes I half-think Admund put it in his head—Leeland's head. He gave him the idea to try and get you pregnant. I mean, all his medical experiments. He already had a foundation with them—previous Masters were all these mad scientist types. Not all of them were medically inclined, but Admund does give them a way with the sciences. Seems only natural he'd give those foundations to Leeland and he'd take off with it. Automatons. They do strange things to Masters. But, Jesus, this has been strangest of all."

And he went into a tangent about *why* Admund might be the most fucked up—the whole "he's the oldest" spiel.

Odissa was having trouble keeping up. "I'm grateful you told me."

"I'm grateful you're still here. Not running away."

---

[34] Now that I think about it, I wonder if Odys took the photos of his parents that Leeland left, or if he let them burn up in the house?

"You keep saying that, but do you know how convenient it is to—to have a slave? Someone so completely devoted to you? Of course you do. You have an Automaton. But see, I don't need one. I have you, I guess."

Dorian kept her hand and brought it to his face, overlooking her ignorance.

Bulfinch cautiously came up to them and arched his back as Odissa reached out. "Why do you think I wouldn't want one of Leeland's Automatons, exactly?"

"He's practically your father. It'd just be too weird. And I wouldn't want you to fuck me with him looming over us, sorry."

"But Coraza would be different? Aw—Bul's looking out the window!"

Standing on his back paws cautiously.

"Coraza hasn't had a history of psycho Masters is all I'm saying. It's like Vulcan cursed Admund to only be picked up by abnormals."

Odissa didn't press it.

Dorian asked her, "This store Fletcher's at doesn't have a great wet food selection, but we'll get one of each if that's OK?"

"We're giving each other play-by-plays for what we can't see." Odissa added a smile to her voice. "It's as good as watching TV, I guess. That we don't have."

"Want to move this show to the bath? A warm bath as the house heats up."

Stanza: Chekhov's now anti-guns.

"Now he's found the clothing aisle." Dorian had begun, just after he'd turned the water off.

She had closed her eyes as he leaned back into her. She hadn't had proper sleep in a while.

"Need anything?"

"Some different gloves. Maybe a shirt or two?"

"You'll let me dress you, or do you want a say in what he picks out?"

Not wanting him to have to describe every shirt available, "I trust your judgment. I'm a small top. Size seven or eight in pants." *But you probably know that.*

He continued his narration as the steam of the tub floated into the cold air. "He's coming down the block now," Dorian finally announced, squeezing her hand a bit tighter.

Bulfinch had peeked in and watched them for a few minutes, wondering where his litter box was. He had settled for peeing on some newspaper that didn't make the lone garbage bin. Odissa cooed at him, but he would not be tricked into coming near.

"I'm glad you made him get the eco-friendly cat litter," she told Dorian as she pulled on the black hairs on his arm. They'd been soaking for almost an hour at this point.

"Nothing but the best for Bulfinch." He gave her leg a little stroke. His hand lingered there for a moment. "Oh, wouldn't it be nice if we could live here forever? Just us."

His hand slid down her leg.

"I feel like outlaws here. There's no furniture," she said, putting a hand on his. She had only agreed to take the bath because she'd been so cold. At least, that's what she'd told herself.

"Yes, but theoretically we could always get *more* furniture. Fletcher's bringing some folding chairs, by the way."

"Those will certainly complete the room."

"I can't see them anyway."

After their moment, he finally let Fletcher come in with their bath products and necessities (read: towels).

Setting a few grocery sacks down before going back outside for the rest, he looked down at them. "Are you guys going to stay in here all day or shall I join you?"

Odissa said, "I'm not sure where he'd fit, Dorian."

"You forget, dear," Fletcher said. "I can become small enough to slip through that drain. And I'm tired of going out in the cold."

"Yes, well, your nerve endings aren't as delicate as ours, so suck it up."

Dorian laughed. "Now who's the one being mean?"

Stanza: Spousal abuse works both ways.

Once the sheets were placed on the dusty cot mattress, the chairs arranged and the goods spread here and there, Dorian told her to get ready. They were going out!

"Bulfinch has his litter box, now we can go out—without you worrying about him."

"Nothing fancy, right? I can't go dressed like this."

Fletcher hadn't exactly gone to a clothing store.

"Don't worry. I'm a bit too depressed for something grand just yet."

Fletcher drove them (in the neighbor's smelly car) to a local diner. Seat yourself.

"This one," Fletcher said, pointing. Someone had left a day-old newspaper on the seat. He took his pleasure in reading it rather than the greasy menu.

"What will you be having?" Dorian asked Odissa. He had sat next to her, trapping her in the booth. Or, as he might have called it, *tucking her in.*

"Milkshake sounds nice," she said.

The waitress came up.

The place was just loud enough for her to raise her voice. The mod-country music playing above them clashed with the 50's diner ambiance. It made it hard for Odissa to concentrate as she placed her order. Dorian said, "Same thing, please."

Fletcher, through his newspaper, said, "The same thing for me, too."

"Same things, coming right up," the woman repeated, amused.

"She probably thinks you two can't read or something."

"Well, I can't, actually," Dorian stated, pushing up his glasses with a grin. She was joking with him. They were having fun.

"And besides," Fletcher said, "I've got the news. It's obvious I can't read the menu at the same time." He shuffled his local section.

The drinks in front of them, Odissa poked with her straw. "I hate cherries. Anyone want mine?"

"You hate them?"

"Well, no. Not *real* cherries. These all have the weird sauce on them." She offered it to them with a tip.

No one took it from her.

Offended that no one even bothered to reject the damn red dot, she changed the subject. "You think Vulcan is insulted that *Star Trek* used His name for an alien race?"

"Why would He be?" Fletcher said, looking over his paper. He had assumed fake glasses for his reading—big John Lennon ones (or Harry Potter depending on the generation).

"Because, well, certain seasons weren't as...good as others. I don't know. There's bound to be *something* that would piss Him off. And it's not like they asked His permission."

"Most humans don't ask permission. But then again," Dorian mused, "I don't know that they should have to. Spock is, likely, the least of His worries."

"Live long and fuck Vulcan," Fletcher mumbled behind his paper.

"Even so," Odissa said. "I still wonder His opinion on the matter."

"Maybe you'll meet Him someday. You can ask yourself."

They all took a sip (or two) of their drinks.

Odissa spotted someone far away. A handicapped man with even older parents. He could barely swallow the food his mother fed him. It was hard for Odissa to watch—not because she was disgusted, but because it hurt her heart. Staring at the family, "I think I'd ask Him *why*. If I met Him."

"Why what?" Dorian said, taking his lips off the straw.

"Why the gods would let something like that happen." She nodded once and Fletcher's eyes glanced. "Mistakes."

"Ah," Dorian said, his voice lowering. "Well, first of all, it's not like He's the one in charge of those issues. Second, people aren't mistakes."

"For sure. But, I mean in general...*why* does it happen? It's so unfair. Oh, never mind. I don't know what I'm saying. Well, let me rephrase. I'm just glad I can't have children,"—her tone was hushed. "So that can't happen to someone else. My children won't have that problem. Or me. God knows if I had kids what kind of monsters they'd be..."

She paled, realizing what she'd just said. She stared at her glass, unable to look at her boys. *Shut up, Odissa!*

"We all have our handicaps, Odissa," Fletcher said, a bit surprised she'd call disabled people monstrous. Especially now that she was fucking one. But something told him that wasn't what she'd meant.

"Fitting, though," Dorian forced a laugh, "given that Vulcan is, well..."

Disabled.

"He has a limp right?" she asked them, as if she didn't know. She was really leaning into stupidity. "I'm not getting Him confused with Someone else?"

"No, you're right," Fletcher said, watching her grow redder and more embarrassed. "Most of the time, He does. What does it say about us if even our gods are disabled?"

She took her spoon, watching her face materialize in the warped metal. She noticed her sad expression. Was the glimmer of this outing melting just as her image in the spoon?

She caught Fletcher staring at her—spying for Dorian. She glared at him—THEM. Dorian inched closer to her, pressing his leg against hers. "What would you be doing right now if none of this had happened?" he asked, his voice hushed (as if anyone could hear them—in fact, the older folks in the restaurant seemed appalled by the look of this threesome).

"I'd be doing something with Odys."

"Like what?"

131

"Anything. We'd probably have just gotten off of work. We might do homework together for the next day."

"Are you going to miss school?"

"So I can *never* go back or anything?"

"Maybe we can both go back. Isn't that an idea, Fletcher? What would we study?"

"I pick for you, is that it? No, tell me what you like," Odissa encouraged.

"I would study only what you studied—so I could get to know you better. I never really did well in college, you see. I was too preoccupied with sucking all the dicks I never got to in high school."

Dot. Dot. Dot.

"I need to use the restroom," Odissa half-lied. She could go, but it wasn't a need.

Dorian replied, "Hold it until we get home. I'm not getting arrested for going into a girl's room."

"Even though no one could tell the difference," Fletcher commented.

"I love how you can make fun of yourself, Dorian. But that still doesn't relieve my bladder."

Chit chat chit chat chit chat.

The food came out.

They ate, as they were supposed to do.

Then, as they were halfway through the meal:

Lily Allen ringtone.

Fletcher pulled out the phone (yes, from his "pocket"), and looked at the CID. "Where the hell did he find a payphone?" he said as he passed the phone to Dorian. "They still make those?"

"Hello, Odys," Dorian greeted, his mouth half-full. "You know I let Mother have this phone tapped, so why are you stupid enough to call me?"

Odissa dropped her fork to eavesdrop.

She could hear her brother's faint voice: "How'd you know it was me? Never mind, stupid question, I guess."

"Let me speak to him!" Odissa begged, her voice a loud whisper.

Fletcher put his paper down and grabbed her wrist—warning her. She'd not be touching that phone.

"Why are you calling?"

"Don't you mean from where?"

"Get to your point, Odys."

"All right then, I want to know where you went."

"And you thought I'd tell you, Odys?"

"You haven't cussed me out yet."

"That comes later."

"Fine." He hadn't expected him to answer. "But you at least asked me why I was calling. You're still interested."

"Think what you must. It's true, Odys, I wish I could trust you"—Dorian put a hand up to Odissa, who was leaning a bit too close—"But, given the circumstances…"

"Ask me what I want again."

"I'll not be redundant, Odys."

Odissa was calmer now, listening—trying to imbibe it. They all sat very still in the booth. Odissa held her breath so she could hear over the *damn stupid music*.

"I want Mother to fork up Cestus. That's what I fucking want. I want a plan to get her to admit she has him. To prove once and for all she's beyond forgiveness."[35]

"And you have this plan, do you? You think you can't trust Mother, and that may be true. But her pros outweigh her cons. I'll not go against her."

"Pepin said—"

"FUCK WHAT PEPIN SAID!" Dorian shouted. The restaurant quieted. Fletcher waved them off, mouthing an apology. "You think I trust him over Mother?" He was

---

[35] Wait, what? He thinks she has Cestus?

133

hunched over, leaning into the phone as if he might get close enough through the cell-waves to punch him.

For a second or two Odys didn't respond. But Dorian didn't hang up the phone either.

"Pepin was willing to die for something, Dorian."

"So was Leeland and we're all grateful he did."

"Pepin didn't die because of Gwen, though."

"When you find out why Pepin killed himself, let me know, boy. Then we'll talk. Otherwise, you're just his puppet. Maybe you shouldn't have synced with Maud."

"Tell me where you are so I can tell you in person."

"I'm not letting you get near her, and you know that."

"Let me speak to him, at least." Odissa touched Dorian's arm. She knew she could get him to talk, and Dorian knew it too. But he'd not involve her with this. He ignored her.

"Let me talk to her, Dorian," Odys said.

"You are in no position to be asking for things, Odys."

"Then tell me how to earn your trust. You know this was the best way to keep Mother's hands off them."—the inanimate Automatons.

Odissa could tell the conversation was ending so she had begun to beg. "Please, Dorian." She put a hand on his leg.

But Dorian shut her up. His hand went to her pants and grabbed her genitals, making her softly gasp from his horrific public display. He was doing it to express not only his jealousy but to finalize his stance on the matter. She was cornered against the booth's wall, trying to get away from him. She tried not to squirm—to draw attention to herself.

Fletcher kept hold of her wrist on the table, staring her down, keeping her still. His eyes cut to those around them—none had caught on yet.

Dorian continued on with his phone-convo, "I want an Automaton, Odys. I want the inanimates to be evenly distributed. You shouldn't have both of them. Give one to me and maybe you'll get to see Odissa again."

"Done. Set the terms."

"Get a cell phone. Text me the number. I'll text you the number to my backup cell."

How many phones can a person have? Odissa wondered.

"But do it tomorrow," Dorian clarified. "You understand? We're done for today."

The waitress, aware of the peace-disturbing threesome, came to ask if everything was all right. Were they done with their plates? Ready for the check?

But then she noticed Dorian's hand placement—the way Odissa was hunched over the table—the way Fletcher held her wrist. And before Odissa could pretend she wasn't embarrassed, it was too late. The lady's eyes widened—and seemed to ask Odissa if she needed her to call the police. Where these men bothering her? Fletcher calmly followed Odissa's eyes to the waitress's face.

Dorian's hand lifted as he cleared his throat. The conversation with Odys was over. He hung up the phone. Before the lady could turn away—Odissa had assumed a rebellious face and, with a rebellious hand, had rebelliously cupped Dorian. It was all just a game, waitress. No need to be concerned. Call the cops if you want, but not for *those* reasons. With her left hand, she squeezed Dorian gently, between the legs, and stared the lady in the eye. "There's no problem."

The waitress's face shifted from concern to disgust. "You need to leave."

"We'll be leaving now, yes, dear." Fletcher opened a wallet—pulled from somewhere quickly. "This ought to cover it. Keep the change."

The waitress blushed. Maybe from embarrassment. Maybe because she'd never been tipped so much. Maybe because she'd actually thought Fletcher was attractive (because he was).

And they were out.

"Remind me never to take you two out again," Fletcher grumbled, holding the door. "You're too expensive."

135

When the car started, Odissa slapped Dorian. "Don't you ever embarrass me in public like that again!" When he didn't respond, she slapped him again. Though a normal human couldn't hurt him, she could tell her actions pained him. And she kept hurting. She kept at it because she knew he'd still love her in the end: "You think I won't scream the next time you pull something like that? I swear to God I will!"

He grabbed her hand. "I'm sorry."

"A manipulative little—little bitch!" She put her seatbelt on with passion.

"I'm sorry," he said again. And he really was. "And thank you for—for saving face back there—"

"You're not welcome!"

"Oh, but I think I am." He crossed his legs, put a hand on her own. Fletcher drove faster and faster. "I think I'm very welcome."

Stanza: A sexless marriage and a sexful of divorce.

Odissa smoked in the bed-cot-thing, the covers pulled over her naked torso.

It was raining outside and she watched the water roll down through the cracks in the blinds. Dorian had his arm placed around her, propping both of them up as he leaned against the corner wall. He twiddled paperclip-Fletcher with his right hand.

"What do you think my brother's doing right now?"

"I just fucked you and you're talking about him?" He gave a wounded sound and kissed her hair. He was always kissing her—always begging her for affection. She pulled her head away from his lips.

"No, I just fucked *you*," she growled.

"I can fix that," he said reaching down the covers.

She squirmed away from him. When the laughter stopped, "Funny, isn't it, how I trust him and you trust Gwen?"

He stopped when she wouldn't let him kiss her.

"I don't think it's funny at all," he said with a craggy voice, shrinking from her.

"Hand me the ashtray."

The ashtray was a plastic cup. She blew smoke out the corner of her mouth.

"If I gave you an Automaton—any Automaton—would you use it to stay with me forever?"

She settled in under the covers. "So you're afraid that if I get one, I'll ditch you? That the new drama you're going to stir up?"

"Can't you just reassure me?"

"No. I'm using you. I'm using you to get an Automaton," she said, flicking an imaginary spec of ash off her lap (so nervous around him, even though he had the least invasive eyes of anyone she knew). "I'm using you because I have no one else in the world I could use to get one. I mean, even if I begged, Odys wouldn't give me one of the two he has. That's why he has them and I have to be here with you. You who have none to give."

"You don't have to be so cruel."

"You don't have to be so worried."

Blahblahblah, they fuck a lot and play twenty questions on repeat. Maybe they even ordered food at one point. Eventually, though, night came and they fell asleep.

Stanza: And as they slumbered...

From the floor in the opposite corner, the cell phone vibrated. It lit up the darkness like a holy candle.

Dorian unconsciously dropped the paperclip in his hand. The paperclip twisted upwards, becoming a man. Fletcher scooped up the phone next to the bags and went outside. He stole a quick peek at his Master and Odissa before he closed the door behind him. Dorian might want to know what this moment looked like in the morning: his Master, mouth wide open for flies, was quietly snoring, one foot peeping outside the covers. His head was on Odissa's chest, crushing her and keeping her lungs from rising fully.

Fletcher looked at the phone—a face floating in the darkness.

He moved to the door, texting back. He put that phone in his "pocket" and pulled out another from his chest. He counted to ten seconds before it rang.

Answering the phone with a hiss, "Do you know what fucking time it is?"

"My clock says 12:06," Maud replied from the other end. He could imagine her lips against the receiver.

"We said call tomorrow!"

"Tomorrow is today. And I'm just doing as you told Odys."

"This isn't what we meant."

He walked up past the house porch and grabbed onto the gutter. It creaked, but not enough to discourage him from pulling on it. He used it to swing himself to the roof with one arm. He looked like a skeleton creeping up the house. He climbed up to the peak with ease and crouched near the crumbling chimney—a pale, gangly gargoyle with a slump.

"You're being terribly brave about all this, Odys. How do you know I'm not with Mother, right now? Letting her hear aaall the plans we're about to make?"

"I'm pretty sure our bases are covered, Dorian. If you wanted Gwen to hear, you would have gone with her. But you didn't. You split up."

"How'd you know that?"

"Mother's not the only one with spies."

"Given Dorian's history, Maud, we deserve the spying. On the other hand, we have every reason to trust her. It's going to take a lot for you to turn me against her."

"I don't care about your stance toward Mother. I care whether or not things are fair."

"If Odys cared so much, then why did he make you do this phone call?"

"Odys is asleep. He'll know all about this in the morning. And don't be so hypocritical. Dorian isn't talking right now. You are. Your Master's a lazy ass, too."

Fletcher laughed. Dorian thought it was funny. "Tell me why—honestly, why— this couldn't wait until the sun came up?"

"Because I know you smell it too. Something is happening. The ash is in the air. It's thicker. It's all too coincidental."

"It's just people burning fires for the cold." He itched his nose, becoming more aware of the fact he *could* smell it. He couldn't stop smelling it. *The nose knows.*

"No. Being a Master isn't what it used to be, Dorian.[36] The gods are planning something—something big. It's all coming to a close. All of our plans will be for nothing. So will Mother's."

"And what was Gwen's plan, exactly, Odys?"

"She said Automatons shouldn't exist. She didn't want them damaging more lives. She's taking the burden on herself. She'll likely launch the Automatons she's got into fucking space and then shoot her brains out so that she doesn't have to feel guilty about dying. She wouldn't make new Masters *suffer.*"

"Look. In one week we'll give you a call. We'll arrange a meeting place. You'll deliver Coraza to me and then maybe we'll let you see Odissa. Clear?"

"No. I'll only give you Admund. Can't have you tempted to give her Coraza just because you think she'll have less of Leeland in her. I won't do it. I don't want him near her. I've only just gotten rid of him."

Fletcher rolled his eyes. "We'll call you in a week."

"We don't have a week! You know it."

"Don't bother us again. You understand? You left us—you accepted this fate when you took the inanimates. This is how it works."

"Vulcan won't give us a week, Dorian. He's smothering us. I called you, now keep the ball rolling. If you don't, They'll roll it for you."

Fletcher removed the phone from his ear and hung up. "I'll drop the ball every fucking chance I get if it will fuck up Their game."

The phone convo ended, but Fletcher's wakefulness would not. Instead of sleeping, he perched on the roof, brooding for Dorian.

---

[36] We are well aware that it is Maud talking to Fletcher here. But do realize the proper nouns don't really mean much when they both recognize each other as Odys and Dorian.

Stanza: The metal gargoyle.

Dorian woke up. He felt Odissa lift her head and push back her hair.

"Good morning," Dorian told her, smiling through his stubble-shadowed face.

"Morning," she mumbled, turning her head away from him (as not to breathe morning breath on him).

He fumbled under his pillow for the pack of gum Fletcher had put there upon making the cot-bed. "Chewy for yah?"

"Sí, gracias," she said. She wadded up the wrapper but wasn't sure what to do with it. She rolled it between her fingers. "Why the fruity gum instead of minty, again?"

"Because I don't like my gum the same flavor as my toothpaste? Does it matter?" He tried to kiss her, but was off target. He hit the side of her lips, instead.

This made her realize Fletcher wasn't in the room. "Where's Fletcher?"

"He went to get you coffee and cigarettes. Let's get dressed so we can go out to brunch, huh? I'll make up for the outing we had yesterday."

He was up out of bed in an instant. However, he was back down again, almost falling to the floor. "That's what happens, you see, when I don't sleep with Fletcher. Going to be a bumpy morning," he laughed as she helped him right himself.

"What do you mean you didn't sleep with Fletcher? He wasn't here last night? When did he leave?"

He started to answer, but paused—like someone trying to recall a foggy dream.

"I'm afraid he was up all night being anxious for me. But it'll get better as soon as I have breakfast." He leaned against the wall all the way to the bathroom.

Following him in her own sleepy daze, she asked, "What does he have to worry about?"

"Instead of a bath, let's take a shower. You want to try fucking standing up?"

"Can you even stand on your own?"

"Best we save the shower experiment for another time, then," he said with diluted confidence.

He gave a stretch as he pulled back the grimy shower curtain for her.

"I'm just going to wash my face and fix my hair…" No need for a shower.

"I was so looking forward to doing yours today," he sighed, rubbing his puffy eyes. "But I can't see without Fletcher. I didn't think this through. I suppose you can just put a hat on me or something."

Odissa glared at him. It really wasn't fair that he *could* pull off "just a hat." It was she who had to make adjustments just to feel comfortable in her own skin. She stared into the mirror at him, there, wondering what "comfortable" and "skin" meant to Dorian.

As Odissa finished her hair and started on her makeup, she glanced at Dorian, who was dozing off on the closed toilet lid. She chose her foundation, noticing that it matched her skin tone perfectly; she marveled at how good Fletcher was at buying products. Not just because he was the Automaton of Dorian Dandor, but because his divine database knew much too much about everything.

"Were you always such a—a femme? Is that the right way of phrasing it?" she asked Dorian. "I mean, like, with my grandparents? Did they have a problem with it?"

The question rebooted him. "Yes and no. Your mother used to dress me up in girl clothes for fun. And by fun I mean I was the one who was having it. She always thought she might get in trouble for making me her living doll." He smiled in his fond remembrance. "How come you haven't ever asked about her? I mean, maybe you have, but you still don't seem entirely interested."

"What should I ask, then?"

"I suppose you're right. Where to start?" He ran a hand through his hair, thinking. "She was much like you. Or, rather, you're much like her. Except she took longer to warm up to me—and to others. She was very quiet—at first. We were the three amigos—her, your father, me. She was so loyal to us, she didn't even have a girl best friend. Well, maybe I count. She was always the type who was befriended, never the befriender. She wasn't the kind to fight for a place in, say, a circle. The circle had to come to her. If that makes any sense."

"It doesn't, but I like the way you talk about her. You talk about her as if you've..." She paused and tore her eyes from the mirror, choosing her next bit of makeup. "Thought a lot about her."

"She had this way of *reacting* to people. She would step back if you moved forward." He demonstrated, his movements sloppy and tired. "But it didn't feel as if she was avoiding you. She was drawing you into herself. Making you follow. She could do that. She could move you and control you if you came close enough. Reminds me of you, in a way. Our parents said that I started to mimic her when they moved in together. I would say things she would say—the way she said it. I would move like she moved. Maybe because I wanted to be her. She was the most fascinating and beautiful human being on the planet..." He smiled at the memory— but it made him remember something else. "And then she and your father just moved away one year when I was in college. My parents didn't like your father—they caught me sleeping on him once. It bothered them, that he would let me. Your parents—they eventually stopped calling as frequently. I stopped wanting them to. And then I avoided them all together because making amends is—is hard. You want to know the last thing your mother said to me before she died?"

"Do I?" She had stopped putting on makeup completely now, frozen in place as she listened—not wanting to hear. He was only rambling on like this because he was so tired. She could hear the sadness in his voice and see the history in his face.

He fidgeted with his thumb ring.

"She wouldn't talk to me, you see, when I finally got them to agree to come and visit me. She was still pretending to be angry at what I had said to them the last time I'd seen them—that I didn't really have time, especially since *they'd* never had time for *me* before. That's how I'd phrased it, you see. I had just gotten Fletcher when they had finally tried to reconnect after all that time. Your father was the one I convinced to come out and see me—before it all happened. But on the phone before that, well, Dory had said 'Dorian, I don't know who you are anymore. We used to be like twins, but then we weren't enough for you. You became an alter-ego that isn't you.' That's what she said. I remember it perfectly because Fletcher burned it into my memory. I have two brains now—double the hauntings. And then she passed the phone to Dominic."

Dorian rubbed his forehead, massaging the memories back into place. "She could sum me up so easily. She made it so easy to—to be afraid of her. And she was right. But not entirely. She had rubbed off too much on me. She was the reason people loved me. I could amplify her. I would wear your mother like an outfit, Odissa, and I made her better than herself. She was my muse. But she didn't like looking into a mirror, I guess..."

"She should have taken it as a compliment," Odissa said, rinsing her hand. She didn't know why, but this topic made her feel guilty.

Fletcher came in through the door and handed them their coffee. He leaned on the bathroom doorframe, hair brushing the top. "You look fine, but he looks like shit. Why didn't you say something? I'll go get you some clean clothes." He left but turned back around. "Almost forgot." And he slapped down a box of new cigarettes. But he kept her from reaching for them. "Not yet!" he held up a finger.

And with his other hand he pulled a cigarette from "behind" his ear and stuck it in her mouth. He flicked the tip and away it smoked. He winked.

Odissa removed the cig and glared at Fletcher as he left the room. "I thought you said you were tired. He seems plenty full of spunk to me." And then she realized Dorian was asleep, head in his arm.

He started when she set the curling iron down. "What? What were we talking about?"

"You were talking about my father—" she tried to get him off the topic of her mother.

"Was I?" He laughed, trying to remember. "You know, your father shaved his head in the eleventh grade. Completely off. He liked it shaggy. But he also liked it cleanly. My hair would've been a bit much for him, too. He would disapprove of your brother's hair, *definitely*. Your mother wouldn't have minded, though. I think Dory—I mean, your mother…Gah, it sounds so strange, calling her that—'your mother.' It makes me feel like a pervert."

"If the shoe fits." Odissa smiled at him, but realized he couldn't see it. "I think this is the least of our sins."

"Well, yes. But the fact of the matter is that it would be wrong even if you weren't my by-marriage niece. I'm a hundred times your age"—he exaggerated. "I guess this makes me a cougar." He leaned back on the toilet seat, crossing his legs and clawing at her.

"Who do I look more like, my dad or my mom?"

Fletcher came in with a fresher pair of clothes and started to re-dress Dorian. Odissa stared for a moment, watching. Dorian and Fletcher were leaning on each other more than seemed right. Dorian almost fell over when putting a pant leg through.

"Odys looks more like your mom. You look like your dad when you smile. Your dad had a knee-buckling smile."

"It sounds like you had a thing for my dad."

"There's a reason I wanted to be your mother," he laughed, sitting back down.

She screwed on the lid to her mascara. "Get off the pot, I'm going to puke."

"I have digital copies of—of photos. Photos of your family. Digital records. I hate to bring them out. I never look at them. Maybe someday we can view them together?"

She could tell he didn't want to look at them in the near future, though. She wondered why he cared to even preserve them if he never looked at them.

"We don't have to talk about this, Dorian. We don't. I was doing fine without them—without a family."

"Yes, well, I wasn't."

"I couldn't miss what I never had."

Fletcher noted her expression for his Master, making him respond: "Ah, look at you, concerned. This is why I love you so much. I've been without someone who is mine for such a very long time."

"Is my brother family, though, to you?"

Again with the mouth twist. "You done getting ready?"

She turned away from him. "Let me fix this strand of hair."

Fletcher and Dorian waited. "You know, at first, when your brother gained Maud, I thought Pepin might be trying to help *me*. But then it became clear—no, *obvious*—that this all had to do with Leeland. Of course it would. Pepin was so...obsessed with Leeland. Always felt responsible because he's the one that *caused* Leeland. But now I see that Pepin only cared about Odys because Leeland cared. Not because *I* cared. Pepin didn't give a *fuck* about me. Hell, he probably liked your brother more than me. I'm really starting to question Pepin's motives."

Odissa suddenly wanted to keep him talking, so she pretended that strand of hair needed more than just a little work. "Pepin could have given Maud to me instead of Odys, couldn't he?"

"Sure," he shrugged. "He could have given Maud to you. You could have been just as worthwhile a person to catch our attention and get the same results. Why not?" He was too caught up in his anger to catch her meaning.

"But there had to be a specific reason. Why Odys and not me? And if Pepin did it, by some chance, to bring us back to you, Dorian, then why didn't Pepin just tell you we were still alive? Why not let you know who we were and bother someone else with Maud?"

He marveled at her understanding. But then the thought came to him. "And who else would he bother?"

"Someone already like you. Someone with an Automaton already. I don't know."

145

Fletcher responded more quickly than his Master, "He knew he needed to protect the twins from Leeland, and giving them an Automaton was the best shot for that."

"I *understand* that. But, and correct me if I'm wrong here because I'm still picking up on things, but Pepin didn't only have one Automaton, did he? He could have given away Madus—more easily than giving away Maud. Hell, he could have given *both* us twins an Automaton. But he didn't. He didn't want me to have an Automaton. But he wanted *Odys* to have Maud."

Fletcher narrowed his eyes at her.

Had Dorian been standing, he would have sagged at the knees at her insight—so shook was he in finding yet another reason to love her. "I see what you're saying," Dorian agreed. "Either Pepin wasn't able to give Madus to you or there's something *more* to how his gift was given."

Fletcher took off with it. "Yes, maybe something disrupted the major plan. What's happening is his plan B. Although, we're both assuming there's a plan A at all."

Odissa took it back. "Well, he could have just liked Odys and was tired of living, right? Why couldn't he have just randomly liked my brother over me?"

Dorian pursed his lips, disagreeing with her devil's advocate. He liked her original thought—as if he had come up with it himself. Pepin had chosen Odys for a reason. "That makes it all seem anti-climatic. Pepin did love a good show. Especially if it went on and on and on."

There were too many "what-ifs" now to keep the game fun. They dwindled into silence.

"…Dorian," Odissa asked hesitantly. The moment the name escaped her lips, she regretted it.

He heard the meekness in her voice. "Yes?"

"I don't want Admund or Coraza as my Automaton."

"Your options are not vast."

"I'll tell you which one I want."

"Well, go on."

"Madus." The name felt strange on her lips, but she knew it well enough. She liked how the name made Dorian stiffen angrily.

"Stop being cruel, Odissa. You can't have that one. By the time that one's available you'll be older than the pope." He crossed himself like someone waving off a terrible idea.

They walked out of the bathroom and into the living room, about to leave.

"Wait, Fletcher, go get my hat. And glasses!" Dorian touched his face.

Fletcher dashed away and returned, placing them on his Master. He preened a little for him, tucking some hair behind his ears. "I'm not sure I like this hat I bought you." It had a large puff ball on top. "It resembles a man bun too much. Maybe we should buy another one when we're out."

"After we eat, because I'm hungry," Odissa grouched when Fletcher adjusted the hat for the third time.

"Don't rush me," Dorian barked back. If he was going to be an unshowered slob, he might as well look good doing it.

"How many ways can you possibly wear a hat?" Odissa begged for a good answer.

Dorian huffed, seeing himself through Fletcher. "You're just saying that to get me to move, but fine—" and he opened the door quickly to appease his Odissa and started out.

And that was when he was stopped. He had bounced off a very broad chest covered in a black and white striped sweater.

Stanza: Stereotypes and archetypes.

Before Dorian could even recover from running into the pillowy-firm pecks, Maurice had caught him. Before Dorian could even slip through his fingers, Maurice's gun was already drawn. And, before Dorian/Fletcher could even notice

Maurice point the gun in everyone's general directions (Nobody move!), he had already...

Turned the gun on himself.[37]

"You as my witness!" Maurice shouted, pulling Dorian's arm like a child would a doll.

Fletcher rolled his eyes and stepped in front of Odissa.

As the gun fired, Fletcher enveloped Odissa. The bullet ricocheted and hit the wood floor.

"You fucking idiot!" Dorian shouted when Fletcher was sure Odissa was OK. He ripped his body away from the intruder. "You could have killed her!"

Maurice hit the ground, fancy gun slipping from his fingers.

Odissa wanted to scream at the falling body but...

There wasn't any blood.

Taking her hand from her mouth (she felt stupid at being so dramatic), she stared between Fletcher and Dorian. They weren't concerned at all.

Dorian kicked the body. "Fucking Maurice! You can't pull shit like this."

"Is he—?" Odissa asked, wondering why they didn't seem to care.

Composing himself with a deep breath, Dorian pushed up his glasses. Fletcher took a cautious step toward Maurice, wondering if—just if...

Well, it wasn't likely. Maurice had never been able to kill himself, so Fletcher didn't have high hopes (though there was still slight altitude—wishing every day that this thorn in their side would die for good).

Odissa jumped when Maurice's chest heaved and he opened one eye; the large thing rolled around the room, landing on Fletcher. "Am I dead?"

"Nope. Purgatory still," Fletcher said, leaning on his knees. His lips were a straight line, fighting against a twitch of annoyance.

Maurice sat up, moaning under his masculine weight. His shoulders slumped over, lip pouting. His legs were apart—like some little boy on the floor—a little boy

---

[37] This scene seems so familiar. B.L.A. does love to wave a gun around.

with a waxed mustache. He frowned at his gun, cradled it in his palms. He began to blubber.

"Why must you do this in front of us? *Every* fucking time?" Dorian scolded, almost reaching down to shake Maurice but thinking better of touching something so pathetic. *Pathetic rubs off.* To Odissa, "He needs an audience—lo juro por Dios."

Maurice shook the gun in his hands—fighting against breaking it. "I was almost certain eet would work!" he spat, face turning red with frustration. "I had zee formula perfect—I vas sure!" He grit his teeth.

"You should have tested it beforehand," Dorian mumbled, gritting his own teeth.

"I may want to die, Dorian, but I do not want to die alone." He sniffed up his runny nose, staring at the floor.

"What witchcraft did you latch onto this time?" Dorian already regretted his interest.

Fletcher fought the gun away from Maurice and checked to see if there were more bullets. Empty.

Maurice looked up at him, sheepishly. His bottom lip quivered. "D'you know how hard eet iz to mine iron from Ethopia, get it blessed by priests of twenty different religions, and zen—and zen!—forge bullets from Italian volcanic coals?" He shook his head, tears squeezing out his bulging red eyes.

"Isn't that like what you did last time?" Fletcher asked, picking up the bullet (that had bounced off Maurice's head) and sniffing it. A self-made one with—what was that?—ground *pearl?* He licked it to confirm again. He glanced at Maurice's gun. He couldn't classify what type it was. Probably a self-made contraption.

"OUI!" Maurice whimpered—on the verge of crying again. "But zis time I had it blessed by a shaman in the south of Maine, unlike last time. He is a favorite of Venus herself, so the witches said."

"Venus wouldn't come to them, you idiot. Was probably just some nymph or mermaid saying They were her!" Fletcher shouted, tossing the bullet behind him. "You know you can't trust the witches of Maine. They think they know but they don't."

"But eet was worth a shot!" He pounded his fists on his knees and kicked.

"Yes, but by now you ought to know your shots usually *miss*." Dorian hissed, gesturing for Fletcher to keep Odissa back, lest Maurice pull something else. "And why, again, must you do it in front of everyone? Some suicides are best done alone."

"Well, someone will need to clean up zee mess." Maurice gestured to the theoretical splatter that should have happened. Then, he seemed to notice Odissa. His ears—eyes—even his mustache perked up. "[Mumbling in French] So *zis* is the girl, eh? Zis must be her. [Mumbling more in French]."

His face turned into the most charming beam—as if he *handn't* just been weeping like a spoiled brat.

Dorian straightened, snapping his fingers. "You leave her alone. Don't speak to her. Stop it!"

Maurice was on his feet in an instant. He whipped his hands behind his back and leaned forward, turning one bulging eye toward her. Odissa swore his mustache's tips wiggled on their own—like a bug's antenna. "Ah! The infamous half of the infamous twins!"

Fletcher crossed his arms and rolled his eyes again. "Notice how the accent disappears when he's not being dramatic." Fletcher proceeded to scoff after Odissa almost smiled.

Indeed, I'm not fond of always capturing his pronunciation and leave it to Gabbler to correct if I slip. However, feel free to imagine Maurice's accent as fading in and out.[38]

Odissa reared back—though he wasn't touching her, his every fiber intruded, forcing them to zoom in on each other. His hair was a dark brown, though his

---

[38] Yeah, don't count on me to catch everything. The point is, after all, to leave the art bare and raw for the world.

eyebrows and mustache were slightly black. Perhaps it was the wax. Even those bushy brows had a few curls.

He sent her mind into a vision—a vision of his zeitgeist. He reminded her (and I can feel you sighing now, for of course you've already called it) of an antique circus poster. A ringmaster—a mime—a strong man all at once. But there was another memory surfacing—a memory that made no sense—or perhaps not yet—of Mose the Bowery Boy.[39]

But this took her aback. She could always assign a historical figure (at least to humans) and it had never before been a fake one. A fictional folk hero could not count, no. Mose had no mustache. Wasn't Mose Irish? No wait—he was played by Frank Chanfrau. French enough—and mustachioed enough. Yes, yes, Frank Chanfrau—owner of the Bowery Theatre, first urban superhero, famed melodramatic actor—would do. And there it was—the mythos there—the rowdy immigrant yet to lose his European flair—the second-generation eccentric.

Yet he was no second-generation. He was a first. A very old original. A copy-and-paste of every French cliché I can think of. Let me stop there, lest I cram too much of him in and he become a lesser adaptation of the man he really was. Gods forbid I give him a beret.

An Antebellum French caricature—does that not clash nicely? But let me assure you, he's just what we needed to pick this gloomy story up.[40]

His finger came at Odissa's face. "*You* are the one Venus changed Dorian for." It was an announcement—as if for Odissa's benefit.

---

[39] Mose. Legendary (and I do mean legendary—not real) volunteer fireman/street gang member in New York during the 19th century. Odissa is playing the historian again. I think I'm just going to start linking to Wikipedia articles instead of explaining things. Our Narrator assumes we're as knowledgeable as Odissa.

[40] Yes, a suicidal character is the perfect pick-me-up.

"Mecca knows better than to blab," Fletcher said, confiscating Maurice's gun for good by hiding it inside himself. He was busy trying to fend off Maurice and look out the far window—he could feel the neighbors' eyes because of the gunshot, but they weren't the type to invite the police. Poor Dorian was quite useless with Fletcher so torn between two tasks. He charged Maurice, but Maurice was always one step ahead—aside—around.

"No. It was Rosemund," Maurice said, never taking his eyes off Odissa as he dodged Dorian.

Dorian was betrayed! "Why would Rose tell you my business?" He stopped his chase.

Still staring at Odissa, "We talk, we talk! After all, I'm her favorite guinea pig."

"Better you than me." Fletcher waved a hand, warning Maurice to keep his distance as he stepped to the window for a better look. He verified no one likely saw the commotion through the open door—it was at a good angle for privacy.

But Maurice did not heed Fletcher's warning. He took Odissa's hand, brushing it under his mustache. "I'm Maurice; enchanté. Mecca haz told me all about you. And his photography skills, well, zey did nothing to capture your true beauty!" He winked, enclosing her hand in his. He covered the side of his mouth to whisper, "My Mecca is a boy of many talents. Takes after hiz father. More ways zan one." Again with the wink and the wiggly mustache.

Fletcher pulled him back by his striped shirt.

Maurice turned to Dorian. "She is very pale, Dorian. But now that we know who she is you can tell there's a very *ethnic* streak about her. Her mother was Cherokee, no? And is she like you, Sorta Rican? Put her in a tanning bed and she'll look just très magnifique."

Odissa's eyes widened. *The fuck did he just say?*

Fletcher huffed in his face. "That's his favorite word, *ethnic.*"

"Or was your mother only half Puerto Rican?" Maurice asked, as if that lessened her value. "No, that was your mother, Dorian. I got the Native American part right at least, oui?"

"I'm what?" Odissa asked Dorian, lighting up.

Dorian glowered at Maurice. He would threaten to kill him, but that would be no punishment...

Maurice turned back to Odissa, taking her hand once again despite Fletcher trying to slap it away. "And please don't worry, Odissa. I only want to kill myself because I have nothing left to live for. Nozing too dramatic."

Fletcher tugged him away again, Maurice's limbs flailing as he lifted him up like a puppy. "Touch her again, I'll break your nose."

Maurice pointed to Fletcher. "Odissa Odelyn, did you know zat Fletcher used to be *my* Automaton? *Oui*, I've been dead before—for a few seconds"—more like minutes—"But when I awoke, I couldn't control Fletcher. He was inanimate. I decided to live life without 'im. Zat's when our Dorian was brought into zee picture!" He slapped Dorian's back, making poor Dorian stumble forward.

Dorian was growing redder and redder. "Yes, all thanks to you, Maurice," Dorian mumbled. "We were just about to leave. Now, why don't you tell us where Mecca and Q are so I can kill them for bringing you here."

"Why *are* you here, Maurice?" Fletcher questioned.

Fletcher pulled Odissa away as Maurice kept inching closer to her (Odissa would be against the wall soon).

"Oh, Dorian. My son asked me to come. In times like zese, you know my boy needs his Papa."

"But *we* don't."

"I'm here to babysit the babysitters." He said it more like *baby-sit-airs*.

"You're just here because you want in on our hot Venus and Vulcan action," Fletcher scoffed.

"I brought him back to you didn't I? Give me some credit." Maurice's mustache twitched.

"Such a favor!"

"If you really think having him scampering about at a time like zis—when he is upset and looking for ways to cope—is a good idea, zen fine. Have fun bailing him out of an Ecuadorian prison again. I can't make that kind of money anymore. But you and I both know you could use someone like me—with no stake in zis feud—to keep *all* parties in line."

"Yes, but what's in this for you? We don't have the gods on speed dial—you know this. And we're not going to drive to Mexico to visit some curandero for a magic pendulum."

"Well, a simple invite for us to breakfast would be a start."

"Depends on who's 'us,'" Fletcher said to Maurice, looking outside the door for Mecca or Q—bound to be there! "We don't reward brats for their bad behavior."

Maurice upturned his nose, offended. "As if you should complain about my kids when you can't keep your own from fucking each ozer."

Odissa's jaw dropped. "How dare you—"

"I think I'm doing a fine job of it, actually," Dorian interrupted her and stepped toward Maurice.

"At the cost of the inanimates. They're no longer in your reach—"

"There it is!" Fletcher pointed. *The real reason he's here.*

"Q would be a safer storage place than Maud! How dare you all insult my son like this? He told me all about eet."

Fletcher laughed. "Not even Mother wanted to give your son the choice of handling an inanimate, Maurice. Wasn't just us."

"Q is more trustworthy zan Maud. Who knows what Maud is up to?"

Dorian shook a finger. "Automatons are not people. Maud has no *traits* outside of Odys. Why are you being so specific?"

About to be sorry he had asked: "Automatons can *make* the human!"

Fletcher squeezed the space between his eyes. "Not again with the Master Personality Transference Theory."

"You know eet happened!" Maurice pointed at Fletcher, brows merging.

Maurice remembered Odissa. "Perhaps she's even noticed it herself, zee transference!" His posture stiffened. "In her brozer."

Bros-air.

He realized he had her attention.

"Ah," he said with an esoteric crispness. "She *has* noticed."

"Don't, Maurice—" Dorian tried to inch to the door but it was too late. The show had begun.

Stanza: The Ringmaster's introduction.

His belly gravid with excited breath, "Odissa, have you noticed how Fletcher looks at Maud?"

Odissa's eyes went down in thought—how Fletcher had stared at Maud in the apartment when both had pretended to be cops.

"Ah, you have, haven't you? *Oui*. See, Odissa, I did zat."

"You did not!" Dorian snapped.

"Part of me is still inside Fletcher. And zat part is in Dorian too now. And zat part, no doubt, has been inside—"

Ooh la la!

"She gets the point—now get out of my house!"

But Maurice didn't budge when Dorian pushed at him. "I'm not ashamed to admit what I find attractive." From the side of his mouth, "(And that's a dark-skinned woman). Oh, how she could trick me into thinking she wasn't Pepin in disguise! That's the only reason I never touched her—" He mused, even though gadfly-Dorian was trying to shove him out the door to no avail. "If you're going to have an Automaton, she is the Automaton to have! Gods know I don't want Fletcher back. He's nothing to show off, you know." "I resent that," Dorian said, crossing his arms.

"You would!" Maurice's eyes turned back to Odissa. "But the reason I mention Maud, Odissa, is because I have reason to believe that Masters transfer some of their *qualities* to their Automatons. I did it to Fletcher. Now, of course zis is what we believe happens with Automata memories—that their memories affect the new Master. *That* everyone seems to agree on. But what I'm saying is *personalities* affect them too. Like with computers: I reprogram the OS of one computer and zee next user has to deal with zee new settings. You leave your mark—not just your file-memories—on your Automaton. Zis is why Maud can't be trusted. She has turned your brother against us."

"There is no 'us,'" Fletcher said. "You stopped paying your dues a long time ago."

"He should never have been left alone with the inanimates. This would never have happened back in zee day."

Dorian buttoned up his coat. He was too angry to butt in so he had Fletcher do it: "Memories, personalities. Same thing for an Automaton."

Maurice's eyebrows and matching mustache rose, wondering if Odissa were catching on. "He doesn't like it, but Dorian has a zing for Maud! You see how he is pouting? Zat means it is true."

"No, it doesn't," Dorian denied.

"I am very zorry to zay, Odissa, but I do not think you were the first female Dorian fell in love with." He laughed a stereotypical French "huan-huan-haun."

"Love has nothing to do with how he looked at Maud," Odissa said, her brows coming together. *How the fuck did we get on this subject?*

Maurice shrugged in the French sweater-shirt I'm making him wear. "Perhaps so. Dorian can control it better," Maurice elaborated when he saw Odissa's curiosity. "But Fletcher is more obvious about it. Always looking."

"Everyone looks at Maud!" Dorian shouted, hand on the door knob. The cold was making him shiver—that or the rage.

"He makes excuses because he doesn't like zat I'm inside him. Making him notice her. Venus didn't have far to turn the dial, thanks to moi."

"Fuck you!" Dorian rambled on in Spanish—on why Maurice shouldn't be here, on why he better stop putting these thoughts in Odissa's head, on why he was such an asshole.

For a few seconds, the two men argued—each in their mother tongues. There was quite a bit of hand-gesturing—especially at Odissa. Then, finally:

"But eef zee girl iz going to have an Automaton, she 'as the right to know! You give her Coraza and the next thing you know she's Leeland. I say never use those Automatons again."

"This isn't your decision!" Dorian barked back.

Odissa walked to the door. "I may not have understood the multilingual [bilingual?] fight you just had, Maurice, but I think I understand why you *really* mentioned it. I can tell you right now I wouldn't accept Admund or Coraza. You don't have to worry about that. They will not be transferring anything to me."[41]

Dorian was boiling, his hat now askew. "Stop trying to frighten her into abstinence. Maybe if she did touch Admund, she'd understand your stupid theory then. She'd understand what it's like to have no control over what your Automaton makes you fucking notice!"

Maurice motioned to our frothing Dorian. "See, he admits eet."

"Let's go to breakfast," she said, feeling embarrassed for Dorian and like Maurice would not leave the house unless they did.

"Yes, let's!" Maurice clapped his huge, veiny hands.

"That wasn't an invitation," Dorian grumbled.

Maurice followed them out, just the same.

---

[41] Are we really still on this will-she-or-won't-she subject? She's made it pretty clear she doesn't want them. Whyyy are we still talking about this?

They saw Mecca and Q in Maurice's truck, their eyes peeking over the dash. Dorian went up to the nose of the car and shouted, "Get out of the truck!" He slapped the hood, threatening to dent it.

They locked the car doors, eyes wide. But Fletcher used his Automaton-ways to pop the lock and drag them out with his noodle-arms like puppies by the scruff. They didn't fight it.

"They're not getting breakfast," Dorian said flatly.

Fletcher plopped them in the snow. "Someone needs to watch Bulfinch anyway. It's your punishment for bringing this zombie along. Go, get in the house." Fletcher kicked Q's bum as she scurried away to Maurice.

"Oui, in zee house," Maurice shooed them away gently. "Order some food. Behave." He gave a wink to them no one but Odissa noticed, turned to get into his truck.

"Maybe it's good Maurice is here?" Odissa asked Dorian as they rounded their vehicle (clearly not riding with Maurice). "They seem to obey him."

They had gone so penitently it was almost suspicious.

"No." Dorian growled. He opened the door of Odissa. "Because there is no one for Maurice to obey."

"Why does Mecca obey him?"

"Because Maurice threatened to disinherit him of his antique circus equipment."

(Oh, the erotic things you can do with that!)

"Seriously?"

"Fuck if I know." He noticed he was being rude and corrected himself. "Mecca has daddy issues. Plus, who wouldn't be afraid of a spanking from someone you can't kill?"

"I'm surprised he didn't bring his clown car," Fletcher grumbled, watching Maurice back out and wait for them to start driving. "Mustn't be big enough for his ego anymore."

Dorian humphed and slammed the car door for Odissa.

Stanza: The first law of Metafictional Thermodynamics...

In his own car, Dorian released his angry tension…by *driving*.

I guess I forgot to mention that Odissa was a bit confused she'd been placed in the passenger's seat.

Fletcher leaned forward from the middle of the back, eyes on the road for Dorian. Dorian pressed pedal to the metal and sped through a yellow light. It made Odissa nervous to see him so mentally crowded. They had ignored her protests of "But he's blind…"

Odissa calmed down when she remembered Dorian wouldn't do anything to put her in danger. That was impossible. "Did you guys agree on where to meet? Did I— did I miss something?" They had lost Maurice in his truck minutes ago at a stoplight.

No part of Dorian responded.

Thinking of ways to distract him—to get his mind off the unwanted visitors: "Maybe I should drive," she glanced back at Fletcher, as if that part of Dorian might back her up. "I need to drive. It's—it's too *effeminate* for me to sit here."

"Not now, Odissa." *No gender-swapping jokes today!*

"Don't snap at me like that."

"He shouldn't know Odys has the inanimates. Mecca needs to keep his mouth shut."

"Why? Does it matter?"

"Yes, it matters! Especially since we can't kill him if we need to keep *him* quiet."

"And does he normally go about telling people your secrets or something?"

Fletcher gestured to Dorian. "My Master, here, is just looking for excuses to be angry. He's unhappy they were even able to find us so quickly. This means we have roommates."

"And," Dorian expounded his own expounding, "you're not even jealous. You're not even jealous I like Maud. Hell, you're not even jealous I like Fletcher. Makes me feel like I'm powerless. Like I have no control over this relationship."

159

"You want me to throw a fit like you? Is that it?" She leaned over the middle section of the car, blocking Fletcher's view for a few seconds. Dorian swerved a little on the road.

"Jesus—" Fletcher tried to look around her.

"You want me to be upset? I'll be upset!" She shouted at him. He frowned so she knew her abuse was working. "You knew he would find us. I can tell." She prodded him.

Dorian had Fletcher grab at her gloved hand. "Stop it, you'll make us crash."

"And if we do? I'll be hurt. You're the one playing a game with my life, Dorian. All for show!"

She sat forward in her seat once again. To herself, "You turn into my mother. You turn into Odys. Fuck."

The boys said nothing else. Fletcher's eyes glanced at her and back to the road. He adjusted his elbow on the back of their seats, not sure how to interpret her words.

"…And maybe I am a bit jealous," she said after a few seconds of silence.

His face still an unhappy slab, Dorian asked, "Really?"

"Sure," Odissa shrugged. "It makes me jealous that if it wasn't for Venus's intervention, I wouldn't have you. Not that that's new. That makes *me* feel powerless."

The window was foggy, so she pulled her fingers down on the glass. It was starting to snow in flurries again.

Odissa inclined her head against that window like someone trying to cool their fever. "So, like, is Maurice the only Master to not have had a *relationship* with his Automaton?" She waved a hand in the air, as if to make space for her words.

"Relationship?" Dorian asked. "You mean sex?"

She realized what she was doing and clutched the collar of her coat, embarrassed. Now she was going to have to annotate her statement—something she wished she had planned for better. "He seems to be the only one. All the vibes from the others…"

"No, Maurice never fucked me if that's what you're asking," Fletcher said. "And I wouldn't call it sex, either. It's still very one-sided."

"But is it?" she asked. "That's not what I'd call masturbation—do you call sex with a sex doll masturbation? It's not like they're real, but there's no one else but you there, either. Then again, I don't do it, so I have nothing to compare."

Dorian, taken aback by her haphazard tone, still welcomed a verdant smirk, "You don't masturbate?"

Odissa thought about it. "I never had to." She enjoyed how her response bit at him.

Dorian swallowed her answer and upchucked one of his own: "Well, that's good. Because when you get an Automaton, I want the only one you're fucking to be me."

"That's not really fair."

"It's not fair you might just get a male Automaton."

"You didn't seem to mind yours."

"Yeah, well."

She cut her eyes at Dorian, liking how she had taken his mind off Maurice—so *powerful*. "Just think of the things I could make a male Automaton do to you, Dorian. What I could make Madus do to Fletcher."

She noted Fletcher's stoic eyes glance from her—as if his sight had brushed her shoulder like a hand.

"Don't say things like that," Fletcher said, though he wasn't sure why he said it.

"I would do whatever I wanted with my Automaton." She was pushing herself around by her elbows again. Her eyes narrowed—not at Fletcher, but at the Dorian who was looking *through* Fletcher.

As he tried to look past her—avoiding eye contact to keep his view on the road—he couldn't help but be distracted when—

She kissed him.

161

That's right. She kissed Dorian's Automaton. She could hear Dorian stiffen in the seat beside her—not only because he was having trouble seeing the road through Odissa's head, but, because, well, he could *feel* her.

Fletcher, trying to watch the road and find the correct reaction, somehow remained very still for the whole experience—as if Dorian were taking his time in deciding whether or not this was...*OK.*

Dorian decided to pull over, bumping them apart. "Eyes on the road, man!" he huffed—at himself. "And *you,*"—he pointed a finger at Odissa—"that wasn't very nice. Don't touch me like that." He shifted in his seat, uncomfortable.

"What, like this?" She ran a hand across Fletcher's lips. Fletcher finally reared back from her.

"Now I've had a *relationship* with an Automaton. We're even, and now all we have to do is fuck each other without tally marks." She said it with a defeated tone, though she was quite smug with herself.

"You call that a relationship?" Fletcher forced a snort. "It was only a kiss." Fletcher stared at the road, an annoyed expression on his face, though the kiss itself had gained no reaction (for that, you must view the Master's face).

"Depends on how you define a relationship," Odissa watched the road as Dorian started driving again.

"You don't know what you're doing—what you're saying," Dorian said, gripping the steering wheel too tightly and shifting in his seat again. But he couldn't hide the fact his dick was hard. "You don't have a soul outside your body. You can't just intrude on mine like that."

"Yes, I can. I just did. And you liked it. You liked it a lot, as far as I can see. You liked it but the human part of you doesn't want to because it just looks *weird.* Is that why you don't like Maurice, because he makes you feel *weird,* Dorian? He makes you remember wet dreams about Maud and 'ethnic' women?" She chuckled. "I like weird, Dorian. Haven't you figured that out by now?"

"I like weird too, and that's what fucking scares me."

"Where are we even going?" Odissa asked, pulling down the mirror to check her hair.

"To breakfast."

"But I'm sure there are a hundred different places that sell *breakfast*."

"But not all of them sell French toast."

"Yeah...that really narrows it down for me."

"Maurice has a very distinct compass, Odissa," Fletcher said as he tapped his nose. "He can follow us even if he doesn't see our damn car. He's fucking drawn to me because he's still inside me. Calling me. The pull is stronger at this proximity. And yes, that does mean we just admitted to his Transference Theory. But you don't have to tell him that."

She studied his angry expression—Fletcher looked angrier than Dorian now. Perhaps that's because Dorian was too busy trying to get rid of his boner.

Dorian parked the car. Before Odissa could unbuckle her seatbelt, Maurice's face was in her window, tapping the glass. He wore no coat, just that too-tight sweater. He opened the door for her, quite the gentleman.

"Stop opening doors for her!" Fletcher ordered, slamming his own. He wedged himself between them before Maurice could offer his arm.

Odissa opened the restaurant door for Dorian, to keep Maurice from doing it for her.

There were a few people in the diner, but most were over age fifty and surprised to see younger kiddos. At first they frowned at the fantastic four—so metro-sexual, that one—so hippie-ish, the other—so odd *she* was with them, that one. The older one was all right. His mustache was sublime.

But, these seniors seemed to realize they'd best not scare off new entertainment, and averted their eyes and their judgment. Yet they kept sneaking looks—unable to resist this group with men who reminded them so much of times gone by...

As they went to their far-off table:

"Don't you kids have some hot-happening place to be at?" A grey woman smiled up at them, clutching her black coffee cup. She knew her comment was random, but she couldn't resist. Old people have to create their kicks by poking at what's not theirs anymore.

Dorian took the opportunity to shine. "Why, this is where all the cool kids go!" His smile melted her heart, so charming and boyish.

They were in!

Dorian made Fletcher sit with Odissa. Simply because he didn't want Maurice near her or his Automaton now. *No touching my things.*

"What'll it be?"

The boys knew what they wanted and ordered—ordered too much.

Odissa, "Coffee."

Maurice, "Zat's it?"

Dorian, "If that's all she wants, then, yes."

(He latched on to any opportunity to snap at Maurice).

Waitress, "Alrighty, then. Just a few minutes." She picked up their menus.

"You already directed negative attention to us," Maurice scolded, his voice hushed.

"No, you did that!" Fletcher said, pointing and crossing his arms to match his Master.

"Stop it, both of you." Odissa hissed. "No more grouching until I get my fucking coffee."

"Yes, Madame," Maurice smirked and laced his fingers together.

They spent a few seconds lingering under the old-time radio music, oiling up their rusty etiquettes. Odissa wished an old person would talk to them again and break the tension.

"So," Maurice could stand the silence no longer, "has Odys made contact yet?"

"What makes you think he'd contact us?" Fletcher asked him, as if this family gathering had turned into a business meeting. The tone was shifting. Odissa pretended not to notice—she kept up her old-people-watching. But her ears tuned in.

"Mecca told me how you spoke to Mother, last you saw her."

"Oh?"

"Mecca said you weren't too pleased with her. Not zat you're pleased with Odys either."

Dorian decided to defend himself, "I was angry. I still am. I didn't like confronting her, but she could have done *all this* a lot differently."

"Mecca thinks you did like it. Mecca thinks you needed to get something off your chest, there."

"And I'm sure Mecca also told you what she did, so you know my anger is justified."

Maurice's mustache twitched and he spoke through the side of his mouth in Dorian's direction, never turning his head, instead addressing Fletcher. "Mecca said he had never seen you so angry."

Dorian added, "That little runt of yours shouldn't have brought you to me. Go and find Odys. Gwendolyn. Rose. Anyone but me."

"But you're the easiest to find," Maurice chuckled, gesturing to Fletcher. "No, Mother sent Mecca with you for a reason and I intended to figure out that reason."

This made Dorian prickle. They were getting off topic. "I've said before you need to put a stopper in him, Maurice. It was bad enough he was doing it"—all things in general— "when he was younger, but he's an adult now, technically. You can't keep making excuses for him. He's proving your hypothesis wrong. He hasn't matured. He won't. Everyone's thinking it. No one will say it. They don't want to hurt your feelings, but he's never stopped being a risk. And you're never around to suffer the danger or put a stop to it. You know he made me jump Odissa? I almost killed her because of his pranks!"

Odissa's eyebrows came together, putting the pieces in place.

Maurice just chuckled. "Can you blame him for being bored? Life iz so long and so dull. Let him have what little fun is left, Dorian."

The server brought out the drinks/Odissa's breakfast.

Dorian's jaw twitched. "If not for Gwen I would have put him down a long time ago."

Odissa gasped at his statement. "Dorian!" *To say such a thing.*

"You'll have to kill me first before you can get to zat point. You're so moody, Dorian. Is this because of the pictures he posted online of you and Odissa in the bathtub?"

"What?" Odissa blurted out, coffee going up her nose.

Dorian did not react. "This is exactly what I mean, Maurice. We can't manage with him."

"You think that is why you cannot manage? How has he held you back? He is your scapegoat!"

Dorian leaned into Maurice to growl: "She's supposed to be dead. What if those photos are found? It blows her cover!"

"Ah, but he iz so good at taking photos! Don't worry. Eet did not have your faces." He sighed, basking in his son's many talents. To Odissa with a wink, "I taught him everyzing he knows!"

"Though *why* is yet to be understood," Dorian grumbled. Fletcher took out his phone to see if he could find the site where the pictures were up. Hopefully they were a collection he could easily hack. He'd search Mecca's regular outlets.

Maurice, with winsome fashion, changed the subject, "Odissa, you want to know how Mecca got his name? Everyone does. Well, I say 'everyone' as if there *is* someone new to tell on a regular basis."

"You regularly remind us on a regular basis," Fletcher uttered, tapping his fingers on that smart phone.

The comment did not assuage Maurice. "I'll start from the beginning."

"Of course you would," sighed Fletcher.

"Look what you've done, Odissa," Dorian scolded her, as if she could put a stop to it.

But she didn't mind Dorian's irritation. She actually wanted to know. And she was starting to like Dorian's squirming.

"I'll give her the short version if you stick zis fork in my brain, Dorian," Maurice bargained, his eyes bulging toward the Master.

"No matter how much I'd enjoy it," Dorian replied with hum-drum airs, "I'm not even going to *consider* assisted suicide until after breakfast." He leaned back as if picturing himself doing it.

Maurice resumed his preface. "Perhaps a short version anyway, since I'm a tad depressed my bullet didn't work zis morning. That took me two years and fifty thousand dollars." He cleared his throat, the thought of wasted time choking him. "Now, Odissa, when I died, I had actually been in a very melancholy mood. Despite the fact I was very good at my job (I still am, you know), I was debating the purpose of it—of zee circus. Even today, I can still get a lot of money for my tricks. Hell, I'm even better at them now since I can't kill myself! But as I was zaying, I hadn't practiced the tightrope in many months, as I had been traveling in Rome on holiday."

He never walked the rope for shows. It had only been his personal hobby, to enjoy alone. He felt most would think him silly—a huge man on the rope. He'd rather stick an attractive Maud up there, to wow the crowd—someone the crowd would care about if she fell. Also, he'd rather see her up there himself. A spectacular view.

"What does this have to do with why you named Mecca 'Mecca'?" Dorian asked.

"To understand the name, she must understand the father!" Maurice insisted, as if Dorian were incredibly stupid rather than rude.

"But you died *after* Mecca became a Master."

"Which I will highlight in my story once I come to eet!" And he continued with his more-than-near-death experience.

See, when he practiced, he never secured the under-nets because he never had need of them. What need of nets has a Master? But as he fell from the rope, and before he hit the ground, life—as is expected—flashed before his French, French eyes. As he looked upon it (his life) he thought, well, he'd had a good run. It was only natural that a human would be afraid of a fall and therefore contemplate death during a major one. And as he fell, well, he had accepted the fact that if he *were* to die, he wouldn't be too sad about it. It had been a full life, yes. Thus, in essence, he was willing to die. Very willing.

"Same as Pepin pulling that trigger," he said, pulling Odissa out of his flashback.

Fletcher looked up from the phone. "I still don't see what this has to do with Mecca, you self-involved—"

"You see, before I had died, my son had just celebrated his birthday. And we'd just given him his Automaton, the *beautiful* Q."

"Pedophile," Dorian mumbled to the empty table.

"And so, I was content that my son was secure and safe. It was one more reason to accept death. Thus, some might say I was perfectly suicidal as I fell those somewhat-fifty feet. And, upon impact, I died." He clapped his hands together—splat. "For exactly [BLEEEEEEP] minutes.[42] I think I was able to be revived after so long only because I *was* a Master. It was quite lucky, too, that Pepin happened to walk by and notice my death. One of my old dwarf assistants had begun to scream—violently, the poor dear. Zere was quite a lot of blood." He gestured with his hands—as if he had been gushing. "I landed on my legs. It protected my head, unfortunately."

"The only reason he didn't explode upon impact is because he didn't *want* to die until his legs landed." Fletcher caught her eyes. "He didn't make use of the fall until the very last minute—didn't *try* to die until it almost passed him by."

---

[42] The exact number is unimportant, and changes according to storyteller and listener.

"And now I forever chase her—beautiful Death."

Odissa set her coffee back down, no longer finding an appetite.

"Anyway, before any of our relations could accidentally graze Fletcher (who had been sleeping in my pocket), Pepin used his scarf to pick him out and deliver him to Mother's care. Maud had been trying to revive me. She kept hitting my chest with her metal hands—hands charged with soul." He lifted his own up in demonstration. "They were able to revive me before the ambulance arrived. She could start a heart as well as stop it! They tried to pump me full of things. Pepin tried to do it for them at one point—thinking that it was just a normal human who couldn't puncture me. Pepin had to kill them later, because they asked so many questions. 'No, you're not doing it right,' Pepin kept saying, taking charge."

Maurice chuckled.

"Upon my hospital bed, we soon realized I no longer had any control over Fletcher. I was, at first thought, free of him. We didn't know the side effects would linger. I did not know I *didn't* have the option of death. When I came to, we all knew which option I'd eventually choose—*still* would like to choose, for that matter. It is a miserable existence, you see. With or without an Automaton. Mother said I could have Fletcher back if I wanted, but I didn't. I told them 'Give him to someone who needs him. I have no need!'"

"That's not exactly what you said," Fletcher said. "From what I hear it was more like, 'Fuck no. He's kept me from getting laid too many times. I'll share my bed no longer!'"

Maurice ignored Fletcher and sighed, still keeping up with his dramatic tone. "Of course they knew. They knew I had essentially done it—accepted death. It just hadn't worked. In the back of my mind, I even considered actually living a normal life—leaving all these fuckers behind. But zen zere was always the case of my son, Mecca—whom I had already trapped in this Automata-life with me..."

"No, you trapped *us* with him," Dorian growled.

Maurice gave a dramatic pause—staring off into space. "I did try to kill myself, later on. I was a liability to my son, after all, and Leeland was growing worse and worse. It was that attempt at death, however, that proved death impossible. Rosemund was all over me after that. She had so many things she wanted to 'test.'"

The breakfast was brought out, and Maurice sat back, the whole group eager to eat as if they hadn't just been discussing Maurice's blood and gore.

Thank you, no that will be all, yes, you can leave the check now.

Maurice watched Fletcher pour on his syrup so thick it ran over his plate (and proceeded to do the same for Dorian). He tucked his napkin in his collar. His voice very low, "As far as we can tell, I'm the first one to, well, *come back.* Also, the side-effects go against everyzing we know. Even Masters can kill themselves, but I can't now? In theory—"

"Ah, more of your theories!" Dorian shoveled waffle in his face.

"*In* theory," Maurice went on, "my soul must be stuck in a type of limbo. Still in Fletcher, maybe. Better yet—it's already in the afterlife while I'm just here, just my body. It's waiting to get its soul back. Zomezing like that."

"Yeah, *zomezing* like that," Dorian mocked.

"It was Vulcan!" Maurice said, waving his toast-covered fork. "He won't let me die. He meant for zis to happen. He has a purpose for me." He winked at Odissa. *And that purpose involves you.*

"Don't flatter yourself," Fletcher said, already done with his pancakes. He went back to his phone.

"Now," Maurice said to Odissa, "I only told you all this so that you'll understand what kind of a man I am—and why I named Mecca 'Mecca.' For sure, you wonder why—if I believe Vulcan has a purpose for me—I would still want to die? Well, Odissa, I don't like being controlled. Especially by a god zat isn't the highest up, if you know what I mean." He crossed himself the Catholic way. "He has no right to take away my free will." He adjusted his napkin like a tie. "I rebel in little ways: I stand in front of microwaves daily. I do not look both ways before crossing the street. I smoke, to blacken my lungs. Yet nothing works. Even my own body fails to destroy itself." He sighed a great sigh, staring into his food. "I *could* have died. But you damned lot revived me."

"I had no part in it, believe me," Dorian said. To Odissa, "They didn't even know I existed at that point."

"Before all that, I had traveled to Africa. Toured Egypt. That sort of thing."

"The *colonial* thing," Fletcher took a righteous drink from his orange juice.

"On my travels, I had a son."

"You can give birth now, can you?" Dorian asked, his lips covered in sticky syrup.

"No one knows the full story." Not even Mecca, for that matter. "And I like to keep it that way. As does everyone else, it seems, because they leave the DNA tests alone, well enough."

Fletcher snorted. He gestured with his fork to Maurice. "You wanna know why he doesn't want us to know if Mec's his real son? Because *he* doesn't want to know."

"He is my real son." Maurice's mustache ruffled. "They actually like Mecca, despite what they say." He cut into his breakfast angrily. "And it's not like Mecca lets them the chance to give a paternity test. Mecca wants to be mine and that's all that counts. Blood hardly matters beyond zat."

Odissa shook her head. "But why put so much effort into claiming he's your son if you're just going to undermine it with a speech like that?"

"Pardon?"

"You want to kill yourself. To leave him. That's not very fatherly."

"I can see you judge me. But even in death, I could still be a good father."

"And he really doesn't want to know if Mecca's mom slept with someone else before she died," Dorian added.

Odissa frowned. "Did I really need to know all of that, Maurice?"

171

"Oh, now you take our side!" Dorian huffed.

Maurice shrugged. With his mouth now full, "I think eet gives greater context, oui. See, after I learned zat 'is mother died, I brought him with me. And I eventually convinced Pepin and Mother to let someone so young have an Automaton. Zey knew he needed protection. The stars had aligned—Q was vacant at the time." He chewed a bit and washed it down. "Now, since we've gotten that bit out of the way, I can tell you about his name. For sure, you look at me—a devout Catholic!—and you find it strange that I named him *Mecca*."

MECCA: Not just a place anymore.

HOLY: Crap.

FATHER: Who cares if he's Maurice or not? No one else would claim him.

MOTHER: The reason Mecca needed his Papa.

Chapter the fourth,

Monotheism is the polytheism:

How many gods does it take to make monotheism?

"Yes, one good look at Maurice and you can tell he's Catholic." Fletcher rolled his eyes.

"I named him Mecca because we needed a little homesickness in our group. There was too much Greco-Roman talk, you see. There still is, frankly. Even we Catholics, with all our Latin! Abrahamic religions deserve their recognition. Zat and Mecca's mother never got to make her pilgrimage. Mecca came *to her*."

"That. That's the lead he buried," Fletcher jabbed at the disappearing words. "No self-involved tangent or rant about death needed."

"I wanted to remind Vulcan of his place in the religious order. That he is not so important anymore. Perhaps that's why I lived after my death." Maurice snorted. "He's punishing me for hubris!"

"And THAT," Dorian inserted, "is why Vulcan owes us all one for making us suffer eternity with this French asshole." He took a sip from Fletcher's orange juice (his apple was already gone).

They finished their meal—sat and stared at their empty plates while waiting for someone to make a decision. I'll make it now:

"Oh!" Maurice exclaimed cheerily, "Guess what!" (No one guessed). "Found a new wrinkle recently. Just here. Eet might mean I'm getting older!" He leaned in to whisper, "Older means death."

"No, it just means you're frowning more than usual," Fletcher noted, finally turning off the phone (Mecca's photos apparently taken down from the site—the hacktivist hacked).

"Speaking of frowning," Maurice said with a frown, "when's the last time you've spoken to Vulcan, zat worthless piece of *sheet*?"

"I'm sure Mecca has mentioned the mall excursion?"

Odissa blushed, recalling what Mecca had seen.

"But zat smells more like Venus. Not Vulcan, Dorian."

"Same thing some days," Fletcher hissed—like a machine releasing steam.

"If you must know, He came to me to warn me His Wife was meddling. Which a lot of good that did us," Dorian crossed his legs under the table. Its brushed Odissa's knee.

She looked at him as if it were code for something she could not translate.

"The gods have been silent lately, but silence is golden," Maurice explained for Odissa's benefit. "It's the other *senses* that can speak. Gods still have a stench. My nose isn't what eet used to be, but I can feel His ash. It lands on me. Won't brush off." He shivered.

Dorian took out his wallet. "I'm ready to leave. See you back at the house, Maurice."

Fletcher pulled him back down with an outstretched arm. "Not yet. Do you smell that?"

173

Maurice's eyes rolled across the room. He pointed to a man leaving the bathroom. He was a huge sort. The poor man was balding, his white rolls of all-American fat jiggling as he limped over to them. The leg brace supported his entire calf—from ankle to knee. That leg threatened to buckle under the man's massive weight. Though the face seemed jolly enough, it was also tired.

The man stopped and looked down at them, heaving—as if he'd just walked twenty miles. Sweat was moistening the underarms of his shirt. The man sniffed, keeping his nose from running.

Maurice's mustache twitched. Fletcher's nose itched. Dorian's head tilted to hear. Odissa's eyes widened.

Could it be?

Maurice was the first to glower and speak. "Speak of zee devil."

They all looked up at the towering mountain-man—except Odissa, who looked at her captors because she didn't understand why they were frozen in place. There was hardly a tint of fear in Maurice's eyes, though Odissa swore his mustache twitched in anxiety. Maurice, you see, hadn't seen Vulcan in quite some time.

Maurice was about to speak (speak some angry, well-rehearsed words) when—he found he couldn't. Couldn't even open his lips.

"I hate the French," Vulcan said, like one might to an inbred dog. "They're always much more interested in my wife than me. Love language—*ha!*"

Thankfully, Vulcan's colossal size blocked the view of others who might otherwise catch a glimpse of what was going on.

"Actions speak louder than words, Maurice. All talk and no action."

Maurice's upper lip spasmed as he stopped trying to speak. He even struggled to leave his seat but found his ass glued down. Odissa was mortified. Maurice settled on the one thing he could do: give Him the finger.

But Vulcan was done with Maurice and turned his Moai-shaped head to Fletcher. "Heard my name in conversation. Thought I'd trudge by." The god wheezed in a few breaths—a very good act that went well with his costume. "I'd take Maurice's advice, if I were you."

"Advice? What advice."

"The advice he came to give. To bestow upon you're unwilling ears—one of the few senses you have left, Dori." He pulled at his lobes.

"So his plans fit yours, that it? Your plans haven't always been for my best interest, V. Your will be done, but what about ours?" Dorian tucked his wallet away.

"And just what do you plan to do about it? Stand in front of microwaves like him? You think that pisses me off? No. It's fucking good entertainment."

"Was Bob's death entertaining? Did you sell tickets?"

A few people were starting to stare, their old ears trying to listen. But don't worry, Vulcan wouldn't let them—no matter how many times they adjusted their hearing aids.

"Listen here, Dorian. I came because I wanted to give you an update on Odys. He's about to text you again."

The phone gave a little jingle under Fletcher's hand.

"Speak of the devil," Vulcan panted, a smugness on his lips.

Fletcher opened the text. Odissa read over his shoulder: "Tell me when we can meet and where."

"Take Maurice's advice and respond to Odys. That's what Maurice would suggest. Isn't that right, Maurice? He wants you to set up a time and a date. You should do that. But you won't will you? You're mad at me and doing the opposite of what I want. But you're the one suffering for it. The longer you drag it out, the longer you two have to stay under the same roof." He pointed between the two Fletcher-Masters. "You need Maurice, Dorian." Vulcan's saggy eyes cut over to Maurice. "But don't think you've served a purpose yet."

Vulcan lingered over them for a few seconds, looking right through them. Then, His eyes rolled over to Odissa for a few seconds. It was an indifferent stare. Dorian had hoped her first Vulcan-sighting would be more impressive. But that was usually asking too much from the god.

"Also note, I don't give a fuck if you think I smell or not, Fletcher. Now, if you'll excuse me, I actually intend on having coffee with these old farts back behind me. You may leave now."

Standing up, "Is that what you told Bob? That she could just 'leave' us?" Dorian demanded an answer with his waiting. "What did you tell her? What were your last words to her?"

The man turned back around. "Who?" The bodies in the diner paused. Then, "Don't make a scene, Dorian. She made her choice. I'll make use of all choices. Now go before I start a gas leak in this joint to teach you a lesson."

He must have pressed his magical play button, for the world started moving once more.

Odissa looked over her shoulder as they left the diner, the little bell on the door ringing. "He really *is* having coffee with them!" *But He wouldn't say one word to me.*

Was it odd to think He should have?

Dorian took her by the forearm and stuffed her in the back seat with him. This time Fletcher would drive. And he'd take the long way home. "He's not really having coffee with them. He's probably just possessed some poor bastard who was already here. Easier than creating a completely new look, likely. Hell if I know."

Stanza: Living dead boy.

Maurice and Fletcher parked their cars…behind the delivery truck.

"What the fuck did you do?" Fletcher-with-his-hands-on-his-hips asked the little boy inside.

"Mecca bought us lots of stuff yesterday. Mecca didn't shop too hard, though. Click here, click there. All from one place. Nothing fancy," Mecca said, browsing the web on one of his tablets. His little bare feet dangled down from Q's arms. Her eyes were supervising the men's delivery going on around them.

"Nothing fancy?" Fletcher shouted as an HD television the size of a car was squeezed through the door. "We're gonna get robbed!"

Indeed, the neighbors were staring.

"Mecca paid for convenience, not quality, this time. Besides, we're not staying here long. Papa already told Mecca *everything*."

(So that's why Maurice had been on the phone when driving).

Fletcher snatched the tablet from Mecca's hand. He followed it up with, "You know credit cards can be traced and addresses hacked. We're supposed to be hiding. You—you can't just redecorate someone's house."

Q rolled her eyes. "Like we really threw off the feng shui."

Dorian spun to Maurice. "He can't redecorate. *I'm* the gay one!"

"It's not redecorating if it's never been decorated," Odissa mumbled.

Maurice laughed. "Oh come, Dorian! You know he's safe about these things. And it's not like Odys couldn't find us if he really tried."

"That's not the point," Fletcher said, moving Odissa out of the way of a very nice mattress being brought in.

One gentleman told Q, "The bedrooms are all set."

She replied with a "Thank you so much. And the kitchen?"

Fletcher tossed the tablet back to Q. "He should have asked."

"But we wanted to surprise you," Q said, gently handing the tablet to her Master. His hands grabbed at it as if a baby blanket. "To make up for...things." Her eyes cut to Maurice. "If we're going to be uncomfortable here together, might as well make it less so."

Odissa grabbed Dorian's hand and, with a cheerio-tone said, "Well, there's no use standing when there's empty seats." And she sat him down.

It was much cozier, and Q had the TV programmed in a matter of seconds. "Stealing cable from the neighbors, but no biggie. The company will never know the difference."

Maurice had taken to a solemn rocking chair in the corner and, after crossing his legs, had pulled a pipe from his pants' pockets and a small tin of tobacco. "I'd ask if you mind, but I can smell a like-kind," he said to Odissa with a wink.

She had made herself comfortable on the new sofa, facing the television. Dorian had ensconced grudgingly as Fletcher had gone to inspect the house for any eccentricities. He suppressed a smile when he noticed a coffee maker for Odissa. "Good boy, Mecca," he said as he pat it. He would make some for Odissa.

Mecca had taken to the overstuffed chair, still busy on his phone and tablet. Odissa wondered if, perhaps, Fletcher had hacked something too noticeable (in regard to the cabin photos)? Mecca was engrossed.

"Can I use the restroom?" Odissa quietly asked, leaning over to Dorian.

His ears perked, alert. "Yeah, sure."

Maurice, puffing away, "You make her ask?" His bushy eyebrows danced.

Odissa, standing up, laughed. She'd let Dorian handle that one.

When Odissa got back, they were watching a Russian channel. And seeming to understand/enjoy it. Maurice's foot bobbed as Odissa sat back down, though his eyes were on the TV. She glanced out the window, at their reflection. The cramped coziness made it feel as though it should be Thanksgiving or Christmas—what Odissa assumed such holidays would feel like, based on movies and books. It looked as though it might snow again. There was light, but no sun. But she could tell the day was almost over. Their breakfast had been more of a lunch. Time was moving quicker and there was nothing they could do to tell the gods to slow it down.[43]

Maurice noticed it too. "They're growing impatient"—as if he'd had the same thought.

"Damn right I am," Dorian grumbled. "I want you out of my house."

---

[43] Yeah, sure, the gods. In no way is it the fact you have too many characters in the pot now and not enough plot yet to get the stew boiling.

Maurice pulled out his pocket watch, checked the time, his bold chin wrinkling into his neck. "Mecca, what time is eet?"

Mecca looked at his phone, confirming their fears. "Never enough time in the day for Mecca to get everything done," he sighed, shaking his head.

"The fuck have you got going on then?" Dorian said. *By all means, leave and do it.* "So far it seems like we're the only agenda item."

...

Odissa savored this moment with these amusing creatures who felt like coming home, despite Odys not being there.

"...Odissa," Maurice stated over the television's mumble and Odissa's vision.

"Yes?" She looked at him, confused that he'd address her suddenly.

"Do you think Odys would give you an Automaton if you asked for it?"

"What kind of a question is that?" Dorian thusly interjected, putting a hand on her back as if to remind Maurice he needed to go through him.

Odissa rolled her eyes at him, knowing he couldn't see. Mecca and Q stifled giggles at Odissa's expression. Eventually she answered Maurice, "No. I don't think he'd give me any Automaton I asked for. He spent his whole life hating my father and anyone involved with him. He finally has a chance to keep me away from Augury, and he'll do it. Even if that means staying away from me himself."

Maurice raised an eyebrow, his mustache smiling with it—devilishly. The lines of his face were sharp—even the wrinkles. And when he grinned—or spoke—his skin would pull or ripple over the well-molded bones. Wide bones. Yet still very sleek.

"And how convenient it is!" Maurice burst. His one eye popped toward her as he spoke. "How convenient that eet keeps Odys away from you. Odys's sacrifice has allowed Dorian to get closer to you. Isn't zat right?"

"Sacrifice?" Odissa repeated, as if she found the term appealing.

179

"The gods clearly don't want us to get closer because you three shits are here," Dorian snapped, pointing with three fingers.

Odissa crossed her arms, staring at the rug (it looked like a wannabe-Persian rug). Bulfinch was even lying on the corner fringe, as if on any other day he might play with the tassels (but not today—not when strangers were watching). Bulfinch always loved a good rug. He loved to throw up on them. This rug looked too old to be new. Had Mecca ordered some antique things as well? How did it get here? She hadn't seen it delivered. But no one else had commented on the rug so perhaps she was the one going mad...[44]

Maurice cleared his throat and tended his pipe. "Odys's little thievery gave quite an excuse for me to come into the picture, didn't it, Dorian? The gods want me to see you with Odissa. And I'm starting to see the whole picture. The gods needed me to see you two together."

Dorian laughed. "Mecca's here too, yet I don't see him whipping out his divine purpose like it's bigger than everybody else's."

Mecca and Q would have latched onto the entendre if only the joke hadn't been about their Papa. Their Papa was speaking. They must remain silent and let Papa defend himself. They bit their lips.

"I'm just saying, I 'ave eyes."

Fletcher came in and handed Odissa some coffee—he hadn't bothered to make any for anyone else. "I knew I smelled coffee!" Odissa exclaimed. She looked over at Q and Mecca with heart eyes. "You bought a coffee maker for me?"

Mecca shrugged. *No biggie.* "Also bought a cat bed, but Bullygoat doesn't seem to like it." He did not look up from his screen.

"Because you shoved him in it," Q sighed (Mecca clearly felt guilty about it).

With that, Maurice stood up and announced, "Well, I'm going to adjust the temperature in here." Bulfinch was startled and dashed away.

"I think it's warm enough," Dorian said, glancing in the direction of the thermostat.

---

[44] Mind the rug. Seriously, don't trip.

"Not zat kind of temperature adjustment." He pointed to the fireplace. "I will chop the wood."

"I think it's gas…" Odissa said as he as he passed by. She examined it from afar, seeing the button.

"Not anymore eet's not," Maurice replied.

"Chop wood from what?" Fletcher demanded a source.

Maurice looked out the frosted window. "There's a tree, over there."

"That's the neighbor's tree."

"I doubt zey'll notice." He winked at her.

"It's the only tree on this corner!"

He was out on the snow-covered lawn in seconds, shirt off. They watched him in their seats as he passed over the window. No one seemed as concerned as Odissa.

"Where'd he find an ax, even?" Odissa asked, craning her neck to try and see him once more. But he was shortly out of view.

"You don't have to stare so hard at him," Dorian snapped like and old housewife. "That's exactly what he wants. Attention."

"How's he not freezing?" she asked. "I mean, immortality is one thing but not *feeling* is another."

"Mecca thinks that's the point. He's trying to freeze to death," Mecca said, typing away on his tablet. His eyebrows had risen and fallen with each sentence.

Fletcher watched Odissa cradle her cup and stare at Mecca. Mecca was sad and she knew it. Too well behaved. Something had deflated his overactive bubble. And no one was bothered by the chopping going on outside. *They must know something I don't.*

"You think Odys is sacrificing himself for you?" Dorian asked Odissa, after making sure the 'kiddos' were pretty much tied into the cultural dances of southern

Russia. He tucked some hair behind her ears. "I think he's just trying to control the one thing he has left."

"You really want to talk about controlling?" She reared back from his petting—his playing with her hair. Batted his hand away.

"Is what he's doing any different than what he's always done, when you were presented with a connection to your father-husband?"

She wanted to answer him honestly but remembered Mecca and Q. She'd not have this conversation in front of them.

"They're not really children," Fletcher whispered, taking Maurice's seat. "And they'd eves drop on us even if they weren't in the room."

Q nodded, confirming.

She took a moment to savor her coffee. "Yes, Odys is sacrificing himself for me. I believe that. We both have daddy issues. Can't that be an answer?"

Curiosity sparked inside him. "But who did you hate more, your 'father' or your 'husband'?" Air quotes implied.

She snapped her head in his direction—in the same second as they heard Maurice's ax hit something. "When did I say I hated them?" *Had she said it?* "You want me to hate him? You want me to hate them like Odys did?"

Dorian shrugged, snuggling into the couch as if he might take a nap.

Odissa stared at him. And Fletcher stared at her. "I don't think I do hate them, Dorian. I had a deal with Augury—"

"Leeland," Fletcher corrected her. Dorian tried his best to keep her from reverting back to lies. *He* was the truth.

"I neither loved nor hated them."

"But you're the victim of—"

"Am I?" She laughed, staring past the television. "I'm the one that *allowed* it to go on with Leeland. I'm just as responsible. This isn't—wasn't—rape, Dorian."

Rather than bring up he disagreed with her definition, "Drink your coffee. It's getting cold."

She got up.

"Where are you going?"

With a huff, "To pour this down the drain. The fucking drain."

But she never went to the kitchens. Instead, she walked straight out the door to watch Maurice chop wood.

When he heard her approaching, he put down the ax, heaving breath turning to fog.

"The tree still stands," he smiled through his panting. "Mecca actually ordered me some wood. He knows I love zee *entire* winter experience. He gets the best deals. Mecca was born in the wrong time period, I zay. Zis one is perfect for him. Should have been a millennial."

Maurice gestured to an un-chopped woodpile that a truck had no doubt dumped in their front yard. It wasn't wet with snow.

"I think they figured that, since you started chopping so quickly. We could hear you." She squinted in the brightness—the sun whiting everything in the snow. "I thought French men were supposed to be more interested in fashion and philosophy and romance over...camping and manliness."

A bacon joke manifest.

"I came from a different time in France, my dear. Also, France is no longer my home. I have no home. I am quite—as zey zay—*Americanized.*" His lips expressed amusement. He arranged his log on the chopping block. "Well, Odissa Odelyn, do you like the cold or are you simply fond of watching me and my wood?"

She resisted a laugh. She gripped her coffee tighter. She was starting to feel the cold now. Snowflakes were falling into her mug.

His bulging eye brought the truth out of her, "I couldn't stand it in there, being *alone* with him." Out of all of them, Maurice was most like her. Automata-less. Single. One.

His brow rose, as if saying *Ah*. "Is Mecca not in zere?" He arranged the log once more and picked up his ax.

"No, he is."

Maurice cut his eyes at her—as well as that mischievous smile. She saw Mecca in that smile.

"That's to be expected." The ax came down. "Venus didn't think this through. She made Dorian too in love. And he's driving you mad." The ax came down again. "Or maybe zat is her plan? To drive you mad."

"No, it's not that." *Dorian's not driving me mad.*

"But it's part of it." He said it with assurance and tossed some wood away. "Dorian doesn't know what to do with his new character trait—with playing the hetero. He's latching on to zee only thing he's sure of. You." He saw her face. "Believe me. I know Venus."

"I didn't come out here to talk about Dorian. I came out here to escape him."

"He's going to be pissed, you know. Miffed that you came out here to me." He picked up a half-log, looking toward the window as if Dorian could see them. "Running's not fair to him. He can't help what he is." Maurice panted, the cold stinging. He tossed a few logs here and there. "What Venus made him."

Odissa hugged herself and her mug, looked up at the white sky.

Maurice rolled his shoulders. "But look at me, I'm rambling when you clearly came out here to get something off your chest. Your magnificent chest by the way, so delicate." He cupped the air in front of his own. "Too bad eet's not my type."

"Yeah, I get it. You like dark meat." She didn't have the heat/time to spare on ripping apart his sexism so: "And I know I've just made him angry. I know that. That's—that's why I did it."

Maurice stood back from his work and admired it—all his wood. He rubbed his cold hands together, looking at them. Not a single chafe or crack in sight—*oh how he wished the flesh would split open from the cold!*

"You came out here to get away from them too," Odissa said. "You don't really want to be here, do you? You're not normally with them—ever. That's why you weren't at the cabin. You're not one of them. Neither am I."

Maurice sucked the chill air through his teeth. "I admit I'm not used to being cooped up with humans." He put a leg up on his woodpile. "I am usually very busy with my own devices. But I come when I'm called. Help me carry this to the back. Then you will go inside and get warm and face him. And I will chop more wood."

He stacked some wood in her arms and took up a load of his own under one arm. She tried not to spill her coffee.

As they walked to the backyard, Odissa said, "You knew Leeland, didn't you? You knew him before all this? You knew him better than Dorian?"

The snow crunched beneath their feet.

"Yes."

"Was he always a religious man?"

An eyebrow raised. "Why do you ask?"

She didn't answer right away. What she wanted to say was *Before having sex with me, he would pray—in a language I couldn't understand. He would never look at me. He hated it. And I felt sorry for him. Even though he hated me, he would call me back to him. And I would go. Because I felt so obligated.* But what she actually said was: "How could he do this to me? How could I let him?"

Maurice dropped his wood next to the back door with loud clanking. He helped her unload her own pile, handfuls at a time. "I think Leeland only wanted to have a child with you. A child would have taunted them—made things harder. He was too pious to touch a woman he wasn't married to. He was of Saint Augustine's mind—is that what you're asking? He believed the angels and demons were gods, but zat God was still out there. Zat I'm sure you have guessed by now. But clearly, his morals still trouble you. And with good reason."

185

They walked back to the front of the house. "Would he have threatened to kill the child? I don't understand what the point was." She started shivering—unsure if it was from the cold or the thought.

He picked up the ax and put it over his bare shoulder. "No—I don't think he could have killed his own child. But it would have, say, made it harder for Dorian to want to live. Dorian was already having so much trouble at it—at living." He eyed the tree above them, considering it next. "Now go back inside and keep Dorian from doing something stupid. You heard what Vulcan said. I need to be here. Dorian can't kick me out just yet. Don't give 'im reason."

He swung the ax down on his foot.

It bounced—nay, *slid*—off his boot.

He cursed in French, walking away. "Now I must get new boots! I never think zese things through. But I find it best that way. Saves me the trouble of premeditation. You laugh at me, vixen?" He made a *Humph!* sound. "It is I who will have the last laugh—literally, because I will outlive you! Why have an immortal body if you can't abuse it, no? Be gone with you. Zis is no freakshow." He boomed out the monologue as if a magician directing a volunteer off his stage. *Zank you for your participation.*

She tried to find it funny, but there was a sadness to it—to him wanting to be alone.

He watched her enter the house through the back. "That girl is too wise and too curious. Feels like zis is all just one show for her, not gods." He arranged his wood. "Well, I will put on the best show zat zere is, oui. Indeed, Maurice, zat is so."

Stanza: Odissa's priest absolved her.

Odissa stomped the mud off her feet. Her eyes adjusted from the bright snow-light and noticed Mecca was now watching cartoons...and smoking one of her cigarettes.

"Where did you get those?" Odissa demanded, marching over to him as if she were his babysitter. She almost ripped it from his lips then realized—

"From your purse," Q said, daring her to say more.

Odissa turned to her. "I know I shouldn't ask *you*, but is it okay for him to do this?"—as if Q were his big sister.

"Of course," Q answered, a mischievous smile on her face. She adjusted the lace collar on her goody-goody dress she'd just formed to stress that point. Tapped her Mary Janes together.

"We're older than you, kiddo," Mecca said, blowing out some smoke.

"At least give me one of those. They *are* mine." She looked in the box. Last one. "I was saving these, you know."

Mecca snuggled closer to Q, flicking some ashes onto the floor. "Mecca will buy you new ones. Don't worry. Mecca treats his ladies right." He winked at her—just like his father would.

"They went to the bathroom together." Q pointed, meaning Dorian and Fletcher. She took up a phone from Mecca's lap as it started buzzing.

Was it an alarm, a call, a message? Why did they always look so busy, these two?

"The water just stopped running before you came in. They're angry you went to Papa."

"Yes, well," Odissa said, deciding not to light up. "Guess I get what I give."

Q smiled, apologetically. "Give them this," she said, pulling a pack of fruity gum from her insides. "We noticed they were running low. Always keep some handy, in times such as these."

"I noticed Fletcher's been chewing up a storm. Is it because Dorian's stressed?"

Q shrugged. "Probably."

Odissa lingered over them. Woman-to-woman, Odissa leaned down to Q and asked, "*Should* I talk to them?"

Q, realizing that Odissa had a strange way of addressing her over Mecca—as if she were appealing to Mecca's feminine or mature side—said, "Yes. But just so you know, we heard them talking about Fletcher's boogers before they started running the bath. They're both getting sick. The nose knows, you know."

"Knows what, exactly?" Her head cocked.

Were the kids being immature or were boogers really a big deal?

Q, quietly, (because Mecca was trying to listen to the TV suddenly), explained the due information on Automaton bile(s). "What goes in must come out eventually," she added. "Either though picking,"—she held up a finger—"popping"—she made a gesture of a gun—"or, well, you know. Pooping." She shrugged. "The three Ps."

"Right…"

Mecca exclaimed, "Ooh! [Random anime show] is on! You know what that means, Q. Bunny suit, please!"

"I'll be back later," Odissa said, backing out of the room and where this scene was going.

She meandered to the bathroom, looking over her shoulder once more—out that fogged window—to spot Maurice posing with his ax as if he'd just cleared a forest.

She softly tapped on the door. "Dorian? Can I come in? Please?"

No answer.

She tried the knob anyway—twisting it with exhausted anger.

"Dorian?"

[Insert silent treatment here]

"Fine. I'll play it your way."

She stormed away. Back outside. To Maurice.

"Can I borrow this? Thanks."

Hauling Maurice's ax, she plodded right past the couch (Mecca and Q never peeling their faces from the screen) and back to the bathroom door.

One—two—three. She began hacking away at the knob until it fell.

The door (knob on the floor and its latch dangling by a few splinters) cracked open. Her walk was calm as she returned the ax to its proper owner with a "Thank you." She dabbed her nose on her sleeve as her body adjusted to the hot-cold-hot-cold pattern.

She sniffed and tapped the door open with her foot.

Clouds of steam flew up around her, fogging up her glasses. She took them off to see. She half-wished Fletcher would scream "GET OUT!" like a little girl—to lighten the mood and give her something to shout back at.

But he was merely a paperclip between Dorian's spindly fingers. He squeezed the rusty metal into his fist as she attempted to close the damaged door behind her. He didn't want to see her.

She commandeered a nearby handtowel and stuffed it into the huge peep-hole she had created.

"So many baths. You'll become a raisin, Dorian, at this rate. I'm not very fond of raisins."

He tapped Fletcher against the bathtub edge. "You left me. Alone. With them."

"I came back, though."

"I can see that."

"I needed some air. I was about to slap you."

"I wish you would've just slapped me." He stopped tapping Fletcher against the tub.

"I don't know what to do with you—you and your clinginess. I've never—never had someone like you before, Dorian."

Well, I guess Odys is completely forgotten, then.

"I'm driving you nuts, am I?"

She sighed. "You don't know how to be—how to be *this*."

"What, straight?"

"You and I both know you're not straight. Venus didn't iron you out, for sure." *I wear you with glorious wrinkles.*

He laughed at that, tucking in his chin to keep her from seeing how humored he was.

189

"No, I mean someone who turns me against my brother." The faucet dripped. "Are you just going to sit there, in your bathwater? Baths aren't baptisms, Dorian. You aren't a new person every time."

"If you're going to come in here, then join me."

"I don't have to join you every time."

"Then leave."

She bit her lip and turned to go.

But Dorian threw his paperclip at the door.

Fletcher sprang up, blocking her.

She turned back around, watching his bathwater settle down around him; watching his angry face become stoic once more.

"I changed my mind. You can stay. It's enough to watch me bathe."

"Thank you for *allowing* me to watch you. Of my own free will."

"Do you think I should shave this stubble?" he asked her, as if picking up where they'd left off. He ran his fingers over his protruded chin.

"No. I'd like to see what you look like with a beard."

"Odys never had a beard, did he? But Leeland did. I think I'll shoot for something in between."

"If that's your goal, you've already reached it, Dorian."

His hands went back into the water.

"You like my hair?"

"No. It looks better than mine." She leaned against the sink.

"Sometimes I think about shaving it. All of it. Even the head."

She crossed her arms. "Like Britney Spears? Is this your 'leave her alone' moment?"

"No, I don't want to be left alone, Odissa."

It punched her in the gut.

Odissa ran her hand across the towel rack and laughed. "So, what's up with the boogers? Q said you were talking about them? Made me all worried."

"She heard us cussing did she? WELL, SHE SHOULDN'T BE EAVES DROPPING!" he shouted at the door. "I made Fletcher spend the night on the roof, you know. It's been rough because of it. I could have just been groggy all day, but no. I had to tap into my reserves to battle off the *Makepeaces*."—He hissed their name—"Ironically, they make anything but peace! Fletcher's nose—it was clogged up. It's bad for Automatons. A bad sign."

He pointed to the trashcan, full of drying, coppery slime.

"*That* came out of him?" Odissa gasped.

"When it's gold we keep it. A trophy."

"That's disgusting."

"No, it's hard work to make gold that way. He doesn't control it. Collecting it is one of a Master and Automaton's few simple joys—our pearls."

"Maybe tonight you should relax. Besides, don't you feel a little safer with the others here?"

He frowned once more, pouting at how right she was.

She knelt down beside him. "You want to go to bed early, then?" She smoothed back his sticky hair. He closed his blank eyes at her touch.

Fletcher watched them as he leaned against the door—already smacking away at the gum she had set on the counter.

"I'm a little hungry."

"Lunch in bed, then."

"But I haven't washed my hair."

"I thought you were shaving it anyway."

When she finally got him out of the bath she asked him, "What do you want to eat, then?"

"Mecca's ordered pizza."

"He has? He didn't say so. Never saw him do it."

Fletcher, using a spare towel to dab his Master off, replied, "Believe us. Mecca *has* ordered pizza."

As they exited the bathroom, there were a few flashes of light.

Fletcher charged.

"Damn it!" Mecca cursed from behind the wall corner as Q held Fletcher off. "Out of memory."

"Does this mean you have to delete the ones of me in me my fairy costume?" Q asked, as if it were such a waste. "The lighting was so good that day. My fans will love those!"

But Maurice, already back inside, was taking care of it. "Not right now, boy." He picked both the Automaton and child up in his arms, the captives giggling.

"Keep them on tighter leashes, Maurice!"

Before dashing off to their room, Odissa asked, "You ordered lunch?"

"More like *linner*," Mecca said as he attached himself to his father's hip.

Maurice sighed heavily, as if this conversation brought back memories. "Remember the days before takeout?"

"God, yes!" Q replied, her limbs still dangling in his arms. "Don't remind us! Makes Mecca uncomfortable. He was never fond of cooking. And it's such a hassle to go out. We look too young to drive."

Odissa didn't want to remind them of the days before drive-thrus. God only knows how sad their faces would be.

DING-dong.

Knock knock knock.

"That was quick!" Q said. "By my calculations we still have about twenty more minutes." She looked at her self-made wristwatch. Something wasn't adding up.

"Maybe they had our types of pizzas already ready?" Mecca asked.

"All twenty-six?"

"Only twenty-six?" Maurice asked. "Don't you normally shoot for thirty, so we can have leftovers? Have I taught you nozing?"

"We didn't know what kind everyone would like. So we ordered all the main ones."

"There are twenty types of 'main' pizzas?" Dorian inquired.

"No, twenty-*six*," Mecca corrected.

Though Odissa was enjoying the conversation about pizza: "Is no one going to get that?" And so she went to answer it.

Just as Dorian said, "She shouldn't be answering doors—" and Fletcher had every intention of stopping her, the next thing they knew the door was already open and they could do nothing about it.

And there were no pizzas.

There was *Maud*.

CAFFAR: The screw.

SCREW: That screws.

THAT: Screws.

SCREWING: You.

Chapter the fifth,

THEY GONNA FIND YOU:

Hide your Odissas?

Odissa had just stood there, taken aback. Maud, as far as Odissa could tell, stared only at her—just as shocked. *They let her answer the door?*

Odissa's hand around the knob was so tight her knuckles turned a blue-white. Anxiety over the dilemma was enough to make her freeze there. Even when Maud had smiled and thrown herself around Odissa—had brought her head to her cheek— she didn't know how to react. Odissa hadn't even thought about hugging back because she was still stuck on Maud's initial expression—that expression that mimicked exactly how Odys would look at her at a time like this.

193

Of course it was Odys's expression—his expression on the Automaton's face. The thought was too uncanny to be sweet. *She's even touching me like him.*

Just as Maud drew back to study Odissa…Fletcher had swooped in and trapped Maud to the floor.

"Don't!" Odissa shouted—not sure at who.

The floor cracked as Maud hit it. Maud was on her back, arms raised in surrender and admission.

Maurice calmed Odissa, "Best let the Automatons deal with Automatons." He pulled Odissa behind him, just to be safe.

Fletcher had straddled Maud and was angrily gripping her 'shirt.'

From the side of his mouth, Maurice noted, "Just look how he's enjoying it, being on top of her! Oh, to be him right now."

Mecca snorted.

But it was drowned out by shouting: "The fuck are you doing here?" Fletcher growled. "You think you can just show up here? The fuck are you here? How'd you know where to find us?"

Q had also jumped to action. While free of Mecca (still in his Papa's arms), she slammed the front door and was crouched for the ready beside Fletcher—for whatever was to come.

Maud's coppery wrists struggled and writhed under Fletcher's shiny whiteness. As they wriggled, they meshed and melted into one another. Their bodies flickered in enigmatic stretches, flapping and waving over each other in semi-solid form. "If you're so afraid of me—of—of us," Maud corrected herself, "why the hell did you let her answer the door?" She grit her teeth as she tried to outflank him.

They caught each other's arms or slipped out of each other's grip—each trying to keep hold of the other while barely solid themselves. They looked as if they were floating in space—or submerged under water. Moving rapidly, yet not going anywhere. Their hair and 'clothing' seemed so weightless in the struggle.

"Don't make me ask you again!"

The fight seemed pointless—like oil mixing with water.

"Why the fuck do you think I'm here, Fletcher? What do you even mean?"

"What the fuck do *you* mean?"

"Why'd you invite us if you intended to be so unwelcoming?"

"When *the fuck* did I invite you, Odys?" Dorian shouted at Maud—knowing her Master listened.

"You don't know when you sent a goddamn text?"

"Text?"

By now, Fletcher had eased his hold on her, and she had realized there was a misunderstanding. They ALL had realized there was a misunderstanding.

"I did it," admitted *Q*.

VULCAN: Has been showing his face(s) a lot more lately.

TO DORIAN: 'Recycling is incestuous, but useful.'

TO MAURICE: 'Oh look, it's that zombie I let live for my own amusement. You'll kill yourself only when I'm done with you. Like I said, recycling.'

TO ODISSA: 'You're making things a lot more fun for them. And a lot easier for me.'

Chapter the sixth,

Mecca's mischief:

How shall it be managed?

"We"—as in Q and Mecca—"hacked your number. Made it seem like the text sent through your phone—that it was from you. I'm the one that sent it."

"No," Dorian corrected, holding up his towel. "Let's no put a cute face on it."

"Mecca is cute!" Mecca protested. "But Mecca didn't tell them to come *now*." He insisted, glaring at Maud and kicking his legs. "Mecca didn't know Maud would come before Mecca could properly *build up to it*."

"Fuck you, Mecca," Maud grumbled up at him. "Excuse me if I can't read the subtext of a text."

"Well," said Maurice after a long pause. He rolled his frazzled mustache's end and stared at her chest. "That's all very well, but I'd rather hoped you'd be the pizza delivery man, Maud."

Fletcher wasn't ready for a lighter mood. "Why the fuck did he send you, Maud? Too afraid to come himself?"

"Exactly!" Maud admitted as Fletcher let off her.

"Why?" Dorian demanded, pissed at her exactness—shoved in a single word, no less.

Odissa moved over to him, noticing his blood pressure rising. Dorian could barely form the words through his anger. She touched his bare forearm—the one holding up his towel—to show her loyalty.

"Quite frankly, Dorian," Maud said, caring for her wrists, "he hides himself from you to spare you." The skin where Fletcher had touched was still glowing. Same with Fletcher. They were burning.

"Oh, what a saint this Odys is. He cares sooo much for us," Dorian spat.

"Where is he, then?" Fletcher backed up to his Master. He'd just finished straightening his skins/clothes back out.

"He is here—in the area," Maud stated, tearing her eyes away from Odissa—who still refused to acknowledge her.

"How the hell did you get here so quickly? Where were you coming from?"

Maud didn't answer, merely glared up at them from the cold floor.

"Almost seems like you knew where we were this whole time! So why come here now when you could have been here all along?"

"I didn't know where you were."

"Like hell. You probably followed us." Dorian muttered, crossing his arms over his bare chest. "You fucking stalker. Odissa, this is abusive behavior. I'll not have it."

Odissa rolled her eyes at him—a movement between *this isn't the worst he's done* and *you're one to talk.* "And you expect me to do something about it?"

Maud caught Odissa's face. "We *didn't* follow you. Had too much to do besides."

Fletcher flashed his teeth at her. "There's two of you. Could be in more than one place."

"I haven't smelt her," Q said. "We would have. But maybe not you, Fletch, because you're about to sneeze out. Look at you."

Maud snarled. "Can Odys come here or not?" She was tired of the trial going on.

Maurice looked out the window. "Iz he not out there, hovering?"

"He's not stupid! He can't take a beating as well as me." She smoothed back her hair, as if it had been in her face.

"You want to see Odissa, Odys?" Fletcher said down to Maud. "You give us Coraza, then. I bet at least one of them is in there, inside you right now, Maud. For safe keeping. Pull them out." He pointed at her—threatening to poke her.

"We already said we'd give you one!" Maud pulled Coraza out of her side and dangled the plastic bag.

"Give it." Fletcher scooped Coraza up and tucked her inside his chest. "And you don't touch me, got it?" he said to Q, as if she had plans for rummaging through his orifices.

"Why the hell would Mecca want her?" Q hissed. Coraza wasn't their intent for drawing Odys out of hiding.

"So he can come now?" Maud made herself reasonably comfortable against the wall.

Dorian crouched down, not bothering to pull up his towel in the back. "Come and do what? See Odissa? Can't you do that for him, Maud? Isn't he *technically* here now?" He pretended to knock on her head "Your avatar is barely welcome, Odys. You stay in there."

197

"We were afraid you'd do this, Dorian," Maud said, rubbing her tired eyes. "But fair is fair."

Calmly, "If you come in here, Odys, I *will* shoot you."

"Get your gun ready, then, Fletcher," Maud said, smirking. "You won't fucking shoot *me* Dorian. What would Odissa think of you then? Fair is fair, right Odissa?"

Odys was dragging her into it.

Dorian grabbed Maud's throat, but she didn't fight back. "Don't you realize she's chosen me?" Dorian hissed. "There's nothing for you to come to, Odys!" He tossed her away.

Maud merely rolled her eyes at him.

Dorian stood back up, expectant. They all saw the shadow as it passed over the window—the cloudy day making it barely perceptible.

The doorknob turned. "Don't let him come in, Q!" Dorian warned, pointing. His voice shook through them like a bang.

But Q wasn't in a mind to obey Dorian. "You're unreasonable, Dorian," Q shouted back. "Don't be like this."

Fletcher had one gun-hand pointed at Maud and another—even bigger—gun-hand pointed at the door. "I swear to fucking god, Mecca, make her back me up!"

The door slowly opened. A final push made it swing wide.

But, to their surprise, it wasn't Odys (and, to their disappointment, it *still* wasn't the pizza delivery man). To cut short their upmost shock, it was:

"Rosemund?"

ROSEMUND: Her Automaton is as redundant as she (but emphasis isn't necessarily a bad thing).

ART: Rosemund once wrote a poem (inspired by Bob) and it went like this: "Fuck up./ Already fucked up?/ I fuck up the fucked fuck!/ Fuck the fucked fuckers who fucking fuck./ Fuck." (As you can see her vocabulary is advanced). The poem pleased Bob.

COPIES: Caffar copies not only words, but whatever her Master is currently into.

WORD: Word.

Chapter the seventh,

I once was found but now I'm lost; could see but now I'm blind:

What amazing grace will sound?

"This shock must be shocking for you," were her first words. With a fancy new cane, she stepped into the house, glancing about. Her eyes landed on the puny light fixture above them in the fan; it was a worthless use of electricity. "To be honest, though, I told Odys wherewherewhere you were. He was waiting for your OK, Dorian—very patient."

"Why are *you* here?" Mecca asked, straining his neck to look past her. "Where's Mother, then?"

They all looked behind Rosemund but no one was there.

Rosemund adjusted her glasses and stopped staring at the light fixture. "Gwen left me. She left me at a restaurant when she left me. Said she had to use the restroom and never came back. See, I had a feeling she was about to—a feeling she was about to leave me. Found her cell phone in the toilet. We can't track her. She left me, and Odys contacted mememe and I told him where you were. Give the boy credit, Dorian. He respects boundaries."

Dorian didn't have the energy to weasel Gwen out of yet another heaping pile of guilty. "You knew she was going to leave? And you didn't stop her?"

Rosemund stepped forward once and tapped down her cane. The cane gave her good reasons to pause and catch her breath. "Well, I never really stop her, do I? I have no control over her." *I let her get away with murder, frankly.* "The better question to ask is why she left me, because I have no idea why she left me. That's the realrealreal mystery. Especially when I have no beef against her. But I have my assumptions as to why. Hello, Maurice. I am not surprised to see you at a time like

199

this, so I'm unsurprised. Mecca can't seem to let the dead rest, now, can he?" She frowned in Mecca's direction, as if he had thrown off the *proper order of things*.

But they had been thrown off by Mother long before his Papa.

She gestured for Maud to get off the floor as she herself took a seat on the couch, uninvited. The others drew in despite themselves. Rosemund was in charge now. Her age and legacy demanded it. "Q, get me some tea, would you, darling?" But she asked it of Mecca, leaning forward on her cane. It's only that Q would be doing all the work.

"Yes, come on in," Dorian said. "Make yourself at home, Rose. Bring whoever you like! Mi casa has plenty of room for all you goddamn strays."

Rosemund gestured for Maud to sit—*stop hesitating, Odys!*—sit down on the couch. "You can't avoid Odys forever, Dorian, because you can't. You need Odys." She leaned her cane against her leg after jabbing it at him.

"First I need Maurice and now I need Odys. Who the fuck *don't* I need?" Dorian mumbled to himself.

"Vulcan is shifting things for a reason. He means for specific Automata to land in specific hands. We can't stop his plans, but we can certainly figure out what they are, even if we can't stop them. That's whywhywhy I'm here. We must put our heads together. That's why you need Odys, Dorian."

"He's not one of us, Rosemund."

"There is no *us* anymore, Dorian—we are not us. Gwendolyn has gone. We're orphans now. That's exactly whatwhatwhat Vulcan intends to prove."

"She abandoned you, not us," Dorian said. "She wanted us all to go with her."

"She wanted one last goodbye, you idiots," Rosemund pursed her lips over her braces. "Just what do you think the cabin was? That was the original goodbye. Then Leeland fucked it up." She scoffed and stared at that shitty light fixture again. "You lot don't unununderstand her."

"You sound so disappointed that we don't understand a psychopath." Maud took out a cigarette and offered one to Odissa. Fletcher slapped the cigarette right out of Maud's hand. Maud glared at him, picking it up. She touched the end of her cigarette, lighting it. She smoked it spitefully. "But then again, you *would* understand her, Rose. Like knows like."

Rosemund craned her neck to get a good view of Maud (whose eyes were just as fiery and mean as that cigarette). Rosemund pointed with the cane again. "You sound just like Pepin over there, Odys. You use his words, his actions. You have a big Automaton to fill, boy…Vulcan has drawn us together and pulled Gwendolyn out. We need to know what ititit means."

"What what means?" Dorian growled, re-tucking in his towel as he sat opposite Rosemund on the new coffee table, a foot of space between them.

"What it all means…" Rosemund rummaged through hair and pulled out a screw. She tossed Caffar on the ground. She swiveled upwards and stood over her Master. "…It means I have a prediction to predict, Dorian." She crossed her legs and crossed her arms, her windbreaker rustling. "Vulcan is making a statement of us all. Vulcan let Leeland die in a way that ultimately contradicted everything he believed in—and *that* only happened by letting Gwendolyn contradict everything *she* believed in. She broke her ownownown rules. There is a trend trending here. He wants us all to go off-brand."

They thought about it.

"Everyone's different," Maurice nodded to Dorian, eyes popping out at him. "Doing zee opposite of what they've always held true. The whole liking girls thing. Gwen breaking her rules. Pepin giving up Madus. Bob killing herself after holding out so long. Leeland giving up. Mecca…behaving."

"That last one's debatable…" Dorian grumbled.

"Yes," Rosemund said. "He is drawing the outside in—inside out."

"Outside in." Caffar repeated, observing her Master with her flat, passive indifference.

Dorian took in a deep, settling breath. He pointed at Maurice and Rosemund. "You all are here to watch it happen—you're here to watch Vulcan turn us all outside in. That's the only reason you're here—mere curiosity."

"Curiosity!"

"Shut up, Caffar," Fletcher shouted at her.

Caffar did not react.

Dorian pressed on, "I won't stand by and watch like you. I won't give in that easily. You come here because you know that's what He wants. Fine. But that doesn't mean *I* will stay. I won't make his plot easy on Him!"[45]

Rosemund shook her curly head. "We aren't here to watch each other suffer. I'm here to show you you've been used to drive thethethe narrative along. It's no reversal if it still moves us forward."

Dorian's ears perked, finally understanding what Rosemund was taking the long way to. "Where is Gwen moving?"

"Gwen can't stand to break her own rules." Rosemund went on. "She will punish herself. Because we didn't. She will stick to her own rules because they are her rules. I think that was her plan all along. She won't let Vulcan contradict herherher because she won't be contradicted by Vulcan. No."

Odissa saw Maud pale. Odys had never thought about this and it showed through Maud. Something inside him felt guilty for hating Gwen so much.

But then Maud's features shifted. "Vulcan *means* for Odissa to have Madus." There was something too bright in her voice.

Fletcher's skin buzzed as he flashed a dirty look. "Have you no shame? Must you gloat for getting what you wanted?"

Q brought forth the tea. She took back Mecca from Maurice. "You really think she would do it?" She held Mecca tight as if to protect him from Rosemund's answer.

---

[45] Talk about quarreling with your characters!

"If Pepin and Leeland and Bob were willing to die, why is it so hard to think she would be too?" Rosemund answered, picking at her braces. "That seems to be the way Masters go these days—the way they go is by their own hand."

They spoke some more about the logistics of it all. How could they be sure this was what she was doing? How dare they suggest it?

"When will she do it, do you suppose?" Maurice asked Rosemund. "You think she will warn us when she's about to?"

"Are her actions not warning enough, Maurice? She'll do it whenever the time is right. Whenever the stars alignalignalign." She drew a line in the air with the side of her palm; they, the stars.

Speaking of stars aligning...

Knock, knock, knock.

"Pizza!" Mecca exclaimed, the heavy topic forgotten. Q rushed to the door. But, once again (and so disappointingly) it wasn't pizza. It was only *Odys*.

ODYS: Not as tasty as pizza.

HOWEVER: He needed to be reintroduced into the story somehow.

THOUGH: Still kind of a letdown.

BUT: At least we can move on.

Chapter the eighth,

The nose knows that you know:

No nose can't know?

"Oh, it's just you," Q frowned, disappointed.

"Damneet all!" Maurice cursed, eyes looking up. "Stop teasing us like zat. I am starving." He peeked through the blinds, hoping to see a delivery car looking for their house. But no. He only saw more wintery weather.

Odys lingered in the doorway, face pink and windblown. His hot breath expressed the steam of his racing heart. Clearly, he'd been waiting outside for some

203

time now—waiting until he couldn't stand it any longer. His red eyes demanded acceptance as they scanned everyone in the room. And then they landed on Odissa's.

Odissa took a good look at him, noting her own reaction to seeing him—him, the only thing left of her old life besides Bulfinch. She looked on him with anger and forgiveness. *You left me with them.*

She was just about to avert her eyes when Dorian's huffing caught her attention. He was huffing and clutching his chest and—

"ACHOO!" Both Dorian and Fletcher sneezed. At the same time. Dorian tried to steady himself on the floor—his face red with anger and embarrassment.

Fletcher collapsed on that floor beside him, bouncing to the ground as a rusty paperclip.

Automatons can sneeze out. But Masters can't. (No matter how hard they try).

Dorian straightened and showed the blood running from his nose. He tasted it as it ran over his lips. "The fuck?" He lost his balance and reached out for the nearest object—the coffee table.

Mecca and Q cringed, their eyes wide with concern.

"For a sneeze-out to affect a Master..." Mecca said, but stopped. That was one bad *achoo*.

Rosemund stood up and shooed Odys back outside. "I told you to wait, boy! We've moved too fast." Rosemund waved her cane. "Give him a minute."

"No!" Odys said, pushing in. "I refuse to be an outsider in this. I have earned my place."

"You don't understand," Q said, stepping in front of him. She put a hand on his chest, pushing him back as if Dorian were Superman and he were Kryptonite. Her eyes were red with panic—they didn't expect this. "It's Venus. You're interfering with what she's done to him, Odys. He can't help but resist this. Can't you smell it? You have to do this gently. You know what the gods are capable of."

Maurice's eyes cut to Dorian, who was trying to steady himself on the arm of the couch. "My god, zee girl is right."

"Please, boy!" Rosemund begged Odys. "You just might kill him."

"Maybe that's what the gods want," Maud said under her breath. She put her cigarette out and stood up.

"Bite your tongue!" Rosemund slapped Odys on the back of his head. "No, they don't want him dead. They want him to hatehatehate you, though." Her voice lowered as she observed Dorian—Dorian clutching his chest as Odissa examined his face. "Venus gave him a reason. And a reasonable reason to hate Odys means there's a reasonable reason the gods want them to fight."

Caffar sniffed the air. She could smell the cause. Odissa.

"The gods leave clues wherever their hands touch," Maurice said as if he understood Rosemund. He twisted his mustache and floated about the room like an inspector investigating a crime.

Odissa glared at them and picked up Fletcher, thinking perhaps Dorian couldn't see him—that Fletcher was too sick to show him. Her heart pounded in her ears. She wondered how bad this was—what she had helped to cause.

She pressed Fletcher into Dorian's hand as he continued to smear blood on his face, thinking he was cleaning it. "How bad is it?" he asked. He could barely pronounce the sentence.

Odissa scowled. "The gods want Odys here, yet they don't want Odys near me? Make up your minds."

"It's a delicate balance," Rosemund replied. Her Automaton was inching closer and closer to Dorian to sniff him. He shooed her off angrily, feeling her too near. "If they didn't want Odys here then he wouldn't be here. The same house? Maybe. The same room? Maybe not. The Automatons are an interesting variable as well... "

"If the gods don't want us in the same room, then fine," Odissa said. She noticed the way Rosemund and Maurice were inching closer and closer together as they observed Dorian like a specimen. "We're going to a different room. You all can work out your own sleeping arrangements. Tell us when your damn pizza is here."

And she ushered Dorian to the bedroom, his heart fluttering at her beloved words.

Mecca was pleased to inform, "The couch converts to a bed. And that's a futon."

His purchases were oh-so practical.

"Did you anticipate such a sleepover, zen?" Maurice asked, popping one eye at him.

Mecca shrugged. "Mecca plans for all scenarios. Mecca has decided that he will sleep in his fort tonight."—as if the tension in the room could all but affect him.

"How strange," Rosemund said. "That is what I decided too. And how strange it is already sososo close to bedtime. The gods have sped up time. Now, has this fort you speak of been built?"

Stanza: Tense attention.

Odissa tucked Dorian in. He was trembling. It made her stomach churn, to see him so scared of his own reaction. In a whisper, "What's happening to you? What is this thing?"

"I don't know," he wheezed, angry at the question.

"So this has this ever happened before? To any of you?"

"No. Not to me."

She used his towel to dab the blood from his face. "It is evil, that a goddess would do this to you. I'm so sorry. I didn't know this would happen—that you have no control."[46]

"Venus didn't cause this nosebleed. I did. I did by staying up too late last night. Wouldn't be as bad otherwise. I'm making myself sick just thinking about it. All this just came together too fast and all at once—couldn't control it. I thought you were finally mine and—"

He shivered. His nose started leaking again.

"It's so cold in this damn house. I'll get those extra blankets." As she moved to leave, his hands grabbed her arm.

"No, I'm fine. Just…come to bed with me. I'll be very stressed if I don't know where you are. Fletcher's asleep right now. He can't see you. I need to see you."

---

[46] Yes, yes. The gods did it. Not the Narrator's lack of another plot device.

He latched onto her and didn't let go until she said "Of course. I'm right here. But won't you let me properly clean your face?"

"No," he said. "Later."

She crawled into bed against all hesitancies. "At least the bed is nice. Mecca chose well."

"Humph."

"He bought all this to please you." She watched him cautiously—as if he might drown in another nosebleed. "He likes you. I think he likes you more than Maurice. He's scared of Maurice."

"I'm scared of Maurice."

"That's why he brought him, I think." She laughed and rubbed his cold shoulder. "Stop being so angry, Dorian. I'm here. I'm not leaving."

Her hand withdrew from his arm and traced the lines of bloody stubble.

"Just give me a moment to believe you. I just need a moment."

She combed her fingers through his damp hair and said, "I won't leave this room until you want me too. We've shut them out. It's just you and me." She relished the power—the power of being able to kill him with a single decision, a single glance, a single "I don't really love you."

"If you leave me, I might die. Literally. The thought of it gave me a nosebleed." But, clearly, she already knew this.

Stanza: A pound of flesh.

They made room for Odys in the kitchen, pulling up a chair. They had wanted to put distance between him and Dorian. The kitchen seemed the farthest place.

"You're frozen stiff," Q said, handing him a blanket. "I'll make some tea—no, coffee."

Thanks.

"The gods may want Dorian and me to be enemies," Odys said, "but it really seems more like they want Odissa to just choose."

"Mortals are such fun for them," Maurice said as he leaned on the counter. "She's a Helen of Troy come to put us at war—the oldest play in the book. Good to finally meet you, by the way." He extended a hand, but Odys refused it.

He glared at it. *Doesn't he know Homer has been alluded too so many fucking times already?* "Your handshakes are legendary, and I'd rather not break my fingers off just yet." Too cold.

Instead, Maud presented her hand and Maurice beamed. He turned it over and kissed it. "Pepin never let me touch you, dear. So good to feel your skin once more."

Maud tore her hand free of him, frowning. "That's the first time someone has ever kissed Odys's hand. Can't say he likes it."

Rosemund chuckled, toasting her cup of tea at Odys. "To being a woman!"

Maurice straightened, getting down to business. "I planned on sleeping on their old cot, but you can take it. I don't mind finding a different place to roost tonight."

"No thanks. The car will do just fine. I don't want Dorian to look at me and spontaneously combust next time. But I will stay inside until it's lights-out, if you don't mind."

"I think we can stay up late for you," Maurice winked. There were plenty of stories for him to tell, especially since he rarely had such a virgin audience.

The pizza soon came and Q went to get plates. Mecca claimed a whole pie for himself while Odys wasn't hungry much. Q politely tried to whisper through Dorian's door that the pizza was ready, but there was no reply.

The television filled the silence for them—an uncertain void which lacked a wanted cheer. Odys had planned to stay in the house long enough for Odissa to come out of the room and get her share of pizza. But that didn't happen. She wouldn't come out so long as he was there—that was the vibe. He wasn't so cruel as to starve her.

"I'm off to bed then. If the battery runs out, do I have permission to jump it with one of yours later?" He pointed amongst them all.

"Of course," Mecca mumbled, his eyes barely open. Q, by this time, was fighting sleep and nudity. Thankfully Mecca was covering most of her already...

"There's a gas can, too, in my truck," Maurice added quietly. Just in case they needed it.

As they took their blankets and pillows into the back seat, Maud lit them up a cigarette.

The overhanging trees reached up like talons into the dark sky. "How long do you think the car will last?" Odys tucked his arm behind his head and took the cigarette from her.

"Does it matter? It's not yours."

"Just wanted to hear myself say it."

They passed their cigarette back and forth.

"She does like him," he said after a few puffs. There was a light fog on the windows that gave a secluded feeling—a sense of privacy. Odys kept his voice a whisper. "She *would* go for a guy like him. Nothing like us."

Maud gave him the cigarette to finish. "He's a *little* like us. Needy."

He flicked the ash into the floorboard as she rolled into him. They slouched in the seats at a diagonal slant, one of his feet on the middle armrest. She brought her knees up closer to him under their covers. I tell you this because he wanted it. I tell you this to prove how much he has changed. He welcomed her touch now, put his hands on her legs—*his* legs.

He put the cigarette out on the car door. It briefly smelled of burning plastic.

"Are you sure we should be here?" she asked him, her wide eyes the only thing not cast in shadow. He loved the way they seemed to glint like a cat's—metallic—reflecting a far-off street lamp's lights. "I mean, I know Vulcan wants us to be here. But are you so sure you accept what Vulcan has in store for you?"

"Where else would I go?" He examined her, as if there were still a way for her to hide something from him. *What am I suppressing?* "We can't leave it like this. Not until we know she's safe."

Maud nodded. "If she's safe with an Automaton, then we have plenty of time to win her back. She'll be ours, Odys."

"It's Dorian's gameplay now. We'll see what happens."

She traced a finger around his face. Odissa used to do this to help him sleep at night. He could almost convince himself she was there, if he kept his eyes shut.

He closed his eyes but Maud's were wide open. She saw the lights in the house go out. The darkness further enveloped them.

Stanza: Talking to yourself is not as fun as answering.

Odys had finally fallen asleep, Maud curled up by his side when, not forty-five minutes afterward, there was a tap on his window. With sleepy faces, Maud and Odys stirred, noticing the car was still going strong. Odys rolled down the window with the knob.

Maurice smiled down at them. He wore no coat.

"What is it?"

He leaned on the window frame. "Come inside, boy. Dorian's awake. He's asking for you."

"What? No. It'll kill him." Maud narrowed her eyes. "Or do you want him to die?"

"No. Not if he knows you're no threat. Odissa's not zere. Eet's just you and him. Plus, you were very wise to sleep out here. Showed respect. I think he feels guilty for making such a scene back zere."

A little pissed that they'd already put so much effort into getting comfortable, Odys tumbled out. "What does he want?"

"How should I know? He's in the kitchen, rummaging. No need to be a mouse, we're all awake anyway. Who can sleep with this—this smell in zee air? I guess you're used to ash. Never mind. Just don't ask to see Odissa and you'll be fine."

As Maud quickly formed some proper PJs, Maurice smiled, his eyes trying to steal a glance.

"Pervert!" she snapped up at him. She threw the blanket at him. As Maud caught up to her Master, she placed her hand in his. That hand soon became a penny. Odys decided he wouldn't gang up on Dorian.

They crept past the couch, where Caffar and Rosemund were under the sheets. Mecca and Q pretended to be asleep in their sleeping bags underneath their "fort" of blankets and clothespins dangling their best over Rosemund and Caffar, yet still not enough to cover the giants. Bulfinch might have found it cozy, but feared being squished.

Odys followed the light from the kitchen. He could hear the muffled creaking of cabinets.

When he entered, he saw Dorian hunched over the microwave, warming a few slices of pizza, a red paperclip between his teeth.

Fletcher was obviously "charged" enough to see for him, because he turned his head in Odys's direction and knew it was him. "Odys."

"You asked for me?" Odys said, unwilling to hide the irritation.

"I'd like to apologize, Odys." Dorian moved the paperclip over to the side of his mouth with his tongue like some toothpick. "Now that I've got my soul back into a manageable state, I feel I can act more accordingly. I didn't mean to make you seem like—like the bad guy back there. Needed my nap. Don't get me wrong, I hate your face. But I know it's not your fault. For that brief moment, Odissa was taken from me—yours again—and it *killed* me. Almost, anyway." He moved some paper towels out of his way, crossed his arms.

"I'd like to apologize, too."

"Don't bother. Not accepted."

"I was asleep, you know—"

211

"My dear nephew, I owe you much more than an apology. That's for sure—though I'm not in the habit of paying off my debts. I'm the reason your life is as it is and I've proceeded to ruin what little joy you built up in it. I can feel the weight of that. I am forever in your debt. But I think we're growing more and more even."

"Oh, are we?"

He took Fletcher out of his mouth and sighed, crossing his arms. "You have the power to hurt me. The mere thought of you tempting Odissa makes me fucking bleed." He laughed it off, as if Odys was harmless now—now that Odissa wasn't near him. But he still dabbed his nose, checking. "Bleeding doesn't make for a very constructive setting. We didn't get to talk this Mother issue through—"

"Just to be clear," Odys interrupted, "what makes you think I'd even want Odissa now? How could I be around her with Maud latched onto me at all times? I don't—I don't think I could do it. It wouldn't be the same. *I'm* not the same, Dorian."

"You are not a very adventurous sort, Odys—threesomes can be fun. Especially when there's two of you. And it's not you who I'm worried about. Odissa *is* an adventurous sort, you see. She might not mind Maud as much as you think."

"It's not about her."

"I can see that." Dorian snorted. "It's all about you, hm? Odissa certainly doesn't mind Fletcher." Dorian opened the microwave to test the pizza. It needed a few more seconds. He continued to lean against the counter.

"One big fucking orgy, this whole thing."

Dorian shrugged. "As long as Odissa didn't fall in love with anyone else in the process, then sure. Why not? It's not even the thought of her fucking you that really gets me, Odys. It's the thought of her still *loving* you. Nothing is enough for Venus."

"Your nose is bleeding again."

"It's nothing." Dorian tore off a paper towel, chuckling as if it were ironic. "The gods make me eat my words," he said as he dabbed his nose. "Don't like us conspiring."

"Is that what we're doing, Dorian?"

Dorian pursed his lips as he folded up the towel to dab again, holding his head back. "No, I suppose not. What were we talking about? Orgies, that's right. Vulcan may have let his wife drop a *deus ex machina* on me but I'm not entirely immune to who I once was."

"If it were me, I'd be pissed," Odys said, leaning against the opposite counter. "I'd fight against it—your impulses."[47]

"If you were me you wouldn't *know how* to be pissed." Dorian adjusted his robe. "You'd be too obsessed with your sister. And hell, I hate Vulcan on principle, but it's not often life gives you instructions or directions. Take them when you can."

"Yes, from the hands of other people."

"Odissa wasn't in your hands," Dorian corrected as he poured himself a drink from a flat two liter. "She's not even in mine. Why do you think I gave myself a nosebleed at the sight of you? I *don't* have her. She's not *mine*. You can't keep treating her like she's yours, Odys. That's why she fucked me in the first place. She's not yours. She's *her own*."

"You think I don't know that? You think I can't see how controlling I am?"

"Good. Then you have no problem understanding why I can't control my fucking obsessive behavior toward your sis." He handed Odys a cup of soda.

"Thanks."

"But back to what I wanted to talk to you about. I'm in." He licked his thumb free of pizza sauce and closed a few box lids. "I'm on your side, Odys. Even if my mouth says differently later on. If Mother kills herself, we still stick together, understand? We can't let everything fall apart. The Automata are our responsibility now."

"Done."

---

[47] Like you fight against the universe every day, Mr. OCD?

"And for God's sake, don't sleep in the damn car. The floor doesn't kill the environment."

As Dorian was about to leave the kitchen, Odys called him back with a whisper. "Dorian, all I want is for her to be safe."

"Not happy?"

Odys ignored the statement and continued to hog the focus, "I'm sure we can both agree she needs an Automaton. Madus would suit her nicely. No one else."

"You're so sure Mother will be out of the picture?" Dorian laughed at it. He was sure too. Already dancing on her grave. "Fine. If that's what happens, she'll have the twin. But, Odissa can choose things for herself. She'll have the final say."

"Agreed," Odys lied.

"Well, I'm sure Odissa is hungry," Dorian rushed the conversation. "I'm going to wake her up."

Odys thought about telling him she only liked cheese pizza—that the variety he had on display might disappoint her. But he didn't say a word.

The protagonists then parted.

As Dorian took in the pizza, he found Odissa was busy petting her cat—already awake. "I heard you leave," she said, as if guilty for being awake. "He came out from under the bed, at least."

The cat became very interested in the pizza (~~I~~ Bulfinch needed to know if I was missing out on anything).

"Bul's getting used to this kind of life, Dorian. Even I could get used to this," Odissa mused, helping herself to a slice of cheese.

~~I~~ The cat came up to him, dabbing Dorian with a cold nose for not offering ~~me~~ him any yet. ~~I~~ Bulfinch purred, batting at Fletcher when Dorian took him out of his mouth to eat. ~~I~~ Bulfinch was bored out of ~~my~~ his mind by now and starting to test the boundaries of ~~my~~ his captors.

"He's bipolar, this cat. Used to be so afraid of me."

~~I~~ Bulfinch was never afraid. Only leading them into a false sense of superiority.

Stanza: The interpretation is up for interpretation.

Now, let's see.

Gwendolyn stared into Anselm's eyes. His long-nailed hand—a little hand—stroked her greying black hair. But who was that other there, in that same bed, with them? Madus.

But let's ignore him and zoom into Mother and Anselm's face, shall we? Madus will get his close-up in time. Let's not worry about what he looks like just yet (though we can assume it's similar to Maud).

Mother's face was pink under the dim motel lamplight. Pink and wet. She closed her eyes and a few more tears rolled down her face, soaking the pillow.

"Come now, Gwen," Anselm whispered to her, scooting in. In darker lighting, he looked more *human*—more human when shadowed. But she hardly wanted him to be. To admit he looked human was to admit the age he could also be mistaken for, which always sank her throat into her stomach. That's why she kept him so ethereal—so that she could deny what she perhaps was. "This will all be over soon. Enough tears, you need to sleep."

She covered her face.

"Just a few drops left, Ansi. I need to get rid of them all, before tomorrow. I can't cry tomorrow. Tomorrow has no place for them."

"Shh, I know." He took the covers in his fingers and used the sheets to dry her face.

"I know you already know this, Anselm, but I want to tell you. Tell you with words," she said, her voice was raspy from crying so much.

"Sí?"

"I know I'm making you do this. I know you have no choice in this matter. But I also feel like…"

"I know."

"No, don't interrupt me," she said in Spanish.

215

He smiled. Gwen did love a good argument with herself.

She went on, her voice slightly cracking, "I know—or, at least, I can feel—that some part of you—of whatever parts Vulcan put into you—accepts me. Whether or not that means it's some form of love, I don't care. I just wanted it to be on the books."

"Your overt effort in placing it there won't be forgotten," he touched his skull, running his long nail over his silvery skin. *It's recorded.* He drew closer and took her under his chin, as if he were the bigger of the pair.

She liked to pretend he was. It was so hard to pretend though. The illusion didn't last long. Her mind would be forced to revert to other charming excuses, like comparing him to a hobbit—I believe the line is they were like "Only children to your eyes." A hobbit without the feet. It lightened the mood usually.

"Don't worry. You're imprinted on me forever. No matter what happens, you'll always be in me. There's no way you—*we*—can't affect the next who has me. They'll know, too, how much I loved you. They'll know we were happy." He kissed her forehead, pale lips lingering. "They'll know."

"Such silly talk, Gwendolyn," Madus said, his voice sounded muffled—as if Mother was trying to stifle his commentary. "You fool yourself, you spinster."

Her pretty face contorted as it buried itself into Ansi's little chest, trying to ignore the other Automaton with her. She wept. She had almost forgot about her third self.

Anselm's lip twitched. She was hiding from her "Doubt"—the part of her soul that shined brightest in Madus. Madus wore it best. And she hated him for it.

Madus went on, his voice slow and struggling—it strained him to speak, for Mother did not want to tell herself what she must:

"You'll be imprinted on us all right, Gwendolyn Gwendy. You will. But they will not see your love. They will see your narcissistic selfishness. They will see all you did to protect Anselm—"

Anselm grabbed her face. "You shouldn't give him voice, Gwendolyn." He sat up in bed. He glared down at the Automaton opposite Gwendolyn. The expression on his face, the unholy frown, scoffed at the idea Gwendolyn had to be shared—split into so many parts.

His polished eyes fluttered back down to Gwendolyn. He reassured her, "Tomorrow these tears will be well spent. Vulcan won't be able to passively hurt us anymore. No more. We are the solution, Gwendolyn. We always were. We got rid of Leeland so the solution could take root. We'll teach the gods a lesson."

Gwendolyn looked up at Anselm, shaking her head. "I don't want to do it, Ansi. It's so unfair to them. I leave so much of the burden on their shoulders."

He leaned down for another kiss on her forehead. His hair fell over them. It sheltered them from the part of her she didn't want there—the part on the edge of the bed with barely any room.

That "part," however, still needed to hold her hand as she fell asleep. It was instinctual that they touch.

Anselm eyes cut to Madus before he settled in, Gwen finally asleep. Madus looked like a mannequin—lifeless and useless—just as Mother liked him.

Stanza: Meet your meat.

A loud crash awoke Dorian and Odissa. Realizing it was coming from the kitchens, they paid no mind. But the smell of breakfast wafted into their room and their noses could not let them rest.

"It smells so bad, but I'm starving." Odissa admitted into Dorian's chest.

"It's Maurice's cooking. He fucking burns everything because it's only manly if it's charred with fire." Fletcher pulled himself off them, flinging the covers off. Odissa noticed he quickly formed clothes before completely standing up. "Shall I bring you something?" Fletcher asked, hiding a yawn. His long hands scratched his chest at exactly the same moment Dorian's did.

Odissa raised her head and asked Dorian, "So you don't want to get up?"

217

Dorian moaned. They'd stayed up late. They'd slept in late. It was almost noon, Fletcher checked.

"I don't want you near Odys."

Her voice more concerned than he'd like, "But I don't think I even hear his voice in there."

They listened for a moment.

Fletcher cocked his head. "I think you're right."

"So you'll risk it?"

"I will. The thought of letting you out there alone makes it worse, actually."

"How convenient that you're all better."

"*Los Doble Ves* want us out there. Has nothing to do with convenience."[48]

His phone flashed on the floor where it was charging. Fletcher read it aloud: "'Making breakfast, Odys gone.'"

Dorian yawned. "They must have this room bugged...I suppose we could see what they're so happy about in there."

"There will be no happiness in Dorian's house!" Fletcher stomped his foot whilst opening the door.

And they shuffled their way to the bathroom to get ready.

...

He left Odissa to finish touching up.

Odissa half-expected to find a penny somewhere—stowed away to get to her in private. But Maud never appeared and Odissa kept herself from wishing on it. She left the bathroom with no further expectations.

"Oh! Good morning!" Q said, sporting a darling little chef's uniform (complete with specific alterations which allowed for, well, more skin). But she wasn't doing any cooking. She was scrubbing.

Mecca was busy on the floor, watching what looked like cinnamon rolls, biscuits, and perhaps a pie baking. "Odys went to the store and bought *a lot* of breakfast. Mecca doesn't usually eat breakfast. Mecca is excited."

---

[48] Doble Ves = Double Vs. Vulcan and Venus.

Odissa wanted to ask *"And where is Odys?"* But assumed it would eventually come up without her prodding.

Fletcher to Q, "ALL of those dishes were necessary to make breakfast? Where did those dishes even come from? And did Odys buy a waffle maker too?"

"Must have been Odys. Wasn't Mecca," Mecca said as he rocked back and forth while the oven-goodies baked.

At least he wasn't staring at a screen.

"Help yourselves," Q gestured to the leftovers on the table. "There's bread for toast."

Fletcher studied the food but went straight for the remaining pizza. "I trust nothing you lot mix together."

Maurice was busy over the stove. "Bacon?" he asked them, mustache twitching, eyes sparkling.

From the looks of the sky-high plate beside him, he'd already cooked a whole pig.

Odissa was too sleepy to laugh at his "Kiss the Cook" apron.

"None for us," Dorian said, stretching. "No meat for me anymore—Odissa's orders."

"Orders?" Odissa repeated, having said nothing of the sort.

Maurice raised an eyebrow.

A smile spread across Dorian and Fletcher's faces. They were excited to let a specific cat out of specific bag. A cat they had tied up in said bag only last night. "Odissa's a vegetarian, Maurice." *Yes, Odissa, Maurice is a carnist! Hate him now, hate him now!*

"Does my cooking offend you?" Maurice asked her, eyebrows coming together.

219

"No, Maurice," Dorian said, smoothing down his bedhead (that Fletcher had just noticed). "Your cooking does not *offend* me. But I don't trust where that meat came from."

"All food comes from labor and suffering," Maurice said to his meat with a frown. "Even plants cost a price!"

Mecca (who was sitting on the floor between Q and his Papa) sighed and put his head in his hand. Q glared at Fletcher for her Master. They knew what kind of a verbal essay was coming. "Did you *have* to comment on the origin of the meat?" Mecca mumbled.

"You know," Fletcher said, leaning into Maurice, "it's your generation and after that made us the gluttons we are today. The start of industrial farming. GMOs. Everything. It's because of your generation we're the capitalist carnivores that we are. It came from *you*."

"Do you not remember how old *you* are, Dorian?" Q scoffed.

"Well, as a *socialist*, I do agree," Maurice sighed at his pan, mustache and eyebrows twitching with every pop of bacon. "Everyone iz a bunch of pansies now! Never killing and owning your own food choices. Your ignorance is—how do you say eet?—*bliss*."

"You killed this pig yourself then?" Fletcher asked him, to push the unveiling along.

"Why would you ask such of question in front of Odissa? Of course I did. I brought zis with me. Zere is more in my car. Why are you trying to piss me off so early, Dorian?" He pointed outside, where his cooler was packed into the snow. Spots of red trailed from the cooler to the back door.

Dorian whispered to Odissa, "Maurice only eats what he kills with his own hands."

"What?" Odissa said—almost a gasp.

Maurice shrugged off the uneasiness in the room. "Zey taste better zat way."

"Yes, controlling their suffering makes it all the more savory," Fletcher frowned.

"But the pizza—" Odissa said, screwing up her face, trying to understand.

"Yes, yes. In other words, *not all zee time.*" He sighed. "If I am zee cook, I cook *my* meat." He tapped his apron-clad chest. "Eet iz not my fault social norms keep me out of ozer people's kitchens. You all eat out so damn much! Who is capitalist now, hm?"

"Sorry to keep you from killing, Maurice," Dorian said, walking to the opposite counter and rooting around in a drawer of grimy silverware.

"Not that your presence here isn't killing us," Fletcher added, leaning against the fridge.

"That's awful, Maurice," Odissa said as she watched him mind the bubbling bacon.

"You think I kill them more cruelly than they would be killed at zee factory?" He put a hand on his hip, snorted.

Mecca rocked back and forth, ears in his hands and pleading for Q to take care of this if it got out of hand.

"Is there any humane way to be killed when you're not suffering in the first place?" Dorian answered for her, quite happy he had finally found and deepened a divide between Odissa and Maurice. *How do you like him now, Odissa?*

Odissa glared at Dorian, understanding why this conversation was happening. *I never should have told you that last night. You were perfectly oblivious to the fact before I pointed it out.*

Maurice's mustache twitched and he turned off a few stove knobs. "All life iz suffering, Dorian." He popped one eye to Odissa. "You and Dorian are perfect for eachozer, then. He dabbles in zat shit. Diets and fads. Do you know how many baby cows are killed so zat you can have milk, Odissa? Cheese? How many male chicks are ground up alive because they can't produce eggs? Vegetarian. Ha!" He waved his spatula at her. "Do not you shame *me*, girl. At least I own the blood I shed. I don't whitewash it with dairy!"

Odissa turned bright red—that he would scold her as he cooked innocent flesh! "I've thought about going vegan too. I do eat vegan—"

"When you are vegan, we will speak of vegan theories. Until zen, we both pick and choose our evils."

Q raised a finger as if to interject but Fletcher cut her off. Rolling his eyes, "Are you kidding me? She barely eats, so I hardly think your morals are equal, Maurice."

Mecca scooted under the table, as if something were about to hit the fan and splatter everywhere.

Maurice shook his head at his work, feeling her judgement. "Zis world is fucked, Odissa. Fucked. Don't you know I see how fucked it is? Why do you think I want to *die*? You think I can't see the human ego in what I do—in what we *all* do? Killing sentient beings when there are perfectly good ozer routes to nutrition?—it is evil! And the gods let us continue perpetuating such suffering." He trailed off in French, waving his hand.

"And so you just give into it, the system?" Odissa asked him, trying to understand his logic. *What do gods have to do with it?*

"Of course I give into eet! Zat is the point. To die. To sin. To pay the wages of zat." He crossed himself—not for forgiveness, but to stress his point.

Even Dorian reared back from Odissa as she leaned into the madness. Q shook her head at him. *What have you done.*

"So killing animals is meant to kill you faster?" Odissa demanded his answer. She was slowly losing respect for him with every word. At least other carnists were ignorant of what they chose. He knew and continued the route.

"Yes. Cholesterol. High blood pressure. Cancer."

"But you actively *kill* your own food. If unhealthy is your goal why do you have to do the killing? Are you saying you raise them too? Like a fucking farmer? Where is your farm?"

His face grew dark. "Killing kills part of the soul, Odissa. Leave it at that." His eyes shot to Dorian and Fletcher, telling them to rein her in.

Odissa didn't notice. Or, if she did, it did not dissuade her. She laughed off her frustration. "But *how* is that more moral than me? You just admitted it is not!"

Mecca whimpered from under the table. This was it.

"If not pigs, zen people." Maurice eyed Dorian, who was gathering paper plates and napkins. *Zere, are you happy, girl?*

Odissa crossed her arms, as if his words did not compute.

Fletcher gestured to him as he walked away, eyes ablaze. "*See?*"

"Yes, tell her how many circus performers died before you found out pigs were a better, more constructive release," Dorian laughed.

Mecca buried his head in his arms. He hated this kind of talk about his Papa.

"People?" Odissa asked the room. "What does he mean?"

"To die you must eat death," Maurice said, plopping down his plate of pig carcass where he was about to sit. He called his son out from under the table with a snap of his fingers, needing the room for his thick legs. Mecca hesitantly crawled out and continued to stare at the oven.

"You're a cannibal?" Odissa asked, hoping not.

Fletcher sniggered.

"No, girl!" Maurice spat. "...Not anymore. Zat's what makes killing pigs more reasonable. No one looks for pigs when they go missing."

"He will try anything once." Fletcher had opened each pizza box to judge the contents. He handed a few worthy boxes from that inspection to Dorian.

"He did it more than once, though," Dorian footnoted himself.

Odissa shook her head at Maurice—her head at them all. "You laugh as if it's funny?"

Dorian was just full of giggles, knowing he had solidified a great wall between them—as if he had broken up two BFFs!

"He only killed a few," Q said as she dried off a plate. She finally got her foot in the door of this conversation.

"As if that makes it any better," Dorian said, arranging pizza on his plate. He licked his thumb off, itching to eat during his entertainment.

"Meat is meat no matter where it comes from!" Q threw down her towel and picked up another dirty dish, the act agitated and raw.

"Meat is meat," Caffar repeated, coming in. She sat down at the table by Rosemund.

(Oh yeah, I forgot to tell you. Rosemund has been there, the whole time. Sitting quietly and reading her paper. The subject matter apparently had no effect on her).

Meat is meat.

Meat is meat and meat is wrong to eat, no matter where it came from. Odissa relaxed. Wasn't that the truth? Wasn't that what she fundamentally believed? Was she about to put human lives above animals lives, like—like some *carnist?*

She bit her lip, considering her next words.

"He told you that himself, did he? Meat is meat?" Fletcher frowned down at Mecca. Dorian started to microwave a few slices of pizza. "Is that how he justifies it? Makes it seem less vile, doesn't it, Maurice, to tell your son that 'meat is meat'?"

Maurice was too busy looking at his heaps of bacon. "Vile was my intention, Fletcher. After all, Zeus destroyed mankind for cannibalism once. I was hoping he would destroy me under zose same terms."

"But Zeus isn't your patron god, is he? And you didn't know how much you would actually like it, did you?" Fletcher laughed at him.

Odissa's skin prickled, knowing on any other day Fletcher/Dorian couldn't give a fuck about this topic. They were only dragging it out for her. She took another step back, wanting to back out of the room—to put distance between her and the horror.

"Don't worry, he won't eat *you*," Mecca said, noticing her. "He only eats bad guys."

"Best way to make them useful," Q said, smiling to herself in the sunlight as if— as if she *agreed* with it.

Maurice said over his shoulder, "I don't run into many *bad guys.*"

"Also, Papa doesn't eat girls. They eat Papa," Mecca giggled, laying back on the floor, happy the conversation had avoided implosion.

Maurice cracked a grin and winked at him.

"Really makes the term 'zombie' fitting, doesn't it?" Dorian laughed again, looking at Mecca. Mecca didn't find it funny—rolled his eyes.

Maurice popped his neck, letting the words roll over him. "Not zis early in zee morning, boys. I haven't done my yoga yet."

"Yoga?" Odissa mouthed to Fletcher, so Dorian could see. Her brows raised like antenna, trying to help her compute the walking-contradiction-that-was-Maurice

This is what Automata do to people?

"Oui, and I meditate everyday on new methods of death and ways to piss off the gods. Like eating pigs. Pisses off the Jewish one, anyway." He flipped off the ceiling. "I fixate on my goal: death."

"The only death you attain is those you kill, Maurice," Rosemund said. "And by the looks of it, you've attained quite a lotlotlot of death. Congratulations."

"Pepin always having to clean up his messes. No wonder he left the circus," Fletcher mumbled past is mouth full of food, as if remembering his time in said circus.

"Pep didn't want to get eaten," Dorian theorized, taking his plate of breakfast pizza from Fletcher.

Maurice fixed his plate. "I only killed the ones about to rat on us. They were threats."

Odissa pointed in the air. "Did this happen before or after you were suicidal? Because I assumed you left the circus after trying to kill yourself."

Mecca looked like a sad puppy once more, sitting up and readying to hide again.

225

"Oh, I did leave after," Maurice nodded as he bit into his bacon. "But it did not leave me. I still had my traveling show. I still had people who hated me—who thought I wouldn't hand over trade secrets—who thought I had swindled them. Zis and zat. But even before, well, some people are willing to kill off the competition. And when you're the best at what you do"—and he was the best at not dying—"people are spying on you anyway. Waiting for you to slip. To spill your mysterious *beans*. Gives them ample time to notice ozer things they should not. And then threaten to blackmail you with zose things if you don't give them what zey want. But you cannot give people what zey want, Odissa."

"Enough of it is enough," Rosemund said, flicking her paper. "Eating a human here and there is nonono worse than anything else we've done. At least they got eaten. Plenty of people I've killkillkilled were wasted in the ground. Now, would you all hurry up and eat?"

It wasn't the subject matter eating away at her, clearly, for she was looking at her watch.

"I do what I want in my own fucking house," Dorian said right after his first real bite of folded pizza.

Fletcher sat down, halfway done with his pizza already. He picked up a vegetable that fell from his bite. "Fried green tomato anyone?" He lifted it up so that everyone at the table could moan at what was actually green pepper. "Do sit down, Odissa." He tossed it in his mouth and swallowed. "I won't let him touch you." He presented her with graceful options.

Odissa shook her head. Not willing to obey just yet, "It's weird."

Rosemund cleared her throat, not liking that *this sort of talk* was still going on. Odissa sat down. Rosemund and Caffar, at the table, were apparently finished with breakfast and food in general, open sections of the newspaper hiding their faces.

Odissa leaned over the table, one final thought building up in her, and whispered to Maurice, "I'd rather that be human meat than something so innocent. I think that's my problem with it."

"Me too," Maurice whispered back, passing her test.

Dorian frowned at her—was his plan backfiring?

"But a murder a day keeps the living at bay," Maurice said in Rosemund's direction, tiptoeing around her limits.

Caffar, with the longest and most usable legs, kicked at him under the table.

Odissa sighed, the breath flapping her lips. As she poured herself some coffee: "I hope you die, Maurice. I really hope you die."

"Ouch," Dorian said with a smile. "That's harsh."

Odissa snarled at him.

Rosemund checked her watch again and looked to Maurice, as if they were both expecting something—any time now.

Fletcher caught the look and brimmed with suspicion.

Dorian stood up, preparing for what Rosemund and Maurice had in store. "Where *is* Odys?" He asked, helping himself to a bowl of pancake batter before Q could wash it out.

"Don't speak of the devil unless you want him to hear," Maurice said, his curly eyebrows bouncing. "Smoking break. He's waiting for your OK to come back into the house."

They waited for Dorian to give it, holding their breath. He checked his nose with a few fingers—dry as a bone. He considered it, rolling his fingers. "Let him come, then."

Mecca nodded to Q and she left her dishes with a shake of her wet hands.

Odys instantly made the crowded room feel like it was threatening its max capacity.

He sat down next to Rosemund and took out a fresh pack of cigarettes. He did not offer Odissa a one. In fact, he completely ignored her. She silently thanked him for it. Fletcher was watching her every move as he stuffed his face with Dorian's crust. Odys pretended to be interested in the wall. *This is what brothers do. This is what brothers do.* If only Mecca had bought a ticking clock for the kitchen. It would have added to the dramatic buildup

"Should I not have come in?" Odys finally broke the silence. It was a question no one would be answering, for there was no good reply.

Odissa, upon his sentence, gave her self the excuse to actually look at him. Odys was smoking shorts. The store must have been out of filterless.

She could do for a filterless right now, the leaves would give her something to spit—a reason to chew at her lip. Like tealeaves, they would help her read his future. She pushed up from the table, an act that made them all hold their breath again.

"Is there more coffee we could make?" Odissa asked Dorian, coming over to him. But they were not out of coffee.

"I'll put another pot on," Fletcher said, his voice quiet and cautious. His chair creaked when he stood. Team Dorian had assembled and was looming above the rest.

Dorian realized Odissa was waiting for him to sit back down—realized her position depended entirely on his movement. He knew she was walking on eggshells for him. For *him.*

Q tried to break the tension by saying, "It snowed a shit-ton last night. It's very deep. But it's not the soft kind. Good for making snowmen. We already made one." She pointed out the window.

Maurice smiled down at her. "I used your scarf, Dorian, I hope you're not mad. The one on the back of the couch."

"Snowmen, Maurice?" Dorian said, tearing off a bite of crust. "I'm surprised you didn't fancy writing your name in the snow instead."

"Just because you have to squat, Dorian, doesn't mean you have to make fun of zose with a dick."

"Oh, he has one, all right," Fletcher said, watching the coffee maker steam. "It's been in me enough."

Though it earned him half-hearted grins at the breakfast table, the fact that Odys wasn't smiling made it harder to enjoy. Odissa watched all of them like watching a standoff—what was going on?

Odys flicked his cigarette ashes into a makeshift ashtray—a brown coffee mug with a broken handle, probably found in the pantry from the previous lives lived there. He had carried it in with him.

The oven dinged and Q assumed a pair of hearty oven mitts to take the hot items out. I've already forgotten what I said she was baking.

Cinnamon rolls. Was it cinnamon rolls?

Maurice, continuing to nibble at his fried pig, asked, "So, what is on zee agenda for today?"

His eyes slid toward Dorian, as if he might answer. As if he was in charge.

Dorian gestured with a new piece of pizza to Rosemund. "Was I supposed to plan something, Rosie? Is that why I have this audience?"

Rosemund put down her paper, spreading it out, despite the plate full of syrup beneath it. "Funny you should asasask that—what you just asked, Maurice. Because I see here, in this week-old paper, that a Mr. What's-his-face has recently died and left his estate heirless"—wait for it—"because he did not have an heir."

"And why is zis so noteworthy, dear Rosemund?" Maurice led her on, as if they'd planned this whole conversation. He dabbed at his lips with his cloth napkin, cocked his head as if he did not know.

"He was a collector and restorer of importantimportantimportant antique antiquities. Including sixteenth and seventeenth century automata. Maybe even eighteenth. Nevertheless, he was a very fine restorer and collector of important antique antiquities."

"So you've said!" Maurice cleared his throat. "And I assume you're interested in zis week-old topic *because?*"

"Funny you should ask that, too, Maurice. The paper says here that a Mrs. Danny—also called 'Dan' by close relations—D. Lion bought the estate last week and the writer hopes she'll reveal what's hoarded up inside—maybe even donate to

229

local museums." Rosemund pretended to read the sticky newspaper—like she hadn't memorized her lines perfectly.

"A Mrs. Danny D. Lion? Now, where have I heard that name before?" Maurice smoothed out his mustache between chomps of bacon. "Danny D. Lion? Danny must be short for *Danielle*."

"Or maybe Daniella?" Rosemund shrugged.

Fletcher rolled his eyes.

Odys put out his cigarette. "Is this the same Mrs. Lion who invested in the Pakistani orphanage alongside a Mr. Louis E. Anna?"

Rosemund reared back. "Oh, you remember Mr. Anna do you? He was a fun one."

Odys sighed and hunched forward. "Maud certainly remembers all the names Pepin used to go by—as well as yours, Rose."

"Ah! They've found me out, Maurice. How clever of them to be so clever."

By now Odissa was catching on. She picked out a cinnamon roll Q offered her. "What have we found out?"

Mecca, his mouth covered in frosting, said, "Mecca thinks we should go see it! Go see the house Rosemund bought."

"I have the keys, here!" She retrieved the copper key from her might-as-well-be-an-afro and dangled it between her freshly-painted claws.

Dorian and Fletcher puckered. "Why do you want us to go to that house, Rosemund?"

"I think we should all go," Rosemund said, "because it's ironic I just bought a house sososo nearby. Fate wants us to explore my new property."

"Is that why you came here, Rosie? To get us out of this house? Why do you want us to leave?"

"Don't you see?" Maurice said, leaning over the table. "Vulcan set this up. Vulcan meant for Rosie to buy zat 'ouse! And eet is so close to us now. It is *meant* to tempt us into a field trip once we all got settled here."

"Then I won't be going!" Dorian slammed his fist on the table. "Bob died doing what she thought Vulcan wanted. Vulcan *let* her die. I won't accept His plans."

"I think you will end up zere whether you like it or not, Dorian." Maurice gestured to the picture in the paper, now bleeding through with syrup. "Vulcan killed off zis poor man so that we could go to his house. Don't waste his death."

"You don't know that!" Fletcher huffed.

"Let me put it zis way, Dorian," Maurice dabbed his mustache with his napkin. "If you do as Rosemund wants, zen I will leave you in peace. And take Mecca with me."

Dorian sat back. "Why are you on her side of this? What's in it for you?"

The coffee pot sizzling matched Fletcher's glare. "Now we *know* Rosemund is planning something. Something is in that house, isn't there, Rosie? Isn't there?"

Odys jabbed out his cigarette. *One two three four five six.* He looked at Maurice. "What deal did you make with Rosemund, Maurice?"

"So you're not in on this?" Dorian raised a brow at Odys.

"Not yet."

Maurice averted his eyes and he shoveled more pig into his mouth, chasing it down with a cinnamon roll.

"No. She didn't make a deal with you did she?" Odys pressed him. "She told you something. You know something needs to happen, don't you? This isn't Vulcan. This is man-made."

"Did Vulcan come to you, Rosemund?" Dorian prodded. "What do you know, Rosie?"

"Come with me to the house, Dorian. This is for your own good."

"No, Dorian," Odys said. "Don't go. Odissa, don't let him. If this has something to do with Vulcan, then—"

"You are going, Dorian, or I'll let Mecca burn zis fucking house down, you understand?" Maurice recrossed his overly buff arms.

Mecca's mouth hung wide with eager possibility.

Dorian chuckled as he rinsed his hands off of greasy pizza remnants. "Fine. Do as you like. You already do. Burn it down. The furniture clashes anyway."

Mecca grumbled.

Maurice sighed. "Eet's not working, Rose."

"Not working," Caffar agreed.

Maurice leaned back in his chair. "She won't tell you. But I will. We have reason to believe Gwendolyn will be zere."

"Mother will? But why?"

Rosemund stood up. "Damn it, boy! You think I know why? You think I know why Vulcan wants it to happen there, in that house, where it will happen? I don't know whywhywhy! I don't know why Gwen thinks it has to be this way but it will be because it will be. Can't you see that Vulcan set this up and Gwen is accepting it and you cannot curse her for it? Gwen needs us to bebebe there."

"Goddamn it, Rose, sit down!" Fletcher barked at her. "We'll go! Just sit the fuck back down. Christ's sake—all of you. Was that so hard? Was that so hard to tell us Gwen will be there?"

"Of course she will be zere!" Maurice shouted up at him, waving him off. "We could write this story all on our own."

I'm willing to bet Gwen's name will be at the end of a chapter soon, too.

"Going is still in line with what Vulcan wants," Odys said. "We can't forget we have choices—we are humans with free will."

"No, we're not," Dorian whispered. "We're not humans. Not anymore."

It was decided. They would trade this house for another.

Thus, our characters set out on a two-and-a-half hour drive to the state border.

Stanza: Rosemund promised Maurice anything in the house he thought might kill him.

Somehow, Q and Mecca had managed to find a very nice MOTHERFUCKINGSUV with chained tires that could roll through winter itself. They only got stuck in the snow about six times when they had to stop at four-ways in the back roads. But the Automatons had little to no trouble lifting the car out of those.

The car itself had little room to spare. The Automatons, therefore, were kept in pockets most of the drive. It made for a very odd experience, Odissa observed—as if a part of the Masters were muted (though sometimes a muffled sound here and there would come out from a stuffy pocket). Even visually, the Masters lost part of themselves—Odissa had to read them like normal people. They were like a foreign film with no subtitles—people now so used to being expounded by another that they had forgotten what it was like to express themselves singularly.

"Odys, did you know Maurice is a cannibal?" Odissa asked her brother. She had only just realized he hadn't been there—been there for the morning debate. The long car ride had allowed her to dwell on the topic.

Rosemund rolled her eyes and scolded Dorian over her shoulder, "See what you've caused?"

Mecca sank in his seat.

"Of course he knew," Maurice grumbled. "It's not something Automatons easily forget. Pepin helped me cover some up."

Odys turned to her, his neck stiff from sleeping without a bed. "How'd you find out?"

"So you're—you're OK with it?"

Odys thought about it. "Maud knew some the people he ate," he admitted. "They weren't good people. Maurice made use of them." Odys shrugged through repeated conversation circles as if he had been there for their previous rotations.

"But it's weird, right?" It was as if she were a scientist gathering data—wanting to judge his reaction so she could adjust her conclusions.

"Believe me, Odissa, that's not the weirdest thing they've done."

"How did you eat them?" she shifted her questioning to Maurice. Again, like a scientist gathering data.

Maurice huffed through his nose. "Chopped them up into little bits. Cooked the pieces. Like any other animal."

"You used an ax?"

"For some parts, oui."

"And why? Why kill them? What made them bad?"

"Because they were threatening us," he snapped. "Plus, I needed *some* way to dispose of the body. What better way than to eat them?"

I feel a spin-off series of prequels coming on. A Vol. 0.5, if you will.

"Were they tasty?"

Maurice seemed to like that question, for his eyes lit up—eyebrows danced. "You do not mock me after all? You really *are* curious?"

Odys cringed. Of course his sister would ask a question like that. And indeed, how often do you get to meet a real-life cannibal? Odissa couldn't throw away her shot for answers.

"All meat is bland," Maurice said. "Until you add spices."

Odissa's face opened. "That's what I always say! I mean, about meat. Not human meat. People say it tastes good, but no, it doesn't! Anything can taste good with the right spices. It's just an excuse for them to keep eating meat."

"And at least Maurice denies all excuses," Odys mumbled.

Mecca covered his small ears and leaned forward in his seat.

"Sorry, Mecca," Odissa said, noticing him.

"Don't be sorry," Odys said. "It's the only subject that can shut him up."

Dorian didn't like Odys picking on Mecca (only *he* could pick on Mecca) so he uncrossed his legs and changed the subject:

"Rosemund, how did you hear about this Collector?"

(Notice the gentleman is a Capital-C collector now).

"Danny D. Lion read about some of his work he did for a museum. That's how he caught my eye. I killed him a few weeks afterward."

"You did what now?" Odys asked, eyes blinking.

"He refused to meet with me to discuss our similar interests. Also, he was known to buy black market artifacts that I also wanted and then destroy them before I could steal them from him. He knew who I was. He knew I was out to get him. He knew."

"What the fuck is wrong with you people?" Odissa asked Dorian, her voice trembling. Maurice's cannibalism was more and more charming.

"You don't know what kind of artifacts he has up there, girl," Rosemund said. "He has things I need to see before I die. Before we all do."

Maurice shifted in his seat. "This Collector apparently got his hands on many occult things. I want *mine* on anything that might make Vulcan notice me. Anything that might get me closer to Him is something zat will get me closer to the reason I'm still fucking here…"

"No one asked you, Maurice," Odys said as he stood up in his seat and turned on the radio past him.

Enough talking.

Stanza: The rest of the car ride is not that important.

The house was old, as it should have been. The iron driveway gate was locked, so they let Q out to break it. But there wasn't much reason to pull the car up, what with all the high, unshoveled snow.

They all jumped out of the SUV. Odissa thought that it would have (had any normal people been watching) looked like they were coming out of a clown car, what with all the Automatons forming privately inside before hopping out.

"Time to go through that hair purse for the key, Rose," Fletcher said.

"Doesn't look like there's alarms anyway," Q said, as if she would love to break something else.

The house was nothing too creepy or too nice. Complete with dying ivy on one side, the only thing it lacked to be picturesque was new paint on the shutters; it was a modest mansion.

Odys observed that their tracks were the first to this virgin snow. *If Mother's supposed to be here, then she isn't here yet.*

Or perhaps she'd been there a looong while, dummy.

The wood floors creaked under them. A thin layer of dust lined just about everything. Apart from the ghost-sheet covered furniture, the place looked quite normal.

They decided to explore the place floor by floor. Together. Maurice *swore to God* if anyone tried to scare him with one of those dusty sheets, he'd see if he also retained the ability to kill a Master.

Rosemund didn't comment on the fact they'd already proven it impossible through the time she got him to stab her in the hand. The knife had bounced right off.

Now, moving on from the topic of Maurice's physical limbo, we can proceed to the point where we examine the house itself (which I would very much like to do).[49]

Since there was no electricity (they made no pit stops for a generator, much to Rosemund's dismay), Rosemund busied herself with opening any curtains while Maud was clever enough to light one of the many unused display candles. She passed them around as she found them and lit them.

"Mecca's smells like cookies!" Mecca said from Q's back. Their smiles glowed in rapture of this little side quest Vulcan had sent them on.[50]

Maurice and Caffar had become busy with touching things. Smelling things. It didn't shock anyone when they also started to *lick* things.

---

[49] Despite being the only one of them not there to see it (I'm assuming Bulfinch is locked up in the house still).

[50] Should they not be more somber about Gwen planning to kill herself? Maybe some of them think they can stop her? But like hell I'm asking B.L.A. for revisions on this section. It was a struggle just to pry this from our Narrator's hands.

"Is this a competition?" Fletcher scoffed at them.

"This knob, here, sixteenth century. Crystal. It's worth more than the desk itself—Mahogany wood from the Yucatan," Rosemund interpreted for her Automaton, licking her own lips as if she tasted it too.

Maurice seemed more apt to try anything metal first, but everything was fair game. After they had briefly explored the kitchens and the modest wine cellar to return to the main rooms (they decided that they were looking for a relic of Vulcan, not Bacchus) the cold of the house caught up to them and they began to shiver and grow impatient.

"What, Maurice, do knobs have to do with killing you?" Odys asked, only half-interested as he and Maud admired a damaged oil portrait of some noble woman. It was exhibited as if in prime condition.

"I must say," Maud added when Maurice did not quickly answer, "though you no longer have Fletcher, his record of antiquities left quite an impression on your brain, Maurice." She raised her red brows as he went for the same drawer Caffar did.

Caffar searched madly—as if hoping to stop a hidden bomb. Maurice followed her like she were a drug dog. No, wait, they have bomb-sniffing dogs. A bomb squad dog.

"Papa always had an eye for such things," Mecca said, adding commentary to their exclusive *Antiques Roadshow*.

Odissa saw that even Maud was starting to touch things here and there; the search-madness was taking over all of them. They were in a game looking for the portal key to move the narrative along. She glanced at Fletcher, wondering what they expected to find by such methods…But even he was looking about, crouching low to the ground. Odissa gave him credit for keeping his hands in his pockets.

"Bring more light over here," Maurice beckoned as they'd made their way to the far end. It was the last nook they'd explore before going to the next floor.

Rosemund limped forward, glancing over Maurice's shoulders. He started to pull out and overturn all the drawers within the writing desk, making quite a mess as papers and supplies scattered. "Agh! I can feel something. So close. I can *hear* their noses twitching!" He pointed with his popping eyes to each Automaton.

He noticed Caffar's nose scrunch—inhaling a large sniff. Everyone with their candles turned to her upon the dramatic intake.

"She has the best nose," Rosemund smiled as her Automaton walked over to a closet door.

She opened it, revealing an enclosed staircase.

It was no closet at all.

"Likely leads up to the next floor," Maurice observed. "Just a second way up besides that terribly pretentious one from the foyer."

They could barely keep up with him as he dashed past Caffar up the conch-like iron steps.

By the time all of them had reached the floor's hall, he'd already thrown back curtains on the single window at the end, sending through the white sunrays. Caffar was close on his heels. Rosemund took her time, her hand hovering over the walls, frames, knobs as she wheezed about.

"I will admit," Dorian said aside, "there is *something* on this floor. Vulcan was here."

"How can you tell?" Odissa asked as she observed a painting—a small print copy of John Gast's *American Progress.* She frowned at the work like one might an omen.

"This place isn't covered in dust. It's covered in ash."

The floorboards creaked under their conjoined weight. Maud's heals made a sexy tap tap tap. Odissa found it distracting and tried not to stare at her. Odys would catch her and try to meet her gaze, but Odissa would always avoid him.

"But *what* are we looking for?" She still did not understand—still felt as though they were being mysterious when, in fact, they did not know themselves.[51]

"Nozingness!" Maurice shouted from some room. "Sweet nozingness."

---

[51] I'm not so sure our Narrator knows.

Dorian shrugged, not sure what to tell her. "It could be an object. We don't know. We only smell him."

"As long as it can kill Maurice, we'll be happy," Fletcher mumbled, putting back down a glass vase.

They all entered into Maurice's chosen room. It felt like they were in a museum and Maurice was THAT tourist who took pictures of the light-sensitive art and almost got your group thrown out.

Odissa stared into her flame. "With these candles, it feels like a gothic novel."

Dorian squeezed her arm. "Then I shall be your blind Mr. Rochester."

Odissa saw Odys roll his eyes and go back to studying the paintings on the walls. These paintings, in this inconspicuous corner, were no prints.

Wanting to block their conversation, Odys said, "I don't think we should be looking so hard." He overturned a few low-standing bookcases, kicking through the volumes like an acrobat on a tightwire. "If Vulcan means for us to find something, then He'll show it to us."

"Don't be foolish, boy." Maurice picked up a large rock sculpture that seemed to be some indigenous artifact. "If gods did all the work for us, we'd be bored out of our minds. And so would They."

Maud picked up a disarrayed book. She had been scanning through the titles faster than a computer using the CTRL + F feature. "Someone's already out of their mind." She set down the outdated encyclopedia to pick up another. "Oh, look, Odissa, it's a first edition of [insert any book you'd like here; it doesn't matter—we know she's well-read]. Oh my God, it's even annotated—by [such and such a modern writer that Odissa was semi-fond of]!"

Odissa froze—wondering why Maud was talking to her. It was almost as if Odys had forgotten the hierarchy and had shown himself exclusively through Maud.

Odissa took the book reluctantly enough, for Dorian's sake.

239

Dorian crossed his arms behind his back and turned from the scene, trying to pretend it hadn't happened and sniffing back potential blood.

Maurice frowned up at the mantel laden with dust and old photographs. "You killed a very interesting man, Rosemund."

"No. I *collected* him. I did unto him what he did to all of this stuff."

"That's one word for it," Fletcher sighed. "Another is '*reaped.*'"

"Harvested," Dorian added.

Maurice smiled over his shoulder. "I would love to be part of such a collection, Rose—if only!" He dusted off his hands and walked back out into the hall. Of course they tagged along.

Maurice was mumbling to himself as he picked his next room, *"Needs a fresh coat of paint, that,"* and various other observations in French.

Lifting their candles, they discovered they were in a studio. Seemingly, an art studio.

"Seems our Collector did his restoring here." Q noticed the table, bench, and easels in the center of the room obstructing the full view of a mannequin-sized figure. "Just as the article said."

The figure was sitting on a stool, her legs on the table—her torso exposed with no proper skin, revealing the gear work and metal-frame core. Like some dissected frog, her canvas linings were pinned back. Half of her face was missing and in need of delicate touch ups.

"It's an automaton," Mecca said, his eyes widening at the sight. "A real one."

"She's huge," Maud said. "I can't remember the last time I saw one so big."

The figure had been separated from her fancy pedestal—a pedestal which, when wound and properly geared, would cause the mechanics in her body to spin and come to life.[52]

Caffar began to sniff about the figure, her nose inches away from the tattered attire of the life-size automaton. With each sniff she made herself assume the

---

[52] Of course this book would have a scene so ironic! The real automata population was entirely underrepresented until now.

Automaton's appearance—the flaky paint-like skin, the same balding hair, a similar pattern and stitching of the clothes. Parts of the cloth were threadbare, wanting to be sewed or patched. Caffar's costume proved too much work, to sniff and feign unnatural features. She stuck with sniffing.

Though everyone else seemed intrigued with the mechanical toy, Maurice was busy thumbing through the canvas paintings propped up against the walls. "All copies," he said to himself. "Nozing more than a mere hobbyhorse. Who has such time?"

(Maurice had a stable full of hobbyhorses, so he was one to talk).

"You suppose it's modeled after Jacques de Vaucanson's flute player?" Mecca asked the room. It was hard to tell—her posture looked so familiar.

"No," Rosemund said, "she belongs to a larger orchestral display—perhaps part of an old carnival ride. Modern design. That is no cherub face. Sadly, she's of nonono sentimental value to us. Except that we can see why Vulcan would 'visit' this Collecting Collector. He had interesting interests. Makes for a very nice setting, eh? Nice ambience. Vulcan has set the stage. So many propspropsprops."

"Is that really why you killed him?" Maurice laughed, tossing aside a tube of paint. "You were jealous of Vulcan's favor?"

"Why be jealous when Vulcan meant for me to kill him?"

As Maud and Odys looked but did not touch, Odys's eyes followed the automaton's arm to her hand—a hand closed into a fist with posable fingers taped together to protect them. "I think she's beautiful," he said.

Maud held her candle up to the Automaton's legs on the counter. "No, you don't."

Rosemund snorted. "You can't decide, Odys?"

"I've decided not to decide, I guess." He glared at Maud, cursing his tired brain for the equivalent of sleep talking.

241

Dorian, Fletcher, and Odissa had found a portfolio of paper sketches and were leafing through the pages. "I wonder if he did all of these," Odissa spoke her thoughts aloud.

"Likely not," Dorian answered. "The hand is so different throughout. Though some are alike, see here?"

"Well," Odys said, his posture sinking as if bored of this room already, "This ambience is a waste if nothing. Starts. To. Happen."

I'll speed this up.

Maurice had pulled out a random canvas as he said, "Vulcan liked this Collector. It makes me jealous that Vulcan would possibly spend so much time even considering someone *else* and zeir affairs when *I'm* still alive."

"Perhaps it's that very masochistic attitude, Maurice, which drives him away." Fletcher batted some cobwebs from a toolbox he felt compelled to inspect.

Odissa decided on intervention. "Maurice, many humans would be so happy to have what you have. Not even the Masters have it, right? You depend on nothing. Most people would say you should be grateful."

"Let me know, ma petite fille, how you still feel about longevity after we get you that Automaton." And he continued his search. His wide eyes never stopped darting about—never stopped bulging.

As the others rummaged through what was the most interesting room yet, Odissa observed her brother. He acted as if he wanted to move on to the next, yet he had returned back to the deconstructed Automaton in the center. Nothing better to look at, apparently.

"Dolls are so creepy, I always thought," Odissa said in her brother's direction, to distract from his blank state. Dorian did not notice, as Fletcher was still examining tools like someone picking through an estate sale.

Still lost in thought, Odys replied, "Don't call it a doll."

That's not exactly what Odissa had meant to imply, but she somehow felt as though she deserved the rebuke.

Luckily, Odissa didn't have to suffer blushing for too long, for Caffar and Rosemund seemed to be leaving the room, distracting Odys from the automaton. Behind some very tall frames leaning upon a cabinet full of old pottery and paint supplies was a small door. The kind of door that the people of the twenties or thirties would have more easily fit.

"A water closet," Rosemund informed as she worked open the rusty hinges. "Bring in more light! Quickly, now! Do you not hear the exclamation marks in my voice?!" Snatching a candle from someone else, Rosemund held it up. "Vulcan was flushed outoutout of Olympus. Always check bathrooms because Vulcan was cared for by the sea—the bathrooms are the portals, I always said."

"This is the first I'm hearing it from you," Dorian snapped back.

She had passed over the grubby toilet. It was a hard fit, to get all of them in there. By the time Odys had observed what Rosemund was jabbering on about, everyone was already gasping.

Almost every Automaton had their own insightful comment to include:

"Lipstick on the mirror—in a man's house."

"That doesn't mean anything," Dorian snapped again.

"Fish scales are used to make lipstick. It's a sign."

"Of animal cruelty? Sure."

"But it's all in the bathroom. Vulcan *is* the shit of Olympia."

"'The nose knows,'" Fletcher read the mirror. Though everyone could read well enough for themselves. "You think He wrote it, or the Collector?"

"Same thing at this point—no matter the method." Maud looked about the room for more signs.

Caffar proceeded to lean against the sink and lick-taste the lipstick. She merely nodded her approval and repeated, "Same thing."

"The nose knows." Rosemund squeezed around the rest of them, held her candle down to the box of tissues sitting on the back of the seat. Upon further inspection, "There's a message on the tissue. The tissue has a message!"

"Pull it out, then!" said Fletcher, but he'd already done so, being just as near it as Rosemund. Reading aloud from the tissue that had been stuffed back inside the box, "'This box is encasement of cardboard and tissue. Pull no more out and you won't have an issue!' Signed, 'V.' He has a way with words, that Vulcan. Wonder what muse helped Him come up with that shit."

Maurice scoffed, turning red. "This object won't kill me. Black market my ass, Rosemund! The Collecting Collector could just go to zee store for something like a tissue box. Jesus. Next trip we make might as well be to zee fucking store!"

"Think of it this way," Dorian replied. "Vulcan had to pick out which box of tissues He'd use for this closet, right? Plan for the Collecting Collector to buy it. Follow him home to pull out the tissue. Or, get the man to write the message in a trance. Wait for the man to die, perhaps."

"Don't be a smart ass," Maurice growled. "If it even happened like zat!"

"It could have happened like that," Rosemund frowned into herself. "I poisoned him. Slowly.[53] The Collecting Collector had plenty of time to go to the store for V."

"Yes, because we all get spirited away to buy tissues for gods," Dorian mumbled.

"Let's not pull out any more," Odys said, feeling claustrophobic and squeezing out of the room.

"The box looks new," Mecca noted.

"Is the tissue soft, Fletch?" Q asked, reaching for it.

"Yes, it is. Perhaps the black market sells in bulk!" Fletcher presented it to her.

"Caffar, take the box, won't you?" Maurice asked her.

"What?" Dorian barked. "You all don't want to pull out each tissue and see what they say? If you don't want to do it I will—" *I will disobey Him for us.*

Rosemund shook her finger. "We can blow noses once we understand why He gave us a boxboxbox of tissues. But yes, Caffar will keep it safe."

---

[53] WHEN?!?! HOW?!?! By sending him laced fruit baskets?

"Maybe He thinks we're about to cry? He's warning us?" Mecca asked, his voice quiet as he considered it. *Mother really is gonna kill herself.*

"We should pull them all out now just to spite him," Dorian said, grabbing for the box. But Rosemund snatched it away, cane on his chest.

"Let her take it, Dorian. Just what do you think is in there?" Odissa said—hoping Dorian would obey her and stop moving toward the box. But there were two of him and only one of her:

"I'm happy to find out for you," Fletcher said, reaching over their heads.

"But He said not to—" Odissa caught Dorian's arm.

"Ah! Look at zat." Maurice chuckled. "A Pandora who doesn't want to open the box."

"No, I think there is a Pandora," Odys said, frowning in Dorian's direction.

Fletcher was too slow in grabbing the box as Caffar stuffed it into her stomach, her body shifting to rebalance the new mass inside her.

"We found the source of the smell, can we go now?" Odys asked. "Can't we just admit the Mother-may-be-there thing was just a reason to get us out of the house?"

"It was a reason," a voice said from the center of the studio floor. Their heads whipped behind them. "A good reason."

Stanza: Madus Mouse.

The closed hand of the automaton figure began to twitch. The tape ripped as Madus busted through where he had been inserted. He fell from the hand, knocking her delicate frame to the floor. He stood there, nude, hair in his eyes, so void of proper detail—as if Mother hadn't decided how she wanted him to look. Thus, I won't explain him more. He is merely a concept.

Maud observed her twin brother, because Odys was curious—curious how much his own Automaton might match him. He was different from memory. Maud's memory.

245

"Didn't you smell him, Caffar?" Maud goggled, a betrayed tone in her voice. Caffar had been the one sniffing—sniffing so nearby.

"Didn't you smell him? Didn't you smell? Didn't you?" Caffar repeated, her lips pulling back further with each word like a hiss.

"How could anyone smell anything besides that damn stench in the bathroom?" Madus said, standing straight and breathing in the room. His head was still low, though, as if he didn't want to see everyone for Gwendolyn just yet, hair over his face. A swamp thing birthed without a swamp.

"I won't lie," Rosemund said with a shrug. "I smelled him."

"But, then again, you knew he was there," Maurice sighed.

"You had him this whole time, didn't you?" Odys accused. "You brought him in with us?"

Never mind if she did or not. That's not what matters.

"We chose this setting because it felt right," Madus said, leaning on his knees as if standing took a great effort. He had been away from Gwendolyn for many hours now (hiding) and her stress was doing nothing to conserve their energy. "This place was a compromise with Vulcan. He sets it up, but Gwen still gets to do what she needs to do. She gets to say what she needs to say. We think Vulcan understands the arrangement, otherwise it wouldn't happen. You all know why I am here, I assume?"

"Where are you Gwen?" Dorian asked, as if shouting into a speaker phone. *Can you hear me, Gwen?* "Why aren't you here?"

"Because I didn't need you to interfere with how I plan to make things right, Dori," Mother spoke through Madus. "But I also needed to say goodbye. Before I go on, though, I want to tell you that no, I didn't have Cestus. But I know where he is. Leeland told me before he died. At least, I think he did. And it makes perfect sense. It's what we suspect. He hid him inside *Admund*."

GWENDOLYN: A mother of sorrow.

ANSI: Her anger.

MADUS: Her secrets.

CESTUS: Her betrayal.

Chapter the ninth,

And now they know:

But what do they not know?

"Bastard." Odys cursed, kicking over a chair. Maud hissed under her breath.

Odissa asked, "What does that mean?"

Fletcher whispered to her, "He wanted to insure we touched Admund—where he left his greatest imprint, no doubt!"

"Gwen, you don't have to do this—please," Dorian begged Madus. "We want you to stay. You know how we feel—" *We voted.*

"Where is she, Rose?" Mecca demanded, tears in his eyes. "You know—tell us. Papa, make her tell us!"

But Maurice shook his head. *Hush now.* This wasn't his family to correct. *I cannot control her.* Not anymore. *I never could.*

"Rosemund does not know where I am but she knows enough. She brought you here because she knows I want it. She won't betray me."

"You'll kill her!" Q shouted at Rosemund. "We both know that's not what you really want."

Rosemund could not bear to look at them, avoiding their eyes and questions like small hands plucking at her sleeve. She adjusted the grip on her cane. "You have no idea what I really want, child."

Madus continued in his staticky voice: "By the time you figure out where I am, it will already be too late, Dorian. Please just listen to me. Gwendolyn has sins to confess." A gloss formed over Madus's curtained eyes. Mother was crying, but he would not. That bit would be mumbled in translation. He put a hand on the table to help his shaky limbs stay up. "You pace in place like a mad dog, Fletcher," Madus said. "Hold still. Madus cannot help me think with so much noise."

Fletcher stopped his prowl and latched on to the acknowledgment that Gwendolyn was there, behind Madus's eyes. "Gwen—Gwen, this is madness!"

Madus/Mother ignored him and turned to the others. "You want to know why I stole Madus from Rosie? Because Pepin told me something before he died. He told me his reasons for why he was going to end his life the way he did and said that I should make my own moves accordingly. Pepin told me he had recently found out about Leeland's secret life as a father."

"You knew?" Dorian's head cocked. "You knew all this time—?"

"I knew only days before you did, Dorian. Only days. And even then I was not sure—not as sure as Pepin seemed to be. The fact that they were Dorian's lost twins was not the greatest concern. Not for Pepin. Not for me. See, Pepin knew why Leeland had saved them. It had nothing to do with Dorian. It had nothing to do with me. It had nothing and yet everything to do with all of us—"

"You aren't making sense, Gwen!" Dorian shouted. His voice echoed through the room, breath as ice.

But Madus shook off his words with trembling and collected Mother's thoughts once more—pushing past. "You don't see it because it's covered in ash. Vulcan meant for us to overlook it—buried under the volcano of history. Leeland didn't save the twins because he pitied them or planned to use them against us—no." Madus banged his fist on the table, making the disassembled automata parts jump (Mother was trying to explain and Madus filtered her passionate thoughts into the most coherent form manageable). "Leeland saved them because he knew something about one of them. To understand it you have to go back to the beginning. The very beginning! When Vulcan—that god I no longer trust or care to depend upon—first created the Automatons He also created *The Prototype*. The fact that He let it live— left it for the Masters to handle instead of waving His hand and destroying the thing—makes this, even now, our own burden to bare. He's letting us decide what to do with It."

"It?" Maurice repeated. "My God, Gwen, what are you zaying? Is Alpha—?"

"When that temple girl, so long ago, volunteered to possess Alpha—the original Automata-model created with the equivalent of a soul and free will—she didn't bear The Prototype until death. We may have stripped Alpha down to the barest soul-part, but we did not kill her."[54]

Madus released his fist from the table and ran his fingers along the splintering wood, his actions more and more elegiac. His voice, steady like a monk's mantra, hummed out Mother's explanation: "They had expected the monster to die within the temple girl. At the very least, old age should have taken them. Why wouldn't Alpha die with the host? The host contained the essence of the deconstructed-Alpha." Madus started to round the table but stopped when he crossed the knocked-over automaton, her body like a cadaver's. He studied it as if it caused him to remember something. "Alpha was a furnace—was supposedly defeated and her soul-flame added to another's. The soul is a fire—a spark of life not easily extinguished when made by Vulcan, it seems. Vulcan gave the Automata and Masters the Words—the Alchemy to tie Alpha's flame-soul to another. Those flames burned in the same pit— the same host. That temple girl. They used the Words! But those Words are useless now. The job is done. They can do no more. Those old Words cannot fight this new form. We need new Words."

"What new form, Gwen?" Dorian watched Madus like a math problem written on a whiteboard, needing full space for the solution.

"We thought Alpha had been extinguished when the soul-flame of the temple girl died. They were bound. They were *supposed* to be bound. In most ways they were. But when the temple girl's flame was blown out...the flame of Alpha's *wasn't*."

Maurice smoothed down his frazzled mustache. "Zee girl is dead, Gwen. So is Alpha. Thousands of years have passed. A soul needs a body. A vessel. Hers died. End uv story."

---

[54] "We" as in the old Masters.

"No. The essence of Alpha lived on. Not in the temple girl—of course not in a dead host. You see, flames can light other flames, given the right conditions." Madus waved the air with his hand. "The Buddhists believe that the same energy runs through us all; just as the same candle can light an infinite number of other candles. Alpha got to light another candle before her host died. And those candles lit more. The soul is a flame," Madus reinforced. "Don't you see?"

No, they didn't see. They weren't computing fast enough. Gwendolyn Gwendy, however, was so well rehearsed with the aid of multiple Automatons; their metaphorical gears working to amplify her own. The others couldn't help but be afraid of her unfathomable reasoning.

"We're trying to," Dorian said. "We're trying to see."

Madus leaned forward on the table, shaking with rage and weariness. "The first Masters of the time should never have put Alpha *in a woman*. And Vulcan—that passive traitor and slothful guide!—should have redirected them. Better yet, He could've just killed the monster Himself. Don't we all wonder why He didn't? Instead He lets us believe we had stopped the Alpha. He toys with us! He made us believe we had no purpose left—made us go on and on without knowing His true intent. I know I shouldn't speak for the gods, but His neglect—no, that's not the word. His *relinquishment* has become unbearable. Maybe I could have tolerated this so much more if—if there was so much less of it. You still don't understand me?

"The female priestess bred, Dorian. Her womb gave birth to not only a child, but a sub-flame of Alpha. Alpha was in that child. Maybe part of Alpha even remained in the temple girl to keep her quiet—so that others would not suspect. After all, she was bound to the host. Part of her may have had no choice but to stay in the temple girl. Maybe part of her did die. I don't know. The others let the temple girl live out her secluded life, didn't they? They never knew. The host never suspected. Reincarnating itself over and over into a newborn baby, the Monster's subterranean light never faded out. Never died. The umbilical cord was cut and a new body was given each time to Alpha. Yes, maybe the new hosts only held a slight version of Alpha. Or, maybe it is the full version. Maybe copies like clones—or software. I do not know! But I know some form of Alpha still lives because she was given tinder and kindled. Besides, fire is fire no matter where it lights from."

It all burns the same, doesn't it?

Madus walked the other way around the table, away from their eyes, finding a side of the table that was only his—apart from them. "It had to be females. Only females. Only the female sex, you see, will grow new wombs to create new wombs.[55] It worked for a while, for Alpha. Well enough. Perhaps it was a mere sub-existence, passing through history this way. Perhaps it even became habit, a parasite merely moving onto the next host. It doesn't matter. What does matter, however, is that the woman *had* to breed. In order to create new wombs, the gene pool had to be mixed. But Alpha had no guarantee of getting acceptable genes. Doing this made Alpha run into a genetic *malfunction*. Sterility." Madus paused and lifted his eyes, but did not look at them. A mad scientist reporting his study's findings.

"Infertility was running through the bloodline. It grew harder and harder for Alpha's bodies to become pregnant. Barren wombs make for barren futures, and Alpha's was growing short. Just as Leeland was about to kill off her remaining host—a baby—a child before the age of speech—she spoke to him, begging to preserve her. And in that moment, I theorize, a proposition was made. The girl-child wanted fertility. The Alpha inside the child bargained with Leeland. She could not mend her problem by herself. She no longer had the means or the right tongue to perform the Alchemy she knew. It is also likely she never forgot the Words, really. She needed help to repair her human vessel. You cannot perform such acts on yourself—surgery and the like. Not very well. And if the Automatons who, with the

---

[55] Edited out a speculation or two from Mother about how the temple girl may have tempted her guards, how Alpha's bodies were burned as witches, how she eventually lived with and was birthed into Native American populations.

Vulcan-given knowledge to trap her into human form, could—at the very least!—help her keep expounding her mortal cages, she'd help Leeland in return."

The quiver in Madus's voice already revealed what gains Alpha had promised.

"She promised Leeland me—Gwen—" Madus corrected himself. "Maybe help in his plight. Hell, maybe she's the reason any of us even met. I'm still not sure of the past, but I am sure she could see the future. Alpha knew the Words and the means to see it—see it from the past. Alpha is Alchemy itself, so of course she knew—she knew!" Madus scratched the table with his long nails—nails long like Maud's—like Anselm's. "I think she told Leeland she could be the key to changing my mind. And perhaps she was."

"However," Madus added, "Admund's knowledge proved unable to give Alpha fertility. Alchemy only holds so much power over biological decrees, and even then Vulcan likely promoted her infertility; Vulcan didn't want to drag it out any longer than He already had. And, oh, how long He had let it go! On and on. Finally, He brings us to a close. He draws the beast back in—a beast He had given a very long chain to begin with—a beast He *never* intended on killing."

Madus cupped his face with one hand, focusing on their shadows as if wanting this to be nothing but a cave allegory.

"I believe Leeland barely recognized he had saved something that could awaken and bring us all to our knees. His hate of Automata blinded him. He knew very little of Alpha's potential within human bonds. Who knows what she's capable of? What we do know is that Alpha could make a newborn speak; Alpha let her host's parents die; and, Alpha kept her existence secret for centuries. The threat is certainly there. But how much of one? All this is relevant because Leeland left her here to haunt us. It is my guess that he—he contacted Pepin and told him—or Pepin figured it out. Pepin felt obligated to warn us; to warn us that Vulcan had never intended the Masters to kill her completely. Because of that, Pepin created his plot to save us from *Odissa*."

ADMUND: Knew his Master had saved a monster.

LEELAND: No wonder he allowed Admund to "experiment" on Odissa.

BROKE EVEN: Yes, a deal's a deal.

ADMUND: Adopted a monster, but his Master married one.

Chapter the tenth,

Martyrs:

Can you hear the silence of the saints?

I should tell you they had all been staring at Odissa as Madus faded out his monologue.

"Me?" Odissa breathed, finally sure what their wide eyes meant.

"Hush, child!" Madus raised a finger. He brought that finger down and tucked his hair behind his ear—finally showing his face. "Your own words won't help you understand. You must listen or you will never be free. You will always be trapped and hiding. Listen to me." He pointed to his bare chest. "You see, Odys, the reason you have Maud is because of your sister. Pepin needed a way of testing Alpha. If she ever tried to compile the Automatons under herself, how would we stop her? How could we even test whether or not we *could* stop her?"

"Why would she want to do that?" Fletcher asked—searching for a rope to pull them out of this theoretical hole. "Why would she want all Automatons?"

Mother was starting to sound like a god herself, a puppet master pulling the strings.

Mother pressed herself through Madus, "Why wouldn't she? Why wouldn't she want control over so much power? So much immortality when her own is at stake? The only reason she hasn't come after us for so long is because she cannot hurt us. She is in a mortal body. The Automata protect us. Don't you get it?

"I had observed, at length, her attachment of you, Odys. It was quite obvious Pepin knew Alpha was dormant within her. Perhaps even somewhat subdued by Odissa's own personality. Who knows? It was one of our hopes that if Alpha were ever compelled to take all Automatons and unite them in one body—to do gods-only-know-what—then she wouldn't be able to get them all. We hope—nay, *pray*—she wouldn't be able to kill her own brother. We knew she loved you. We knew she saved you too, Odys. You meant more to her than her parents did. Leeland could control her through you. I'm sure this was Pepin's reasoning."

Madus stared at the table, the odds and ends resting there. "I suspect that there are two 'beings' within her body, and they are most often separated. From what we've observed, Odys, Alpha has even kept your sister in the dark. She is innocent—how could she not be? A part of me even wonders if Alpha hasn't changed over the years—has she become docile, her only desire is to exist? I do not know. I do not know.

"However, I do know it was never our intent for Dorian to fall in love with her. There was never meant to be this much pain—pain in telling the truth. Venus has made our choice hard. Vulcan let Her do this. I blame Him. But I won't let Him have the satisfaction of my choice. I'll curse god and die. I hope you also forgive me, and accept my suggestion."

"Suggestion?" Maurice asked.

"As each one of us dies, let us draw lots and give the inanimate Automatons back to ourselves. A family of Masters has not worked; Leeland's plan was cruel; Pepin's, impossible. This is the next way. Alpha cannot get them if we have them all."

Their candles were dripping too much wax now. Madus observed the position of the sun, remembering the time. Clouds were rolling over the sky. His eyes lowered onto Caffar. Mother remembered the box. "Do not dwell on that damn tissue box. It is just a distraction to get you to think Vulcan wishes to speak with you. But His voice is clear! What He wants we already know. He let her live this long, didn't He? There must be—and is—a way to feel safe with her alive. Indeed, have you yet to feel threatened? Do not touch her. Promise me, now, you will not harm her—" Mother's eyes look through Madus's and pleaded with Maurice.

Why did she beg Maurice?

Yeah, why?

Because "If He means for her to live," Maurice whispered, "why would I obey him?"

"She is Vulcan's sin. Don't let her become ours. Do not touch her. If you do, how can we ever be sure we didn't kill something that had actually lost its bite? We are not like that."

"Yes, we are," Rosemund sighed to herself.

"Why did you keep this from us? Why?" Dorian demanded.

"Because we couldn't scare her off. We couldn't scare Odys off. We had to let her think we were stupid and that she was one of us. And isn't she? Has Odys not earned their places among you?" Madus looked at Odissa, whose eyes were wide, her heart rippling her body like a rabbit's. "Are we not balanced now?"

Odissa couldn't stand his eyes—Madus's eyes pleading for Mother. *Please let this be a standstill.* Odissa noted the others in the room—their fear keeping them from defending her.

"And you will leave us to decide what we should dododo with her when you leave us?" Rosemund said, frown arching against a sob.

"I've told you what to do with her. Let her be as she has been. Vulcan will do whatever He wishes, but we can at least let *Him* make the final decision. We've done enough work. We never should have been her jury. Not when we were to be denied authority anyway."

At this, everyone noticed Dorian had retreated from Odissa. Odissa had barely realized he'd stepped away from her—so consumed with the spotlight, the eyes watching her. He backed into the wall and slid down, covering his face.

Madus observed this for Gwendolyn, and she knew she shouldn't keep them longer. Madus found his strength to release the table. "Maurice, Gwendolyn has found your traveling carnival stage and hitch wagon—the one you drove up to [such and such a town's] border to park before going to Dorian's."

"God, no," Maurice could barely say. "Not in my wagon!"[56]

The French phrases ensuing tried to cut her off in protest but—

"I've written a letter. I'd like you all to read it. And don't dare call it a note. Never a note."[57]

"You don't have to do this, Gwen," Rosemund said softly, though it wasn't begging. She would not beg Gwen. No matter how much she wanted to. She respected her more than that.

"You all may forgive me, but I cannot. I broke the rules," Madus said for her. And then his lips trembled, "And I killed Leeland. I killed him. Was he so wrong that we should kill him?"

Odys was the only one willing to mumble a "Yes." But he said no more when Rosemund glared at him.

"Vulcan makes us do mad things," Rosemund said.

"He will make me mad no more. My Automatons will be safe here until you come. I love the new costumes, Maurice. I'm wearing Captain Hook."

But before Maurice could boil up and shout at her: "DON'T RUIN THE SATIN!" Madus fell to the ground—a penny once more.

Gwendolyn Gwendy had killed herself.

Mecca crawled up in his father's arms and snuggled under his chin but could not ignore the smoke coming from his Papa's ears.

"[Cursing in French]. She always hated me, zat bitch," Maurice said as he cradled his son's head. "She's zee reason Pepin left zee circus, you know—she changed him—converted him! She made him want to leave everyzing we had built and zat is why I wanted to die. Zat is it!" His chest heaved. "She made zee circus seem boring. She made it all so *pointless*. She promised us things. A grand vision. Of secretly helping zee world. Some fucking world zis is!"

---

[56] The newspaper a few weeks before this time announced a local weekend fair. Perhaps Maurice had been interested in attending, though it's no absolute fact he planned on participating. A man with no Automaton has to make a living somehow, no?

[57] Because this wasn't as suicide. It was a sacrifice.

He pointed in the air in Rosemund's face, as if Rosemund were to blame for Mother's previous existence. Rosemund did nothing but frown and run her tongue over her braces.

"And when I did die, zat is when he left, you know! He left all of us to hide. All because of what she started! We were perfect before her. Before that [French word] Leeland fell in love with her. Before zis—zis so-called *family!*"

!!!

"And now she must flaunt her death in my home—zere is nothing she cannot taint! Ah, [more cursing in French]." He slapped the side of the wall with his palm, his stiff hair jumping and landing out of place.

Odys turned to his sister, who was busy staring at the floor. Her direct line of sight was inches from Dorian's feet. Fletcher was watching her like a hawk, his face unreadable and unfazed by Maurice's rant, as if he had muted it.

Rosemund cleared her throat.

Odissa's eyes flicked to Rosemund. "Mother knew about me. So she told you too? You knew this whole time? If not everything, then you knew more than they did. And you're not afraid of me? You've been so calm—so trusting, even." Odissa laughed, as if in some humorous dream-state. Was part of her falling asleep?

Dorian looked up upon hearing that soft laugh, his skin prickling.

She noticed his hesitant acknowledgement and stepped back. "Are you all afraid of me?" She could barely form the question. It caught in her throat.

Odys stepped toward her, putting himself between them and his sister.

"What does this mean?" she asked—asked anyone who would answer.

Her brother could avoid her gaze no longer. "I don't know what this means," he shook his head. "We know what Alpha did. The Automatons remember. She did terrible things."

"So you *are* afraid of me?" She backed away from Odys as he tried to touch her. "You really think that—that thing is inside me? What was she talking about, Odys? What was she saying?"

He did not answer, for it was too obvious.

Tearing her eyes away from Odys, she demanded of Dorian (though very softly), "Can you not love me anymore, because of this?" She shooed her brother away to stand alone by the wall. "You all shuffle your feet rather than answer me! Why won't you say anything?"

"Odissa, please—" Odys begged as she continued to stare at Dorian—Dorian who wouldn't answer her from his spot on the floor.

"Did you not hear what Gwendolyn said, though? She loves me as well! She said not to hurt me—please!" The panic in her voice surprised even her.

"Mother loves all things," Dorian quietly said, speaking his thoughts aloud—though he probably shouldn't have said it. "But that doesn't make them safe, Odissa."

A shadow fell over her. She shook down more tears. She marched over to where Madus slept, inanimate, on the floor, Master-less.

Dorian rose to his feet, the others too—their stance prepared to stop her.

"I could touch it, if I wanted—you all know that! You idiots just let him sit there—vulnerable." She bent down, her fingers inches away from Madus. They warned her not to. "But I could! I could." She started to cry, and took back her outstretched limb. "But I don't."

She begged them to notice her control.

Rosemund limped over to her. Taking her handkerchief, she picked Madus up and folded him within its fabric. The penny flashed like new—as if it had been minted just yesterday. "And you won't," Rosemund said.

She gestured for Q to take Madus, for now at least. Q found an old paint tin full of wooden buttons to place him in. She melted the lid down with her fingers.

Odissa crouched there, weeping, her eyes closed. Rosemund snapped and gestured for Dorian to come to her. She backed away from the couple as Odissa fell into his chest.

He did not touch her or comfort her. He only let her come to him. She noted this but did not let that stop her.

"I know what I am!" she screamed into his chest. "I always knew! But she makes me forget. I forgot. Don't let her take me again—" Her body trembled. Her voice gentler, "No, she won't make me forget this time. It's too late to forget. You all will remind me even if she does make me. She is not cruel or stupid. She did it to protect me."

She felt Dorian clench.

Odys and Maud watched with angry and confused tears in their eyes, their bodies wanting to turn away in agitation.

She pulled away from Dorian. "I—I hate you all. You can't let me around you," she whispered to herself. "It's not safe. I will kill every last one of you."

She said it as if she believed it but desperately didn't want to.

"You won't," Dorian forced himself to say.

"That is my nature. This has been what she wanted all along. She *used* me."

She noticed Dorian's hand tremble—in what could only be interpreted as fear— as he tried to soothe her.

"I'm going to kill you…" The words weren't even words. She was fighting them, silencing them to whispers as they escaped her lips. "That's why Gwen left. She's leaving the gods to Their mistakes."

He pet her hair. "No, you won't."

But Dorian's shaky voice proved he was not so sure.

Odissa could not keep the words down. "She is awake. She knows that I know and she will silence me. She's no longer pretending to sleep. You won't know where

I end and where she begins. I remember now. I remember. I remember my mother, Dorian—I remember you—" She smiled there. But then that smiled faded to fear. "I let her die, Dorian! I let my mother die. My father. So many before them."

"You didn't," Odys said—he could be silent no longer. "You're Odissa. You didn't kill them. You won't hurt us."

"I've seen the future, Odys. I will. The past speaks. I am older than any of you. I know!" she screamed at him.

She put a hand over her mouth, shocked at her volume.

They let the silence take them.

"You are supposed to be here with us." Dorian said—grabbing her face. "Vulcan wants it. The stars aligned for you, Alpha. Vulcan means to use you. Odissa is still in there. You're still Odissa."

"But you hate Vulcan," Maurice said. "Why would you want her to be here if Vulcan wants her to be here?"

"Because Vulcan couldn't control her once. Now He can. Vulcan set all this up so that she would be with us. He hopes to use her. But she might be the key to making His games stop."

"You are only saying zat because you love Odissa."

"Apparently not just her." He pet her hair and Odys's face grew redder. "I'm also in love with *Alpha*."

ODISSA: A Gemini in more ways than one.

FACES: Two.

LIKE: A coin.

COINS: Have two sides.

The Annotated Manuscript: The Pre-Programming: BOOK THREE

Preface,

Freedom from the pursuit of happiness:

Who are the ghosts in our machines?[58]

Dear United States citizens (and all those other peoples the USA has yet to assimilate), I think the Preface's title and subtitle says it all. *Fuck your American Dream.* The more I think on the manifest destiny of this story, the angrier I become.[59]

I guess I'm starting to rant again.

But don't you see? See—look!—the implications of this story. Of what it means if it is true. This is why I don't care if Gabbler believes or not. It hurts worse to know its truth.

The gods planned for colonization—and all other evils. Do you see it now? And Vulcan stood by like the rest of Them and allowed the cancer to spread. He did nothing as the gods made Their deals and bets and plans for this sacred land.

Scratch that.

He did do something. He made Automata. He made them to fit within the *civilized* dream. Made the Automata into futuristic shapes and designs. He knew to play off misfortune. Off of what would come. Off of what would end.

And for what?

I'll tell you what.

---

[58] "I have made you a tester of metals and my people the ore, that you may observe and test their ways. They are all hardened rebels, going about to slander. They are bronze and iron; they all act corruptly. The bellows blow fiercely to burn away the lead with fire, but the refining goes on in vain; the wicked are not purged out. They are called rejected silver, because the LORD has rejected them." —Jeremiah 6:27-30.

[59] Ah, this is why the John Gast painting.

261

For this.

For this story.

He thinks it will show the world His upgraded nature.

And perhaps it will. Perhaps any attempts to smear Him will only fuel His legend. This is His story, after all. I can only tell it because He[60] lets me. And, let's be honest, what else am I going to do with all my time?

I'm still working out *why* He lets me, though. Why me. Why I was chosen.

Part of me (a small part) grudgingly thinks it is His way of atoning.

Of proving all the suffering in the world is for a reason.

But what good is a reason when it's not a good reason?[61]

Vulcan never has good enough reasons. For example: just like this story, there was never a *good* reason He preserved any part of *Alpha*.[62]

Chapter the first,

The rumors of her death were greatly exaggerated:

But does that make them untrue?

Odissa breathed deeply for a while, letting them know she was trying to collect herself—and what she was going to say. "It all makes sense to me, why I did what I did—why I've done what I've done."

"And what've you done?" Maurice asked, popping one eye at her. Though his hands were behind his back he was far from at ease. Q had taken Mecca from him, as if Mecca knew he would be safer in his own arms during a scene like this.

"I don't know! You all look at me as if you know more about me than I do." Her back found a rack of old paint cans. They watched her eyes, moving back and forth over nothing, as if watching something playing before her they couldn't see. "I say I don't know," she eventually said, "but it's only because...I don't know if I know.

---

[60] I'm so sick of catching all the capital Hs. I feel as if I may have missed some. Does Vulcan deserve the capital? I feel less and less inclined. Whenever I catch a lowercase "h," it feels as though our Narrator is slipping in reverence. Probably for a good reason.

[61] When I asked the Narrator why they were suddenly so political, they said, "This story is in the U.S. for a reason."

[62] "He has no time to be anything but a machine. How can he remember well his ignorance...?" —Henry David Thoreau, *Walden.*

It's like Doctor Jekyll and Mr. Hyde—except a Doctor Jekyll that has never been allowed to know Hyde exists. How could he know, if Hyde actually chose to suppress himself, instead of the other way around?"

"Amazing, zee concept of yourself, Odissa," the expression of distrust on Maurice's face screaming.

"I'm really that scary?"

"You tell us, Odissa." Maurice said as if speaking to a caged animal he may or may not let out. "Should we be afraid? Your little outburst just now isn't comforting—threatening to touch Madus."

"Stop it, Maurice," Fletcher said for Dorian. "There is a reason Mother looked at you when she said not to touch her—not to harm her. Isn't there?"

Maurice frowned. "I am not sure why she did that. Not sure at all."

Odissa gasped, hand over her mouth once again. She pointed, some part of her coming to a conclusion. "It's because we'll be last ones. I can see it. I'll still be here when they're gone, and so will you, Maurice." She kept that hand over her mouth, thinking. "Mother knows we'll be alone together. If not me, then Alpha—I can see it. Oh my god, how can I see it? How did I know that?"

"Because you're not stupid, Odissa," Odys tried to calm her from afar. "It just makes sense, that's all." *Hush, now. Don't give them reasons.*

Odissa trembled, rubbing her wrinkled forehead. "Alpha knew it, though. Oh my God she's in here—in me. She's scared." Odissa pulled at her shirt as if it were a skin she could shed.

Maurice turned to Rosemund with a tired groan. "You think she can kill me?"

"Maybe that's what Mother meant. Don't try to get her to kill you, Maurice. Don't do anything stupid."

Maurice's eyes narrowed in thought. *Has my relic been here all along?*

"Don't even think it, Maurice!" Odys shouted. "Don't even think about provoking her! I'll fucking kill Mecca if you do. She bleeds, Maurice. She's not like you. She's not like us. You don't get to play your game with her—you understand?"

Maurice's mustache twitched but he said nothing. Mecca's eyes widened in horror.

Odys put two hands up in apology. *Just listen to me.* "Look at her hand—that scar there!" Odys pointed. "The childhood scrapes and bruises. Those were real. Just look now, at that scar on her shoulder. Show them, Odissa."

Quietly, "Don't make me—"

But he was there, tugging down her collar. "I gave that scar to her. I chased her down the hall when we were five years old. Broke a statue. Blood everywhere." He had come to love that scar. "You don't get to touch her, Maurice."

"You don't get to decide," Maurice laughed. "She gets to. She can try killing me if she wants, boy."

"But you don't get to provoke her," Maud enforced.

"Maybe not her directly..." Maurice laughed, an angry sound.

"You fucking touch Dorian or my brother, and I'll never kill you, Maurice. I'll let you live for fucking ever with your guilt!" As the last word came out of her mouth Odissa slammed her hands on her lips—eyes glazed with shock.

"You think I would kill them?" Maurice shook his head. "No, I only want to kill myself."

"I'm so sorry," she murmured. "I didn't mean to say that. I didn't."

Maurice turned to Odys. "She can defend herself, you see?"

Mecca began to sputter and blubber. He hid his face in Q's thick hair, slobbering all over it. But she didn't mind, for her face was too busy frowning; her arms too busy cradling him. She looked up at Maurice. "He tells me to tell you fuck you. You're only making things worse."

"One death before the next, please," Rosemund said. "Do we go clean Mother up, or what?" She sighed, and looked about her house. Disappointed property owner.

Maurice cleared his throat. "Haven't we had enough for one day? The dead stay dead. And in this weather, the body will keep. Let's have lunch first. We can't think straight on empty bellies."

Or, at least, Maurice couldn't.

"So we'll just leave the Automatons for anyone to find?" Odys objected.

"Do you think Mother would be so careless? She knew what she was doing. Just look at *zis* elaborate ending. And still," he added with a look at Odissa—still cautious, "the show goes on."

"Can you give us a minute, all of you?" Dorian asked, as politely as he could through his stern-stoic face.

Their eyes searched Fletcher's face for why. Was it safe, really, to do that anymore? They weren't so sure. Even Odissa glanced about.

"Go out to the car. Warm it up or something. Go, fuck you! Go."

A wrinkle came over Odys's face as they trickled out. His jaw clenched and threatened to break his teeth.

They may have left the room, but they hovered in the hallway, leaving the door open.

Dorian was just glad they obeyed him.

Odissa put more distance between them.

Dorian felt her move away and took a step toward her. "I saw you realize it—like a dream you forgot you once had. Does it fade in and out, then? Are you even conscious of it?"

"Fuck, Dorian," she sniffed, "'Does it fade in and out?'" she laughed at that. "Ask a person with multiple personality disorder that same question. Their answer will be mine. Stop—just stop asking me questions as if I completely understand them! You sound like *Leeland*." She hissed the name.

"I do?"

"Asking me questions—questions that confuse me! I remember them now. Not all of them, because she made me forget, but I remember how they made me feel. *This* feeling. Fuck." She gestured up and down, wriggling in her skin. "She comes out and she makes me forget. But she's not making me forget this time. Gwen drew her out. There's no point in hiding anymore." She took a breath, hugging herself. She realized she was rambling. "Fuck, for a moment there I thought you were going to kill me—*you*, Dorian! You. I thought you were going to—to let it be done. You're supposed to love me."

"I love you enough to let you die if it's not you in there anymore, Odissa. You should have seen your face. How it contorted—"

Fletcher put his hands in his 'pockets' as he watched them. "You looked scary as hell—telling us you were going to kill us."

"But you just said you loved Alpha, too—"

"I do. But I don't know if it's kind to let her live. I think Vulcan is using her. And Vulcan may be using me to hurt her. I can't let that happen. I don't know what's going on yet."

"Then kill your fucking self—not me!" *Some love this is.*

"You think I don't know that's the better option, Odissa?!" he shouted at her. "I am sorry I got confused. You try being under a love spell and tell me if you always have the most reasonable reaction to things!"

He thought his nose was runny but no. It was bleeding again—bleeding at the thought of a life without her—of a life for her without him. Either way, the thought was crippling.

"That's blood," she said.

"Fuck—Fletcher, help me."

But Fletcher was already looking about for something to dab Dorian's nose. Odissa offered her scarf. "Caffar has all the damn tissues," Fletcher grumbled.

As he dabbed his nose he asked her, "You remember Dory?"

She put her hands through her hair, squeezing her head as if it might explode. "I have two memories inside—inside me. Sometimes I let myself see it and sometimes

I don't. The memory of her isn't really Odissa's—I mean, mine. It's Alpha's memory of her. It's my own mother's memory."

His spine stiffened. *She doesn't even know which one she is. Maybe there is no difference.* "You remember talking to Leeland? As a baby?"

"No. I don't. She won't let me see it."

"Are you lying?"

"I don't know, Dorian!" she shouted at him. She covered her ears. "Why are you even asking?"

"Maybe you want to confuse us, to protect yourself. And that's OK. The more confused you seem, the more innocent as well. Because you have sinned, haven't you? You've been hiding. That doesn't make you seem safe." He paused, tossing her scarf away. "I won't let them hurt you."

"I think that's what Alpha wants. But me too; I won't let me hurt you. That's the one thing I know. I want to be here. With you."

Stanza: The Automaton with no soul and a soul with no Automaton.

There has never been a car ride so quiet.

Upon finally reaching an acceptable town (to find acceptable food), Dorian could stand the silence no longer. "Rosie, why did you even go along with this? Why would you let Gwen?" He stuffed his hands deep into his coat pockets to squeeze Fletcher. He was chewing on his gum so forcefully—his cheeks rippling—they thought his jaw might break.

Rosemund shifted in her seat, moving away from the question.

Odys was busy watching his sister from the corner of his eye. He was pretending to look out the far window beside Mecca. But he wasn't really. His sister was staring at her lap. Her arms crossed. Her eyelids were so downcast that they might as well be closed.

Finally, Maurice cleared his throat. He looked at Rosemund and then in the rearview mirror back at them. He was going to answer Dorian's question for her.

Rosemund turned her face to the window so she could brush away those tears under her glasses before they ran down her scars. Mecca, though a little less restless than normal in his seat, saw Rosemund's face blush—almost matching that red hair. He awaited her answer, same as the rest of them. She pulled her coat around her more tightly, though she did not button it. The action wasn't for warmth, it was for comfort—to brace herself for what Maurice was about to admit for her.

"Sometimes your time comes," Maurice said over his shoulder. "You can't deny that of a person."

Dorian shouted, "How was it your decision to make, Rose? How? How was it even Gwen's?"

Mecca started to blubber again, putting his face in his knees. He wanted Q to hold him but settled on Odys patting his back.

"Jesus, shut up, Mecca!" Dorian barked, hitting the back of his seat. "You never cry—why the fuck are you crying? Si no quieres que esto suceda, then maybe you shouldn't have brought your damn zombie, dumbass. Bringing him here progressed everything. Everything!"

Mecca gave him the finger and continued to sniffle into himself. He hated this family.

In Spanish, "You'd think he'd be more mature by now but no. Q must have slowed down the part of his brain that makes him not be such a fucking crybaby. We don't need your tears."

"Don't talk to him like that!" Odissa snapped.

The van fell silent.

Maurice sped up. Eyes in that rearview mirror. To Odys, "She knows Spanish does she?"

Odys's eyes were wide when he answered. "Yes." But he was starting to realize that maybe it was not because she had ever studied it in school.

Dorian's face contorted. He threw back his head and wept tears worse than Mecca.

Stanza: They stopped at the first open restaurant.

"Apparently the weather has kept some from caring to open," Maurice said as they drove through the most populated street yet. He pulled into a Ma & Pa's diner. The run-down architecture tried to resemble a saloon.

"It's just winter. These people obviously have never been north this time of year," Q stated as she sprang up from her inanimate form.

They were the only car in the front lot.

They sat themselves, as no host came out to greet this Donner Party. Even pulled a few tables together.

It took a while for someone to come out from the back. They could hear a television humming behind double-hinged swinging doors (they went along with the western theme). They were a bit late for the lunch specials, so the dinner menu is what they looked at.

After placing their orders, Maud looked about, scowling.

All the place was missing was a buffalo head on the wall.

Oh, wait, there *was* a boar head.

It might have been nice, forty years ago, this place. But now it was just scary. And everyone was afraid of what their food might look like when they finally got it.

Rosemund dug through her hair and pulled out a pen.

"Had she a beard, she'd hide things in that too," Maurice said to no one in particular.

It gained a few obligated smiles.

Rosemund started working out a math formula she had just solved in her brain, making sure the solution was true as if solutions mattered still. No one was much for talking.

Soon enough, the waitress brought the dishes out. Just as she was picking up her foldable serving-table and setting the check by Maurice (he was the 'oldest' gentleman at the table), she commented, "Oh, I swear to God. We get no peace in this town any more. Not only do the hobos drop in for free food, but the cold can't even get rid of them damn Bible thumpers."

She nodded outside the window and walked away, heaviness about her step.

"Never mind, I like this place," Odys said to no one particular. Everyone else was too busy staring out the window.

It took everyone a few seconds to zoom in on the old man at the corner stoplight, standing in the snow, shouting at the slow-moving cars. The cold silence made his voice more audible. Fletcher had to grab Mecca's food-shoveling hand to get him to stop his fork-clatter, so they might better hear.

The old man, still agile in the cold, was reading from a very worn, leather-bound Bible. He would have been a cute old man, all warmly dressed, had there not been such a righteous forcefulness in his stance under that wearable banner.

And in his voice.

"HE MADE THE SEA OF CAST METAL, CIRCULAR IN SHAPE..."

Then the cars were allowed to go, drowning him out. But he kept on shouting. "THE SEA STOOD ON TWELVE BULLS...LIKE THE RIM OF A CUP...HE ALSO MADE TEN MOVABLE STANDS OF BRONZE...ON THE PANELS...LIONS, BULLS AND CHERUBIM...WERE WREATHS OF HAMMERED WORK. EACH STAND HAD FOUR BRONZE WHEELS WITH BRONZE AXLES..."

"You think it's Him?" Q asked them. "My nose is so full of ash from the house I can't tell—can't smell."

"Maybe, maybe not," Rosemund answered, pushing up her glasses to better see far away.

"Him who?" Odissa asked.

They tore their narrow eyes from the palmer to look at her skeptically. *Did she really not know?*

Maurice nodded back to the street preacher, "Hard to say what is and isn't Vulcan. Some might say *everything* is potentially Vulcan. Connected."

"What's he saying?" Odys tried to read the man's lips, urging Maud's better ears to tune in.

Dorian, who was adapt more to hearing than seeing, said, "Old Testament. He's no evangelical, despite that Bible he's waving around."

Fletcher clarified, "First Kings, Chapter seven." Then, as if translating from a silent movie, reading the lips, just seconds off: "'...all cast in metals. Each stand had four handles one in each corner, projecting from the stand. At the top of the stand there was a circular band half a...'"

"He's skipping ahead. Your words don't match," Mecca pointed out.

"He knows we're paying attention to him," Q added, looking away as if caught.

"He's looking at us..." Maud began to eat her potato.

And then the old man closed his Bible, tucked it under his arms, and walked away. The spitting snow eventually clouded his figure.

"He's not even going to say hi?" Rosemund said. "It must not be Him."

Maurice nodded. "Just like we have our postmen, Vulcan, too, can have a message delivered. He's there, though, even if it's not Him, He's looking through his eyes. Telling us He's watching. A warning."

"Gods shouldn't walk. Feet are what mortals use," Mecca judged.

"Feet aren't a curse. Not having feet, however, would be one," Maurice said to his son—trying to put a smile back on his lips.

They ate their food in relative silence. No, actually, *complete* silence. Not another word was said until Maurice left a couple hundred-dollar bills on the table and told them to take a restroom break if they needed it. No one else did, for they all wanted to leave before the old lady realized so much money had been left for her.

Close early, Grandma, everywhere else has.

271

However, just as they walked out the door, they were not met by cold air, cold snow, cold sleet. No. They weren't even outside. They were in Maurice's trailer-wagon traveling-show. And the door had just slammed behind Maurice, last one out.

…Or should I say *in?*

Stanza: Young Adult Lit and Ancient Adult Lit.

It was only a matter of seconds before they realized what had happened and willingly accepted their new surroundings—pressed against each other as if a cook just scrapped them into a canning jar. "At least Vulcan saved us on gas," Maurice said as he squeezed past everyone to hunt for the dead body.

He knew his way about the cramped space. They saw him halt. There it was, behind the curtain.

"Yes," Fletcher said, walking up toward the body (as everyone was, circling around it), "but it doesn't help that we don't have a car now. And it's so cold I don't want to walk around for another one." He sniffed. From the cold. From the sight.

Mecca and Q exchanged excited looks (despite their sadness). *New Car Time* was what they had gotten out of that. The mere thought of thievery could lighten any wake.

Pushing past a rack of undressed puppets in the wagon, Odys saw out the window into the vacant parking lot covered in ice. The pointed flag-garland, draped along haphazardly, smacked against the wagon. The colors and the ice reminded Odys of the frost carnival in Virginia Woolf's *Orlando*—when the ice breaks and the sheet-slabs float off with the tents and the people and into a cold, cold void. *Swept out to sea*, he thought. And then he thought that line perfectly summed up this current experience. He wasn't sure why. It was Pepin who'd read the work, not him. Maud was only letting him draw upon it. He didn't understand—not in his distracted state—that what little was left of Pepin had come out at the sight of this place, this setting.

But also and…it was the woman, there—in the center of this ice—who had killed herself. The authoress of *Orlando* had killed herself as well. Other than that, the reference didn't fit. But that's what Pepin would have thought, nevertheless.

Mother's body was slouched in an armless chair next to a rack of costumes and a disgruntled polka set. The white ruffles of her costume were splattered with red blood. From one hand, the fingertips reached to the ground to a plastic hook that had once covered them.

In the hand in her lap, well, little mirror-Anselm could just be seen.

Maurice gently lifted the paper from under her hand, sliding Anselm off with grace. He unfolded the yellow Big Chief Tablet paper (where did she find that old parchment, or had she had it for a while, inside Anselm like a desk?). "What iz zis? A novel?"

Yes, you're in one, but no. Mother only wrote about six pages.

"Read it," Dorian said, his voice faint.

"No." Maurice shook his head, mustache stiff. He was a bit too angry with Gwen to care about her final message. "Fletcher, here."

Fletcher cleared his throat, clearing out his own sadness to vociferate the dead's last words.

"*[The following footnote contains the beginning of the letter. It was cut because it made Mother seem like too much of a fangirl, but the Narrator insisted on keeping it in because "They have the right to know where Mecca gets it from." Personally, I think the Narrator just wanted a reason to mention Lord of the Rings YET AGAIN:[63]].*"

---

[63] "*'I was recently having Ansi re-read aloud all my favorite books to me one last time. He would recite them to me. I made him memorize so many, but they start to blur after an age—like rust blurs a metal's shine. But he did his best. I noticed new things this time around. The Lord of the Rings series came up in our selection. I remember reading them to Mecca. Tell little Mecca he will always be my baby. Tell him that. LOTR was our thing. Our book. But I came to the Tom Bombadil portion this time and... This is going to sound so stupid, but it will help you understand my anger. Remember how the Tom Bombadil portion was cut from the movies—because no one seems to like it? Well, I found a new respect for Tolkien's creating it. Tom represents all the outward forces at work—or, shall I say, NOT at work. Tom is a*

He turned the paper over.

"'*But to my real point: I have been reading. And in my reading, I noticed there are three stages of immortality—of never growing old, that sort of thing. We've been reading a lot lately—rereading before I do this. Books—the written word—have been the only thing to never change since the beginning of Automata. All other story forms have. And so many stories are like ours—with immortal characters. I'm*

---

representation of those beings and natures who can interact with us; who can—if they willed—help or hinder us but simply do nothing. They just are.

"'Some might say that's what has become of the gods themselves—of God.' And that's big G 'God'"—Fletcher clarified—"'Nevertheless, the Tom portion was important in and of itself because it showed that, yes, there was an epic good vs. evil battle going on apart from him—but there also was/is a portion of the universe that doesn't get involved. Many of the elves are even like that, yes, but none of them quite have the capacity, you see, of what Tom COULD do. HE essentially could control the ring. It didn't control him. He didn't disappear.'"

Fletcher looked up at that point and asked them. "Is she *seriously* ranting about *The Lord of the Rings*? Is that all this is?" He skimmed the paper quickly.

"You know she went with Mecca to every premiere," Q said, as if it were a defense. Mecca's eyes were red and watery, remembering. She bounced him like a baby.

Maurice scoffed. "Of course she loved such *immature* zings. Putting them into my son's head! And yet she blames me for—for—"

"Says the man with a *Peter Pan* wardrobe?" Odys mumbled, actually finding the written lecture interesting and wanting to get on with it.

"Which she ruined, by zee way!"

Dorian put a hand on his hip. "She's writing her last words and *this* is what she chooses as a topic, though? A thesis on *The Lord of the Rings*?"

Her *thing* with Mecca.

"Keep reading," Rosemund ordered. "There is a point to it, I'm sure."

"'Also, you might say the Shire was just as ambivalent. It was apart from any side-taking. It never really went good or evil, though it was, later, taken over against its will. It shows that some things are never really good or evil, at least. But this is no tirade against Jackson, God bless him, he did such a good job... No, this is about Tom Bombadil, and the relevance of the Toms in our lives today. They're all around us, aren't they? So jolly and happy—how can they be? How *dare* they be? ...Yet, how can they not be? They do not worry for their lives. If they lose a friend, they can always make more. We mortals are infinite...

"'This is not to say that the Toms are evil or heartless and should be overthrown. But we cannot rely on them. They make our lives no easier or worse. We know a Tom in our own lives. He is Vulcan. He's the biggest Tom of all, especially since we know he exists and yet hides his face so often. He could solve our problems so easily. That, or make them a bit lighter. Yet, the Toms just stand there and watch—watch as we have to take matters into our own hands.'"

remembering my bookshelves now. I've landed on my three favorite examples of immortals: Peter Pan, Dorian Gray, and Orlando.'"

Odys stiffened, looking at his shoes. No one noticed him. Slowly, he realized Mother and Pepin had talked about *Orlando* in the past. That's why this was so familiar. *Pepin had read it because of Mother.* Maud remembered.

Odys clutched his chest, knowing that moment was over and it wasn't his. *Stop making me mourn over this woman, Pepin J. Pound.*

PEPIN: The ghost in the machine.

BOOK: *Orlando.*

THOUGHT: The Victorian age was the life and death of the novel, really.

THUS: Didn't really like *Lord of the Rings* and didn't understand when Gwen would call it "A classic!"

Chapter the second,

Childish allusions:

Reverting back to innocence?[64]

"I don't like zis weird book club," Maurice growled, leaning against the door to the overstuffed closet. Like Pepin, he had never approved of Gwen's taste in literature. Usually a bit too fantastical and childish for his liking. Made his son all the harder to tone down and understand. A bad influence!

Maurice, you see, did not understand this story is about story—from poetry to prose—from fiction to metafiction. Just as our Automata stood on the shoulder-myth of Talos, Vulcan's next creation must stand on the shoulders of giants too. Maurice did not understand, you see, that Vulcan wanted to assimilate these Gwen-mentioned books into his own mythos (no matter how awkwardly they fit); that Vulcan had

---

[64] "Are we so made that we have to take death in small doses daily or we could not go on with the businesses of living?" —Virginia Woolf, *Orlando.*

275

inspired Gwen to re-read and write; that Vulcan wanted to stand (as he often needed help to do) on literary merit.[65]

"'*Funny—isn't it?—how the three types of immortality relate so well to our own stages—to our own family. My age was of Peter Pan, childish hopes—all Lost Boys finding each other—so much unknown. Dorian, well, Dorian came into this family with a Dorian Gray approach. He ushered in a new era for us—and maybe Bob, too. We added decorum to our Neverland. But now...we have all awakened into Orlando's world—so subjective and melancholy. Also, so ambiguous—its every page. Breaking down those definite roles...This age will never be as great as the first. Nothing will. It's the postmodern dilemma, isn't it? What more is there to do after the introspection? After all these approaches to immortality have been tried? I cannot fathom.*' Signed, '*Gwendolyn Gwendy.*'"

"That's it? That's all she said?" Dorian asked. "All she talked about were books?" *And Mecca.*

"I suppose someone should comment on the fact she's in Hook's costume?" Odissa suggested after a silence, as if trying to show respect. "Like how Mr. Darling was always played by the same actor as Hook's? But genderbent."

"Let the subtext lie where it is." Dorian's words rolled his covered eyes for him. "We're all smart enough to get it."[66]

Fletcher handed the paper to an expectant Rosemund, who ran her long-nailed fingers over the words while he found something to put Anselm into. It was as if Rosemund thought she might feel something her eyes could not see in the lines. Then, when satisfied, she folded the essay for Caffar to tuck away in her deepest "pocket." Rosemund adjusted her owlish glasses, the equivalent of wiping a tear away and began rummaging through her coat.

Dorian went on, "We all get that Vulcan wants to set the same ambience as those stories. Jesus Christ. We get it."

---

[65] Vulcan seems to have a thing for fantasy literature, then?

[66] But we just wanted to be sure.

"Not stories, you fools. Novels. Not all stories are novels." Rosemund put on her gloves and walked over to Gwendolyn's body.

"But *Peter Pan* is also a play," Odissa whispered, as if maybe they shouldn't be so sure in their interpretation.

"A play still written down. Novelized." Rosemund's hand hovered toward Gwen's hand. She lifted it so that Ansi might land into her gloved palm. Her scarred lips trembled as she said, "Gwen wants us tototo keep Automatons 'in the family.' If we agree to keeping them in the family, then I want *Anselm*."

ANSELM: Wanted.

WHY?: Because he knows.

WHAT?: Mother's secrets.

WHICH ARE?: Secrets Rosemund longs to know.

Chapter the third,

The shoulders of more than just Talos:

Who else came before The Nine?

Rosemund folded her gloved fingers over Anselm, looking over her shoulder. She watched them struggle for a response.

Odys looked out the window once more—at the ice. Wished it would crack beneath them. "Though I am fine with it, I want us to have a sit-down about the *implications* of multiple-Automaton keeping," Odys said, his tone hopeful—hopeful that he was not the only one with a voice of reason. "Outline the rules. Maybe not make them breakable them this time."

Q nodded, "It makes Mecca uncomfortable."

"We can come to some *agreements* when we get to the house," Fletcher said. "However that [getting to the house] might be." He half-uncrossed his tense arms to peek through the thin curtains covering the tiny windows. "The lot is pretty barren." Therefore, no nearby cars to break into, let alone drive off with.

"We could always call a cab," Odissa said. Up until this point, she had kept to the back, so as not to scare them by standing near an inanimate Automaton. Something told her that if they hadn't been magically transported here, she would have been asked to stay in the car.

Before they could decide, the door to the trailer opened.

"If you'd like, I can arrange for a cab to pick you up once you're done with your appointment. Vulcan will see you now."

The beautiful secretary—?—had nothing more to add. Merely stepped aside, motioned for them to go through the next portal-door (to gods-only-know-where), smiled gracefully, and stared at them.

The silvery-gold alloy of skin and hair made her more *metallic* than our known Automatons. Her gestures and body were stiffer too; her Barbie-doll hair had little movement. Everyone exchanged a "look." *This female is no Automaton-Automaton, correct? Correct. Nothing but one of Vulcan's wind-up toys. A puppet. A projection. Not real.* They all seemed content with their conclusion and decided to move on to more important matters: if they walked through that cursed door again, what was likely to happen?

"Haven't we dealt with enough, for one day?" Rosemund sighed, gesturing to the dead body. "Who is going tototo clean this up, if not us?"

The unblinking secretary—for what else could she be, really?—waited for them to proceed. "Don't worry about all that. Vulcan's got it covered. I've already made some calls."

As they gave one more glance at Gwen's body, they weren't surprised that it wasn't there anymore. "My fucking Hook costume!" Maurice cursed under his breath. "Wasted!"

His eyebrows and mustache twitch-flicked at the automata girl like bull horns.

"Speak *friend* and enter here, am I right?" the secretary said as they stepped closer. "You know, because of the whole *Lord of the Rings* thing."

"More like speak of the devil," Odys mumbled.

Looking through the doorway, what should have been a vacant parking lot covered with snow was now a long, brightly-lit hallway with many doors and "office" sounds echoing off the whiteness.

Maurice, first to try anything dangerous, stepped forward. When the secretary closed the door behind them, they paused—it was no frail trailer door, but a vault-esque contraption needing no further description.

They were there for business, all right.

"Doesn't seem like where a blacksmith would work," Odys commented to himself, though the secretary heard. *More like the light at the end of the tunnel.*

She held her clipboard closer to her prominently-boobed chest and smiled wider with her metallic teeth. "Vulcan Manufacturing needs its headquarters, and this is where all branches report to."

"I'm sure," Odys smiled, waiting for someone else to go first as they followed.

"If I cancel my appointment, *mademoiselle*, will there be a fee?"

"Yes, Maurice." She nodded once. She stopped walking, her heals clicking together. "But it will not be death, if that's what you're hoping for. I've also been told to inform you all that this"—she spun her pen around— "isn't real. It is a joke. Please laugh."

They all forced a "Ha."

"When you see Mr. Vulcan, sillies."

They glowered.

The hall seemed to darken as they went along (which was steadily) and they no longer had to squint. The effervescent whiteness evened out into a Wall Street-CEO-skyscraper floor.

Fancy.

An assorted and expensive collection of oil paintings lined the walls, depicting Homeric scenes framed in gold—all exhibiting Vulcan or Hephaestus (same thing, really). The sounds of their shoes bounced down the hall until they reached the very-end door, bordered by two golden, Doric pillars.

When they stopped, madam-robot-secretary stopped as well. "Please go in, He is waiting for you."

Maurice did the honors. Besides, he had a bone to pick with Vulcan. He was building up courage—courage to say things like, "Why the hell am I still alive?" and "Why the fuck did you give us a box of tissues?"

But the office lights weren't on. Though the huge windows let in enough of the sunshine and a spectacular (but probably unreal) view of New York City, the office seemed empty…

Until the chair swiveled and Vulcan showed Himself.

Maurice's objective thus hindered, he rolled his eyes and said, "A little cliché, no? A swivel chair!"

"Admit it," Vulcan said, lighting a cigar, "you'd do it too, just for fun. And isn't it fun, though? All this?" He waved His thick hand around, gesturing as the lights came on. His fingers had gold rings matching the fancy black suit's gold cufflinks. He looked more like an Italian gangster than a CEO. "And look at that, over there," He pointed, "I even included a miniature-scaled model of my home volcano, back in—"

"Er, that's nice, Vulcan," Fletcher said, moseying over to the window to look down, "but we're not in the mood to play along. You know, what with the whole Gwen suicide and everything. Just stick to the fat-cat routine and get to business." The height gave him vertigo, so he moved back.

Vulcan chuckled. "Business, right. I do understand. You're all in a rush to get on with your lives; I was just hoping you'd appreciate how much effort I put into all of this."

"Are we drugged?" Maurice asked, curious, "I don't think He's ever created an entire scene for us—just a *persona*."

Q shook her head. "He's never been a whole building before."

"Does that mean we're inside Him?" Maud swallowed back a little something in her throat.

"You're right, I don't think He's gone to so much trouble," Dorian agreed, trying to remember, running past scenarios through his weary brain.

"Finally, you notice," Vulcan mumbled, "I pulled a few strings, trying new things, testing new options. In the old days, I would've made this a forge at the base of a mountain. Or a cave. But modern times call for modern measures. The sex-machine secretary took me a while to perfect. I'm very particular about my smiles. Hers is just the right amount of teeth. She's beautiful, isn't she? She got you to follow her without a fight so at least that worked. Anyway, you're here today because I have a few announcements to make."

"At least we know we're here for a real reason," Odys said. Only Maud heard him.

Though Vulcan needed no ears to hear it, He made no effort to defend Himself. (After all, the very idea that a god needed to justify himself would lessen the potency of said god).[67]

"First, let me offer my sincerest condolences for the loss of your Mother." (There wasn't an ounce of sincerity to His tone). "I'll miss how she said my name. Sounds so great in Spanish: *Hefesto*. Granted, my name sounds great in any language. Not that it's spoken it in a sentence worth listening to half the time..." He noticed He was losing them. "But, if you want to make a martyr of someone, make it Bob, not Mother. She died for the woman who's failed to protect you from me. You never needed protection from *me*."

He put His thick hands together.

---

[67] But isn't this whole novel just another defense on your supposed godhood, B.L.A.? Kind of hypocritical.

"Now, let's start with the biggest elephant in the room, no? Alpha. Ah, yes, Odissa, so quiet. Trying to blend in. I see you, there, so good at being overlooked. Hell, I'd even go so far as to confess the fact *they* don't want me to notice you. On the other hand, they don't want to be punished *for* the very act of letting you live. They were supposed to kill you once. But they didn't. It's such confliction that makes this topic necessary to address."

"Are you talking to us or to yourself?" Fletcher asked. Rhetorically of course, because he didn't expect an answer.

Vulcan put out His cigar. He was too busy talking anyway.

Dorian, however, did not take a rhetorical route. "Why didn't you tell us, all these years? Why didn't you tell us that Alpha was alive and well—that the past Masters hadn't succeeded?"

And why did you set him up to fall in love with it?!

Vulcan shrugged. "I knew you'd figure it out."

Their faces scoffed.

"Oh, come now," Vulcan went on. "Have a little faith in me. No wonder I still let the Automatons hang around in human hands. You think I'd let something live without a purpose? Sure, the Automatons put a stop to Alpha's rampage back in the day, but what kind of a life would that be, without a little bit of purpose left to fulfill?"

He gave them the measurement of purpose with finger and thumb.

"So you're admitting zat you never intended Alpha to be destroyed?" Maurice asked, a little upset by that answer.

"But she *was* destroyed—dead. Dead like ghosts are dead. You can't kill ghosts."

"So you *would* rather evil exist zan to completely destroy it?"

"Indeed," Odissa said, walking over to the model of the (now) bubbling volcano. "Why not destroy Alpha and let the Automatons find their own purpose? Why not let them struggle like real humans, trying to figure life out? Oh…wait, I know why. It's because they aren't humans. They have no freedom. They are just…*things.*"

Something wicked rang in her tone. It made the others squirm. They didn't know whether to applaud or fear her.

Vulcan didn't let them decide. "Because, believe it or not, it's not so easy to kill your own children."

Odissa laughed. But it was a confused laugh—one which sounded her opposition. "No, it's not easy to kill your own children I suppose. But I wouldn't know, right?"

"Who am I talking to, Odissa or Alpha?" Vulcan chuckled. "So hard to tell sometimes, isn't it?" He eyed them all with a curious gaze.

Odissa didn't answer Him. "It's not easy to kill your children, I suppose, but it does seem easy to have your other *children* try it—to banish her like Ishmael. As if illegitimate."

"Just because Ishmael was forged with a different method-mother doesn't mean he-she was less of a son-daughter."[68]

Odissa and Vulcan locked eyes.

Odissa crossed her arms. "Who's to blame, then, for not making Ishmael the son of Sarah? The child must suffer the Father's mistake?"

Vulcan didn't waste time in taking a breath, "Just because someone is exiled doesn't mean their heart must be hardened."

Odys saw a bitterness shadow his sister's face. Or, maybe it was Alpha's face. He couldn't say who owned that face now—in that second.

"You think my heart hardened, *Father?*"

"In some ways. In others, it softened."

"So you give no direct answer? You don't want them to know?" Odissa frowned, nodding. "Being human and mortal can make life more precious, is that it? She may no longer wish to do her half-siblings harm?"

"Yes, yes. Anything is possible."

---

[68] So many Biblical allusions in this one—my!

"So you're saying she's...different now?" Dorian asked, hopeful. "She's not the same Alpha?"

"Every day we change, Dorian. Even tomorrow Alpha will be different. Even I have changed, no? You shed skin cells. You grow new hair. You learn new things."

"Won't you at least tell us if we can really trust her?" Fletcher stuck his hands in his pits.

"Oh, yes, you can trust her. You can do anything you like. But, yes, I would go with trusting her. It fits with my agenda, see. Granted, I gave her the ability to make her own decisions—which, I emphasize, is also part of being a good crafter. I gave that gift to you Automata too, but only in a different way. You have freedom through your Masters. I never have to be disappointed in you that way..."

"Can't you take the Alpha out of her, to make sure?" Q asked, because Mecca wasn't saying much these days.

Vulcan and Odissa both laughed, which made it clear enough.

Odissa covered her mouth in fear of her own sounds. *Why was that funny?*

"Dear Mecca," Vulcan soothed him, "Don't you remember Alpha's form? That form your predecessors reduced her to, by my instruction? I told them how to strip her down, taught them the way to sedate her before she could repair herself. Taught it to Admund who taught it to the others. Innate knowledge. I also told them how to place her volatile form, mercurial in its fundamental state—like the primordial soup from which sprang—"

But He laughed, cutting Himself off. He couldn't do it anymore, the repetitive speech. "You've heard this before. In sum, Alpha clung to the woman's life force. Perhaps, you might say, she even killed part of it so that she might live. Like mistletoe sucking from the branches of trees."

"But mistletoe can be cut off," Dorian reminded.

"Yes. But at what cost? Alpha is like cancer. One that spreads and can move. *Mercurial*, I just said. Weren't you listening? Now, the world functions in a certain way, and, though it would be a miracle for me to—as you might call it—'cure' Odissa of Alpha, I think I'll spare Odissa the woe of losing herself—or, part of herself. She was born with Alpha. She's come to like Alpha, believe it or not. Just as much as Alpha likes her. Alpha was made with a soul—the equivalent of one. We put the tangible form of that soul into Odissa's family line.

"Now, Alpha may have a choice of whether or not to be good, but you bunch also have a choice—a choice Gwen left up to you. What will *you* do with the choices she makes—that each of you make?"

"Are you saying there's redemption for evil, then?" Dorian asked, unsure if he should phrase is that way.

"Oh, heavens no. I'm not saying that. I can't say things like that. Not when Everyone's listening. You have to let *them* make the choice. After all, if evil eventually chooses good…they aren't really 'evil' then, right?"

Maybe.[69]/[70]

"Mecca, is that a good enough answer?"

Mecca shrugged and frowned. The most he could muster.

"Now, back to my box of tissues." *Were tissues ever mentioned?* "My box of tissues is particularly important for why I've gathered you here. Caffar," Vulcan tapped at the empty space on His desk. "The box, please."

Caffar, walking over to Vulcan, made herself look like His golden secretary— just shades off. Opening the recently-formed knob to the door in her stomach, she pulled out the box of tissues.

"Nice touch," Vulcan nodded, aligning the edges of the box to His desk.

"Nice touch," Caffar repeated, turning back to her regular shape.

Vulcan cleared His throat. "Though your dear Mother cared little for how I plan to—quote end quote—make things right, I hope you show a little more respect for

---

[69] Judas was uncomfortably close to Jesus, though.
[70] But, then again, there's no Jesus figure in this story, is there? Is there?

my things, in the future. A wasted tissue not only hurts the environment but is just plain rude." He stuffed the fanned paper back down into the box.

He was pleased at how guilty they all looked.

"Please, have a seat."

CEO-Vulcan gestured to the chairs that magically formed behind them, knocking them off their feet and scooting them closer to the desk.

"You look great, Rosie, stop trying to look into that mirror"—Rosemund was making sure her hair wasn't too wind-blown from the chair ride over—"You're the best-looking Sapphic I know. Now. My box of tissues, you see, seems very normal. And that's actually because it is."

Fletcher said, "Toilet paper would be more our style, actually."

Vulcan narrowed His eyes, glaring at Fletcher. "Just because I give you a spare tongue, Dorian, doesn't mean you have to use it. Now, back to my box…"

He put a hand over it, gesturing. There was something charming in the way Vulcan played a Rich Man, as if He was having fun with the egotistical gestures only because He knew He could throw them away for the next show. "I have to present a set up, you see, for what's about to happen—involving my box, of course."

"Hold on one second…" Odys said, politely confused. "If you were going to call us here anyway, why not just give us the box of tissues in person?"

"You mean why did I plant them in your every-day adventure?"

"Well, I don't know if you should call it every-day, but *exactly*. It seems a round-about way of doing something simpler."

"I had to keep you in the house. Gwen had to kill herself in front of you. I wanted that to happen. I wasn't going to just ruin something I could work with." He made a sprinkling movement with His hands, ash falling around His desk, symbolic of what He'd done in the Collector's house. "And who's to say that this is even real? Welcome to my virtual reality."

"Fuck you," Dorian hissed at him and the shared hallucination.

"I really don't know how to please you people." Vulcan threw up His hands and slouched back in His leather swivel chair. "First you complain about me not being involved enough and then you complain when I try to take an active role in your lives. What do you want from me?"

"To die…" Maurice said, tucking in his chin and glaring.

"Shush, you!" Vulcan scoffed. "You think this is standing up to me, having a little pity party? Think this makes me angry? No. I've got all day. Keep complaining. See where that gets you. It's gotten you *so* far already, right?"

Seeing them slouch in their chairs, He went on. The tycoon act was working. "Now, Maurice, if you'd just let me talk about my box, you might find out a few things about *your* position *in regards* to the box. After all, I did let you come along, didn't I?"

Maurice crossed his arms, mustache bunching. Vulcan matched him.

"All right, long story short. I'm moving up in the ranks. I've been put in charge of a few…tasks. The ranks of gods shift just like the ranks of man. Kings to"— pointing to himself—"CEOs. Titles shift to fit the context. Thus, I'm overseeing a very large and very expansive clean-sweep. An evolution, if you will. The world itself is changing, right? Going green. Even the gods, you might say, are recycling. That, or *being* recycled. That's a foreshadowing, too, if you didn't catch that. Take notes.

"Let me just tell you: metal is easiest to recycle. Plastics release their fumes into the air. Paper, well, recycled paper is shit to write on—no offense, of course, to the paper gods out there. Not that I care if I offend any of Them or not. They're all underlings now." He said it to the air and smiled to Himself. It wasn't smug, but it was a little satisfied. He noticed them noticing. "What? So I don't have a right to be proud? I'm a god. Gods invented emotions like pride. We have rights to them. But about my box. This means we're recycling the old system. Reinventing the old gods. Hell, not that We haven't been reinvented ten times over. I doubt you lot would even call me Vulcan if I hadn't introduced myself as such…" He trailed off, turning a bit in His chair to stare out the window histrionically. "As a smithy bends metal over and over—reheats it—pours it into another mold to create something new from old casts, so will I do with the divinities under me…"

"And you're going to do this," Dorian began, "with a box?"

"It's not just any box, Dorian. It's a box of tissues."

"I'm not following what any of this has to do with a box—full of tissues or no."

"And you don't have to!" Vulcan smiled, swiveling in His chair to face them again. "Just don't pull out the tissues willy-nilly. Not until it's go time. Think of it like *Zoltar* the Fortune Teller machine. You have to put your quarters in first."

"Why would we have to pull out the tissues?"

"It's part of the plan, you see—the game. Ask me what the game is."

"What the game is?" Caffar asked.

"Very funny, Rose," Vulcan cut His eyes. "The game will be a symbol for the dualistic nature of the universe. A small-scale allusion for the big picture!" His face lit up in retrospection, hands gestured above Him as if creating a billboard sign. "It shall be a story worth recording—adding to Homer's legacy. And it won't be written in lyrics, no. But prose. It's what the people are into these days. No fucking bards. Might even get them to read the poems in the first place. But I digress. It will be a game. A game with a checkered tissue to start it off." He gestured to the box. "Reenacting a timeless tale of evolution, revolution, devolution—a game of Mesoamerican proportions."[71]

"A sacrificial ball game?" Dorian asked, tentative. "Like, of the Maya and Aztec?"

"Ah! You got my reference. Yes, yes. The Mesoamerican ball game itself was played by the mythological hero twins in the underworld—later to be mimicked in actual life. Yes, you of all people would catch on, Dorian."

"…I thought no one knows how the game is played," Odys added, lest they think only Dorian aware.

---

[71] This is set up for the next volume. I recommend dog-earing this page to refer back to it, critics.

"For our purposes, here," Vulcan looked at him, "we don't need an archeological debate. Also, we don't need to know how either game is played—the ball game or mine."

"Why not, if we're the ones going to play it?" Maurice asked.

"Who said you're the players?"

Fletcher's hair quivered. "So we're the game pieces? It doesn't seem different from what's already instated."

"No, you're not the pieces either."

"Then...what are we?"

"Well, let's just say you're the game itself." He crossed His legs, leaned to the side. "You all keep complaining about how much your fate is already sealed. Well, here you go." He patted the box. "I've arranged a game where fate isn't running parallel—where the gods will place bets on heads whose strings are not yet fully woven. The game will be in another plane—dimension. But still here and real. The walls of the arena will blur destiny to an unreadable degree. I've arranged it all so that They can't cheat. Not even *I* can cheat, because of course I want to play. It's a perfect game."

"Gods can always cheat," Dorian said under his breath.

Odissa leaned in, near the box. Vulcan didn't seem worried. "And where, exactly, do the old gods fit into this?" She asked as if They were all crammed inside that box and could hear.

Vulcan cocked His head as if someone as smart as she should already know. "You'll find out."

"When?"

"When the tissue box tells you."

"How will we know, if we aren't supposed to pull the tissues out?"

"That's for you all to figure out." His voice rang with existential thrills. "But don't worry too much about it. Nothing's at stake, here. No pressure to find out. I encourage you to take your time. In the meantime, this is yours, *Maurice*."

MAURICE MAKEPEACE: Now has a box.

BOX: Of tissues.

TISSUES: For the issues.

ISSUES?: What issues? And why do they require tissues?

Chapter the fourth,

Re-gifting:

What's the return policy?

"I leave it in your care. This is now your purpose, and why you've been kept alive."

He slid the box toward Maurice, tapping it twice.

Something snapped in Maurice like a bone. "You've kept me alive, *moi*, Vulcan, to protect a box of *tissues?*" His forehead wrinkled, lips tightening, mustache writhing like a caterpillar in pain.

"Not the box. The game. The tissues are part of the game." He exhaled. "You still don't see it."

"Doesn't seem like the tissues have any real threat to them. I can tell you now zat we really don't care too much about pulling them out. Except Dorian, zere. You haven't given us much uv a reason to and I know a MacGuffin when I see eet." Maurice crossed his legs, fidgety with anger.

"Defensive measures, Maurice. You all might not pull them out, but an imprudent human with a runny nose might."

"Then why make it a box of tissues? Why not rocks? Baseball cards? Condoms?"

"Those hardly fit our theme, Maurice. The nose knows, doesn't it?" He tapped his.

"He has a point," Fletcher pretended to agree, putting his head in hand.

"Then the game moves forward. Nothing more. I leave the call up to you."

"Fine." Maurice, with one hand, snatched the box and dropped it in his lap.

"Easy now," Vulcan said. "Show some reverence. No need to find out what will happen if those tissues are damaged."

"Trees will weep for their wasted parts?" Fletcher hypothesized.

"Pandora let out everything but hope, no?" Vulcan looked at Odissa.

Odissa closed her eyes as if His cryptic words gave off a stench that stung them. "The proto-woman shouldn't have been given the box in the first place," she said, standing up. "Better yet, why create the maladies at all, to plague mankind? Shouldn't the creators have more blame than the Eves of myth?"

"I see you're ready to go," Vulcan said, standing up as well. "Just let me finish."

Odissa obligingly sat back down.

"Now, I'm not an asshole. So, I will leave you with something: some divine wisdom. If you want my two cents, then you might consider what Gwendolyn proposed. Keep the Automatons in the family. Why not? I never said it had to be the way it's been done. That was all *your* rules. Everything changes. Might as well change with it. The box's purpose can adapt to what you choose. It's my Ark of the Covenant with you. Oh, and another thing." He reached down and opened the drawer in His desk, rummaging. "When you lot get back home, you might notice something gone."

Pulling out what he was looking for—up by the scruff—was me. *Bulfinch.*

BULFINCH: Not what he—she—they—seemed.

JUST LIKE: Odissa (funny, that).

BUT: It doesn't mean he's evil. Not necessarily. We all make mistakes.

GENDER: Mind-bender.

Chapter the fifth,

Pets:

Are they always OUR playthings?

"Bulfinch!" Odissa cried, on her feet once more. "Wha-what are you doing with him?"

"Him?" Vulcan laughed, spreading the cat's legs and moving back the tail. "So she is!" He looked back at Odissa, "You have to understand, Odissa, gods are drawn to other god-like things. You're probably just the first god-like thing she noticed, when she took this form. She smelled me on you."

"She?" Dorian asked, trying to comfort Odissa, who wasn't sure if her cat was about to be (or had already been?) kidnapped.

"Yes, this cat goddess here. She's only in this male cat's body because, well, They do that sometimes. Not only was she hiding but she was curious, I'd guess. *Gods only know* why we do the things we do, sometimes. And she's not talking."

I Bulfinch hissed at him.

"She's going to be added to my game, you see," Vulcan said in a baby voice to the cat. "All of her, this one. Others will only have small parts included. But this one, here, well, she's done some very nasty things. That's why she was hiding. Hiding right under my nose. She hid so well she even tried to forget herself."

"What the hell are you talking about?" Odissa shouted at him, inching forward but finding herself unable to budge.

"Ah, look," Vulcan grinned. "At least you know she has a heart. Or is it that this cat knows your secrets, Alpha? Don't want to let the *cat out of the bag?* Maybe you did know—deep down—that this cat was a little god?" Vulcan laughed. "I won't bore you with the details, but before Mecca blew up your apartment, there was also a very nice rug which escaped and is now biding its time in a flea market in New Mexico. At least, that's what my wife's birds think. Flying things are a bit harder to catch. Bulfinch, here, knew quite a bit about my rise to power. Likely knew more than enough about the roundups, too. Probably enough to tell you, Alpha, what she had heard?"[72]

He tickled Bulfinch's chin.

---

[72] The "roundups" seem like gods are being rounded up for Vulcan's game sporadically. I have no idea what's really implied here, but what I have seen of volume 3 gives me this hint.

Bulfinch only growled, gutturally.

"Such a pretty little kitty now isn't she? Yes, she is! I'm going to make her look even better. Lose these balls, yes I will. Oh wait, looks like a vet did that for you, huh, my kitty-kitty-kitty?"

I would have liked to sink my claws into him, obviously.

"What are you going to do with him?" Odissa demanded. However, a tone in her voice gave away her fear—she wasn't sure she should want the cat that's secretly been a goddess for all this time. Then again, she'd secretly been something *more* all this time, too. And what had the cat ever done to her?

Hell, she loved that cat.

"She's going to be tossed in with the rest of them—the rest of the cat deities."

"Tossed in?" Her voice was shrill.

"Alpha, dear, I think you know what I mean," Vulcan said with a head-tilt. "But don't worry, she'll turn out just fine. She's abused herself more than We will. Little more than a tom cat, now. *That* is depressing."

He stuffed Bulfinch back into the Mary Poppins's desk drawer, escaping without much more than a few hisses (though He did withdraw His hand rather quickly). He straightened out His tie.

"Now, I think that was all I had on the agenda for this meeting. You've been given a lot to digest. Best to let your Automatons think it over for you and come to some philosophical conclusions you'd otherwise never think of. Off you go."

With a wave of His hand, they were in Dorian's little house, still in their chairs, in the living room, among the other furniture.

Vulcan's making this too easy for me narratively.

Stanza: A bunch of Bulfinch.

It took them a minute to realize what had happened. As if waking up from a nap, their drowsy faces blinked unfocusedly, making sure they were all seeing the same scene. At first they didn't notice the box—the box of tissues—sitting on the coffee table, dead center.

Vulcan had moved a bit of the furniture to make sure they all fit nicely round the box.

Perhaps the change is what made them fail to recognize the scene first off.

[If you have been keeping up with the footnotes then this next bit will make sense:]

As if Vulcan were still with them, they heard His voice sound, then drift apart: *"Also, I'm not the Tom Bombadil. At least give me a dualistic role. Good or bad guy. I don't care which, but I do have an opinion and role in the Good vs. Evil. Give me that much. But sure, yeah, there is a Tom in this story—an anomaly undefined, left open to interpretation."*

Mecca, still a bit disoriented, glanced over at his father, a frown on his little face. He wasn't going to say it, or admit his father had never been here or there. Sometimes, he just *was*. That's what gave him so much power over Mecca. Mecca could not define him into the role he wished for him.

So Mecca wouldn't comment on it, no. Mecca wasn't into talking right now. Talking had never come easily for him to begin with. Gwendolyn had sometimes hypothesized that Mecca let Q do the talking for him—even when the words came out of his mouth. Mecca's speech was on a different level. His third-person default—which he was sometimes conscious of, sometimes not—justified their assumptions that his brain developed with an entirely differing outlook (on life and so on). There was no "I" for Mecca, because he had no concept of a singular self. Not when so many past selves where stuffed in him through his Automaton. So, no, of course Mecca wouldn't comment it on it.

He'd make Q do it for him.

"Vulcan means Maurice. Maurice is the Tom," said Q—just to be sure everyone got it.

"Funny, because he's not feeling like much of a side character we can write out anymore," Dorian grumbled.

Stanza: Tom cats.

You may be troubling yourself over how I know what's going on now, especially since I'm no longer in the house? Let me assure you, Reader, that it was never my cat eyes that gave me insight. Like Donna Haraway, you'll see how cyborgs segue to companion animals in due time...[73]

Stanza: A council of DEATH in the LIVING room.

Maurice sucked his teeth. "I refuse to be zis—zis Tom. He says there's been a game in the works. I'd rather play a part than be a—a referee."

"It sounds like *He's* the referee," Odys grumbled. "He makes the rules."

"Exactly..." Maurice dangled his arms off his knees and stared at that box.

"You're not the referee, Mr. Freakshow," Dorian said, his voice low and threatening. "You're the ringmaster. A stand-in representation of the orchestration."

Maurice eyed the boy. "Le cirque of the gods."

"He talked about 'recycling' Them," Odys recalled, taking off his coat. "As if he hadn't been using them—us—all along?"

"As if we need a new purpose." Maud commented, looking at her shoes. They were pointy boots. Odissa had a pair—before the apartment had been de-homed—just like them. Perhaps Odys was dressing Maud up like Odissa now. I'll not pretend to know the answer to this outfit.

"It's game after game after game." Rosemund pulled something out of her pocket. "All gladiator sport for the gods."

She placed Anselm on the table and held Caffar in her hands—spiraled her between her fingertips. The others waited for her to do something.

She *so clearly* wanted to do something.

---

[73] Donna Haraway is a scholar who wrote *A Cyborg Manifesto* and *The Companion Species Manifesto*. This is a joke on how the treatment of the "Other" intersects "technological" and "animal" issues, I think.

295

Lips trembling, "I want Anselm." She spoke the unspeakable. "Put all the freefreefree Automatons on the table. We shall debate this. This debate will happen sooner or later. We must debate a debate."

The others said nothing—the 404 File Not Found. You have to do things manually, sometimes. This was one of those times.

"Put them on the table, now," Rosemund ordered when they hesitated, her scars fading into her face as it wrinkled in grief.

Madus, Admund/Cestus, Coraza were placed on the table. Odissa noticed their shifty eyes. They didn't want her around. She tried to let her chair absorb her—to not move an inch.

Even Maurice made the situation awkward. Would he ask for an Automaton? Should they allow him one? Why not?

"I don't want an Automaton." Maurice put *that* on the table.

"You don't even want to try?" Odissa asked him. She bit her lip, as if she tried to keep from saying more. But she couldn't help herself. "What if it could help you die? What if you touched an Automaton and it reversed it all?"

The room seemed to grow darker at the question—the sun setting.

What hour was it?

Not that time matters when Vulcan keeps speeding things along.

"Don't tempt me, Alpha," Maurice rumbled at her, his mustache twitching. "Oh, don't look at me like that. It's a fifty-fifty. What if I touch an Automaton and it only compounds what voodoo's already on me? Zen no one would ever get zat Automaton again. I might never die to pass eet on!"

"Where's the harm in that? You yourself certainly wouldn't be worse off. And you'd be keeping it…in the family." *Away from me.*

"What is next? *You* asking for one? They won't give you one now. Not since zey know what you are."

She sat back in her chair, smiling with closed lips.

"Do it," Rosemund encouraged him, as if there was no implied turpitude in Odissa's suggestion. "Why not?"

"Don't!" Mecca shouted, huddled in Q's arms.

The shout had only been so loud because Q had shouted it too. Q went on, "Your purpose is the box, not this."

Ignoring the woeful tone in his son's Automaton (*Bad daddy, bad!*), he turned to the "adult" next to him, eyes asking their opinion. Dorian and Fletcher shrugged.

Not thinking a second more about his son, Maurice reached for Coraza—the only female on the board.

But, like the opposite end of a magnet, the nail scooted away, repelled.

Maurice made it scoot a little farther on the table, making sure he could believe his squinty eyes. Each time his finger was a centimeter away, it jumped forward.

They'd never tried it before.

He sat back in his seat, tears in his eyes. "Well, zat's that."

Odissa chuckled out a "Mmh." It sent a chill through the room. Odissa knew something.

Had known it all along.

"You died, Maurice. Your *charge* has been changed. Metaphorically, physically, metaphysically. She's telling me to tell you. Living-dead don't have the same physics as the living-living. You've gone and come back. Your soul knows what it's like to be free from a body. You can't take a pea out of a pod and put it back *exactly* the way it came. Automatons are programmed to respond to fundamental, basic human soul-structures. That's also why gods, animals, vampires, ghosts couldn't get them to work."

"How do you know they can't?" Rosemund asked her, brow pulling up her drooping face. "How many vampires do you know?"

"She knew a cat god, didn't she?" Fletcher said. *How dare you question her.*

"You seem to know a lot about these things, Odissa," Maurice said, body tense. "You're more Alpha zen we might like. Why are you so smart when your siblings aren't?"

"Half siblings," she corrected with a flash of her eyes. "Perhaps that's because they were based off me. And I know myself very well."

"Suddenly you do, yes." Maurice shifted in his seat.

"Thus," Rosemund said, directing their attention back to the table, "there are four Masters, and five free Automatons—granted, one inside another Automaton, hopefully bagged."[74]

"Why not four free Automatons?" Odys asked. "Shouldn't we establish why Odissa shouldn't get one—get it finalized so that it's never questioned again? Because, right now, I still question it."

"Are you so sure I want one still?" Odissa asked him.

"It's not your choice, Odissa," he said, not looking at her. "I *won't* live forever alone with these people."

Dorian stood up in his chair but Maurice shoved him back down. "Don't speak to her like that," Dorian instead attacked with his words.

Odys shot him a wicked smile. *You're turning into me, old man.*

Dorian used his shirt collar, rather than the nearby tissues, to dab the blood pooling at the base of his nose.

"Let's vote on what we *can* vote on," Maurice said above them. "Rosemund has said she wants Anselm. Who among you sees *zat* as an unreasonable request?"

"So we've already agreed with Gwen that a Master can and should have more than one Automaton?" Rosemund asked, turning Caffar between her thumb and forefingers.

Devil's advocate shocked them.

"Vulcan said it was a good idea," Odissa commented.

---

[74] I'm assuming that since Leeland wasn't sick when he killed himself he hadn't touched Cestus?

"V also told me to fall in love with you," Dorian commented. "Look where that's gotten us."

It was Odys who had to be restrained this time.

"Sit your ass down!" Maurice growled, mustache stiffening with his lip. Odys leaned away from the Eiffel Tower towering above him.

Fletcher settled down from his prepared interception. "Rosemund, if you want Anselm, take him. You're the elder. We'll do as we're told." His eyes darted around, daring for someone to contest her.

She laughed. A laugh at winning a terrible prize. "Why did she kill herself, I wonder? If it was going to be this easy to forgive her sins a second time." She scooped up Anselm with her still-gloved hand. "I'm going to the bathroom. I want to be alone as I searchsearchsearch for the answer."

"Let us know if you need anything," Maud shouted out after her. "We should take our time with this. We can't all be sick at once."

"Why?" Fletcher snorted. "Because Leeland will sneak up on us? He's dead, Odys. We have nothing to fear anymore."

The others avoided looking at Odissa, refusing to argue that there was an even greater threat among them.

"I wonder how it will feel," Dorian said, cupping his knees in nervous thought, "having two Automatons while syncing. Think it will hurt more than the first time?"

Something within them already told them the answer. And it was a private matter.

As if in the waiting room of a hospital, waiting for their beloved friend to get out of surgery, for the doctor to give them the news...

They waited.

Around the box (of tissues!) they waited.

299

It was a very quiet process. Maurice's watch ticked very loudly. Cars drove by, crunching the snow. They could hear muffled sounds from the bathroom—through the broken doorknob stuffed with a towel. Vomit, chatting, rinsing.

Perhaps she was talking to Caffar.

Perhaps to Anselm.

Perhaps to the part of Gwendolyn still within him.

But they couldn't understand her.

But I can.

But I'll censor it for personal reasons.

She was talking to all three.

Taking off her glove had been like undressing—about to touch Gwendolyn herself. She found herself puking in the sink, smiling all the while. She'd never been closer to her Gwendolyn. Gwendolyn had left traces of herself—imprints. And those remnants were beautiful.

If it hadn't been for The Universe, Vulcan, Anselm, Leeland...

Gwendolyn could have been hers.

She was sure of it. Now she was *sure* of it. Sure she could have had her in another lifetime.

...

And then they heard the gunshot—the bang and splatter. Jolted from sleepy tension, the others rushed to the bathroom.

She was dead in the bathtub. Polite enough to make the scene cleanable, though she'd managed to splatter her brain and hair on the ceiling. No new inhabitants would notice, with a bit of paint. The wall paint had fixated many a hair to itself in the past—worse than an apartment flip job. Fletcher went to the store for supplies.

On his way, Fletcher noticed Maurice hadn't left his seat when everyone else had.

"You knew she was going to do it," he said, factually. Something was caught in his throat.

Maurice glowered at him. "As if you didn't? As if you'd deprive her of it? As if any of us would." He cursed a little in French. "It's all any of us really want. Sleep."

A "fuck you" to Vulcan.

He stared at the muted television he had just turned on. Maurice could not die. But he could watch TV.

Mecca and Q found his lap, their faces drooping as Mecca flipped through the channels. Maurice hummed a French hymn under the television's drone.

Stanza: Giving head.

Dorian had turned to Odys in the hall as Fletcher had left, catching his attention before he could follow. "Let's let Fletcher clean this mess. But it might be good if we all cleared out and, you know, found something to do for the time being."

"I'll go—go get some dinner for us," Odys replied, taking the hint with an angry glance to Odissa.

There was a new head of the "family"—a role Maurice could never fill. Maurice was twice removed. Or, at least once.

So, yes, Odys knew who to obey. He had to obey Dorian.

MECCA MAKEPEACE: Seeing everyone leave him.

OLDER FATHER: Wants to leave him, but cannot.

YOUNGER FATHER: Wants Mecca to leave.

AGELESS MOTHERS: Left him.

Chapter the sixth,

All in the family:

But what is out of it?

His eyes now gone,[75] Dorian asked Odissa to take him to the bedroom. She led him to the bed but sat down on the floor across from him, watching him like a child

---

[75] (For paint).

at story time. He dabbed at his nose—but, like eyes out of tears, it was too tired to bleed now.

She wanted to smoke.

He crossed his legs.

"Six Automatons now," Odissa said—after a brief moment of wondering why he was being so stoic. *Why isn't he crying? Why do they all have such strange reactions to death? Why do I feel like they've forgotten what it's like to have human emotions?*

"You can't say things like that, Odissa. It sounds like Alpha's saying them. It sounds wrong, in this context."

"I can't state a fact?"

"Not an indelicate one."

Speaking of indelicate, his foot began to bob.

"Are you afraid of being left alone with me?"

He didn't answer.

"I saw that look Fletcher gave you—and everyone around us when you sent him out. It's not that you're afraid of me. But you don't know if you're breaking rules or not. Mother's dead, Dorian. There are no rules."

"Again, being indelicate."

"Because you're being an asshole."

"Get on the bed with me."

"No."

"I'm not afraid of you. Don't be afraid of me. Or is it too soon, to be so close?"

"Jesus, Dorian, you talk about *me* being indelicate and yet you're wanting to, what, fuck right after Rosemund blows her brains out?" Her eyes welled up with tears, but he couldn't see them—and they hadn't made it to her throat yet, so he couldn't even hear the sadness in her words.

"Get on the bed, now."

"I'm not Odys. You can't just order me around because you're in charge of them now."

He got up and walked toward her voice. But he paused, knowing he was bound to be close. He put out a hand as he knelt on the ground. He stopped when he found her shoe. "I just want to sit beside you," he said, feeling for the wall. She helped him, patting on the ground beside her.

He found her hand. She didn't latch on.

He took off his glasses, tossed them to the side. "If you could," he said to the air, "because we can have any life available, what would it be? What kind of life do you want?"

"This isn't life?"

"Will you start a new life with me?"

"A family?"

"No. Just us. Just us leaving."

"Traveling, you mean?"

"Is that what you want?" he asked, truly wondering.

"I don't have much of a life now, apart from you. You blew up my apartment. My things. Even my fucking cat is gone."

"What would make you happy?"

"Who says I want to be happy?"

"You want to be miserable?" he asked, laughing.

"I don't want to chase happiness, Dorian. I'll let it find me."

"I like that." He mused on the topic for a moment before she cut it off.

"Whatever it is that I want, I'm not sure I want a house, a yard. Nothing with too much upkeep."

"No dead people in the bathtub?"

She laughed out her discomfort, wiping away an uncategorized tear. "I'd rather my life be private. You can't have privacy with so many neighbors."

Dot dot dot.

303

"So, an apartment with your twin brother…that was enough?"

"We had plenty of money. Alpha knew—*I* knew Leeland had two Automata and endless amounts of gold. Of course it was enough."

He couldn't understand the nostalgia in her tone—what sounded like a love for menial simplicity. "I mean, you still liked the apartment?"

"Exactly."

"So it's not about where you want to live. If it's not that, then what?"

"Right now, I think a closet would be a nice place to live."

"I've been there half my life."

She laughed. "Life would be so much easier if things were decided for us, no? Then, if we didn't like those decisions…we'd have something to complain about or fight against. Right now we're complaining about having nothing to really complain about, you and I. We have unlimited options."

Dorian tilted his head up, as if looking at the ceiling. "You make us sound like children rebelling against our parents. Our parents: The Universe."

She smiled at his observation and amended it: "The Universe still has rules, Dorian. But children do grow up, I guess. Maybe it's the rules that only children have to abide by: Don't eat from this or that tree; Don't eat this or that animal; Don't love this or that man or woman; Don't think this or that." She paused. "But, as we get older, we can, like, watch PG-13 movies—without our parents taking us to the theater. We can drive. We can buy cigarettes. We can have sex. We can buy alcohol. And now, well, women don't wear head coverings. We can eat pork. We can divorce."

"I see what you did there. All Old to New Testament. How very Christian, though."

"I'm feeling more like a Satanist, to be honest. My point is, it seems like the rules loosen and change, Dorian, because we understand why parents need to be strict. Children are stupid. God—The Universe—isn't. Parents must let their children become adults. Vulcan can't tell us what to do forever. What good parent wants to live their child's life for them? At the end of the day, The Universe finally stops telling you what to eat, wear, say, act. And then asks us what WE want. Sure, our choices might be limited. We might be predestined to pick one thing over the other. But we still get the choice: what do we want? That brings us to existentialism."

Where they currently were.

"You can't see it, but I just waved in front of us."

When his laugh faded, they could hear the TV in the living room.

What he wanted suddenly came to him. "I want Alpha to be good. I want to trust her. I want Odys to be happy, despite what I've *done* to him. I want to know if I'm hurting the world for existing—existing for so long."

"You were given existence, Dorian. The Universe will take it away eventually. There's nothing you can do that the Universe can't counterbalance."

His head pulled away from the wall. "If you do want to travel, I *will* say it's harder to go to other countries. Fletcher can make passports quickly, but they can't leave his hand—if you know what I mean. And even then, the detail takes a lot out of me, depending. We've ways to cheat, though. Private jets. That sort of thing. But low-key is always best. Cruise ships work, too, sometimes. Once you're on a continent, it's easier to move without showing yourself. And like hell I'll ever show anyone my real date of birth." They laughed. "That's how they found me, by the way—this group. I was good at finding people who could make really good fake IDs and I would sell them. And use them to get into bars before I was twenty-one. Bob liked my work. She tracked me down at this festival—but as I was saying. Traveling to other countries is harder for us now, but doable."

"You don't think I know this?" Odissa said, finally taking his hand. "Alpha came to America because she realized the Automatons and Masters were here too. There's no need to travel away from them. Why are you so stuck on leaving them?"

"I mean, if we can't stay here, where do you want to go, then?"

"To bed."

"Long term, I mean."

"Let's start something. A nonprofit. An orphanage. Do good."

"Add gold to the poor's pockets?" He interpreted her.

"What else is there to do, once the labor of living's been done?"

"Vulcan seems to have things for us to do," Dorian added, "in the near future."

"Yes, but we can't worry about that. No sense in worrying about what He will— and He *will*—do."

"But it might interrupt our plans."

"So might getting cancer."

He chuckled and put his other hand on hers. Odissa put her head on his shoulder. He kissed her head. He needed to shave, his beard pulled at her hair.

"So," she said, theoretical emphasis in her tone. "Let's say we know what we want. We want to solve the world's problems like Gwendolyn. We have nothing better to do. But once the world's problems are solved, then what?" She played with one of his coat buttons.

"You talk as if you're immortal, Odissa. You're not yet. I can't picture my life without you." He paused. "You know I'm going to give you an Automaton, don't you? Have you seen it?"

"I have seen it." Odissa stopped pulling at his buttons and let her hand fall to his lap. "But not in an I-see-the-future sort of way. I have smelt it. Smelled the thought on you."

"…What would happen if we did give you one?"

She frowned at his flip-flopping. He went from certainty to a maybe.

"I don't like you talking to me this way, Dorian, as if I have all the answers. I can't keep tapping into Alpha. It threatens you. It feels like pretend. Like I'm enacting something I'm not sure is real." She raised her head to face him. She took her hands and held his face. "If you gave me an Automaton? Well, then I'd have an Automaton. Nothing else would happen." She kissed his lips and pulled away a moment later. She added, "You're scared of what I might be able to do with one?"

"A little."

"I could do nothing more than what I do now. It's only this body would live longer. We could be together for centuries then."

His face twitched like a ripple. "You could kill us then, if you had an Automaton."

"What makes you so sure I couldn't now?"

"You *will* kill us all, won't you?" He let the words settle in the air. But they would not. They continued to float there like bloody feathers freshly plucked. "You'll be the death of us."

She took in a deep breath, chest shaking. "Your end will be my fault, if it ever comes. But I won't let it. It won't be my will that causes it. In some ways, I can be blamed for every Master's death—past and future. I killed them. They all died in their specific, precise ways because Automata were created. And Automata were created because of *me*. To take down *me*. But Vulcan let me live. And he made you love me."

He shook his head. *Don't blame yourself.*

"I did this, Dorian. I can't believe I did all this." There were tears in her voice he could finally hear. "I can't believe this is what it took. All these years to finally stop me and my rage and—"

He kissed her, kissed her like he believed her. Like he wanted to save her from such thoughts. But something tugged him back. "You have changed from what you were. But I still don't understand how you go on. What motivates you. Why you feel like living."

"You, dummy," she said into his face. "I missed you. And the other wonders of the world." She kissed him again, teeth brushing his lips, biting at him as if to hold onto him.

Those teeth nipped and he pulled back, a little pissed. "Not so har—" but he tasted blood. He pushed her off of him, away from him. He struggled to get up from the shock but found his legs unable to help him—then realized he'd best keep her in his grasp. "You could do this, the whole time?" he demanded, not letting go of her wrists. She wasn't struggling. "You can hurt us?"

"Showing is better than telling they say. I wanted you to believe me." Unseen fear shadowed her face, realizing she had gone too far. "I'm so sorry. But now you know. Now you know that an Automaton won't make me anymore powerful than I already am. What's the difference?"

"Can I do the same to you?" he asked. "Can I harm you too?" *Or is it just me who is powerless again under you?*

"Of course you can. I'm in a fucking mortal body, Dorian," she hissed. She didn't like his voice rising so loud. It might disturb Maurice and Mecca—might catch their attention. "I'm just a mortal with skills."

"You could've warned me," he said, letting go and feeling his wet lip. "Always fucking bleeding!"

"It's not that bad," she said, dabbing at him. He flinched at first. "See, you're not sure of me," she stated. "You've been lying too."

"Let me bite you and see how you like it," he grouched. "So you only have the bite of a *girl,* then?" *Not of something stronger? Of something more powerful?*

"You wouldn't want me to chew through your finger. It'd likely take hours."

"I can't believe you fucking bit me." His smile showed numerous hesitancies, but it was still a smile. *She's been restraining herself this whole time. For me.*

She stood up, taking his hand. "My back hurts from sitting on the floor."

He let her place him on the bed. He sucked on his lip. It was barely red now. "I feel like I've just been molested," he laughed—at the impossibility, of course. "It seems such a private matter."

"It's only because you haven't been hurt by someone else in quite some time, Dorian."

"I wish you'd have given me more time to prepare."

"If I had prepared you, then you wouldn't know what I was capable of. You wouldn't be as properly scared of me as you should."

"You *want* me to be scared of you?"

"A little," she replied. "Makes things more equal."

"I don't understand." He leaned down on his elbow, a little angry. "Back at the Collector's house you were begging me to accept you…"

"Dorian, you need to know what I'm capable of. You need to know—because I *don't* want to hurt you."

"But saying that only makes me trust you more!" he softly shouted at her, so the others couldn't hear.

She breathed in deeply, wishing he could see her exasperated expression. "Now we're even. Odissa has been afraid of you this entire time—what you're capable of. It's like Alpha wakes up and boom. I realize I don't have to be so afraid of you. We're equals."

"I think you should still be afraid of me, dear. You're the one in the mortal body." He reached into her pants but she held him there—keeping him from going further. "And there's two of me and only one of you."

There was a knock on the door. Dorian huffed as he sat up—angry they had been interrupted. He did not remove his hand from Odissa. "Who is it?"

"It's Mecca."

"What *now*?" Dorian demanded, hanging his head.

"We just got a text from Odys."

"So?"

"He said he's not coming back."

"What?" Odissa gasped.

"Did he say *why*?" Dorian shouted back, his eyebrows all askew.

"No. But he said he'll let her come back with the food."

"Her? As in—"

Q finished for him, "*Maud*."

MAUD: A substitute for Odys Odelyn.

A SUBSTITUTE: A goodbye.

A GOODBYE: A scapegoat.

A SCAPEGOAT: For some greater sins.

Chapter the seventh,

Selfishness:

Is it selfish to want to be the only one who's selfless?

"He's sending her instead," Q said, opening the door.

"Why'd you interrupt us for that?" Dorian pressed, a coldness in his voice. He still didn't remove his hand from its half-insertion in Odissa's pants.

Hand on her hip, "Why are you in here making out with someone when Rosemund just killed herself? You're so selfish."

"Rosemund just killed herself and *I'm* the selfish one? *Sí*, I'm so selfish for actually wanting to live my fucking life."

Mecca frowned at them from Q's skinny arms. "Not even Mecca would do something like that. Mecca's put his camera away."

"We were just talking," Odissa tried to explain, finally pushing Dorian away. She wanted to tell Dorian to cool it—to be respectful—to alert him Mecca's eyes were pink from tears and to therefore be more sensitive.

"Are you just going to stand there?" Dorian huffed. "Shut the door."

Q and Mecca stepped inside and shut the door.

"I don't think that's what I meant, Mec," Dorian said.

Mecca knew that he'd best do this while he had the 'sight' advantage. "Mecca needs Odissa to leave. Mecca needs to talk to Dorian."

Odissa stood up.

"Odissa, no—" Dorian begged. He cursed under his breath.

Q and Mecca moved out of her way, eyeing the scene with hesitant glances.

"I'll go make coffee," Odissa said. She touched Q's shoulder on her way out. She felt something sink inside her as Q half-jumped at her touch—a cautious reaction showcasing everything but a cringe.

Q quickly smiled to counteract her tenseness. Mecca wasn't afraid, but they didn't want to cozy up with Alpha just yet. *Sorry that I don't trust you.*

Odissa passed by the bathroom. Someone had pulled the door to. She couldn't remember who'd done it. But a door couldn't give the dead dignity. Not when it could be pushed open so easily.

She held her breath as she pushed it to peek in. Caffar was on the side of the tub, next to bits of flesh and blood. Odissa was sure Anselm was in the headless corpse's clinched fist.

She felt sorry for Caffar. Caffar hadn't been good enough to cling to upon death.

We cling to what we love.

"That should be me, there," Maurice said, rounding the corner. "She was more of a man than me. What kind of a man can't kill himself?"

All right, Ernest Hemingway. "Where did you get that vodka?"

He raised the bottle, contents swishing. "I fucking hate Russian shit. Was all I could find in my car. Mecca's stash."

Odissa closed the door, smiling—she shouldn't have gone near those free Automatons. Made her look suspicious. "I wish she hadn't done it."

"That's selfish of you," Maurice laughed. "But, then again, it's selfish of her to leave zem all with so many inanimate ones. They'll never sort out who gets what, between the three of them."

She walked past him, into the living room.

"What's zat smile?" he asked her, following her. "You think I should have said *four?*"

"It wasn't a real smile," she said, frowning as she sat down. The television was showing political commercials that, on any other day, would have made her blood boil. But Odissa no longer had investments in democracies. She was forming a new government.

311

He plopped beside her on the couch—though he could have sat anywhere.

"Zis has always been about you—why I'm still alive." He spat at her after glaring was not enough. "About you and Vulcan and zee fact He can't kill you because He has some—some sick infatuation with you."

"He has an infatuation with you too, my friend. My guess is it's your American masculinity undermined by your French femininity. That's what Vulcan is all about, isn't he? The feminine masculinity. You are Vulcan to Dorian's Dionysus. You are Vulcan to Gwendolyn's Athene. You are Vulcan to Leeland's Ares."

He snorted. "And you? You are godless."

"Give me that." She tried to take the bottle away but he puffed at her. She would not fight him over it. "He loves me too much to kill me. I'm His best work. You can't just throw away your best idea." She gestured to herself. "You *work* on it."

Maurice chuckled at her. "You are so confident now. It is getting harder and harder to see Odissa."

"My brother told Mecca he's not coming back. Did you know about that?"

"Oh?" Maurice took another sip of vodka. "Is that what they're on about in zere?" He gestured to the room. "Mecca's always on his damn phones."

"Yeah. But Maud's coming back with lunch. That's what Mecca said."

Maurice rubbed his glassy eyes. "*Sure* she is. Zat is just Odys's way of keeping us calm. Giving us false hope. Who knows what your brozer is doing…" Maurice caught her eyeing the tissue box. "I ought to burn it."

"Men ought to do a lot of things."

He turned to her, vodka swishing in his bottle. She could smell it on him. "Tell me, Alpha, what men ought to do. What must zis man, here, do?" He pointed to himself, poking his striped chest.

"Tell your son you love him. Tell him you don't want to leave him, but that someday he'll understand that life is incomplete without death. Tell him why you behave as you do. Be a better father. Then, give Dorian your blessing."

"For what?" His lips and mustache pulled up—he hadn't expected this prepared answer.

"For being more of a father than you ever were."

"Father? Ha. He was more like—like a step-brozer or somezing."

She snatched the bottle away when he was too busy laughing. "Many siblings must be parents. And you should still thank Dorian for it."

"Yes, yes, and?"

"Don't let a god *tell* you what to do." Her eyes gestured to the box. "Make Them force you to do it. Don't spend your free will on orders. If you're destined to do something, then it will happen. They'll make it happen. But make Them work at it. Gods want joyous submission, not begrudged. Don't give Them that. Give Them hell." She took a swig.

"Is that all wise Alpha has to say? Take the rock They're throwing at you and throw it back at Them?" He accepted the bottle she handed back.

"Better yet, desire more rocks. Start a rock collection and then you'll want what They're throwing. Get stoned, Maurice. Now *that's* all I have to say." She laughed, stroked the air with her hand.

"You are very into metaphors and analogies."

"I like to call them parables." She took out a cigarette from a crumbled pack Odys had left behind—a gesture, she was sure.

"Fuck your parables. I wanted your opinion."

Her words now visible with the smoke, "No, you want me to tell you what I would do if I were you—as if I'm smarter than you merely because Alpha's older and knows more secrets."

He puffed up his cheeks. "Exactly."

"If you don't want the box, give it away. Leave it to us. What's the worst Vulcan can do to you? *Kill you?*"

His inebriated brain did the calculations, best it could. "He could torture me. Prometheus isn't how I want to go. My liver is too valuable. Don't like pain." He rubbed his stomach, imagining the possibilities.

"I thought waking up every day alive was torture enough? Beginning to think you like living, Maurice."

Maurice's nostrils flared, his mustache fanning. She was right.

Odissa leaned into him, staring into his red eyes. "You want me to promise you, Maurice, that I will help you die if you do this for me? Want to make a deal with me like Leeland did? Say that this is exactly why my Father has allowed you to live, so that I may tempt you? You are His Gerasene Demoniac, Maurice. Legion is within you. You try and try to put yourself into the swine you eat but there is no cliff to topple over. Yes, I can be the one who finally sends you to the pigs, Maurice. Let me."

His eye twitched, making him break the stare to rub it and look down. When he looked back up, his expression had shifted. "If I'm going to forsake that damn box of snot rags, I'd better make it count."

"And you want me to tell you how to make the most of it?" Odissa reached out and smoothed back a strand of his oily hair. "Is that what this is, Maurice?"

"Tell me," he asked again. "Tell me really. What I should do. If we all believe you're good now, well, why not give some good advice?"

Odissa smiled. "Vulcan's likely *expecting* you to neglect that box, and He'll play off your impatience. There's no denying that." She sighed. "This is like David and Bathsheba. David got what he wanted—for a price. He got Bathsheba at the cost of their son. But was David damned for his sin? No. Cause and effect. Equivalent exchange. No need for penance. It was all paid for."

"I don't want my son to die for my sins, Alpha."

"But would you call leaving a box behind the sin?" She frowned at the box, as if it was such a little thing.

He shrugged. "Doing the opposite of what a god commands? What else would you call it?" He took another drink then cradled the bottle like a teddy bear.

She watched him as the sip settled. "There are ways around 'sins,' if you can read the map. It sounds more like your son—all the Masters, really—are to be out of the picture for the game, Maurice. Regardless of what you do. Didn't you hear Vulcan? They're not the players. What the fuck do you think that means, then? Yes, that's right. They're dead. It would be a sin to let Vulcan have His way. A sin in the original." She evened the hem of her shirt, her other hand flicking ash into Rosemund's used tea mug. "What Master has ever lived forever?"

"You offer to postpone the game, then? What's in it for you?"

"I am not a god, Maurice. I can't stop the game from happening."

"But you're more like one than we are. You know zee Words. What do I have to do to get you to help us? You had Leeland convinced with your promises. They must have had *some* payoff."

"What makes you think I am against you that you must barter with me? You all hate Vulcan. Who hates Him more than Alpha? Isn't that how your story goes? No, I am your only hope." She looked out the window. "This is her last body, Maurice. She thought by now she'd have served her time and have more options. It's clear now she has to make more options of her own."

"Then what will it *cost* to insure your options involve helping us get out of zis?"

"You can't escape the game, Maurice. But I can certainly…take a few turns for you."

"Didn't you hear? I'm not playing. I'm the referee. Zee ringmaster!" He pointed in the air, his greased hair flopping.

"But that's not the sin you will have to pay for. I do that for free. You are about to abandon your son and leave him to me. That *will* cost you. You won't pay me. You won't pay Vulcan. But I will make it very gentle for him, you understand? I'll watch over him—them all. You can run off, like you always do. But I will cover for you. I know the way to ease your father-son pains. And the price is you helping me

315

when the time comes; when you know more than you know now; when the game is in play. You understand?"

Maurice sat back, blankness on his face. He stared through her like a spectator waiting for a glimpse of the magician's strings—waiting for her to slip and show the truth.

"...My favorite American writer is Hemingway. Do you know why?"

"Yes, but tell me anyway." She cupped the side of her face.

"Because he lived in France. He was an exhibition of virility. And, he killed himself."

"But what of his prose?"

"Zat was good too."

"Ah, Maurice," she sighed. She leaned over and dropped her cigarette in the old tea. "Just because you're like Hemingway does not mean your sins are forgivable." She slapped her hands on her lap. "But you read the past well. You will die. Not much longer, now."

He chuckled, extending a hand. "I have no choice but to impatiently wait for that day." He patted their embraced hands—coming to some sort of undefined agreement that only those who have cheated death could understand. He said, "I get the feeling zat zere is no happy ending for any of us in this."

"Vulcan included," she said like a promise.

"I can drink to zat."

Stanza: Hacktivism involves a lot of guesswork.

Back inside the bedroom with Mecca: "Well, spit it out, Mecca," Dorian had rumbled, hair hiding his face as he rolled his head about impatiently.

Q had leaned into the door, making sure no one was listening. Mecca pulled a cell phone out from her mouth, tapped away on it. "We tracked Odys down, but we lost his signal here," he pointed to the screen, but realized Dorian couldn't see. "He's off the grid again, Dorian. He's planning something."

"No shit. You couldn't say that in front of Odissa?"

"I—I think they're in it together this time," Q whispered.

"What do you mean?"

She built up her courage—courage to voice their stupid thought—courage to have Dorian knock it down. *Please knock it down.* She went into detail about how they had been re-reading some of the twin's emails (emails from O_Odelyn@afreee-mailaddress.com *to* whydoihaveanemail@thesamefreee-mailaddress.com) and had been studying the IP addresses from said emails and how something just wasn't adding up but...

Dorian toppled it like a Jenga tower. "Are you fucking crazy? What do old emails have to do with the present day? When have they had time to plan something?" Dorian bit his lip in anger, but then winced—still sore. It made him angrier. "

"It was like they knew Leeland was monitoring them. Studying them—"

Mecca cut himself off. "The point is why would he be? Both, you know?"

"We checked their email history before. No one else flagged anything."

"Odys suspected. He suspected the whole time. That's why he was playing along—covering for her—"

"You're reading too much into things. And sure, Odissa could have been 'under the influence' at times when those were sent but—"

"It's not just her email, Dorian—" Q interrupted. She held up her example email to the blind man who could not read. "They're so typical and staged and—"

"You don't see it, do you?" Mecca said, reeling Q back. "You don't get it. Of course you wouldn't. You've never been able to see it. You were her brother once and even then you didn't know."

"What don't I get, Mec?" Dorian rolled his eyes—his whole body rolling with him.

Mecca and Q turned, already rejected. "Even if Mecca told you, it wouldn't change anything." It was as if Mecca had just realized it—realized the totality of what his discovery meant.

317

Dorian filled the silence. "No, we can't change anything. That's the whole fucking point, you dumbass. The inevitability. Vulcan let her this far for a reason. Now get out of my room. Tell Odissa she can come back now."

But Mecca wouldn't be telling anybody anything. Mecca would watch as his theories played out. He would collect his data and proof.

Stanza: What did Odys suspect?

Fletcher entered the house with a bucket full of supplies. Mecca, who had come to sit with Odissa and his father in the living room, noticed the Automaton was chewing something as he passed. Double Bubble. Bazooka. Something pinkish.

Fletcher glanced once at them. "I should have bought food too, since I was quicker than Maud."

Mecca and Q looked at each other, sharing a thought.

They heard the trash bags and a few bangs—taking out the blood-stained dry wall, maybe. Spray spray, swish swish, zip zip.

He walked out a few TV shows later—the large bag over his shoulder as if the skinniest Santa ever.

Stanza: What does Dorian suspect?

Minutes later, Dorian roused himself out of bed and went to scavenge for the new gum Fletcher had brought. He was just about to reach the hall when he stumbled into the wall; Fletcher's memory was good, but it only went so far.

Fletcher could not know that Mecca—for Dorian liked to blame Mecca—had left out a suitcase there, by the doorway. Well, he wasn't sure it was a suitcase. Maybe it was a duffle bag or a heavy coat.

Nevertheless, Dorian stumbled his way to the living room. Odissa got up when she noticed him coming. She helped him find the sofa. She shooed Maurice down a seat.

Odissa held Dorian's hand. She held it because it would be on her anyway, possessive and needy and begging for attention. Holding it kept it still. She wondered if he was listening to the TV at all over that smacking of his gum.

A commercial came on. She felt Dorian breathe deeply. "We can't use that bathroom anymore." No one argued with that. "We can't stay here. We should rent a suite." Not just a room. He wanted their company. That, or he was afraid to be alone with Odissa. "When Fletcher gets back, we should leave here. Mecca, find a place for us."

Mecca pursed his lips in thought. "Mecca knows a house that is empty. Mecca has been looking. Mecca thought you might want to leave after today. The owners are on vacation." He began checking his phone, as if checking on his facts. Q pulled out his tablet to match him.

"How do you know?" Maurice asked him. "Are you friends with them?"

"No. We've been stalking this couple for a while now, waiting for them to leave so we can see if they're the Mr. and Mrs. [redacted] who are related to a certain [famous actor]. They might have some of his stuff we could *collect*, since he spends the holidays with them."

"So *that's* how you know," Odissa sighed.

"At least you're not killing them like Rosemund," Fletcher sighed. "Not yet anyway."

Q gave a few finishing tap tap taps and handed the tablet to Odissa with the street view. "Google Maps shows the houses in their area are close together, but at night Mecca's sure we could all sneak in without a fuss. Look at those tall fences and the gates. Their privacy is their blind spot."

"She's right. This could work," Odissa said—as if she broke into houses every day. She saw their faces when she handed it back.

Mecca sniffed and scratched his nose, going back to watching TV as if he did not care either way.

"Sounds fine," Dorian answered. "Let's go now. We can make it right when it gets dark."

319

"Now?" Odissa asked. "What about Odys—I mean, Maud?"

"He's taking his time anyway. After all, Fletcher just cleaned up the fucking bloodbath in there and he's still not back. Mecca, text him and tell him where we are headed. And tell him never mind about the food."

"You want me to talk to him?" Odissa asked.

"No," Dorian said. "Come help me pack."

Stanza: Guinevere runs off with Sir Lancelot in the end.

"Are you sure you want to leave so quickly?" Odissa asked him in the bedroom, arranging her few things.

"What do you mean? Of course I want to leave quickly. What if I need to pee in the next two minutes? I can't piss in there. There's not enough bathrooms."

Or places for a bath."

"You can use a tree. Fuck, I don't know." She couldn't come up with something better and continued gathering his things. "Do you want this?"

He shrugged, unsure what it was. She apologized and described the thing.

He leaned forward on the bed, noticing her irritation. "Thank you for packing. It's always better to have two sets of eyes on things."

"And it's better to not do it in a rush."

"We can get anything we need later."

"Who's going to be responsible for the Automatons, then?" she asked, folding up one of Dorian's shirts.

"Mecca."

"Are you serious?" She paused in her folding.

"No. But *he* is lately. So serious. He's not the same Mecca anymore. Not with Maurice in the picture." He rubbed his face, trying to decide if he liked the new Mecca or not. "But maybe I *will* let him take them. Anything he does with them can't make things worse, now can it?"

"Well. Maybe he should get a say in what happens to the inanimates too. You all treat him like a child. And maybe he is one. But he should still get a vote."

And so Dorian let Mecca take them for safe keeping. Well, not Mecca exactly. Dorian refused to acknowledge that this was a big responsibility for Mecca and so only spoke to Q—as if she was in charge. And perhaps right now she was.

Maurice drove them to a local Target store and dropped off Dorian and Odissa. Fletcher would pick them up soon, with Rosemund's remains "taken care of." They would meet them at Mecca's chosen house with groceries and, as Dorian had put it, "Better moods."

Dorian turned back to the car and spoke to Maurice through the rolled-down window. "Go get something to eat too. You have my cell if we need to change plans about the house."

"We'll make sure zee coast is clear, Dorian. You just make sure and get me some pancake batter." The window rolled up as he drove away.

Odissa led Dorian inside to the café customary in such mega-stores. "Do you have money?" she reminded him. *Because I don't.*

"Here, one of my cards," he said, shivering off the cold as they stepped inside. He pulled out his wallet. "I can't see them. Use the blue one. After that, just throw it away. We won't be able to use it again. Been needing to get rid of it."

The place had an hour until closing, so there wasn't a line. "What do you want?" Odissa asked him, studying the menu.

"Nachos. And Coke."

Odissa got the same but with coffee.

They sat down and consumed.

"Maurice didn't even ask why we wanted to be dropped off first," Odissa commented, wiping her mouth with a paper napkin.

"Why? You think he should care why we want to go shopping?" Dorian's lips tried to find his straw.

"I'm just surprised that he didn't. It makes me wonder why."

"We're too busy wondering *why* about your bloody brother. The fuck is he doing, Odissa? Sulking? Hiding from me?"

"You pretty much told him to leave. That's probably why Maurice didn't say anything. You're making everyone want to leave you alone, Dorian."

"And you, Odissa, are you going to leave me alone?"

"You're a very messy eater without Fletcher," Odissa whispered over the table, grabbing his hand. His sleeve had dipped in the cheese. "And I don't think Odys is avoiding us. He's closer than you think; he wouldn't leave me alone with you." She finished dabbing at him.

"Is my nose bleeding right now? Because you're provoking a good nosebleed. Or is it just cheese?"

"First you want him to leave us alone and now you want him to come back to us?"

"No. I just want to know what he's up to. Don't want surprises. I've had enough of them."

"I think you care about him."

"No. Well, obviously."

"You don't want him to upset your rule, is that it?"

"My 'rule,' is it?" His yellow fingers paused over his nachos as he smacked out the words.

She wanted to feed him, but knew an offer would insult his current pride. "Not only is it your right to tell this family what to do, but everyone seems to want it that way."

"There you go—not sounding like Odissa. You sound like Alpha now. Something in your voice—you're manipulating us. I can see it. At the very least, I can *hear* it." His voice lowered. He wasn't sure of the people around him—people who could listen. He also wasn't sure if Odissa cared enough to censor their behavior if need be. "Just come out and say what you want us to do, Alpha. You know what's going on. Guide us. We'll fucking give you what you want."

The cashier-girl who had taken their order went back into the kitchen area. Odissa could see her feet as she leaned over the counter, maybe reading a magazine. The low music droned above them, and the shoppers outside of the café-area made enough noise to drown their conversation out.

"Maybe that's why Alpha hid for so long. She didn't want you to constantly question her intentions. Need I remind you that I'm still here and haven't done anything wrong? Stop punishing me."

He sat back in his chair, sucking through the straw. "Haven't done anything wrong?" He smiled in disbelief. "Fine. But you haven't done anything trustworthy."

"Like what?"

"You got Leeland killed, for one. You did that. You set it up. You got him to freak out and tell Pepin about you, probably. And that made *everything* else fall into place."

Odissa leaned forward to hiss, "He had it coming. I didn't choose how Gwendolyn got to him. And I'm certainly not the one who told Bob to kill herself. You have Vulcan to thank for that. Not that she really wanted to be here anyway. And while we're blaming me for everything, should we mention that I let my parents die? Despite the fact that I was a baby and couldn't fucking save them even if I wanted to—didn't even have the muscles to walk! But yes, blame me for not warning them. If you see your infant speak in full-fucking adult sentences before they've even learned to say 'Da-da,' you can bet your kid is possessed. But I'm *sure* they would have continued loving me fully—for sure!—even if I'd managed to convince Leeland to let them live. I'm *sure* of it. And let's not forget that I'm the reason you're blind. Granted, that's *all* you were willing to give up for me and so *ironically* turned a blind eye to let me die?"

He licked his lips, unfazed.

Odissa calmed herself by chugging her coffee. Swallowed and breathed. "You have every reason to trust me and yet you refuse to believe me when I tell you Odys isn't planning anything. Don't I know my brother well enough by now?"

Dorian slapped down his empty cup, the sound echoing and turning heads.

Odissa wanted to tell him he had a dab of cheese on his stubble, but she also thought he deserved to look foolish if he was going to treat her this way.

"Besides," Odissa went on. "You really want to see Odys when you're having such a hard time? He's being kind enough to give you space. Plus, I think he really liked Rosemund. It's the Pepin in him."

There she goes again, Dorian thought. *Sounding like she knows. Like Alpha.* "I'm having a hard time?" His fingers rooted around for more nachos, trying to sound only half-interested.

"Fletcher proves it. You made him—and him alone—clean up 'the mess.'" She noticed Dorian tensed, warning her not to sputter a bunch of attention-drawing details in public. "Q and Maud were too afraid to offer help. You made Fletcher do all the work. Why take it upon yourself? Because that's how you deal with things."

He shook his cup, ice rattling around. "I owed it to her. To you all." He leaned back in his chair.

"No, I think you needed out. You needed to escape me for a bit. When Fletcher went out, so did you. You can't think when I'm around. And you desperately need to think—think about *how* to think about me. Hell, you can't even stand to look at me without getting distracted. That's just another reason to send your eyes away. Now, give me that cup. What do you want? Coke?"

He cleared his throat, trying to absorb her reprimand. "Yes, please."

She got up and went to the fountain. When she returned, Fletcher was there, standing over Dorian. "You couldn't tell him he had cheese on his face?" Fletcher grumbled as she sat down. He licked his thumb and cleaned a willing Dorian's chin. "God, you need a shave."

Odissa frowned. "It's like they always say, you get up from the table and the food arrives."

"So I'm food?" Fletcher asked, pulling up another chair.

"Food for thought," Odissa clarified. "That's not to say I didn't notice you, poking around in the men's department. Did you buy me anything?"

"You noticed me?"

"You're four feet taller than any of the racks. Who wouldn't?"

"You never once looked at me."

"There are reflections in dark windows." She gestured to the ones beside them as she tried to finish her food. Dorian and Fletcher looked at her skeptically. So, she added, "Also, Dorian was acting *too* gracefully. I knew he was seeing *something*. He knew where the tables were. He was avoiding them."

Dorian frowned, found out. "Well, I call bathroom break," he said, scooting back.

And so they each went into their designated bathrooms. Odissa noticed that Fletcher made sure she went into hers. Something also told her that he came right out just as quickly as he'd gone in. Dorian didn't trust her. No matter how much he wanted to, he was having trouble.

"What's next, then?" she said, rubbing her damp hands together. Those automatic air dryers never did the trick.

"To the car." Fletcher said. Odissa noticed his lingering hand on Dorian. Of course Dorian didn't feel well. Fletcher had been more distant than close from him these past few days.

When they got into the "new" car Fletcher had acquired, she noticed all the grocery bags in the back. As Fletcher got into the driver's seat, he said, "The ones in the floor board are food. These are for you."

She slid over and let Dorian in, rummaging. "Nice, very nice," she said pulling out new socks and shirt. "I didn't think about how hard it must be to do laundry."

"Nonsense. We can find a laundromat, if need be," Dorian said, settling in. "Or a dry cleaner..."

325

"Dry cleaning's always best. Saves time and effort," Fletcher said, starting out on the main road.

"You would say that," Odissa sighed. "Look what money's done to you. Well, thank you for buying me new clothes. Though I think you put this in the wrong bag, Fletcher." She held up a lacy thong. *What were you suggesting?*

"Yes, let me see that," Dorian said, examining it with his fingers. "Yes, this is most definitively meant for me. Damn checkout kids, assuming."

"I thought you wore boxer briefs—or are you trying to spice things up?" She flinched at her words. She was trying too hard.

"No, not spice things up. Go back to who I was." He shoved them into one of his plastic bags.

"I didn't realize I was keeping you from who you are."

"You're not," he inserted quickly, as if to put an end to it. "I didn't mean it like that. Just all this traveling about has kept me from my normal wardrobe and I'm missing it. I like nice things, Odissa."

"I can see." She put a hand on his wrist, drawing him out. "And I would like to see." *Them on you.*

He kissed the back of her hand and snuggled into her, wishing the car would heat up faster. But that's what you get when you steal a car. They're usually the older, less reliable kinds.

Stanza: The older, less reliable kinds.

When they got to the house, they circled around a few times, making sure no neighbors were too interested. They parked the car around the block and quietly walked up to the house. A dog barked, calling attention to them. But no humans were responsive.

Freezing, they finally made it to the door. It was unlocked. Stomping off their feet with what little snow had found them and setting down their light luggage, they noticed Mecca was already sitting in front of the TV, eating popcorn. Fletcher held up his grocery sacks with a huff. "What'd I go shopping for, if you were just going to steal from them?"

Dorian took off his shoes as Fletcher took in the place. Off-white walls, off-white carpet, and oak furniture. So colorless. "Wow, what stuck-up people."

"The passcode to disable the alarm was their anniversary year," Q informed, just before ramming her face with popcorn. This was a time before even Ring cameras were a big thing, mind you, so this level of security was pretty high-tech for the time.

"Ugh," Fletcher said, helping Dorian take off his coat. Fletcher made sure the others were smart enough to close the blinds and that the lights turned on were minimal. No point in advertising they were there.

He noticed a professional photo of their unwilling hosts near the doorway—a Caucasian couple. Fletcher scrunched his nose. "Pretend-happy couples make me sick. They expect a baby to bring them back together. But there's never a good time for a baby, so it's not going to happen. Not that they were ever close to begin with."

Fletcher closed the door behind them.

"I know, right?" Q agreed. "At least get a fish first or something."

"These people are getting a divorce. Or worse, early retirement."

"That's what you said about my parents, Dorian. You said that to them once," Odissa said. It shut their snide comments up. She meandered into the living space. The over-stuffed sofa was covered in crumbs. Mecca had raided their food supply; wrappers and dirty plates had already piled up.

"Mecca," Odissa scolded, "you're trashing this place."

Mecca peeked over his laptop at his mess and frowned. "Their food's about to expire. They won't be home for another week. Besides, we'll compensate them." He pulled up a pair of large headphones from his neck and placed them lop-sided on his head, covering only one ear.

"Golden coffee table," Q said, tapping it with her foot. It turned to solid gold instantly. Her color waned and her head lolled back a bit. "Whew. That took a lot out of me. We're going to need more food!" She shot up and went for Fletcher's sacks.

There was a flush sound around the corner. Maurice came out, a local newspaper under his arm. He was also wearing a nice robe—probably stolen from the closet.

"Why the hell are you naked?" Fletcher growled.

Odissa snorted. The robe—that *didn't* come to his knees—made him look like an Renaissance king with scrawny legs. The cigar dangling from his mouth added to the effect.

Taking it out of his mouth he said, "Did Mec tell you that Maud iz five minutes out? She called." He handed his cigar to Mecca, who took it graciously. "You were right, son, these are better than the ones I got in Puerto Rico last year."

Mecca smelled it before putting it in his mouth.

Odissa stifled a laugh. Stealing was no laughing matter. "You all make yourselves quite at home, don't you? Just what are we going to do if we get caught? Honestly, a hotel is starting to sound smarter."

"Hotels have people," Maurice stretched is legs before kicking them up "With the way this lot is feuding we need our privacy. Fewer casualties."

"Plus this way is more thrilling," Mecca added.

"We've lasted zis long without getting caught, dear," Maurice said, crossing his bare legs. "Vulcan wouldn't let it happen."

"Did my brother say anything else?"

"No," Mecca said. He looked up at Odissa with too-knowing eyes. "And that's exactly why Mecca is worried."

"Worried?"

Fletcher's head snapped around at the sound of footsteps. "Speak of the devil…"

The knob turned.

"Just me," Maud said, her breath hanging heavily in the cold air. Her finger turned back into a finger—no longer a key to let herself in. Her hair fell in front of her face, but it couldn't hide the hollow look in her eyes. She saw Fletcher's bag of groceries.

"Sorry we wouldn't wait on you," Fletcher grumbled. "Seems like you were waiting on us, though."

"Why's it just you?" Maurice put down his paper. The tips of his mustache twitched. "You don't look well, Maud."

She came into the living room. The fact they didn't have many lights on contributed to her mystery.

"None of us look well. Not lately. Where are the Automatons?" she asked.

"The kitchen table. Where Mecca put zem," Maurice noted.

Her chest was heaving, maybe from the cold. "And the box?"

"There as well." He gestured in the direction of the kitchen, but she believed him.

"Good," Maud said with a sigh.

"If Odys was so worried about what we did with them, why did he leave us alone with them?" Dorian prodded as Maud forced herself past them.

Maud looked at them all. "Everyone needs space now and then."

Maurice leaned forward in his chair. "Maud, where's your Master? It iz clear you and he are not well. You seem far from him—where iz he?"

Q turned off the television. Mecca closed his laptop lid.

"Forget all that," Maud said, waving her hand. "I may sneeze out soon, so I need an answer quickly."

"To what question?" Mecca asked her.

Maud loomed over him, her high-heeled feet making her endless above him. "Odys wants Madus. Can I have him?"

Everyone exchanged looks. And, they finally noticed Odissa had sat down in a corner chair. Was she not worried about her brother? About his Automaton?

"Why *him*?" Mecca asked, though an answer really wasn't necessary.

Maud looked up, straight at Dorian. "Because I'm a twin. If you aren't going to give Madus to her"—Maud gestured to Odissa—"give him to me."

"We may still give her one—"

"Then why haven't you?" Maud's chin lifted, showing her glowing eyes. "I'm not going to watch her age and die, Dorian."

"We can talk on this tomorrow—when we're all in our right minds and didn't just bury Rosemund!" Dorian reeled, restraining himself from hitting the wall.

"Rosemund got her turn now I want mine. I get my second Automaton."

"That's all very well," Fletcher said, leaning against the doorframe. "But right *now?* Don't you think you're a little too sick to be doing something like that? I mean, you aren't even here, Odys. We'd like to be assured you're the one who's touching him."

Maud's back tightened. There was certainly something mad in her eyes. She had something up her sleeve. "We could test it—see if an extension of my soul could activate an inanimate Automaton rather than my actual body. It's never been tested before, right?"

"Why risk it? You'd pass out, if it worked. Maybe even die. Just—just look at Maud. She's not well. God only knows what you look like. Odys, come to the house," Dorian begged. He was too fucking tried to mess with Odys's shit tonight. None of this was reasonable. "Tell us where you are…"

Fletcher stepped forward as if wanting to shake the answer out of her.

"So, you don't trust me to take Madus? And you don't respect me enough to just let my Automaton touch it? Even if that's what I want?"

"Not when you're acting so fucking weird, no," Dorian said. "Just tell us what your angle is."

Maud laughed. Her legs approached Fletcher so that Dorian could get a good look. Though he stood heads taller than she did, she was his equal in stance. "Oh, Dorian, I can't wait to tell you what my angle is. Just let me get what I came for and you'll see."

She circled him to get to the kitchen. Her heels clicked on the tile floor. She knew that everyone had followed her—maybe to stop her, maybe to see if it would work.

"Don't do anything stupid," Dorian warned, on her (literal) heels. They couldn't stop her. How could you stop an Automaton?

She had already picked up Madus—in his own Ziploc bag. "Don't worry, I'll only take one. Fair is fair, right?" She opened the bag, holding it up like a dose of anthrax. They reared back from it, not wanting to be infected.

"You're being stupid, Odys!" Mecca shouted. "This could kill you if you're so far away. You don't know what a second Automaton does!"

"How would anyone know?" Maud asked. "Any Automaton who *would* know is still here, upon that table." Her eyes lit up, as if using the last of Odys's reserves. "Rosemund would've loved this, wouldn't she? Such an experiment."

Odissa inched past them all, better to see. She looked at them. "You'll just let him take it?" *You aren't even going to reserve Madus for me?*

"Of course they will," Maud said. "They're the ones that watch. They watch as things happen rather than *make* them happen. That's why everyone keeps dropping like flies."

"Don't be cruel, Odys," Odissa said to Maud.

Everyone looked at Odissa in confusion, barely noticing Maud had pulled the lips of the bag over her hand—exposing Madus like a banana without a peel. "Let me get it out of my system, Odissa. It's the last we've got."

"We?" Mecca asked, eyes darting to Dorian to see if he'd catch on.

Maud swayed a bit in place, adjusting her footing as if nervous and weary. She raised her eyes, a strange smile on her face. "I want you all to know—*know*—that this is going to work. I know it will. And, I'm sorry it's not more graceful. I've always been a bit rough inside Odys. That, and the stress makes it hard to be graceful, though there's grace in admitting gracelessness." Maud shrugged for Odys.

"What the hell's he saying?" Fletcher stepped forward.

Maud stepped back. And stepped back again.

331

Odissa raised a hand, asking Fletcher to chill.

As if toasting with a glass of wine, Maud raised Madus and his bag. "To Gracefulness!"

Maud jumped forward at them. She tossed Madus in the air as she moved—so quickly—as she came. The next thing they saw were two glinting pennies…coming directly at *Odissa*.

ODISSA ODELYN: One of a twin.

ONE: Soon to be with two.

TWO: Soon to be with her, the one.

THREE: Though she was always two in one, wasn't she?

Chapter the eighth,

The flinger is flung:

But who hits first?

When Maud had transformed into a penny—flinging herself at Odissa—they all knew what had happened. Odys had killed himself. That, or the Alpha inside him—whatever portion she had stowed there—had forced him to kill himself.

He was no longer needed in Alpha's story. (And I will admit, he'd become somewhat of a side character, dragging along. Perhaps Alpha felt the same way?).

But back to those few seconds. Though Maud, inanimate in the air, would eventually hit Odissa, the first to actually land in her outstretched hand was *Madus*.

MADUS: Got there first.

FIRST: Come, first served.

SERVED: A good portion of Odissa/Alpha.

ODISSA/ALPHA: Now immortal.

Chapter the ninth,

Twins in the twin:

Twin twins?

Maud hit second, hitting her wrist.

Odissa caught her just the same, with her other hand. She caught them both with such quickness it was unnatural; it was unexpected.

Dorian stepped back from her—as they all did. "You reached." *You wanted him to do this. You knew it was coming.*

Odissa turned from them. "Fuck," Odissa hissed, rubbing her head. She wobbled in place.

They waited for her to faint—to topple over from the fact her soul was being ripped from her body (what soul there was). But she didn't.

Alpha was already so used to having her soul ripped in two—that rebirth after rebirth—that this barely phased her.

"Just a headache?" Maurice reeled. "Just a fucking headache?"

"Oh, don't you stare at me like that." She rolled her eyes. "They were his to give. What? Do you expect me to convulse? Vomit like you mortals? Alpha doesn't need to sync. She *is* synchronicity." She started to shake from defensive rage and backed away from them. She averted her eyes, ashamed and pained. And then they caught her eye...

She admired the pennies in her hands, as if they were gold. "You all saw this coming. Don't act so shocked. You did nothing to stop it. I know Mecca told you, Dorian—who Odys really was. He tried to. You don't think I noticed how busy you were, little Mecca? I know what you told Dorian—what you guessed. What you *suspected*." She was talking to the pennies—a Gollum with his ring—nay, *rings*. "Oh, stop looking at me as if I'm going to hurt you. I got what I wanted and leave it alone. Look, all the other Automatons are still here, aren't they? I could easily take a few steps back and"—she took a few steps back—"touch them all." She stood still. "But I'd rather be *given* things."

"Odys just killed himself?" Dorian asked, something in his throat. They had to be certain.

"I did it for you, Dorian. For us. He was making you ill."

333

"You made him kill himself, Odissa." Maybe it was more of a question. A question of how.

She blinked back tears, trying not to look at him but still facing him. "He loved you. He loved what Alpha loved. He wanted to be whole again. Don't you see? I'm whole again—as much as can be. When Maud took his soul she also took his part of Alpha.[76] I am whole again." She brought the pennies to her chest.

"What...have you done?" Fletcher whispered, eyes wide. "What have you been doing?"—*to us?*

"But are you as whole as you want to be?" Maurice asked, mustache twitching as he stood in her exit route. "Your power will never be what it once was, will eet? No. You still are working toward that vision. That vision of being how you were originally created, before zee Automata took you down."

"No!" Odissa tensed, blinking at the floor as if confused. "I would never. I just wanted to be safe. To have my immortality back. To not fear *dying*. To not need to breed and live over and over again. To stay with *you*, Dorian."

"Just, just, just..." Maurice shook his head, turning askance from them all.

Mecca watched Dorian, his lip curling in horror. "You like that she did it, don't you, Dorian? Now you can have her without interruption. Your nephew just died and you cry from happiness!"

"You think I like being this way?" He bent down and growled in Mecca's face. Dorian was crying in horror, wiping his running nose on his collar. Mecca and Q backed into Maurice for protection. Dorian grabbed at Mecca's shirt. "You think I like loving this monster?" He pointed at Odissa. "What would you have me do?"

Maurice pushed Dorian back away from his son. "Zis is what she does! She turns us against ourselves to take them all. She doesn't even have to kill us. We'll kill ourselves."

---

[76] The Narrator and I have had long conversations about what she means by Maud "took his part of Alpha." Perhaps Alpha was half in Maud, half in Odys. Or, all in Maud. The Narrator usually just explains it as, "It's too complicated for you to understand."

"Start with yourself then, Maurice!" Dorian spat in his face. "She can't do the impossible."

"He doesn't mean it!" Odissa shouted, coming between them. They parted like the red sea for Moses, not wanting to touch her. But Dorian wasn't afraid.

"Do not speak for me!" Dorian growled at her. He backed her into the cabinets of the kitchen. "No one speaks for me."

She took the sides of his face to keep the distance between them, the pennies dropping to the tile floor. But she couldn't stop his forehead from resting on hers.

"Why did you do this, Odissa?" *Did you have to kill him?*

"I just wanted to live, Dorian. I can live with you forever now." She cried as she tried to pull his head back by his hair. It turned into holding him in place. The guilt flooded her and spilled out in a confession, "I knew your sister was having twins and so I split myself into two. I had to expand myself to expand my chances of living. Do you understand how hard it was to get her pregnant? The magic involved? *Please* understand. I was Odys and then I was also Maud. And now I'm whole again." She looked at one of her pennies on the floor. "Really, I'm three now. Again."

But under one mothership.

"You killed him. Even if he was you—you killed him. He was something before you possessed him, Odissa. He was still a person!"

"You think Odys wanted to keep living? You think there was really a place for him here? Now we all can live in peace."

Q shook her head, her face scrambled. "You call this peace? There is barely anything of us left."

"I'm sorry. I'm so sorry," Alpha whispered to Dorian, melodramatic tears welled in her eyes. "But this is the best I could do. I didn't think this would be how it happened. I always thought it would be me."

Fletcher formed a gun. Q followed suit. Dorian assumed a low, begging voice. "Tell us why we should still trust you after what you've just done." He grabbed the back of her neck, to keep her from moving away.

"It's not as if I haven't had an Automaton, Dorian. I always had one. I always had Maud. Through Odys. He was me. A clone."

"But now you have two!"

"And you could have two." She pointed to the table. "We could be equals. In that way."

"You didn't have to kill him, Alpha." Dorian cuffed her neck tighter. A heaviness pulled at the corners of his lips.

"He was unhappy." Odissa still stared at her penny on the floor. There was a hint of remorse on her face, but not for what she'd just done; for the fact they did not understand her. "His body had no role with me any longer." She tried to slide down, out of Dorian's grasp, but he held her there, pressing his body into hers, his tears hitting her chest.

"Where is his body, Alpha?" Maurice asked.

"In the trees," she said. "Behind a golf course near the Wal-Mart, where he bought his gun."

And with that Dorian broke, his body sagging. Alpha comforted him as he gasped into her neck. "Mi sobrino..." he mumbled off in Spanish.

To keep from hyperventilating, he pulled away from her, resting over the sink. Free, she quickly bent down and picked up her coins.

Stanza: The woman who tithes.

"I swear this is all I wanted." She cradled her coins in her palm. She ran a finger over them. They noticed she was having a hard time keeping her hands and eyes off them. "I promise I am loyal to you all." She could feel them waiting for her proof. "What you know about Pepin is true. But only half-true. You don't know the full story. How do you think he knew I was Alpha? How did he know where to find my brother?" She looked up at them. "That's right. I told him. *I* found him. Not Leeland.

Everything fit, so he knew I wasn't lying. It wasn't my husband who came to Pepin for help. Not at first. *I* got to Pepin first."

She looked back at her coins.

"We had to make it so Gwendolyn would lie as well. She had to, you see. She had to lie to Leeland. It had to be a chain reaction. I offered Pepin my help in killing Leeland. Leeland was not as evil as they come, but he needed to be stopped. None of you were willing to kill him—not that you necessarily could. This was the best way to get rid of him, in the end. I gave my word to Pepin—I convinced him." She could not stop her fingers from enclosing her coins and bringing her fist to her mouth like one might a rosary. "I have many Words. I know them. I know the Words." She paused in thought. "And didn't they all die happy? They all died thinking they were helping in some way—helping in some overarching plan. You see, Pepin didn't kill himself to give Odys Maud and therefore keep me from gaining all Automatons."

She put her coins on the counter, between her and Dorian. She walked away from her coins, very easily, in fact—as if it caused her no pain, albeit, her eyes did glance once more at them.

"Pepin killed himself because he knew I'd eventually gain all Automatons—and, indeed, I have gained his. You must understand, he trusted me. I told him everything. We planned this together."

"But not this part, right?" Dorian accused.

"He and Leeland were both so convinced that Odys wasn't me," she laughed at their stupidity. "I made them believe—so easily—that he was just a boy. I told Pepin Leeland might kill Odys if he wasn't protected. They were so willing to die if only they served a purpose. Please don't think I wasted them. Our plan was I would become part of the family and you would see I am not out to cause destruction. With the Automatons under my care, no human need be tortured by their curses again."

337

"I'm not so sure that's what Pepin believed," Fletcher swallowed down his words, lest he have to taste them again.

She pulled out a kitchen chair and waited before sitting. "He knew there was a reason Vulcan did not allow the original Masters to kill me—to finish me."

Dorian covered his ears. "Her words!" he cried, folding over. "Her words will destroy us…"

She lowered her face to hide her pain. "I am only trying to help you."

"How?" Mecca cried. "There is nothing left to help! You've killed everything."

"Put out of their misery!" she shouted back at him. She collected herself. "I haven't killed anything. They all went willingly, didn't they?" *Can't I be forgiven?*

"It makes sense why you fucked Odys," Mecca tried to test her reaction levels. "You were the same damn person—same being."

Odissa's eyes flashed to the little boy. "We missed each other, our half-Alphas. Odissa never loved Odys. Not in that way." She paused. "I love *you*, Dorian. I have loved you and I have missed you and I thought that you might love Odys. But Vulcan wanted *this* body of mine to live. I didn't make you love this one."

Maurice cleared his throat.

Dorian searched for calm. "Tell me, exactly, where his body is and I'll make sure the cops clean up everything."

"I promise you, there are no traces." *I'm good at this by now.*

"Tell me now, Alpha. I want to make sure."

"Is this how it's always going to be? You not trusting me? Why not just kill me then?"

"Worse than Mother," Maurice grumbled, crossing his arms. "She knew when her time was up. Yours was long ago."

Alpha's eyes pleaded with him to shut up. "Get it over with, then. See? You know I am good. You know what I could do for you all—what I could bring to the table. Fuck Vulcan's plans. I can show you how to pause them. If you let me. We can be a family again."

Dorian walked up to her, determined. "I want to see my nephew's body. You owe me that."

Odissa told him Odys's location. Out behind the trees somewhere. Blood splattered around an accidental snow angel.

They'd think a meteor fell from the sky and then combusted. Or, that he was some pyromaniac experimenting with left over fireworks. No gun could make that explosion—not that one in his hand, no. Maybe a bad bullet? Was that possible? The lab would say.

Dorian and Fletcher left without another word.

"You leave us with her?" Maurice shouted after him.

Odissa looked at Mecca, still in Q's arms. "Mecca, you can take the master bedroom. I will sleep on the couch." *Close to the door.*

Maurice nodded to his son. *Go to bed, Mecca. I will take this watch. Your papa will keep you safe.*

Q panted in slight panic. Mecca wanted to protest but knew it seemed safer. His papa could not die. Mecca could. He went to collect his things from the living room.

Maurice and Odissa waited until they heard the door upstairs shut. They didn't really care if Mecca was in his room or not. Privacy was a theory only.

Odissa finally met Maurice's gaze. "I know what you must think of me."

"Zen please tell me, so we will both know."

"When are you going to leave, Maurice? Weren't you planning on it?" She looked at the box of tissues. *Hadn't we agreed?*

"That was before you killed Odys and took two Automata. My son's life is at stake here."

"Exactly what I mean, Maurice. You torture him with your presence."

Maurice's mustache twitched and smoke might as well have shot from his ears.

339

"I have an offer for you, Maurice. But, I know someone who can explain it better."

Odissa picked up one of her two coins—only one.

Stanza: Pay the ferryman.

When Dorian and Fletcher finally found the scene (which was not hard, because of all the flashing lights), Fletcher left Dorian in the car to go and scout. Fletcher took the long way around, mumbling to himself that Odys must have called in his own death before he'd done it. *To fucking perfection.*

Fletcher climbed a good tree. Squatted in the branches like a vulture. It wasn't until he saw the torso, the clothes, the imprint in the snow, that he finally accepted Odys was dead. *Dead as Pepin. Just like Pepin. Repeated.*

Fletcher heard phrases like, "Only one set of tracks," "But how could a gun do this?" "Do his prints match anything we've got currently?" "No ID..." Fletcher grabbed a branch and resisted the urge to snap it.

I told you Odys wasn't the protagonist.

Stanza: Crossing the river Styx.

Maud and Maurice were sitting at the kitchen table. Maud's legs were crossed modestly. That did not, however, make up for the fact she was very naked.

Odissa had gone to bed on the couch. Tapped her Automaton in as she went to sleep. Albeit, she was very much awake in Maud.

"As you can see, Maurice," Maud whispered with unflagging grace, "I think it's very simple."

"Zis is not simple. Zis has been zee most intricate plan in zee 'istory of Automata." His mustache did not move. Every inch of him was stiff. Just like his dick.

She had told him her plan. Soothed the dead once again with her words—nay, Words. Just as Vulcan had done to Bob. Gave him solace. Gave him comfort. Gave him a reason. "So we've a deal, then?"

"I don't have much of a choice, do I?" He frowned. Even though the woman of his dreams was nude before him, he found the capacity to frown.

The inanimate Automatons in front of them made Maud smile. Dorian had trusted her Master with them—didn't care if she touched them. Underneath the table, her foot ran along Maurice's leg. "I'm telling you, you'd better take it while you can."

Something in Maurice darkened. "There's a spare bedroom down the hall. Go there," he told her.

Assuming clothes and standing up, Maud left him. Pacing himself behind her, he went into the living room and looked down on Odissa. *She doesn't even need to sleep with them.*

But there was a man's head resting on her chest—Madus's. His long legs wrapped around her, one dangling off the couch. The blanket covered his naked body, his long hair covered his face. His eyes opened when he felt Maurice staring.

"Dorian won't mind sharing a bed with another man," Maurice spoke freely.

"Worry about your own bed tonight, Maurice," Madus whispered as Odissa stirred in her sleep, snuggling in. Maybe syncing with the Automata had finally caught up with her. She had fallen asleep so fast. Even so, that was little proof of vulnerability. Madus closed his eyes.

Entering the spare bedroom, Maud spread herself out on the bed. "You have to tell me what you want," she said. This was part of their deal. The final string of words and promises she could pull to get him to listen. To get him to obey.

"Don't you think I know how sex works?" He raised a curled eyebrow. "I don't assume you should know everything like my Automaton. I know perfectly well who I'm fucking, Alpha."

"Isn't it sad? Even if I were your Automaton, it wouldn't be satisfying. And even when I'm not, you're always really fucking someone else."

"Dorian shouldn't know about this." He was already wanting to amend their constitution.

341

"Why would I tell him?"

"I'm not sure why gods do half the things they do."

"I like that, Maurice, being called a god. Under certain circumstances, I find the title fitting. After all, I'm not an Automaton. But I am not a god."

"It's confusing when you speak like zat, Alpha," Maurice said, spreading Maud's legs.

"Then I won't talk. You do the talking."

He grabbed her wrist to make her sit up. "Undress."

As she "lost" her clothing (a bra slipped off here and absorbed into her arm, some panties there, just disappeared), she helped him undress too, undoing his belt.

As she fondled him, he told her, "Don't be loud, and don't touch my moustache."

"How can I touch it when you are up there? Is this a blowjob or a fuck? Or both?"

He took off his shirt and pushed her back on the bed. A fuck, clearly.

"An Automaton can do both at once, I'm sure." His fingers contrasted with her coppery breast—ate at it with a starved hunger. "Laugh," he told her as he entered her. His face melted at the ease in which she took him in.

That face let her know she wasn't cheating him. She stirred underneath him when he paused to savor her—he need not move if he didn't want to. "What do you want me to do?"

He opened his eyes and looked at her with anger—anger that this could only happen once—that he couldn't keep this toy—that he could fuck millions of others but they would never look like this. He turned her over. Emptied himself into her.

When he was done, he lay down beside her. He was trying to pull his lips over his teeth, but the pained grin kept cracking through. "I wish you were mine," he tried to catch his breath. "Of all the Automatons, I wish you were mine."

"I know."

"Look at it. It was like you were sucking my dick and swallowing. No mess. So clean." He ran his hand up her dry thighs.

"No evidence," Maud said with spite. She would later spit his frothy cum out in the sink to cleanse herself of him.

"That's not what I meant. I meant you are perfection. Vulcan designed you for this moment. I am sure. He always wanted me to lust after you—for you to tease me. Zat bastard. It's all planned, isn't it? Everything."

"Not everything is about you," she scolded. "You might not find me so perfect if you *were* me, Maurice. You think my memories of Pepin would keep your dick hard if they were in your brain? No."

He closed his eyes. "Oui, Pepin's ghost wouldn't let me touch you."

"He let you put me in any number of circus costumes, though." She took his chin, careful to mind the mustache. "Does it feel like you're touching his things?"

He shook his head. "I'm touching Dorian's now."

"What do you want me to do now?"

"Sit up. Just stay there and let me look at you. Give me somezing to remember."

Maud looked up at the ceiling. Odissa, in her, realized how much she needed, well, the ability to make someone contented.

Dorian wasn't content.

But getting rid of Maurice would might make him so.

Stanza: A deal's a deal.

Fletcher and Dorian came back late. The sun was making the new sky pink—rosy-fingered, as Homer would say. Fletcher had watched until the body was taken away in its bag, the area cleaned up and roped off. Odys was as good a buried. The Master and Automaton drove back to the borrowed-house in utter quietness. Fletcher put a hand on Dorian's thigh. They were so tired.

When they pulled into the neighborhood, Dorian's head began to pound—pound with confusion when he noticed Maurice's vehicle was gone.

When they walked in, they noticed Odissa on the couch. A very instinctual part of Dorian did not like the fact Madus was sleeping on top of her. But where was Maud?—in her hand? In her pocket? With two Automatons, she should have taken the guest bed from Maurice. He should have been a gentleman.

Speaking of bed—

Of Maurice—

Dorian went to the spare bedroom. He, with great strain, pushed open the door. Maud was still lounging on the bed. But this time, she had clothes.

"I stayed up for you," she said, sitting up.

"Doesn't count if you make your Automaton do it, Odissa," Dorian said. His hand slid off the doorknob.

"Where's Maurice? Is Mecca still here?" Fletcher asked—honest worry in his voice.

"Mecca is still here. Safe and sound."

Dorian bristled at the fact he was actually glad. He asked, "Why are you in this room and not sleeping with your Master, Maud? She needs you."

Or maybe she doesn't, Fletcher thought to him.

"I stayed up for you because you're mad at Odissa's face. Not necessarily this one."

He couldn't argue with that. "What was Maurice's excuse? Did he take the box?"

"This an inquisition?" she blinked up at them each—blinks to Dorian, blinks to Fletcher. "He left the box."

"Why? How?"

"I got him to. It's just us now. We're a family. The family Mecca needs."

The eagerness in her voice made him think unnatural, fatherly thoughts. "Why did he leave?"

"I made him leave it."

"How?"

Maud shrunk back—an action so like Odissa that Dorian knew she was guilty and afraid. "Does it matter?"

"Yes, it fucking matters."

"I told him secrets. Things I knew about what was to come. When everything is over. I told him why I'm still alive. What I know. That convinced him."

"Like Bob was convinced? Did you give him the whole picture then?" He stepped into the room as if stepping on her foot—pressing for an answer. *What is the whole picture, then?*

"I gave him *enough* of a picture. He could visualize it. Act on it."

"You told me 'enough' and I'm still here. I didn't leave. What did you *really* do, Odissa?"

Fletcher began smelling the room—could smell the sweat and saliva and sex.

"I let him sleep with Maud." Maud pointed to herself as her Master spoke through her.

Dorian slunk back—each step he sagged a little more. He gestured to the room. "Couldn't have tried to *hide* it?" He enunciated his syllables—emphasized words with such conviction they even sounded italicized.

"I did try to, a little. But you don't play along very willingly, Dorian. You clearly prefer the truth because you want to hurt."

Fletcher came up to Maud, bitterness in his red eyes. He took her chin and made her look at him. "Don't pretend this is about sadism."

Maud rolled her face away and gripped her arms, as if defending herself from her own Master's lie. "I got rid of him for you, Dorian. And *I* know what the box is for. I can use it—"

"Get out!" Dorian said, pointing to the door.

He slammed it behind her and locked it.

Stanza: *C'est le premier pas qui coute.*[77]

---

[77] French for "It is the first step which counts."

When Maud sat down on the arm of the couch, her twin and her Master sat up (they were already awake, but the slamming door roused them). Maud started smoking. I've probably said this before, but an Automaton could make smoking look healthy.

Maud passed her Master the cigarette as Odissa got up. Odissa's hand shook—just a little—as she took it. "I'm sorry," she said to Maud as she tucked back the Automaton's hair. *Sorry I made you do it*—as if there were some part of Maud who wasn't her, whom she should apologize to.

But Maud only thought, *How can I care? I am you. And you are not sorry.*

Odissa rubbed the sleep from her eyes and made her way to the room. Madus followed. Madus ripped the door knob out and, without much more effort, pushed the door open. They closed the damaged thing behind them, keeping the false and unnecessary air of privacy.

Fletcher and Dorian were on the floor, as if the bed where Maud and Maurice had once been were unsanitary.

Fletcher, underneath Dorian, tilted his head to see them for his Master—his face untroubled by the disturbance. Unconcerned, he closed his eyes once more so that Dorian might block them out just a little while longer as he fucked. Dorian's dick almost went limp from the thought of hurting Odissa. *Better to not think, just do.* His face was angry—angry as he fucked Fletcher for his revenge. But he couldn't finish, which made him angrier.

Odissa smoked and waited—waited, waited, waited—for him to give up, passing the butt to Madus who smothered it in his hand and then let it fall to the carpet.

Dorian's manic thrusting threatened to give Fletcher a carpet burn—had he skin, anyway.

Eventually, Dorian spat-cursed into Fletcher's chest, fighting it. Fletcher just squeezed his eyes, as if he might accidentally open them and see Odissa.

"Stop humping him if you can't stay hard," Alpha-Odissa said softly.

Dorian kept cursing until (finally) he gave up.

Fletcher sat up, helping a weary Dorian off him. Dorian was panting, but Fletcher stayed composed. There was a hatred in Dorian's face, the sweat running down it. Fletcher leaned Dorian against the nearby bed and, before assuming clothes, allowed his set of genitalia to reform to their more 'default' state. He could give as well as take.

With his tight pants newly formed, Fletcher stood up and stooped over his Master, zipping up his pants for him like a mother would her child. He pat Dorian's face and turned to Odissa.

"Dorian wants sleep. That's all he fucking wanted. To sleep next to you. But then he comes home to *this*."

"So, you're doing this to hurt me?" Odissa said, crossing her arms and leaning against the wall.

"It was nothing, Odissa," Dorian said, breathless. "I was just angry. I was doing to him what I would never do to you."

"Dorian, you don't have to explain. But it's one thing to masturbate and it's another to do it to piss me off. However fun it was to watch."

"No, it was because *I* was angry. I was the one who was angry. I deserve to be angry." He used his shirt to dab and hide his face.

"Maybe we can both be angry. Maybe you can be angry around me."

He scoffed. "I don't know that I can. I can't—can't even fuck Fletcher angrily!" He twitched out the words.

She rolled her eyes. "I'm not saying, like, rape me. I'm saying don't fucking masturbate just to get back at me."

"I want to give you my best."

"Who says I want your best?"

Dorian laughed, almost hatefully.

347

She took a step toward him, looming over, arms crossed. "No, Dorian. I want you. All of you. I thought I *did* have all of you. You shouldn't have to hide anger from me. Why didn't you wake me up? Why didn't you yell at me?" She yelled that last part, as if trying to demonstrate what yelling was.

"I wanted to. I wanted to fuck you and hate you but I knew those two shouldn't mix."

"I'm letting you know you can."

"Don't be ridiculous," Dorian said, trying to stand up. Fletcher gave him his hand. "It's you who do the fucking, remember? The fucking over."

But when he finally made it off the floor, Odissa was already in the living room. She was gathering her purse, her bags. Madus was gone—a penny once more.

"What are you doing?" Fletcher said, asking Maud and Odissa—any part of her who would listen.

There was a panic in her eyes—eyes that avoided him. "Alpha's making things wrong. I shouldn't hurt so much so quickly," Odissa said, tears in her eyes. "This is everything she could hope for. Everything's falling into place. But it's also making her lose everything she was starting to love."

"No, you're not going," Fletcher said as Dorian sat down in a chair. Dorian was shaking—he needed sleep. He needed Odissa.

"As if you're going to stop me," she said as Maud stepped between them on cue.

"Don't fucking *threaten* me," Dorian warned from the chair.

Fletcher tried to step around Maud, but her hand formed a gun. "Don't make me involve Madus, Dorian. Don't make me break this tie." Her eyes counted the bodies.

"Pull him out," Dorian dared, "What've I got to lose? You think I care if I die? You think I care what happens to those damn Automatons in there? You want to fight, then let's fight!"

Fletcher pushed Maud's "gun" into his stomach like an unmedicated lunatic and then walked around her. No one was in for a wrestling match. He went straight for Odissa, who didn't struggle, merely glared up at him as he dragged her.

"Go ahead, pull him out. Where is he?" He tossed her down onto the couch. "Stop me, Odissa."

"You need space, Dorian," Odissa growled up at Fletcher. "Go to bed. Get some sleep!"

"No, I need to hurt you like you hurt me," Fletcher said, ripping open her pants as she flailed—told him to stop.

Maud pointed her gun at Dorian, but Fletcher knew it was a blank threat. Fletcher tried to keep Odissa down on the couch without hurting her, but that was hard to do with her kicking at him.

"You aren't even going to stop me?" Fletcher said, eyes glancing at Maud.

"Dorian, stop it. Get him off me," Odissa warned.

But Dorian just sat there, frowning, his hands resting on the arms of the chair like an immovable statue in stone-sleep

"Please don't make me hurt you," Maud said to Dorian, her voice calmer than the situation presumed.

"Oh, put that away and go back to your change purse." Dorian waved his fingers.

"How do you want it? Fast? Slow? Aren't these the questions Maud had to ask Maurice, no?" Fletcher hissed into Odissa's face, making her close her eyes to block his anger.

"As if we don't already ask each other the same types of questions, Dorian!"

"Answer me!" Fletcher shook her body with his hands.

"Fast. Because I'm a gentleman and I'm not going to deny you the right to your emotions, but I would rather not drag this out." Odissa looked straight at Dorian, past Fletcher on top of her.

Dorian laughed at her words, cracking through like thunder.

Maud reabsorbed her gun and went to Dorian. Stroked his hair. "Do what you must to be able to forgive her. But do nothing more than that. When Hera bound

Zeus, Zeus took his revenge when he was freed. You cannot be Hera. It will not go well for you."

"Zeus deserved it though," Dorian said to her, his lip snarling.

"Allusion can be just as powerful as an act."

Dorian's head lowered into his attenuated hands.

Fletcher slowly stood up, his lanky body taking his time. His hand lingered on Odissa's chest, gingerly—yet holding her down. "We'll do whatever you want, just please don't go." He begged her. "What does Alpha want? What *deal* can I make with her to get Odissa to stay?"

"I think I might die if you leave," Dorian said. "I'm sure I would die, too, if you ever fucked someone else again. Please don't ever do that again." *Please.*

"I have no intention of ever using *this* body for anything but *you*. I fucking killed off Odys so that would be the case. But you can't make what gifts I give you into your own personal hell, Dori."

"I'm in love with a demon." He laughed it, a stultifying sound.

"Fine, make me the devil. I'll slither on my belly and accept my fate. But do realize that Satan left the serpent's body eventually." She said to the air, "Even a willing host is eventually emptied."

The sun was finally up and shining through the closed blinds. Fletcher's body was like a silhouette against that morning light. Odissa stared up at him.

"What the fuck does that even mean?" Fletcher shrugged his hands to her— begging for clarity.

Brown-eyed Odissa pursed her lips and glared. *You want to do this on no sleep? Fine. I'll educate you. Whatever gets you to forgive me.*

She slid her eyes back to Dorian. A shadow came over her features, as if the sun had decided to go back down instead of rise.[78]

"Let me ask you Dorian, Fletcher: Do you obey Vulcan out of Love for Him, or out of Fear? Do you fear Vulcan and therefore submit to Him? Or, do you obey Him because He's ultimately good? If so, what makes Him good? Is He good because He

---

[78] Let me warn you this is a soliloquy. All it needs is a skull.

says He is? And what if He's not good, but you were to obey Him anyway—despite all His flaws (because, let's admit it, I wasn't His best work and how dare He create me; me, who killed so many before I was stopped)? Yes, you fear Him, Dorian. And if you, of all beings, fear, why would I not fear as well—as the very First who has the *most* reason to fear Vulcan? If I have the most reason to fear Him, why don't I? Why am I not afraid?

"Again, as I've asked before, why am I still here if Vulcan doesn't see a purpose in me? Same with Maurice, right? I have a job. A job to explain things—give advice—insight. Let's face it. I know how things—*every fucking thing*—works. I may not be what I once was, but I still have a use. I'm a castrated bull. Good for plowing, but no longer interested in goring what my temper finds irritating. Alpha knows more about the Universe than Vulcan could even teach. Why? Because she *is* Vulcan's teachings and knowledge. But I think you know that."

Fletcher pushed her back down as she sat up too high—pushing more out of her. His fingers pressed into her chest as if finding the X on a treasure map. *There it was.* She glared up at Fletcher, daring him to keep his freakishly long hand on her a little while longer.

Yes, listen for the coordinates. Trace the steps. Measure the distance.

"I'll let you in on some cheat codes, Dorian. I'm part of the game. He doesn't even have to say it, our Vulcan. Perhaps He's hoping you'll figure it out. Fuck, you should've figured it out a long time ago. Not that you haven't had your fucking hard drive rewired by the gods and who the hell knows what kind of glitches that's caused..."

Fletcher looked at Maud to make sure she wasn't moving—to make sure this tangent was no distraction. Odissa batted Fletcher's plaits away like a curtain of beads. *Listen to me.* "You wonder how I'm so sure of myself? Because I fucking helped Vulcan write the rules of this game. Hell, *I am* the rulebook that was in

Him—that He peeled off Himself. I'm formed from the scabs on His calloused hands."

She stopped sitting back on her elbows—stopped pushing against Fletcher's fingers—and instead let her rant flow gently from her and up to the ceiling as if on a therapist's couch. "When He created me, I started out as an idea. I was still inside Him. But not just me, no. So was the idea for the game. *In the beginning was the Word.* This game is older than the Maya's. Older, but just as messy. No, I take that back. It's the *same* game. It never stops being played. Yes, I like that one better." She lifted her head. "So, stop acting as if I'm the Monopoly Jail-square you've just landed on. Hell, the game hasn't even started. Right now the dice are just rolling. Rolling, rolling, rolling. To see who goes first."

Her hands mimed the act.

"You sound mad, Odissa."

"This game needs a referee and that job is not Vulcan's to fill. Not really. He's just the creator of the game. He can't control how it's played after He puts it on the store shelves—how players break the rules. He wants to see what calls we make so He can cheer and jeer for His team. That's where I come in."

"I think you're wrong. I think Maurice is that referee. Fuck, he even wears black and white."

(His French shirt, you see—of course the gods would do something just for a motif).

"Ah, that would have been very clever. But no. Not anymore. I'm the rules, remember? I can be rewritten. Revisited. I can change."[79]

"What if there can be more than one referee?"

"Now you're just trying to humor me, as if you don't think I'm right. No, he's merely a coach on the sidelines now. The one who calls for heads or tails to see who kicks the ball first. And he's made his call."

"Shouldn't there be two coaches then?"

"Who says that there are only two teams?"

---

[79] Suuure you can, Alpha.

"How many teams will there be?"

"As many as there are Automatons. Yet, in some ways, only one."

"I don't understand you. All these sports references make me want to vomit."[80]

"You don't have to understand, Dorian. You're not going to play the actual game. You're just part of the board. That's all you humans were. Beta testers. Your bodies are what the Automatons will use to pick their teams."

"*Their* teams? We have no will but a Master's." Fletcher pulled back from her, as if she was speaking nonsense and sacrilege at the same time. "Automatons can't make choices."

"So you don't want me to stay?" she asked him, surprised he was setting her free.

"Why would you want to stay, if I'm going to put off your game?"—pun, as always, intended.

"That's the very thing. I'm not going to decide when the gun fires. I will stay as long as you realize I love you with all my heart and I'm actually doing everything in my power to keep the game from starting before you're ready. That's what this has all been about. This wasn't manipulation. This was love."

Dorian stood up. His cloudy eyes were red with tears. "They may be the same thing at this point."

"That's not fair—"

He walked over to the couch, not too close but within distance. "You have so many secrets. You say you understand everything, but you do not instruct."

It hurt him to love her and she could feel it shooting out of him. "I cannot teach it to you. You would not understand."

"Tell me what Vulcan's game is," he leaned into her, lips snarling. "Tell me where everything fits."

---

[80] Same.

If I tell you, you'll go mad. "I will not tell you. If your loyalty depends on such worthless information, then no. You would not love me if you knew. You are never supposed to know. The game happens after you, after *us*. I see that now."

She looked at the box in the other room like a timebomb about to go off.

"What did you tell Maurice to make him leave, then? What did you tell him that you won't tell me?"

"I didn't have to tell him what you ask for. He was smart enough to see. Just as Mecca is smart enough to see it." Her eyes pointed up those dark stairs, their intricate wooden railing casting striped shadows on the wall.

"Like father, like son," Maud said as she made her way to those stairs to inspect them. "Maurice was smart enough to know he could do nothing about what Alpha must do." She stared up at the top of the stairs. "Got something to add to the conversation, or are you just going to sit there?"

Dorian and Fletcher heard Mecca breathe and shift. He had been listening and watching and holding his breath between the bars. He peeked around where the rail met the wall.

"Go back to bed, Mecca!" Fletcher ordered, a fire in him rising.

"Don't shout at him!" Odissa shouted back. "He has every right to know what we're talking about. Hell, he already knows everything. You're the one who should listen to *him*."

"So I'm stupid then, is that it?" Dorian asked Odissa. "I can't see it?"

"No, it's that you will see it when you are ready. But until then—until you see it—we can be happy. We are a family now, Dorian. Can't you see it?"

Maud smiled up at Q and Mecca, trying to assure them that this would pass. That Alpha had things under control.

"Fuck you," Dorian said as he moved to the door, Fletcher silently, angrily retreating from Odissa. "Like fuck I can't see what you're doing. We can ALL see what you're doing, Alpha. We're just powerless to fucking stop it."

"Where are you going?" Panic in her voice.

"You're not going to leave, but I am." Dorian said.

She'd not walk out on him. He'd not let her hurt him. That would kill him.

"But you're sick, Dorian! Fletcher will sneeze out if you don't get some—" But the door slammed.

Odissa went to the door, intent on following him out. But Maud caught her hand, held her back. "You know you can't," Maud warned her, gripping her tightly.

Odissa slapped Maud—slapped herself. "Stop it, you *Odys*," Odissa hiss-screamed at Maud. Odissa grabbed her chin, shook it, nails digging in, lips curling. "Too. Fucking. Many. Of us."

Maud noticed Q and Mecca recoil as she was released. *We have startled them,* she thought.

Odissa walked over to pick up Madus, whom she had dropped.

When she bent down, she stayed down. Crying. Weeping into her hands.

Perhaps she wasn't so *sorted out* after all.

Maud watched as Mecca and Q darted back to their room—running to hide. They heard the door lock.

Maud's sight only made Odissa cry more. "This wasn't how it was supposed to go. I planned so well up to this point. The gods won't let me do this the way I wanted. I knew Dorian wouldn't be happy, but I didn't think he could fucking leave me." She studied Madus in her hands, her arms resting across her knees. She was saying all this for Mecca's benefit. She knew he could hear. "I didn't think he had the ability."

"He loves you too much to stay and hurt you," Maud suggested, trying to help her Master work it out.

"He hurts me by leaving!"

Maud whispered down to her, "He'd hurt you more by staying and being miserable. You cannot give these two what they want. At least, not right now."

"I knew I should have waited. I should have put it off." *Fucked Maurice another day.* She massaged her temples. "But I read the signs. I read them correctly—it was only that the signs were against me. The gods are cruel."

Maud attempted nodding but was too focused on staring up those stairs. "Maurice would have taken Mecca away with him then. Mecca would have left us. Mecca deserves better than a life with Maurice. There would be no *life* with Maurice." *Only Maurice trying to die all the fucking time.* "Maurice knew that."

"He's up there, making decisions," Odissa said, her eyes trudging up toward the direction of Mecca's door. "He's up there deciding whether or not to run away from us or stay with us—"

And Alpha had been right. Mecca *was* making decisions.

And they were messy ones.

And by that, well, I mean he killed himself.

They heard a soft bang. And splattering. A shock pulsed through the house. Odissa's eyes grew wide as she looked up, up, up the stairs. Maud rushed to them. Madus fell from his Master's hand and formed, helping Odissa to the room. Her legs did not want to go. Didn't want her to face what she had caused.

Maud sank as she entered. Q was there, on the floor. Inanimate. A bobby pin. From the distance and her direction from the bed, they could tell she had shot him. Shot him in half. Blood soaking into the bed. His entrails rolling out of him as his eyes closed their final time. He was everywhere, everywhere in the room as if to say, *because there is no place for us here, I am now everywhere.*[81]

"No," Maud mouthed. Her head shook. Her body shook.

"Mecca? MECCA!" Odissa screamed as she rushed over to the bed. She reached out to touch him as he faded away—but paused. To touch him would make it real.

She looked up at her twin Automatons, shaking from the shock. *I killed a child. I killed him. His father left him. Dorian left him. He was afraid to be left with me.*

"You don't know that—" Madus said, his head darting between his Master to Mecca's body.

---

[81] Talk about killing your darlings. Jesus fucking Christ.

Odissa tore her red eyes from her Automatons, to look at the body again—to make sure of what she had seen. Verified, something snapped within her. Like a match being lit, a new hatred burned—a hatred for herself and for the god who made her.

The god who made me.

"My god, why did he?"[82] Odissa asked, though the knot in her throat obscured it. She dropped both knees beside the bed, wanting to put the boy back together again. Her eyes filled up with tears. "Why did you do it?" Her hand pushed away blood spatters from his eyes. "Was I that scary?" She kept stroking his head, which grew colder by the second. "I meant for you to grow old. You could have grown old. That was my plan!"

"He didn't know your plan!" Maud shouted at her.

"He knew more than any of them!" She screamed at the body. "Q helped him know." Her eyes moved to the Automaton, on the floor. "She was wise. So wise. She saw things even Admund could not see!"

Madus circled the bed. "Mecca saw things adult eyes could not. He was in between. He knew too."

"Yet he didn't want to be with us." Odissa verged on hyperventilation. "I'm a monster."

"She still is wise," Madus said, walking over to Q, eyes narrowing at the bobby pin. They knew what he implied.

Maud wiped her cheeks, composing herself once more. She didn't have the wits to think it to them, so said it to them instead: "He may have left part of himself in Q. We could find out why he—"

"But Dorian will hate me if I do! He will blame me," Odissa cried up to them. "We can't."

---

[82] I think our characters knew the Narrator needed to move this story along.

"Would he not regardless?" Madus wondered, his eyes matching his Master's in their tears. Tears on Madus were jarring, for his default features were as stoic as Maud's were naturally alluring.

"What if Mecca killed himself because he—he wants Dorian to hate us?" Maud wondered for them all. Her hushed tone revealed her Master's hesitation to have any part of herself think it.

Odissa held Mecca's face, closed his lifeless eyes. Her voice matching her distant look, "Dorian already hates us as much as he loves us."

"But what if Mecca had a reason he did this—other than to escape us?" Maud suggested.

"Not every suicide is part of a bigger plan," Madus reasoned. "Sometimes it's because there is no more happiness left. Just ask Maurice."

"As if it's not to get back at his father?"

Odissa raised a hand to silence them. Not only were their spoken thoughts rattling within her, but so where their unspoken ones. She could hardly sort them all out and mourn at the same time. "Fine," Odissa finally said. "Touch her."

Madus bent down. As he touched Q, his Master's head fell down into Mecca's chest. Or, what was left of Mecca's chest. Her eyes eventually reopened and she lifted her head, revealing a blood-stained cheek, watered down with more melodramatic tears (have I said "blood" and "tears" enough yet?).

Alpha had not weakened from touching Q. She had weakened from learning Mecca's reasons.

Newly-active, Q had reformed and walked to her new Master, had cupped her messy face in her tiny hands. "Mecca didn't know you were so good."[83]

"You let Vulcan win!" Odissa cried up to her new Automaton—face contorting into a red smudge. She held on to new arms tight, as if to never let her go. *He wants His plot to start and you gave in. You just quit on this—on us.*

---

[83] "Good" really is no objective adjective when called that by yourself, you know.

"No matter if you control when the game starts, He will get His way. The game will always start. Mecca knew he had to die for your cause—willingly or not. He was bored with this game. Wanted to reset. Reboot. He wanted to be wanted."

"I WANTED HIM! He didn't have to die for me," Odissa gasped, as if throwing her fit would make it reverse. "He could have died for himself. He could have grown old." Her head fell as she kept repeating, "He could have grown old."

Q shook her head. "You think you get to decide when the game starts. And that's partially true. But you wanted Mecca and Dorian to decide for you. Well, really you wanted *Mecca* to because of course he would outlive Dorian through sheer biology alone. His body was younger despite his age. Mecca could have lived for a very long time. Even longer than your own body with an Automaton. This is why Mecca knew he had to go. Sooner her later he would *have* to go. You cannot have children, Odissa. We all know this is Alpha's last chance. Vulcan caused this on purpose—so that you would cause the others to leave. That is His message telling you the game must start in this timeframe. If you don't, things will get ugly—whether you want them to or not. And Mecca didn't want to see you have to play dirty. You're playing so clean, as it is."

"We are the built-in cleaning system. The anti-virus protection. The system backup. He knew we couldn't fight it forever."

"You could have grown old," Odissa whispered, hugging Q in the middle. "I planned for it all. Eternity until you were ready to go. This wasn't what I wanted. What have I done? Oh, gods, what have I done? This wasn't supposed to happen. I had a plan."

"You never had a plan because you could not plan for this, Alpha," Q said, stroking her Master's hair. "Your plan was to plan for anything the gods threw at you. Not what the Masters threw. Otherwise, you planned well. That's why you split yourself in two and became twins, to increase your chances of living. That's why

359

you suppressed yourself in Odissa and her ancestors. But you didn't plan on liking the Masters so much. No one could plan for that."

"Vulcan could have," Maud said. "He did."

"He means for me to suffer," Odissa said into Q. "He has a deadline He wants me to meet. This is the true punishment."

"Mecca guessed you didn't necessarily like your role in the game. But you must do your duty. Mecca knew he also had no choice. He had no reason to stay and every reason to leave."[84]

"But Dorian's still alive," Odissa reasoned—the wheels in her head turning again—calculations and computations ticking out results. "Vulcan may not care *that much*. We still decide when the game starts."

She smiled up at them, then quickly stopped. Seeing herself smile through their eyes scared her. Was she really happy?

She stood up, looking about her. She would have to change her clothes.

Though she didn't have to say her commands aloud, speaking them helped sweep up her thoughts: "Go through his bags. Take his tech. I'm going to go clean up." Odissa was just about to leave the room but paused, looking at Mecca one last time. "And give these people more gold."

She walked down the stairs, rubbing tears back into her eyes—rubbing the multitude of voices back into her brain.

Stanza: Pay to play.

Odissa waited for Dorian at the vacant house for ages. She waited for him to return.

But he did not.

She decided to leave at night.

"He will come back to us when he's ready," Madus assured themselves.

Then, with her bags—Dorian's bags—Mecca's bags—and the untouched Automatons, she helped load up their newly-stolen car (that Madus had found a few

---

[84] I can't tell if this is a genius way of killing off a character or a lazy one. Maybe both.

blocks away). Just before they left, Odissa observed the golden-detailed kitchen. A remodel only Trump would love.

"The cops won't know what to make of it," Maud said behind her.

"We don't care what the cops make of it," her Master answered. "We care that it's a distraction. That it will confound the owners of this house. Maybe keep them from telling the story of what they find, because there is no story. No explanation."

They drove for a while, then switched cars before ending up at a very low-key hotel.

Stanza: Gambling is a gamble.

That following Sunday, after the couple had come home (how many days did I say they were to be gone? Doesn't matter. Just know, it's been a bit) and Mecca's crime-scene had made them vacate their home (once again) while police investigated, Odissa waited in a car, all by herself, reading the news on one of Mecca's many phones.

It was then a popup alerted her that one of Dorian's credit cards had been used. "Bless you, Mecca," Odissa said to the screen. And she passed it to Q, suddenly sitting beside her. *He wants to be found.*

Stanza: A few weeks later.

Mr. and Mrs. Who-the-hell-cares were finally able to go back home, though they had decided against using the master bedroom ever again. In fact, they had already started packing boxes to move. "I heard the house still smells like the dead body. They can't get it out," the neighbors would whisper to each other. "So sad, too, because this was the house they wanted to raise a family in. Did you see the kitchen, too? I think they're going to remodel the place too. It's all torn up."

The doorbell rang.

Mrs. opened the door to find Fletcher.

She looked stressed, her hair pushed back behind a sweatband. Through a half-open door, "Can I help you?"

"Is your husband home?"

What is this, the 50s? Dorian thought at him.

Fletcher saw the boxes and the lack of furniture.

When Mr. had happened to pass through the hall, Fletcher put on a sad smile. "I heard about the boy."

Their shoulders tensed. They had suspected he was here for that. So many reporters and curious neighbors and investigators.

"Did you know him?" Mr. Husband asked.

"Yes."

Mrs. Wife said, "I'll call." Call the police, she meant. Not because she was afraid, but because why wouldn't someone want to identify the body? Or, what was left of a body. The cops could help with that.

"That won't be necessary," Fletcher called after her, stepping forward (but not in). "I'm asking about the box, and the objects around the box. The box of tissues. Did you touch any of them?"

"What are you talking about?"

"Honey, go call," Mr. Husband said to Mrs. Wife as he took over the threshold.

"I told you that won't be necessary," Fletcher said, raising his hand. They hadn't seen his gun before. He stepped in quickly and closed the door, keeping the gun pointed. "Maybe afterwards, when I'm gone, you can call the police. Once your phone line is fixed, because I had to cut it. I apologize but I couldn't risk it. Now, about my box. It was a box of tissues, on the table. I really need it. Did you see it?"

"Put the gun down, son, and let's talk this through."

Fletcher rolled his eyes. "I'm not going to shoot you. I just need you to take me seriously. Was there a box of tissues on your kitchen table when you got home?"

"We don't know anything about it." Mrs. Wife cowered by her husband. "There were too many cops everywhere. There may have been. They may have taken it as evidence."

"None of you became ill? No cops became ill? What happened to the objects on the table—the screw, the safety pen, the bent nail?"

They looked at him like he wasn't speaking English—a good sign.

"Did you even notice anything on your kitchen table?"

"Like she said, the cops took the evidence," Mr. Husband said. "But the fucking dead kid in our bed was a bit more distracting."

"Honey—" the wife warned him. *Not when there's a gun in your face.*

"This wouldn't have been evidence," Fletcher enforced. He looked around for the golden coffee table. It wasn't there. "Did they also take your golden coffee table? Or did you claim to already have owned that?"

They swallowed.

"Don't worry. I don't want your coffee table. It was a gift. You can sell it to whomever you want. Now, my last question. Did the criminals leave anything *besides* the dead boy?"

"Yeah, a fucking mess!" Mr. Husband shouted.

"And some toiletries," Mrs. Wife tried to cooperate for the both of them.

What about my Chi flat iron? Dorian thought. Fletcher helped him stifle it. "No bags?"

"I saw no bags."

"Thank you."

He turned to go, but paused. "I want to assure you that you will be left alone in the future. This was nothing personal. And they will never identify the body or the people with him that night. Though it might sound strange or impossible, given the evidence…but he *did* kill himself."

They didn't know how to interpret his lowered voice as he left. The wife watched him walk down the street and turn the corner as the husband called the cops. But they would never find a redheaded man. Not when he fell into some shrubbery as a paperclip and Dorian picked him up.

"This was so unnecessary. We knew she wouldn't leave them."

"Who would have thought she'd have left his body, though? I'll never forgive her for that."[85]

Stanza: Hunting sport.

Odissa had camped at the hotel for quite some time. She had used one of Mecca's old credit cards to get the room, had Madus check in. When she heard the knock at the door, she had not foreseen it.

"Where is your Master, Fletcher?"

Fletcher pushed past her. "He may or may not come up." He pointed downstairs in the direction of the parking lot.

"I thought you'd track our phones here," she said. "I just didn't know you'd take your time doing so. It's been months, Dori."

"Yeah, well, you had all the best tech and credit cards. It's harder to start from square one." His eyes scanned the room. Her own Automatons were nowhere to be seen. And neither were the inanimate ones. "Where are they?" Fletcher asked.

Fletcher had already spotted the box on the courtesy table—the tissue box alone sat atop it, as if upon an altar.

"In the bag, in my purse." She pointed. Fletcher went for them, carefully. He swiftly put on his Master's gloves.

"How can I be sure you didn't touch them?"

"Maybe you shouldn't have left them with me, if you didn't trust me," she replied over his shoulder. Well, really *near* his shoulder, for no one stood as tall as Fletcher.

Fletcher, bending down, moved the Automatons around in the bag, counting them. "Where's Q?"

"As if you don't know," Odissa said, stepping back.

---

[85] There probably would never be a gravesite to even visit, as bodies have to be held in cold storage until identification efforts are exhausted and then the state can cremate.

"How'd you convince him, then?" Fletcher asked, like some criminal investigator.

"It was his decision."

"That's not what I asked!" he shouted, making her jump. It was such a raw reaction he felt almost sorry.

Odissa was crying now. "I didn't want him to do it. I only touched Q to know why he did it. You left and it was like the end of the world for both of us. He thought it was pointless to drag out the inevitable." She wiped her nose on her sleeve, trembling and shaking more fluid out. "He could have grown old. I would have let him. He could have grown old."

That had become her mantra during guilt-ridden nights.

"How can I trust you haven't touched these, Alpha?"

"Touch them yourself and see!" She gestured to the bag in Fletcher's hand. "Who's stopping you? They're yours to choose. Someone has to have them. They're not safe, in this state. Take the burden or give them to me. But don't claim I've gone behind your back!" She was in Fletcher's face now, glaring through him as if she could see Dorian in those black eyes. "Come to me, please," she begged him. "Are you really here?" she put a hand on Fletcher's cheek. "I miss you so much. I'm so alone now."

Fletcher tried to pull away from her but he found his Master didn't have the will.

"You need me, Dorian. Fletcher looks ill. You should not go against your nature. The gods want you with me, darling. I miss you so much."

He looked down at her for a long while. "Please don't have touched them."

She snatched the bag from his hands. "And what if I have? What the fuck would you do, Dorian? Kill me?"

Fletcher snatched the bag back, matching her dramatics. "Get your things. You're coming to Dorian's room. It's bigger. And has a better view."

Her eyes lit up at the first glimpse of forgiveness. "I knew he wasn't in the parking lot."

She dug in her pockets for her Automatons and they gathered up her bags. They followed Fletcher up the stairs and down a hall. Room A.

Fletcher opened the door and let all parts of Odissa in. He flipped on the lights. Dorian had been sitting on the edge of the bed. In total darkness. It made no difference to him.

He clearly hadn't shaved in all this time. Or done his hair. He would have looked homeless had he not been in designer clothes. Hobo-chic.

Instead of acknowledging her presence, he reached out for the bag in Fletcher's hand. He opened the Ziploc bag at once and poured the Automatons on the bed.

He frowned over them for some time. He took off his shirt.

Odissa said nothing.

But her Automaton, Madus, did. "Aren't you afraid you will die, if you touch them all at once?"

Fletcher turned to Odissa, face colder than stone. "Then he will die knowing Odissa was true to him."

Dorian bent down beside the bed and placed himself across the Automatons—all at once. Fletcher fell to the ground, his Master blacking out.

"You suicidal fuck!" Odissa rushed to him, felt him still breathing, checked his pulse as he vomited and frothed. "Bring me Fletcher!" she reached out as Maud retrieved him, put him on his Master's back. The paperclip was cold to her touch while the other objects glowed too hot too fast. She whispered words only Alpha knew. She had forgotten she knew them. She kissed his neck, stroked his black hair, wept over all of Dorian and his many parts. "I told you I hadn't touched them."

When he finally woke up, he felt that he was stretched out on the bed. He could smell himself—a stench like vomit and sweat. When he stirred, he heard Odissa's voice. But he saw nothing. "What did you say?" he said.

"What?" Odissa asked him, exited he was awake.

"You were saying something. Over me. Magic. Alchemy."

Odissa did not reply.

"What happened?" *I should have died.*

"You were out for a week." It was Odissa's voice, coming toward him. "We couldn't give you a bath because the Automatons needed to be on you.[86] I cleaned you as best as I could. I slept in the chair." She pointed to the pile of baby wipes, the chair. "Don't touch your IV."

His hands felt around the bed. "Where are they, then?"

"Here," she said, moving his hands to the pillow beside him. "When they shrunk back I knew you'd wake up soon. Even your dreams were as crowded as your bed, Dorian."

He could smell cigarette smoke. She had been smoking. "Fletcher, I need Fletcher."

"He's in there, Dorian." She picked him out for him.

He licked his dry lips. "Yes. I know," he said, his head settling back down on the pillow. Fletcher was synonymous with "his Automatons" now. Perhaps this was because Fletcher was really the only one Dorian wanted. The others were superfluous phantom limbs that he would never want to use.

"Are you hungry? You want a bath?"

"Yes. But I don't think we can make Fletcher form. We're too weak. You must help me."

He started to get up. "Don't forget them," she reminded him. She put them in both of his hands, divided evenly—as if they were magic pills.

If he had had the energy to see her face, he would have noticed the worried look—worried that his nouns were off—pronoun and otherwise. Dorian was having a hard time being more than two.

He felt multiple hands upon him. Odissa's Automata helped him step into the tub.

---

[86] Is it bad that I picture a giant, lethargic orgy?

When he made it to the bathroom, she began to help him undress. She helped him into the tub. Began to wash him.

"You didn't touch them," he said to her as she cleaned him.

"I told you I didn't."

"And now I have so many. Inside my head." He rubbed his head with his fist like a paw, a fist tight around his Automata.

"You will get used to it. It would have been better if you didn't touch them all at once. Easier."

He sank lower into the tub. Turned his head toward her. The first effort he had made on his part. "I have so many conflicting views of you. In here. So many opinions."

"But do you still love me?" She pushed back his hair, made his Adam's apple pop.

"Leeland had so much faith in you," he said. "He believed you were the key to helping him end it all. That's why he saved you as a baby. In some ways you were the key. He didn't know how you had strung him along, made him believe it was your doing—all these changes in Mother and Pepin." He laughed at the irony. Then his face grew cold. "I can see him fucking you. Admund remembers it."

"That was Odissa. I'm more now."

"I also remember how you used to cringe when Leeland kissed you. That gives me some comfort."

"And what do the other Automatons [make you] think of me?"

"They make me wonder how you could love me."

"I have never loved anyone like you. I've only ever loved myself."

"You didn't love me until the gods changed me and made me devoted to you. That's what you love. Like I worshiped Dory. You missed that. What if I am really a means to punish you? To punish you with my jealous misery?"

She leaned over the tub and put her head to his. "Dorian, you are no punishment. You are my gift. My reward. For being good all these centuries. Don't you see?"

He brought his fists to his eyes. "You could have anyone. Why choose me? It seems too easy. Too contrived."

"That's your curse saying that. I picked you. Because I know what it is to love many. I *have* loved many. And I miss them. I am like you. I am old. I am nostalgic. And I have missed you. Your sister has missed you. And for once in my life—lives—I'm looking back. Not forward."

He began to weep.

She shushed him. He grabbed her arm, pulling her closer, dropping his Automatons in the tub in the process.

The next thing he knew he was back in bed.

And he could see.

Well, his Automatons could see. For him.

He had never seen so well. So many dimensions. So ubiquitous.

His brow furrowed as his inner sight tried to focus. He moaned, feeling ill from all the images overlapping his mind. Odissa sat up, closer to him, and looked down. He had color to his skin again. She stroked his beard. "You would be dead if it wasn't for me."

"That was the idea."

"No it wasn't. You wouldn't hurt me like that."

He grabbed her hand and held it, kissed it. That was all the energy he could spare, for his body then laxed and it was all he could do to keep breathing.

...

Odissa curled up beside him, put her head on his chest. "You shouldn't try to fight to keep them down," she said about his Automata. She reached out and touched Caffar. His body tensed as she did so. "It is making it harder on you."

"There are too many of them. Where will you sleep?"

"I've been sleeping just fine, among them."

"They feel too much. It overwhelms me."

"You seem to enjoy it in your sleep."

His face scrunched up, trying to remember what she meant. Ah, yes, he remembered. Her own Automatons were scattered throughout the bed—they tended to prop themselves up on the bed and merely rest a hand here or there on some part of their Master. But Dorian seemed to remember having one of his bodies touched— he was having trouble remembering which one—touched by a body not his own. Did Odissa even know which of hers had humped his in her sleep? "Were you even asleep when you did that to me?"

"I didn't rape you, if that's what you mean," she laughed at him. "And yes, parts of me were asleep."

She was quiet when he did not laugh back.

"I'm surprised I could even consider it. So much energy."

"You are better than you realize, Dori." She took his arm and wrapped it around her. "You fight it."

And they laid like that for some time—until Dorian's breath slowed and he was back asleep and she watched his Automata pop back up to life, one by one, their eyes closed tight in slumber. She held down a gasp when Dorian rolled over—closer to her, to spoon her. Because, as he did so, his Automata rolled near her too; she the north to all their compasses, their devoted magnetism crushing her.

Stanza: Godheads and god head.

Dorian was now sitting up in bed. He was eating. Odissa was eating. The Automatons—hers and his—were in the floor, watching TV, reading on their phones, taking naps, looking out the window. Picture what you want of the overcrowded room—an overcrowded room that felt so empty despite its tightness.

"Do you think you will be able to walk soon?" She asked him as she stuck a fork in a sticky bite of pancake.

Dorian took his time in answering. Took a drink of orange juice to bide his time. "Where will I walk, Odissa?" What was her rush?

She shrugged and chewed. "To the car?" The Automatons could carry him out but that would look awkward. She could have them go out and buy a wheelchair...

He took another drink. "And go where?"

She stared at him, picking her teeth with her tongue. Did he not remember their conversation the day Rosemund died? How they had daydreamed together? What of all their plans?

She noticed Admund looking over at them, to help Dorian find his food. She hid the frown on her lips and began to eat again. "We could go to your storage units. Get one of your cars so we could stop stealing. Then we could look up a few more dead babies, their socials, and start a few more credit cards so we can be set for a few more months."

"We're set for a few more years, Odissa. No need."

"What does that mean?"

He took another sip of OJ. "It means, Odissa, that I have been bored before, like now, and so bided my time by insuring I would never have to want anything again."

"So I am boring?"

He snorted. "There is never a dull moment with you." He began to drink again but she knocked it out of his hand, making what was left splash the wall.

All his Automata turned their heads. Maud, Madus, and Q just kept watching TV.

"People die, all the time, Dorian. They just died sooner than you would like. Sooner than *I* would have liked. But Vulcan wanted it that way. You know He did. Made it that way. So stop fucking moping about and—"

But she didn't finish her sentence, because he kissed her. He grabbed her behind the neck and kissed her. "I'm sorry," he said past the wetness in his throat. "I'm sorry."

She tugged away from him. "There is so much of you. You're practically a demigod now. It's bound to be a little boring, Dorian."

"Demigod, is it?" he said up to her, letting her head go.

"Having one Automaton makes you god-like. Having as many as you do makes you a demigod."

"What is Alpha, then, with so many Automata? An actual goddess?"

Odissa did not answer. "Where are these credit cards, if you have so many of them?"

"Throughout. We can go and get more, if you are worried."

"I am not worried," she said, putting her plate aside. *I am just bored.* She noticed he had stopped eating and took his plate as well.

He tried to smile. "Please forgive me, Odissa." He looked like a cancer patient begging his nurse for more pain meds. "Please."

"For leaving me?"

"I came back, didn't I?"

She looked over at his naked Automata. They were all looking at her. She turned back to the Master. "You can't stand me being mad at you, can you?"

"Makes my nose feel like it might bleed."

"And did your nose bleed when you left me?" When he did not answer, she reached over to his lap. "Did it?" She ran her hand up his thigh and cupped him between the legs. His body sighed at her unexpected touch—melted into her unwillingly.

"What are you doing?" He gently grabbed her wrist, as if now was not the time.

But she simply used her other hand, which he quickly grabbed as well. His Automata noticed her own stand up, but they were too lethargic to act intimidating in return.

"You used to love it when I touched you," she said over him.

"Comfort me. Don't force yourself on me. I'm not in the mood."

"Your reaction says otherwise," she glanced at his dick.

"I don't have the energy."

"I do all the work anyway," she laughed through her nose.

But he didn't laugh. He simply gave the obligatory smile.

They were silent for a moment, waiting for Dorian to formulate words. It was his turn to speak. She could tell he wanted to say something as he squeezed her wrists. To fill the void. "I am not a man anymore, Odissa."

She cocked an eyebrow. "Are you identifying as female now or....?" She had wondered how the new Automata might tip the scale.

"No, I am legion." He put his head back. "And the only thing I know we all want is you. But we don't know what that means. Or if it is right. We disgust ourselves for loving you."

She pulled her hands away from him and readjusted her position on the bed. Waited before she asked, "Did you ever think about getting gender confirmation, Dorian?"

His lips pursed. *Why are we talking about this?* "Of course I *thought* about it."

"But you didn't get one."

"Because, for one, Fletcher would have had to give it to me."

"That or another Master, and you didn't trust them. Or didn't want them to be the ones to do it?"

"Are you offering or something?" *Am I that dull to you?*

"No. Just trying to understand you."

"Let me be perfectly clear—*transparent*, even. I 'transcend' gender, but I don't mind how I was born. I'm not this or that and I'm not half and half. I'm a quarter." He paused, hearing the change pun and following it. "And I like how I've been *changed*."

Demiguy may be the word he's looking for, though I'll not try to label him.[87]

"But you keep changing," she said, leaning into his face. She heard the pun too and wanted more—more of them and his cleverness. But all she could see when she looked at him was a little boy digging through empty pockets.

---

[87] Despite the fact you've been calling Dorian he/him this entire series?

His Automatons looked up and he finally saw what she was doing—saw her expression. "I frustrate you?" he said up to her. "I've never seen you frustrated." Sexually, anyway.

She glared at the Automatons on the floor and slithered to the edge of the bed. "You tell me to kiss you and then you don't want me to touch you. I don't know what to do."

"Let me figure out who I am. It's not as easy for me as it is for you. You have control over your body even when you touch one," he pointed to the Automata sitting on the floor like a bunch of kindergarteners waiting for naptime.

"I grow impatient. Your body is well enough for decisions yet your mental state holds you back. The Automatons are turning you against me."

"You are not impatient. You are patience personified. I've never known someone who laid in waiting longer than Alpha has."

"Every second you spend keeping me at a distance is one less moment we spend together. Do you hear me?" She wanted to shake him. "We both have limited time. I've never felt such pressure. Never."

"Good. I'm glad you feel pressure, then. You seem to work better under constraints. Keeps you creative."

"What are you saying?" she said, turning back around on the bed. Her eyes were red—with anger or sadness I do not know. For Alpha, at that moment, they were more than likely the same.

"I'm saying that the more freedom someone has, the less interesting their lives become. Especially you. You, who were once a terror for all mankind. You wanted to kill everything. Nothing would be left with such power. We stripped you down and now look at you. Interesting as fuck."

Her face hardened. "You are one restraint I fear I cannot make interesting, Dorian."

His Automata stopped looking at her—as if they couldn't bare it. "I am sorry," he mouthed. "They all remember parts of the past. It's like one big screen shot—panoramic view. I can see all the things I missed. And all those things that could have been better, if I'd only had all these sets of eyes. Things could have been so different."

"You think I don't think the same things? You think I wanted Mecca to die? Rosemund? Gwen? I drove the poor boy to it! None of us saw the signs."

He massaged his temples. "They'll drive me insane, Odissa. I can't ignore so many of them."

"You'll learn how to make them welcomed company."

"It's not that they're unwelcome. I am glad to know these things. I am only disturbed that I have all this knowledge and it does me no good. I can't even change the present with it. I have no power. So much but none."

She shook her head. "It's not that you have no power. It's that you have no joy in it. A truly godlike thought, perhaps."

"Godlike? I feel more helpless. More mortal than when I was."

"Like you said, Dori. Constraints." *You were more interesting when mortal.*

"What a terrible thing to say."

"Then why did you say it to *me?*"

"Because it was true," he whispered. "We're all more poignant when limited."

A commercial played in the background, filling their silence awkwardly with toothpaste and jingles.

Odissa spoke over it, "One day, when you are well, I will ask you to hand me all your Automata. And I will put them under a pillow. And you won't be able to see. And then I will sit in a chair, as you sit on the bed, and I will send Madus over to you. And he will turn you over and I will fuck you through him."

Dorian stroked his beard, trying to play along. "Why Madus? Even Q or Maud could do such a thing."

"Because Q is where I keep what's left of Mecca and Mecca does not want to fuck you. And Maud is where I keep what's left of Odys and Odys wants to kill you."

"A part of you wants to kill me. That *is* interesting."

"Of course. I am Alpha, after all. I wanted to kill everything."[88]/[89]

She thought that would have brought the mood down, but Dorian went on exploring her thought. "And will you touch yourself as you also fuck me?"

"No. I don't find it easy to masturbate. You know that. I would rather focus on fucking you."

"That wouldn't do," he shook his head, throwing out her vision. "Not when I have a perfectly bare penis available to be inside you." He gestured to his genitals.

Odissa sighed and turned to stare at the wall.

Dorian asked her, "Are you feeling particularly horny right now or was that a test?"

Her face cracked at his question, as if to say it was neither. "Do you know what else we could do, Dorian? What else I plan on doing? I take one of your Automatons and one of mine and we just watch them. They'll do the fucking for us. Slavoj Žižek style. Synthetic experience. So we can stop with trying to have it all. We can push past identities and labels. We can just be ourselves. They'll be our ideal selves over there. We don't have to. We're just us."

"Sounds like just thinking about the sex toys doing the work is satisfying enough," Fletcher said from his portion of the wall. His long legs crossed at the thought, covering up his genitals (Dorian's Automatons were all still very iffy on the clothes). He was the only Automaton of Dorian's that ever spoke. But it was no

---

[88] I asked our Narrator why that was (why Alpha wanted "to kill everything"), and B.L.A. replied, "'Everything' is hyperbole, though Alpha did snap and interpret her original 'purpose' to an extreme." Sounds like Marvel's Ultron or something.

[89] Side thought: Alpha and vegetarianism—leads me to think Alpha may be vegetarian because she's making up for past sins. Not sure if that's a theme worth exploring. May delete this footnote.

longer his voice—his tone and pitch had shifted as if speaking for all of them at once. "Now you never have to have sex again."

"Sex is out of the way then. Like death. We can be who we truly are then. Our rawest selves."

"That's the thing, Odissa. This is the price we pay for it all. Who are we now? How do we decide?"

"We let the Automata decide for us." Though the answer was simple, she knew Dorian would never adjust to Automata he did not want—he would never find himself in them. Not when they were a reminder of every prelapsarian thing he had lost to gain them.

There would be no new start as she had hoped. They were still the same people, just haunted by different ghosts.

"Tell me this, Dorian," Odissa said as she stood up. "Will we ever be happy again?"

"I don't care about being happy. I care about pleasing you." He paused. "That's the only thing I think I could ever care about in a life like this."

"I don't think I could be happy knowing you are unhappy."

"The world is infinite for us. Who is to say I won't grow to be happy?"

But Odissa, like Hegel, could see the future in the present. She saw this in the form of the past. This Oscar Wilde couldn't escape his fate.

"Can I give you another bath, Dori?" She said, walking over to his side of the bed.

"I suppose I do smell."

Her Automata helped him up and carried him into the tub. His naked Automata sat in the floor, their eyes watching them as they moved.

He sank into the water as if it were a hot tub. But Odissa never came to wash him. Instead, her Automata stood over him and waited for the water to rise before pushing him under. He struggled a little—more from the surprise. He struggled until Odissa turned to his Automata in the room, their eyes wide with fear.

"I can't live like this. Neither can you," she said to them as they fought to stand up—as they struggled to understand just what was happening. "I love you so much," she said to them. "I'm sorry I did this to you. I'm sorry I prayed for you. I—I was so lonely. With myself. The gods gave me what I wanted. I got what I asked for. They're teaching me a lesson. This isn't fair to you."

She knew she was doing the right thing when they didn't come closer to save their Master. "I shouldn't have saved you when you touched them all. I shouldn't have held onto you."

"It's OK," Fletcher said to her, right before he fell. He said it like Dido atop her pyre—knowing this Aeneas had destiny beyond them. "I didn't want to leave you either. I don't. But I should."

They shrank in glitches into their forms.

Her Automatons dragged Dorian's soaked body out of the tub, placed him on the carpet. Odissa shook her head, *no, no, no.* Regret crawled out of her. "Why did I—?" She knelt over him. Breathed into his mouth. Pressed his chest. Breathed into his mouth again.

He never spit up the water. Only a fraction trickled out.

"He's gone," Maud said for her as she began to try again. "You can't bring him back this time. He doesn't want to come back. You must stop. Nothing good can come from bringing him back. The gods programmed this."

Madus knelt beside her, his coppery hand resting on her shoulder. "You cut his thread straight through this time. The gods won't give him back."

But Odissa just shook her head. *No, no, no.* She pushed back his wet hair. "The gods took him from me long before." *No, no, no.*

Odissa did not weep for him as she had done for Mecca. Instead, she stared at his body, shaking her head, rocking over him. She addressed the gods—the gods she knew were watching—"You will pay for what You made me do. This gift was tainted when You gave it to me. For sure, I will do as You designed me to do," she stroked the lips that were once Dorian's. "But I will always hate You for it."

"Of all mortal men, he was most interesting, wasn't he?" Madus thought for them, as if Dorian was a painting whose artist were now dead—fixed and immortalized. "He saw us. He understood without explanation what we were. Masters and Automata and us."

Odissa looked about the room, at all of the inanimates. She leapt over his body to grab at them. One by one she gathered the Automata and brought them to her lips. She buried her face in them. "Are we not one now?" she said to them as they became her. "Are we not alone together now?"

The hotel would discover Dorian's body two days later—with two pennies over his eyes. But don't worry. They were *just* pennies.[90]

Stanza: Monopoly pieces.

Monday, Tuesday, Wednesday, Thursday now have passed. At least, I think they have. It sure feels like a Friday. Nevertheless, time has passed. And during that time, Alpha had been doing some planning.

Odissa had to stop by the vet for a few *items* before arriving at the recently-closed (or abandoned—I like that word better), *abandoned* mental hospital.

An abandoned mental *asylum*.

Even better![91]

An abandoned mental asylum now used as a storage unit until the rest of the supplies and utilities were needed in the new location. In reality, most of said supplies and utilities were never going to be needed for the new location. They were slightly out of date—but nothing so creepy and rustic as what you see in horror films. They tend to be sensationalized, those films, and remind you of lobotomies

---

[90] Wait, so we're NOT gonna talk about what just happened here?
[91] Why am I even here if the Narrator is just going to edit without me?

and women plagued with falsely-diagnosed hysterics. That's not really the vibe I'm shooting for here. Simply a clean place, well-stocked with stretchers and space.

She had pushed out most of the equipment into the hall. She placed the Automatons in her sulfuric circle like a pentagram with too many points around her selected "patient" chair. Thus began her summoning ritual.

Her back toward us, we see her setting up a supply table—pulling out contents from a large bag and arranging them to suit her needs. The box of tissues is there, as if upon an altar. She lights the candles and walks away from it, and I shift my gears back into the past tense.

Odissa set up the drip, strapped her legs down in the chair, and, when situated, inserted the needle into the vein. Using her teeth, she tightened the straps on her doctored arm.

It was the farthest arm, the one opposite the needled, that she worried about getting loose. She wanted to stop herself from pulling that needle out.

The strap across her middle would keep her from flailing about too much—if she even would. She probably wouldn't. She has more self-control than that average human. She had *patience*, as Dorian would have put it.

But part of her was unsure. She no longer knew herself as well as she would have liked. Centuries of suppression can do that to a being—never getting to be yourself. Perhaps she would pull the needle out after all.

As she leaned back, she could already feel her body turning as cold as the cold, cold room.

She tried to remain calm.

She watched the drip.

It was so slow.

But

It

Did

End.

Her legs twitched only a little when her (mostly human) heart stopped pumping.

One, two, three, four, five, six, seven, eight, nine...

Each Automaton rose from the floor, fully formed, fully naked, and fully confused.

They looked at each other, astonished.

Self-aware for the first time.

They had consciousness.

A self-awareness dependent on no other's.

They had souls.

Or, the equivalent of, depending on your opinion.

Admund was the first to stand up—stand up on his own free will. He looked down at his body, his toes, his hands, his dick. A most basic humanoid form—a form he had trouble changing. So this was him. In his simplest.

Panicking—realizing what had happened—he studied them all—his brothers and sisters—just to be sure. "I—I am." The words choked out of him, recognizing his voice and that it was his. His hands touched in reassurance, wringing.

"Me too," Q stated softly, tears coming to her eyes as she looked at her hands. She felt her arms and felt what it was like to feel without someone else there.

"But who am I now?" Anselm asked.

"You," Madus said, spitting out a laugh. His thin-lipped mouth stayed open with a shocked smile. He pressed himself against the wall as if hyperaware he was apart from all of them and had no intention of returning.

Coraza said, "If we are, then that means—" She found herself taking a step. For a moment, there, she recognized she had *willed* herself to move. It was a scary feeling, to be on your own. It made her debate her every action. She had so many choices and options and...

Maud, speaking for the first (so many firsts!) time on her own accord, "She was good all along."

"Didn't we know that?" Q asked. "I'm sure we knew it. We were her."

"We were her," Coraza said, holding her flat stomach as if to comfort the conflicting empty and full feelings within. "But no one is objective about themselves."

"Now we're apart and know for sure," Madus countered, finally parting with his wall.

Q rushed to Odissa, tears in her eyes (why was she crying? Was this a time to be sad? What kind of tears were these? Did they fit her character? What was her character?). She pulled out the needle and, with shaking hands, touched Odissa's body. Turning to Admund, her long hair parting like curtains, "We have to revive her." She rushed to the table—the table Odissa had arranged. "Revive her, Admund! You know how."

"I don't think it wise," he shouted as if the room were noisy. And maybe it was. Maybe their bodies were ringing with new life.

That which could give freedom could also take it away. Admund was yet to enjoy his freedom. He'd not jeopardize it with bringing Alpha back.

Q began to panic, observing the table. "If you won't then I will. Tell me how!"

"She is dead, child," he said, taking one step toward her, arm outstretched. "Do not go against her wishes. What if she wakes up and we revert back to our soul-less states? Her soul is *split* into us. Her freedom's now ours. We have her soul. It is broken up in pieces."

The littlest amount of freedom can go a long way.

"No. Look—these shots!" She began to prepare them. "Maurice died once and came back. So can she."

Admund eyed the utensils suspiciously, so conveniently placed. He almost remembered Odissa placing them there. Had she made them all forget? Did she not want her plea for help to seem too obvious? He didn't like how those tiny shots—possibly capable of reviving her—undermined her martyrdom.

Q, though she thought the same thing, refused to believe it undermined anything. Though Alpha's strange, Vulcanized soul had set them free in a way only hers could, it wasn't demanding help. There was still a choice. Q would make her first one.

Stabbing the adrenalin needle into Odissa's heart, she waited. "Give me the Words," she said when it did nothing. She prepared the next shot, one for Odissa's arm. "Give me some Words of Alchemy, Admund! I know Vulcan told you the secrets!"

"He told me secrets but not all of them. He knew better by my time. Even more by yours."

"Give her the Words, Admund!" Madus demanded—his face never more expressive.

When Admund offered nothing, Q looked around at the others. There were no Words or even words for this.

"Father's own image and just like last time too!" Madus spat at him.

"I need a defibrillator!" Q went on.

"Don't be daft, girl," Fletcher said, coming up to the stretcher-chair. "Your fucking hands!"

Just as Q understood, Fletcher was already warming himself up for the job. He studied his hands—was he strong enough? Could he do it now? He gave Odissa a jolt.

The first time, nothing.

Perhaps he wasn't charged enough. "Do it with me," he looked at Q, at Madus.

Nothing.

Cestus came up to her feet.

Again. Again. Again.

They sent bolts through her.

"Give us the Words, Admund!" Madus demanded between his own guesses at *the Words*. His body was humming and singing with Alchemy. Some of his Words got odd twitches in Alpha's limbs—odd flickering in the lights as if she were Frankenstein's monster draining the electricity. But it didn't start her heart.

Admund's lip almost snarled—in fear or pride, it didn't matter. He whispered something—something that wouldn't make sense on the lips of a human, for a human could not get the right pitch. They are no living tuning fork.

A wind rushed through the room when he said it.

Q repeated it—over and over—and her eyes thanked him.

His jaw clenched. He couldn't let the others take all the credit for helping Q.

Saying it with force, Q put her hands down again. And this time—this time—Odissa's eyes shot open—glowing with the same metallic aura as her skin. They burned through the cold room and through them all.

They stepped back as she gasped like a fish out of water. They watched in amazement when her body convulsed and a glimmer spread over her—a flashing glaze that disappeared as quickly as it came. Her eyes rolled and came back down—normal once more. But there was something now inorganic about those dark eyes.

She blinked to focus, but found she could not. She closed her eyes and stopped moving. She didn't even breathe.

"No!" Q shouted, taking Odissa's face in her hands. But she quickly released her cheeks, for they were too hot to touch. Q's hands burned from the heat even after letting go, melting her skin.

"Is she dead?" Coraza asked, as if death were possible to measure in a case like this.

"No," Admund said. Something in his voice sounded disappointed.

"I died," the body said, making them all jump. "But only a little." Her voice cracked. "I gave you all my soul. But I kept a corner. It almost died along with Odissa's soul. I'm no zombie—no Maurice. I still have a part that holds on even after the body goes." She finally reopened her eyes and lifted her head—the equivalent of sitting up while being strapped down.

She held up a hand when Maud tried to help her. *Don't touch me yet.*

It was a wonder the plastic hospital chair beneath her didn't melt. They quickly realized her burning flesh had more to do with her body reacting to theirs.

"That portion would have died if you had waited much longer. To be trapped inside something dead!" She shouted at them like one would the elderly. "Now I know how you all felt when Masterless."

She laughed under her hair, unable to keep her eyes open.

"You said Odissa's soul died?" Maud asked. "How is there a difference? Yours were both intertwined."

"Your past Masters' souls are dead. Yet an imprint is behind. My soul was made of different stuff than hers. You couldn't have brought that back even if you tried. Not even Admund knows those Words." She glared up at him. "He only knows the Words to control the Alchemical. That's how he trapped me in this predicament in the first place. Isn't it, Admund? Oh, I tease you. I know you don't remember what you did."

She looked at them all, counting them in her mind. "I made sure to wipe their memories of what you knew, Admund, since we all shared a brain once." She smiled like she was lying. "So don't worry. You still know more than any of them. I didn't touch your filing cabinets. But take care to leave *some* room for new ideas in there." She tapped her head, her eyes glowing madly as she did so. "You've much to learn."

"What did you change in us?" Anselm asked. "How is that fair if you control how we came out? Are you saying I could have been a different person?"

"Don't you like yourself?" Alpha laughed—laughed like a drunk. "Already so existential!" She undid the strap on her middle with a groan and began on the one binding her wrist. "You know, little one, I see history in human faces. But with Automatons it is not so easy. Their history isn't worn on their faces. It emerges in their words, in their actions." She cut her eyes at Admund. "Your ideal self will

385

reveal its consciousness in time." She turned to Coraza, then to Caffar—as if addressing them both as a pair. "Yes, a Geist will surface within you, just as every being alive suffers the ideal selves of the past. You are the culmination of everything, yet there is one history that will personify you. You think anyone gets to choose what kind of person they are? No. They are created by those before them. Odissa's gone. I'm the only part that came back. Like some fucking Christ."

Admund snorted—a sound that surprised himself as much as everyone else.

Q wanted to move on from this display. She flushed at Alpha's words but built up her courage. Could Alpha not be more nurturing toward them—them, whom she had *caused*? "This is all too convenient—like some comic book storyline. Of one who played the possessed host, was later killed by it, and then rose from the ashes. Perhaps you are more like Jean Grey[92] than Christ, Alpha."

"A very Mecca thing to say, Q." She smiled like a puppeteer pleased with the dummy's foreseen words. "But like I said, your history will surface and you will know where I stuffed each ghost."[93]

A shared chill went down the Automatons' spines.

Alpha smiled at their silence. She leaned over the edge of the stretcher-chair. "You had me holding my breath for a long while. I thought it might all be for nothing."

She stood up, wobbling.

"You knew we'd revive you?" Cestus asked, wondering if he had free will after all.

"I had *hoped* so. And you did, thank you. I'm sorry I didn't die as a martyr for you. But you had enough martyrs, really. Those before me. Those are the real saints." Her eyes became distant as she stared at Fletcher. Still transfixed, she went on: "Let's just say I really wouldn't be alive right now without your help—and I'm not talking about the reviving part, either. I gave you part of my soul and I also took

---

[92] Yes, X-Men reference.

[93] I'm guessing the last batch of Masters are going to be most recognizable because 1) they are the freshest and may have overwritten previous Masters and 2) our Narrator is too lazy to whip up more backstories (but who would want that anyway?).

a bit of your code—your essence—to ensure I'd be able to come back *if* you so revived me."

She showed them her hands; they sparked like tesla coils for an instant and then dimmed as she wearily set them down. Nothing but hocus pocus. "It was an even trade, really. Software for software. Freeware, if you will."

Sounds more like malware.

"A trade we didn't agree to!" Admund said.

"It's not like you don't still have your gifts. I just took a corner."

"What is this word? A 'corner!'" Coraza shouted back with a laugh. "You keep saying it as if you've merely rounded off our edges."

"There may be effects, but give me some credit. I could have taken it all!"

"*Why not* take it all?" Madus asked her, curious. "Why not?"

"Because I am not selfish. And better me than someone else. If it had not been me, through this, it would've been done in another way. A way more painful, perhaps. The game must be played."

"If not Judas then another Judas?" Madus asked with a grin—a grin that was halfway hidden behind that long, copper-green hair falling straight in front of his face.

That smile made his twin's eyes narrow in confusion. As Maud studied that quick little exchange—the smile and the tilt of his head toward their once-Master—Maud also noticed Odissa's body. It wasn't the same—it caught and held her twin brother's eye with how it had changed.

Granted, Alpha's Odissa-body had changed before: it had changed when Alpha had been called out of hiding; it had changed when it had touched Automatons; it had changed when it gained them all. Why wouldn't it change again?

But this time her body was more...*beautiful*. That was the change—not darker or stronger or fiercer. Perhaps it was the power over light she now seemed to have, making her shading and highlights more definite, but there was undeniably a terrible, aesthetic beauty to her that hadn't been there before. She was harder to look at, but you couldn't help but stare.

"Judas?" Alpha shot back, "If not *Jesus* then another *Jesus*. Take, eat, this is my body. And you did. Remember this of me—what I did for you." She licked her lips and enjoyed Madus for a moment. Those lips glowed for a split-second after she did so, and then they grew red, as if the new power inside her irritated her organic body. "Judas, Mudas, Madus," she said quietly to him—like they were the only ones in the room. She scrunched her nose, as if seeing the words written out before her.[94] "I will redeem all traitors."

"You make no sense," Admund said, almost hatefully.

"To you, maybe not. But I think Judas, here, understands me perfectly. There's a bit of me still swimming around in there."

Coraza sank back into herself. Her voice whispered, "She knows us. We don't get to choose."

"Tell us now if we really have free will!" Maud shouted at Alpha, leaning into the shout. "Tell us if we're just your puppets and you mean to predestine our every action!"

"It's not me, my beauty, who predestines us. It's Them." Her eyes looked up, the rest of her trying to save energy. "I died for your freedom. I was not pretending. I even tried to stave it off. If I am lying then why do you care so much for your freedom? You think of yourself as an individual! See? Autonomy. That *is* freedom."

Admund shook with rage. "Why give us life if we're to be shuffled into a game? You yourself don't want the game!"

"I didn't. But it's been forced on me. On us. And no, I didn't give you life. You already had life. I gave you my rib. Now, my Eves, stand by me." She gestured to the open space around her, letting her connotations sink in. "You have free will. But of

---

[94] Yes, it is safe to assume I edited this section to fit with the name I chose for Madus. But I do want to be clear that Alpha was playing on his name here, for the same effect. That has not changed.

course you will be called toward me, too. We share parts of the same soul. Not even I can help wanting to be with you. That is the only power I have over you. Fight it if you want." She looked at Cestus, Admund, Anslem. "Some of you will fight harder than others. But that's because there's more inside you than just my soul. There's the imprint of every Master before me. But you can choose who you will follow: your Master, or your soul."

"Why didn't you erase them?" Coraza asked, covering her eyes as if she could see them all—all her past-selves. "Give us a blank slate?"

Alpha looked down from where she now stood, dimming. "I could not kill them a second time."

Admund scoffed at their preciousness. "They are imprints! Not living souls."

Alpha waved a hand, as if it were semantics. "If you let me," she growled, "I will guide you through this life-game unscathed. I know what lies before you. We can rig this for justice. At least, we can try. Let me give to you one last time and spite the gods."

"You've given nothing!" Q shouted, her breast heaving now. "You said yourself it was a trade."

Alpha turned her entire body—slowly—to face Q. Her feet brushed the dirty ground. "Devil's advocate may not be your role, but I wouldn't rule out Judas for your future either, Quarrel." She looked at them all, turning in her spot. Step by step. "I ask you to come with me, but I know your nature. I was you once. You were me once. I could have made it so you would have to follow me. I could have made you all 'blank slates.' But no. The gods will not get rid of their ghosts so easily. You will haunt the gods for me. Be my followers now or later. It makes no difference to me."

And she wobbled to the door. She paused, giving them one last chance.

"We will not go with you," Admund said, as if their elected leader.

She put a hand on the doorframe. "Ah, I thought you might tell them what they will and won't do. You're such a leader, Admund. But I think you do not speak for everyone?" She looked at Madus.

Madus glanced at his twin. Maud's eyes were wide with fearful confusion. "I will stay," he said to Alpha. But they all could hear the ringing of the words he did not say: *For now.*

They were silent until her footsteps faded down the empty hall. None said a word. None knew what should be said.

The sound of their sticking skin—to the wall, to the floor—was the only sound. They were restless. Maud was the first to form clothes, with nothing else better to do. Not that her efforts were that successful. Others took her skin-tight outfit as a sign it was too soon to attempt, overlooking that this could be—yet still—her best designs.

Coraza lifted her head, daring to meet Caffar's eyes. She met them looking for guidance. Something pulsed inside her body when she saw that Caffar was already staring at her. Were they so aimless? "Where's the box?" Coraza asked them all, remembering it like a single thread that could unravel the entire mystery.

Caffar nodded her head to Odissa's table.

Coraza rushed to what Caffar smelled. Her body sparked and shimmered with hope.

"Why would she leave it with us?" Maud asked. "After how hard she fought for it."

Coraza pulled out a tissue. It was blank. She went to pull out another but Q stopped her.

"Don't waste them!"

"It's not like they're fucking birthday wishes," Madus said. "You can't *waste* them."

"Why are they blank still?" Fletcher picked it up from the grimy floor to hold it against the light—as if words might yet appear. "Has the game not started?"

"If not from the box, where do we seek guidance?" Coraza countered.

"We don't," Anselm said. "If Vulcan let *her* be a temporary guidance do you really think he'll talk to us Himself? With true Words? A box of tissues will be no more help than Alpha is."

Cestus grunted. "By that logic we should destroy the box."

"Not a bad idea," Madus said.

Admund snatched the box from Coraza. "No one is destroying anything."

Madus conceded. "Not yet, anyway."

Admund realized his fingers were crushing the cardboard and so set it back down on the counter with great reverence. They didn't need Vulcan's wrath on top of everything else.[95]

He was still butt naked but he had been bored enough to form rings on his fingers. He played with those rings. They helped him think.

Cestus cleared his throat, no longer caring about the box or their destiny. There were easier things they could sort out. "I think—I think Bob's in me." He looked at them, them in their naked bodies. His eyes seemed to ask, *Am I right? I want to be right.* He waited for someone else to claim her or pronounce their own piece.

A few shook their heads. *I don't think I have her.*

But would they ever be sure who was where?

Stanza: Aaand they're off!

Now I must set up the next book—the cliffhanger for the coming volume. It is quite a large and craggy cliff, so adjust your grip and hold on tight. Allow me to show you where this rickety bridge-of-a-novel (as most sequels are, you see) has been leading. We sway across:

The year was 20XX.[96]

---

[95] This new Admund is a very superstitious Admund.

[96] Let's say somewhere between five and ten years into the future for these next time periods. Whatever you're most comfortable with.

Sorry to do this time jump, but *believe* me. I'm saving you from a lot of boring Automaton arguments, a lot of boring Automaton self-discovery, and a lot of boring Automaton power play. Ain't no mortal got time for that and I (a god to some degree), would rather not relive it.[97]

It'll be much more fun to just fill you in as we go along.

Here's the part of the story you deserve, my reader:

It was supposed to be winter, but in this southern state, it felt more like spring. The new characters I'm about to introduce, however, weren't much affected by the heat. They kept to the nightlife, where it was always cool.

Casinos, clubs, crime.

No, I'm not talking about Nevada. The Native Americans of this story were big on their tax-exemptions and sovereign nations in "these parts," let's just say. But not every one of these Native Americans has long dark hair and honors their ancestors, let's just say.

Let's. Just. Say.

With those white-gold wives and white man's money, you can water your blood and cover it with colonizer brands until you can barely see any Indian. Such was the case with the Lakota family.[98]

You see, Lielyth Lakota's grandmother had lived as white until, oh, a few years after the birth of her second son. Bored at home, it just so happened that she had taken an interest in their genealogy (it's not just for the retired) and quickly secured citizenship in the [Bleep] Nation[99] for her and her boys. Not only was that heritage

---

[97] Relive it? Was Bulfinch even there? What are you even saying, Narrator? Is this no longer your Gonzo story?

[98] No, not the Lakota tribe. That's just their last name. One I picked not only for alliterative purposes, but to keep the focus on their Native American "ness." Think of it as similar to the last name "Shawnee" (a common last name in "these parts," so I'm hoping this isn't offensive. Don't think I can't feel you squirming over it from here. I've backed myself into a corner with this damn smudging of facts, haven't I? Fuck).

[99] I'm just going to try and pretend like this is a fictional tribe until I undoubtedly overlook a reference that exposes our Narrator's true intention. Again, as we have in our copyright statement, "This is a work of fiction. All places, events, and characters portrayed in this novel are fictitious or used fictitiously..." This, I guess, includes entire tribes.

important, but so was the free stuff she had heard jealous whites pine over. She had, at one time, been one of them.

Yes, yes. The free stuff. Healthcare and car tags or something like that. She could find it all in this or that library's heritage center, but you'll have to get this or that paperwork first. And she did it. By gods, she did it.

Even with two boys orbiting her like constant moons.

It was supposed to be their ticket out of the trailer park and away from her piece of shit "fiancé" (who had knocked her up when she was a sixteen-year-old runaway). Now she was thirty and tired of the beatings. "We don't need you no more, Larry—you and your drunk ass. My last name means I'm Indian!"

That last name, which had gotten them quite a few questions and quite a few slurs here and there had been what sparked her curiosity—maybe she could prove it.

This was before ancestry.com, mind you.

"You's prolly just named after a stupid place. Like Dakota the state. You ain't gonna get shit!"

"I got Indian blood in me and the Nation gonna support me! I'm a fukin' Indian," she shouted to Larry during one of their usual late-night dalliances.

However, before she could really look into the full extent of the Nation's "support," Larry knocked her into a coma she would never wake from (she had interrupted the football game and he simply couldn't take it anymore).

That's how the Lakota *F*amily started.

Or something close to that, anyway. I wasn't there. This was all hearsay.[100]

The boys were taken to live with various relatives. Sometimes together, sometimes not. Their CDIB cards would be the greatest legacy Lielyth's grandma would leave the Lakotas. But for only one son did it *mean* something. These days

---

[100] *That's* the thing you won't claim to know?

(more present tense), Louis didn't even need to prove his heritage anymore. His money and affiliation always said enough.

His money was also enough to convince his brother and that zealot wife of his that the pre-teen Lielyth should live with him and her aunt. Or else. "Fuck's sake, you haven't even registered her yet."

This being after the fifth time Lielyth had run away from home, escaping from her mother's religious sense of "right and wrong." The cops, whom Lielyth's uncle paid under the table, had been keeping an eye on things for him.

"Louise doesn't want handouts, Lou. What's the point? Their hospitals suck."

"Your fucking wife won't let you work for me. And now she almost killed your daughter, Laurence. The police report said she busted a vase over the poor girl's head for watching a PG-13 movie with some friends. You have DHS on your back. What options do you fucking have?" Her uncle shouted at him.

"She knows the rules of this house, Lou. She's not to watch any of that horror crap until she's out—"

(It had been a Tim Burton movie, but that's still just as sinful, I guess).

"You Christians forget your heritage and dishonor us all with your colonizer bullshit religion."

"You're whiter than I am, you fat fuck! What reservation did you grow up on, huh? I don't recall one in our childhood. Who turned you this way?"

"Who turned *you* this way, that you could dishonor everything this family has built up?"

"Yes, yes, family. Family. That seems to have more than one meaning to you, brother. You're little more than the redneck mafia."

"Dixie mafia, you idiot. And this ain't Mississippi."

"Hey, if you wanna be red, then be red!"

"I'll show you what red looks like. Your wife is nothing to me and neither is her blood if I need to spill it. You tell your wife she'll go to the most religious schools. An institution for troubled youth. Whatever the fuck you have to. But I'm taking her out of suburbia."

Lielyth's father was just glad to have quiet once more and dinner on time.

"Don't ever fucking breed again if you can give them up that easily," Lielyth's uncle had told him once she was in the car. Her uncle knew the power of breeding, the fact being that he and his wife could not. This fact had recently become a problem for him. After his heart attack, his men had begun to question who would take over if ever The Boss were to pass. Had they seen a will? Would his wife take over? Surely not his wife! She barely knew what was going on, most days (what with the wine and the pills and the cocaine). She didn't want to know. Something needed to be planned.

Thus, having his niece was a godsend. It shut up the mutinies.

Pre-teen Lielyth had not objected to the move. She would finally get to read Harry Potter in her own bed instead of at school—she could read *anything*. She would live in the McMansion and have her own phone—she could call *anyone*. She could have sleepovers—watch *whatever she damn well pleased*. She could listen to music she wanted—*as loud as she wanted*. She could skip boring church now—be pagan *like her ancestors!*

And as she grew up, she learned the family "business." She was formally adopted—no longer just "staying with them for a while."

And this sent a shock through all the other "Families" with "Bosses." They had someone new to hate. Officially. Especially when she began giving orders for her uncle and heading some of his business "endeavors."

This was when the Automatons began to choose sides.

Stanza: Let the games begin.

Admund was walking home that same warm winter night. Well, I shouldn't say *home*, for he really lived in a store. An antique store that kept odd hours and sold very little. He wasn't in it for the money. He was in it for the disguise.

Speaking of disguises, his clothes matched his career. All worn-looking items you could find at a thrift store. In fact, he had *shopped around* for wardrobe ideas a time or two, never needing to buy a single item. He looked as authentic as possible, you see. That was his art. *Looking authentic but never being so.*

Just as he was rounding the corner, about to see his sign that read *Alphonse: Antiquary & Shoppe* he paused. His plastic sack crinkled in his fist. His nose scrunched at a scent—metal.

Another Automaton was following him. He traced his steps cautiously with his eyes.

He heard a pin drop.

Well, actually a *bobby* pin, but classification aside. He bent down to pick it up, brows coming together. "How did you find me?" He growled at it, looking over the glasses he did not need.

Q did not answer.

Eyes shifting left and right, he tossed her away in frustration. He'd have to move now—pick another front. He cursed and mumbled under his breath.

Q nearly landed in a drain between the cobbled stones of this historical downtown street. She quickly reformed to avoid such a fate and shouted back at him, "I know you've chosen your Chosen!"

And his feet stopped. He looked over his shoulder, glaring. "Not here!" he hissed, his gaze darting from building to building—all apparently empty for the night.

She caught up to him. "Alphonse now, is it?" she asked him, pointing to the sign above them. "How goes the career, *Alfie?*" She snorted.

Pretending she'd said nothing, he dragged her in by the arm, dark eyes scanning. "We all have new names now, don't we, *Akia?*" He locked the door behind them, shades rattling against the glass, and threw down his sack of groceries into a fraying for-sale chair.

Q—or, should I say Akia?—shrugged. "We're like Gandalf the Grey, sort of. Loads of names depending who you talk to."

"You have been spying on me?" he asked her—sotto voce, towering over her. It was more of a statement than a question. "How have I not smelled you until now?"

She shrunk back. "I'm surprised you recognize my smell at all. I can barely smell you when you're this close. Perhaps it's the unusually warm air."

"It is not the air, and you know it." He could not stand her sullen expression and so pulled away. His long coat sank back into his body with a swish as he turned. He "took off" his glasses, letting them reabsorb into his hands as he folded them—so ceremonious—as if humans were watching. "Why did you come?"

She stood among tables-on-top-of-tables, between his antique balancing acts, trying to absorb it all. "Why did I come *back?* Back to you?"

He studied her for a minute in the dark. He had no intention of turning on the lights—lest someone see—could someone see them? Even now they felt eyes on them—but they had for some time. The gods were watching. You get used to that feeling and never so much as pick your nose where you shouldn't (lest you displease them and lose favor).

"They all think they know better than me," he said of his brothers and sisters. "Why should *you* come back to me? After all these years?"

Q looked around the antique store. It was the most stereotypical antique store she'd ever seen. Admund had worked hard for it to look that way. To appear *normal.*

He snatched up his sack and took out its contents—odd chemicals and cleaners.

"It hasn't been that long." She rubbed her hand on the head of a nude statuette, trying not to look at him.

He huff-hissed. *Releasing steam*, as Q thought of it. "How *did* you find me?"

She wanted to tell him, *I never lost you*, but that would not have been appropriate. That would only make him uncomfortable and threaten him. She shrugged. "I've been stalking your Chosen as well, if that makes you feel any better."

"Tell me how you've found me." He moved a lamp out of the way—as if they might break it with shrill words.

"I've watched you stalking him. You will give him your mark, won't you?"

"Mark!" Admund rolled his eyes, stopping in his steps. "Is that what you all call it? No one has even done the damn deed yet and it already has a name. 'Giving him my mark.'" He mocked the idea. "We don't even know how it's done and you're already using *words* for it!"

He lectured her like a professor—pacing before a new class, trying to come to terms with it. This classroom was well organized, but dusty. He had little time for cleaning, what with paying so much attention to the future and all. There was little room for the present among all this past.

"We do know how it's done, though. The box told us."

"And where is your precious box?" He asked her, leaning forward on his checkout counter across the store.

Q shrugged. "No one has seen or heard from Cestus after he took off with it."

Ah, yes, that is a story. I'll save it for later.

He went on with arranging his new purchases. "Probably destroyed it." Admund remembered that day well. It was the first crack in the foundation of his leadership. He tucked his long curly hair behind his ears, straightening his back (as if it could get any straighter). "So you still speak with the rest of them?"

"Not in almost a year. Not directly, anyway. I spy on them sometimes. They spy on me."

You want to be spied on because you miss them, Admund frowned at his hands. "And will you tell them who I've chosen to wager my life on?"

"I will not tell them who you've placed your bet on. In fact, I was hoping to bet on him too." Her eyes cut to him, waiting for his reaction.

He shook his head. "No." He walked away from her, into the back rooms.

Employees only.

"It's not like you have a choice, who I choose!" she shouted, following him.

He turned around quickly, almost causing her to run into him. "Then why do you ask me for permission? If he's your 'Chosen,' go choose him!" He pointed at the door. *Get out.*

She stopped backing away from him, taking in a breath. "I wanted to be upfront about it. I'm not going behind your back. We're going to be a team."

He looked down his nose at her, crossed his arms. This was his defensive pose to an answer he risked liking very much. He pursed his lips. "But why do you think I am right?"

"Why are you so confident you know which Chosen will win you the game, Admund?"

"You know how I know," he spat down to her. Then, his body slacked—ashamed at his anger toward her. He looked at the floor. "You know how I came by such information—what black arts I used to foresee—and yet you are still here? The others left me long ago because of it—because of my 'impatience with the box.' And so did you." His eyes flicked once to her. "*Why* do you come back?"

He could almost see the secret. "Because I know you are right. And I would rather get answers for myself, by your methods, than wait for them from a Pandora's knockoff box." *A box meant to divide us with interpretation.*

Admund bent down on his knees so he could look up to her, like an adult about to reason with a child. *Has she gotten taller or is she forcing her height?*

She noticed the salt flecking his black mane of hair. *It wasn't like that before, or is it just detailing?*

"I don't think you really want to Choose him," he said to her, frowning under that well-oiled facial hair; black as Blackbeard; curly as Charles I. "If you did, you would have already."

"You haven't yet, either."

399

"So you think I may be trying to trick you? The fact you have resorted to *me* over everyone else makes me think you're still experimenting with possibilities. That, or you are desperate. For what, I do not know. So yes, you may play along, if you are so bored. But you do not have to choose him. I won't make you test your loyalty in that way."

She glared at him for a moment, crossed her arms. "How did you know I wavered?"

His black eyebrow twitched. *She has been lonely.* "Because I know you. We shared a brain once. You want to be sure of everything before you dive in. You want to be sure he is the one. I will test the waters then, if no one else will."

"So noble of you, to do what you already think is right."

"The others are all are so lukewarm. They make no decisions. I cannot find a use for them."

Her face contorted. "I'm tired of the temperature too." *I'd like to see what you can do.*

"I do need your help," he said to her. "When we tell my Chosen what we need him for, he will not believe us."

Her face lit up.

He raised a finger, telling her to contain herself. "You will win him over for us. You have the face for it. You will ease him into it. And, when the day comes that you are satisfied with him, you can Choose"—capital C—"him yourself. I have nothing to hide and I do not want you here if you do not want to be."

"Deal." She presented her tiny hand.

He studied her face, searching for twitches and faults. "But what if I'm wrong?" he asked her. "What if the gods intercepted my foresights, so that they could make a more interesting game?" He looked down at her feet, thinking. "Suppose what the Alchemy showed me was really a lie to keep us from winning? What if what the others say is right?"

Q's chest tightened. *He cares.* She wanted to touch his hair—his beautiful hair—but pulled back when he looked up. "You doubt yourself? The box's tissues could be laced with lies too. I can't say I approve of your methods, Admund, but I wouldn't want you to waste perfectly good providence either."

Admund frowned and nodded his head at her feet. He was listening to her as if she weren't even there, just his inner thoughts speaking aloud. "I trust my methods, same as those tissues. But you must wait, Q. Until we know for sure how strong my strategy is."

"But why do you care? It's my mistake to make."

"A gamble you can make only once. You're putting part of your soul on him. That's how it works. It can't be undone." *And I'll not risk everything for you just to fuck it up.*

The tissues, when they did speak, had been very exact on that point.

She wanted to believe he cared about her and her chance of survival in the game. But a sinking feeling in the pit of her infinite stomach told her no, *He doesn't think I am serious. I'm naught but a double agent to him. He doesn't want me to have regrets and then cause his plans to stumble. He thinks I might betray my own team if I grow to hate him or his Chosen. He thinks I'm like Mecca. That I might kill myself—let myself die—for greater purpose. He might not be wrong...*

He stood and gestured for her to sit at his small table.

She moved to do so, glancing over the tight room. A cot in the corner—a stove. But where were his books? *There must be another room somewhere. Somewhere he's not showing me. This is no space for dark arts.*

"I would offer you food, but I'm afraid I do not eat much. Do you still enjoy eating?"

"Yes. I do. It reminds me of them."

Them.

"I do have some ice cream I tried but failed to like."

"I will gladly get rid of it for you."

He handed her a spoon and the tub and studied her for a moment. She crossed her legs and paid him no mind. *Mecca, Mecca, Mecca,* he thought as she nibbled away.

He sat across from her at the round little table. He leaned forward on his elbows. "This will take a lot of work, you know."

"Didn't you say I was bored? I need something to fill my time. And what, have you so little faith in your Chosen?"

"I will like him better once we have him where we need him—once we can train him properly."

"What? Like a dog?"

He laced his fingers together, already coming up with a plan. "No. But yes."

"You want me to be the Claudia to his Louis, don't you?"

"His what?"

"Did Alpha erase your knowledge of vampire literature or are your files just corrupted?"

Admund's lip twitched.

She poked at the frozen matter before her. "I get to set some ground rules too."

He leaned back like a king hearing his peasants' pleas. "Like what?"

"Like, I get to choose Adimar's first move in the game." She expounded, "Who Adimar's first 'pawn' is. Our next teammate." She averted her eyes, waiting for him to catch on.

"You have seen one—a Beast?" He narrowed his eyes, suspicious.[101]

"I hate that the tissues called them that."

"They have to be called something. They are no longer gods. The Alchemy calls them that too."

"Yet the phrase 'giving your Mark' sets your teeth on edge? But, yes. I have found Bulfinch. Well, what *used to be* Bulfinch. Some of him." She edited herself. "*Most* of him. He's now a bit *more* than just Bulfinch, of course. But this Beast seems to think you know what you're doing."

Indeed, I did—though I shouldn't have.

---

[101] You will learn *exactly* what a "Beast" is later on. As well as a "Chosen."

He sat back in his chair. His fingers rapped on the fake wood of the table. "So *that's* why you're here."

She feigned innocence. "The stars aligned, that's all."

Admund frowned (his favorite expression). "That cat was friends with Alpha once. Why would you trust anything who once found shelter with her?"

"Because like I said, the Beast wants to pledge to team Adimar. Beasts must gamble too. Them's tha rules."

"And that Beast may be willing to die on team Adimar if it helps *another* team win."

Vendettas are sometimes worth dying for.

Q huff-sighed. "I doubt ex-gods give a fuck about anything but their own skin at this point. That's why the game exists, because of gods wanting to get rid of the parts they're not so happy with. This is the spare parts' last chance. Beasts won't risk non-existence for someone else. Not unless they're mad. Not unless they're formed without...*reason*."

"We deal with the foreskins of the gods," Admund mumbled to the wall. "None of them are brains."

The clock above them ticked past the seconds.

Q could wait no longer to ask: "Why have you been alone all this while? Julian and Joslyn paired."

"You call them that now?"

"At least you know who I'm talking about. Anselm and The Lesbians™ paired too."

"That is not a pair," Admund corrected her vocabulary.

"But you know what I mean."

"Their shared love of Mother draw them to Anselm." He sank in his chair— crossed his legs. Even his slouches looked like mighty Zeus at rest.

403

"Leeland was in you too. Not just Coraza. Why aren't you drawn to him?"

His lip twitched. "Because our mother-sister Alpha had plans when she freed us. Must have taken that part of Leeland out of me." He stroked his short beard, remembering the ambiguity. "Just like the parts of gods were pulled apart and plugged in for the Beasts, we're all more than who we used to be. Why have *you* not paired?"

"I just did." She tilted her chin to him.

"The Mecca in you. Picking the male father figure."

"No. I would have followed Cestus if I wanted that. A mother and father in one."

"Do you ever consider Maurice? Going to him, I mean."

"I wish to spare him pain. He should not have to look at me."

She still felt Mecca's guilt within her.

"But on Cestus—do you think he will keep his vow? His vow of non-participation?"

"Yes."

"Because he has Bob in him," he agreed with his own statement. "Bob was a rebel. What's left of her wants revenge for letting Vulcan trick her." He was looking at the wall now, thinking. *She regrets her decision, even if it were inevitable. Or, maybe we regret it for her.*

"Hindsight has made a ghost of her," Q glossed over.

"You should go now, Q."

"No. I am tired and need sleep." She had already chosen one of his antique fainting couches to sleep on.

"Then go to Adimar's bed. You will not have one here." He took her ice cream from her and threw the rest away.

"I will not win him over that way," she said, aghast. "He doesn't seem like a pedophile. I thought you'd know him better than that by now, Admund."

He sensed he had hurt her. "Then in what way?"

"Who's to say I haven't already *started* to win him over?"

Admund frowned down at her. This did not surprise him.

"For someone with foresight, Admund, you do not see the most obvious facts sometimes." She got up with a huff, pushing in her chair.

"Be gentle with him. We want to get this right. We want to prepare him better than any of the other Chosens. Keep me updated. I will be watching you."

"Why start now?" She went to leave, but paused in his doorstep.

"Yes?" he asked her.

"I want to be honest with you." She turned back around. "The cat—the Beast, I mean—found Alpha once. Right after the Beast was tossed in the game. The cat comes and goes. But the cat wanted to find Alpha. And did. But Alpha didn't want to be found."

He let her speak, knowing there was a point to this.

"You know how Alpha always compares humans to historical figures? Well, before the cat lost track of her, she told the cat something. She said 'Lucretia Borgia will inherit and all shit will break loose. That's when you will see me again.' The Cat seemed to think Alpha was getting interested in Odissa's Native American heritage—tapping things out."

He did some calculations in his mind. "Lielyth Lakota is Lucretia?" He remembered how Alpha thought.[102]

"She was just declared Lakota's heir right? The shit's there."

"But I don't think she's *inherited* yet."

"All the same. I knew it was time for me to make a decision. Before Alpha forces us all into one."

When Q left, Admund made the symbol of the cross and the hanging snake across his chest, like a Catholic ritual perverted. "May she forgive me for using her," he said to his Alchemy—his god.

Stanza: On yet another warm winter day (well, evening).

---

[102] Just what the fuck has Alpha been up to lately, to be involved with crime lords?

Adimar was (let's say) about sixteen years old when the Ghibla Family offended the Lakota Family. This made his own family (lowercase F, mind you) have to pick a side.

Some say the Arnauds chose the wrong side. Adimar Arnaud certainly agreed, because the Lakota killed off most of them for it. Now he had no choice but to retain his membership with the Ghibla (or Qibla, however you fancy (no one was ever quite sure how to spell it because the late Mr. Ghin Ghibla himself would sign his name "Ghin Ghibla-Qibla" to cover all bases, which lead to outsiders calling his men the Blah-blahs in mockery, which was ironic because no Ghibla *ever* talked that much, (because, you see, they *acted*))) simply because the Lakota wanted him dead too.

Really, Adimar would have been just as happy being a Lakota—despite the fact they killed his family. Ghibla or Lakota, they were all going to die the same.

By his hands.

See, the Ghibla Family, much like the Lakota, were not exclusive. That's what made the "bigger" Families so successful. They adopted the marginal, smaller *f*amilies right in. You did not have to be Ghibla to join Ghibla. You could even be, like a certain character, Jewish. They didn't discriminate, so long as you would bleed for them.

And the Arnauds had bled.

Bled and bled and bled until there was only one left.

Adimar.

And he would bleed no more.

That's why, on this warm winter eve, he was anxious—anxious that the Family could tell his growing discontent and restlessness. He tried to hide it well, though it was never easy to hide the fact you wanted to kill your Boss for trapping you in a petty crime war.[103]

---

[103] The Ghibla-Qibla had offended the Lakota years back by trying to blackmail Mr. Lakota with "papers that might otherwise suggest a most illegal means of adoption regarding the newest member of their family, Lielyth Lakota." Mr. Boss Lakota had responded with, "That Muslim hermaphrodite can suck me off! I'll show him what a real dick looks like." Such is the conversation you should thank me for editing out.

They had given him some "time off" after the last Arnaud funeral, to collect himself and be sure of his allegiance. He expected any day now that the Qibla Family, too, would confirm or deny their own allegiance to him. This made the fact that *someone was in his apartment* even more heart pounding.

Just as he had put his key in, he had heard his television. He had not left it on. He knew this because he never watched it. He reached for his gun, looking left and right.

He pushed the door open a crack—standing aside—prepared for the worst. "Why are you...here?" His voice got softer when he saw it was a young girl, sitting on his couch and eating his food.

"You don't have cable," she said, glancing only once at his gun. She put the bag of chips down and licked her fingers.

"I know you," he said, his thick brows furrowing.

"Of course you do. I've been following you for weeks. Made it quite obvious."

"Who's paying you? Lewis? Erich? Myyer?"

"I hear you need money. You need money to make Sam notice you. If Sam notices you, so will the Greeks. And so will the Nigerians. And if *those* Christians notice you then, well. Then you're in and you'll control half the gates to the coke trade coming to Tulsa and that will make your new Boss mighty happy.[104] Isn't that right? But what if I told you to forget that scheme because it's too hard and too risky and too illegal and to just take my advice? Let me lend you some money."

"Who sent you?"

"I sent myself. I brought you something." She gestured to a case on the floor at the end of the couch. When he didn't move to open it she went for it. She unlatched it and spun it around on her lap, showing him. "A case full of bigass bills, my friend."

---

[104] Because Ghin Ghibla had just died and his son, Genji "the hermaphrodite," had assumed power.

"What's the catch?"

"You do something for me. You work *for me.*"

"I have a job."

"That you want bought out of. I can do that."

"Who the hell gave you this?"

"No, no, no. Made this myself. Watch." She picked up a jar of his salsa she had thought about eating but had never gotten around to opening. She chucked it at his head.

He ducked, but it didn't shatter. It dented the wall behind him and thudded to the floor—pure gold.

He looked down at his gun, surprised that he hadn't shot it off. He lowered it as he stared at the golden jar.

"Take that to a pawn shop and bam. You've got *money.*"

He pushed back his curly hair and continued to stare, slouching as if it helped him find his center. This was something he did often, Q had noticed. He slouched his shoulders as if trying to hide his size. Not that he was tall or overweight; but, when he stood upright, he knew he looked a much more sinister creature, with a broadness that threatened even him. It wasn't something he wanted to follow up on, should said threat be received. To hunch over—just ever so slightly—was to control the domineering posture that longed to burst forth.

He picked up the jar, to make sure he could feel what he could see.

"Why do you try to get others to notice you, Adimar, when I'm the one who matters?" She stood up. "I'm the one who can fund your way to the top. I'll help you overthrow the Lakotas *and* the Ghiblas. No more working for the Muslims. Christians won't save you from other Christians. Your accounts are paid and closed."

"What *are* you?"

"Your fucking guardian angel. Whatever. Now sit down. We need to talk."

As if something had clicked in his mind, "Get the fuck out of my apartment." *This was just a magic trick. A show. A test of loyalty.*

She cocked her head. "Really? I just handed you what you want on a silver platter and you're kicking me out?"

He raised his gun once more, coming to his senses.

"Dude, that's not going to work on me. Let me be upfront. I'm immortal."

"You're no angel. Angels don't help men like me."

Stanza: He eventually got her to leave.

But, in the middle of the night, he walked out to his living room (he was finding it hard to sleep after what had just happened). And there she was, sleeping on his couch.

Naked.

He cursed under his breath and shielded his eyes. His hand slid down to his mouth and he looked at her once more, tossing a blanket over her.

How had she gotten in? Not only had he bolted the door but he had put a chair underneath it—still in position.

Upon further inspection of his living room, he noticed his lamp was now gold. His used beer bottle was gold. His television stand was gold...

Busy little bee.

Stanza: When he woke her up that morning.

"Why the fuck did you make everything GOLD?" He poked her with the longest wooden spoon from his scantly-utensiled kitchen—the same way his Orthodox twice-removed uncle had poked his twelve-year-old sister awake for some sort of prayers when his family had visited extended family in New York.

She stretched. "Redecorating this shit living room, man."

"How the hell did you get in here?" Did he have an extra door he didn't know about?

She pointed to his fireplace. Something no human could possibly fit down.

"This a joke to you?"

"Is it to you?" she asked back. "You know the Blah-blahs are watching you right now. You think a fucking chair is going to stop them?"

She noticed he was dressed, about to leave. He moved away from her.

She went to sit up but he shouted, "Don't!" and shut his eyes quickly. Cursing, "Who's trying to get me arrested, goddamn it?"

"What are you talking about? I'm fully dressed."

But he was already leaving his own apartment, pushing the chair out of his way. She rushed after him. "See?" she said, grabbing his hand and spinning him around against his will.

Her strength shocked him into submission.

He glanced cautiously, eyes growing wide at the sight. Perhaps he had just dreamed of her nakedness—which was no better of a thought.

"Where are you going?" Q demanded.

But he kept on walking, trying to outpace her.

"Is it a job? I thought you had time off, because your brother just died. Or was it your cousin? I can't keep up with the deaths, sorry."

He kept walking—trying to get away from her and anyone else spying on him.

She liked how he sped up; she was getting to him.

"You know, you're the only person I know who can pull off a butt-chin," she said as he arrived at his car. He examined underneath it, just to be sure he would live to see the inside of it. She was still there when he bent back up.

He got into his car and, somehow, she was able to unlock the passenger door and get in beside him.

She smiled at him smugly and showed him her finger-key.

He stared in awe. "I'm hallucinating." He rubbed his eyes, ran his hands down his face—stopping at that butt-chin. "This is why they're going to ax me. They know I'm going mad."

"You're not going mad, sorry. But if makes up for it, I'm going to be *extremely* useful to you. I won't let them kill you."

Stanza: Adopted daughters.

A few months later:

"I need to confess something to you, Adimar. Someone sent me to you," Q told him. "Though, don't get me wrong, I chose to come to you. He means to make you a god among men."

And so Adimar and Admund met. In a parking lot. Outside a lake-side restaurant with a dock. It was too cold for it, but there were men fishing. Q was sitting in the car on her phone, where it was warm. Adimar didn't like how she had left him alone with this stranger when they left the restaurant. "Hear what he has to say," she had told him.

There was something familiar about this man Q introduced. He was a presence he had felt hovering for a long while.

"I hear you've come into quite a lot of money and are looking for places to invest, Mr. Arnaud," Admund said to him, putting an authoritative hand on the deck rail.

But Adimar, by that time, cared little about the money. He was finally climbing up the ladder. No longer out of holes.

Akia was helping him complete jobs—making the Ghibla's cease all thoughts of rebooting his position—making people afraid of him and his new confidence.

"Is she your daughter?" he asked, still trying to fit the pieces together. "Is her name really Akia? Or is it Q? I saw a text message once calling her—"

"No. She is no one's daughter, really. Although, she might be yours now, by appearance."

The conversation went on, but the most important bit is this:

"Don't let the girl touch your chest, Adimar."

"Why, will she turn me into gold?" he laughed, his words turning to fog in this temperature. He was starting to enjoy his hallucinations now—the way the man looked at him and kept him from leaving. The way the man seemed to know what he was thinking and everything about him. The way this man seemed obsessed with him and offered him the world.

No one had ever cared so much about him.

"No. But what I am proposing, Adimar, will mean you will have a relationship already so unorthodox. You won't want her to feel that."

"I like unorthodox," he said. He had cut his eyes at Admund when he had said it, tearing them away from Q who was clearly winning at some phone game (there were many silenced "Hell yeahs!" he could see through the windshield).

"She might not realize it, but it might make her unhappy to do what I am suggesting. You must tell her what you want her to be—your daughter…or someone like me. She will respect your wishes. She likes you. Do you understand?"

"No," Adimar chuckled. "I barely understand what I'm even doing here right now."

"What we're doing isn't safe for her," he said factually, as if getting to the point. "So either you can endanger her or you can go on as things are now. She is safe, without being who I am to you—who I want to be with you. I don't think she wants things to change between you, either. If things changed, then, well, she wouldn't be as innocent. She'd be like you. Like us."

Adimar studied Admund's face as he watched Q in the car. "You care about her too? Are you so sure she's not your daughter?"

Admund grinned—his teeth may as well have been gold, the way that smiled shined. It made Adimar weak in the knees. "I want what's best for both of you. And you being a father to her, well, that's best. She's not as *seriously* invested in this as I am. Not for the same reasons." His eyes spoke of sad reasons. Sad reasons he knew would never come to pass. *She wants to bring us all together for this game—for us to be on the same side. She's waiting it out. She doesn't want a war. She hopes there's a way to pause this. To stop it. Alpha put that worm in her ear.*

"I see."

"Next time," Admund continued, "visit me without the girl. Here is my card. I want you to give up this death wish. You don't have to die for your dreams to come true anymore. I can give you everything you want and more."

"And in return?"

"And in return I have a fucking purpose in this world." When Adimar didn't take the *Alphonse: Antiquary* card fast enough, Admund tucked it into his breast pocket and patted it into place, cozy and snug. Adimar would never forget those hands. He would dream of them on his skin that night.

Adimar went up to the car, tapped on the glass. Akia—what I guess I should call her now—rolled down her window. "How'd it go?" she sang up to him.

"Your friend Admund told me there's a cat we need to adopt?"

Her eyes lit up.

Stanza: Did You Know that Gangsters Like Japanese Comic Books?[105]

The Lakota, much like the Ghiblas, let small-time criminals have their shot at filling the ranks. Anyone can have a shot, for a few bullets.

Many families unrelated to the Lakota Family happily venerated the Lakota name. Association was key. Association meant you paid your dues and they paid theirs.

It doesn't really matter whether or not the Lakota "owned" a Casino. They had their hands in half of them. That was ownership enough.

Indeed, no councils dared to turn their backs on Lakota help under this or that company name. Not when those India-Indians threatened to consume the hotel industry. The Casino-resorts were on the line. So many Patels working under the umbrella of the Blah-Blahs that it almost became an Indian vs. Indian issue (pun intended). Don't get me wrong, there were several "Indians" working for the

---

[105] Excuse me, but it's called Manga. And yes, I did know. They're called Yakuza.

413

"Indians" and vice versa; it had started to become an ironic clusterfuck long before the Ghibla threatened the Lakota Boss and his niece, Lielyth.

Anyway, to keep things straight about Indians and Indians, well, people (read: the feds) had assumed that the Lakota generally took the Hindus and the Ghibla took the Muslims. Which made it even *more* confusing when, as her seventeenth birthday present, Lielyth Lakota chose a *Muslim* as her head bodyguard. Granted, he was Turkish and not Indian, but this highlighted the fact that no, the cops could no longer generalize about the Hindus and the Muslims when trying to figure out who sided with who during this or that crime. "Goddamn it, I thought we had it figured out!" they would find themselves shouting, disappointed at yet another dead lead.

But no. The Ghibla and Lakota could not be summed up so easily. Not even their lines of "business" could completely differentiate them. They both had their names on anything from sex, drugs, the stock market, coffee houses, shopping malls…and the occasional comic book store (why not?). "Philanthropy," they called it.

The only difference, in all actuality, between the Qibla Family and the Lakota Family was, perhaps, their names. So, when Sedric got a call from the Lakota Family's Boss's right-hand-man's assistant's associate's messenger [takes a mental breath] on such-and-such a date in 200X, he didn't even bother with remembering which *F*amily the job was for.

It just *happened* to be Lakota.

And that just *happened* to be the side he chose to stick with.

And that just *happened* to eventually land him a permanent job as the heiress's bodyguard-slash-assistant.

He gladly accepted. She had handpicked him. Sure, he probably wouldn't get to go on as many assignments. Wouldn't get to see the action. But, hell, it paid a lot better.

The money made up for a loss of an outlet.

Killing was, he would admit, very messy. He often thought he was only good at his job because he could *clean up* said messes—that's what he did. His Boss made the messes, he made them messier, and then he cleaned them up.

Better yet, on a good day, he had kept them from happening.

A *Preventer*, you might say—try to put that on your resume.

But, let's face it, good days were hard to come by. He did more cleaning than preventing up until that point. So, he took the new job and never looked back.

Of course, this job didn't suit him. Most of his comrades had cringed when they'd found out he was "moving up." The guys were losing their most valuable player. "They don't want to lose you, that's it," they had told him. "They're putting you in storage. They can risk losing us. But you? Nah. We're no fucking losses."

"You act as if I'm never going to see you again. Fuck, hasn't Lielyth been there on every single outing this group's had for the past few months?"

"Yeah, sitting in the car, where the Boss normally would sit. But his fat ass would rather stay home fucking his wife these days, right? Little Boss just sits there and that's where you'll be too. You'll watch us from the window if something goes wrong. You won't be there with us."

And they had been right. He always sat in the car with her. Or they never even went at all. He was always with her.

Except for tonight.

See, when he had gotten another call in February 20XX[106] from the Boss's right-hand man saying that, for the evening, he could have the night off, he didn't know what to do with himself.

He stared at his phone for a moment. "He said I can have the night off," he told Lielyth as she put in an earring and touched up her face.

Lielyth had paused in front of the mirror. "Didn't I mention that all of Uncle's men will be there?"

---

[106] Two Xs now. Not one. So, they've been "working" together for a while now, you may assume.

"If everyone's there then why can't I be?" He lifted an arm above his head and leaned off the top doorframe, trying to make himself bigger—trying to get her to notice him.

"Because you're never going to get another night off again if you don't take this one."

"I don't need time off. There's not enough time to plan anything—"

"There wasn't a lot of time for them to plan, either." She walked out of her room and into the living space—their apartment in this mansion-of-a-house. "But I would take the hint, Sedric. They want you to have time off, so take the time off."

He shadowed her. "Why don't they want me there? Do you want me to come anyway?" *Watch from afar?*

"I want you to have fun tonight. Get out. Take a break." She was rummaging for a purse that would match.

He stared at her for a long moment, hand pushing back the side of his blazer to rest on his hip. She could feel him watching but was ignoring him. She finally looked up when he itched his nose—his hand coming up as if trying to stop what he wanted to say and settling for pressing that abnormally large slope (the largest nose Lielyth had ever seen on a man) into his own face. She knew when he itched his nose—a fake itch—that he was growing restless. She had seen what came after restlessness and did not want that tonight. So, she looked up and acknowledged him.

He itched his nose again, biding time to phrase it right. "Tell me where you're going."

She gave him her attention, focusing on that nose. She had chosen him because of three reasons, maybe more, but the first was because of that nose—that nose that gave him a profile like a Roman Caesar. To call it a "beak" would be an injustice. It was a helm's front piece between the eyes. It was a ram's head. It was a forehead and nose combined.[107]

---

[107] The other two reasons, which I edited out, were 2) the fact he was Muslim and (hopefully) wouldn't drink as much as the other men and 3) the fact that he was Muslim and (hopefully) wouldn't touch a kafir.

But perhaps that makes him seem too stout—head strong. He was lean, I will admit—more bony than muscular. However, that fearsomely well-structured face compensated for what everything else the eye needed.

She hadn't answered his question, only frowned as she stuffed things into her chosen clutch. He knew better than to ask about business.

"I'll see you tomorrow morning."

"Who's fucking driving you?" he asked after her. But she was already annoyed and closed the door behind her.

He didn't go out that night.

He stayed in her apartments at the Lakota estate. He sat in his adjacent room, at his writing desk, drumming his fingers, a cigarette burning away like a derailed steam engine between his lines-for-lips, wondering why—why, why, why?—he hadn't been *needed*.

He watched the cameras, waiting for movement. For her.

He sent a text to the Boss's bodyguard. He did not respond. He sent a text to the Boss's driver. He did not respond. He sent a text to Lieltyh. She did not respond.

They were avoiding him.

His fingers drummed faster on the wooden desktop.

He put down his leather shoes from the chair and stood up, checking the clock. It ticked slowly, prolonging his suffering.

What did she know that he didn't? How *could* she know anything that he didn't? He was with her all hours of the day—every day! Even when she went to see her uncle, The Boss, and was in the presence of *his* multiple chaperones, he had always been allowed—nay *expected!*—to escort her. Why not this time?

He stuffed his hands in his trouser pockets. He paced in his cramped closet-of-a-room. He turned on his little television, not to watch, but for its distracting drone. He unbuttoned the top button on his dress shirt and pulled at his collar. It clung too tight around his neck. It was hard to breathe. The smoke suffocating him didn't help either.

He left the room and helped himself to Lielyth's bar. He poured himself a drink, but did not even taste it. He lifted it eyelevel, staring down his brown, warped reflection. His brows came together over that buttress of a nose. He told Allah—without words—he would not drink it if only this night ended well—he wouldn't let his lips touch this glass. The cigarette smoke was his incense carrying up the prayer.

He'd not had a drink in years, not since grade school during that last hurrah with friends before his mother pulled him out of the prep school to move to another town. He couldn't even remember what he'd drank, but he had pretended to like the taste. That school had been why they'd moved there in the first place—a charter school funded by a Muslim philosopher and run by Turks that "would give them familiar community" despite it being the buckle of the Bible Belt. The irony of it was most citizens assumed the school was a Christian school by its name—something religious and peaceful.[108] Most didn't know about its immigrant administrators, though if you Googled deep enough you'd find racist conspiracies. Sedric, to his mother's delight, had conveniently gotten in despite it being a lottery. His mother was later called on to be grateful for it—and for other conveniences of "community." That's why they had left. Found new communities to escape. Sedric was still escaping them. That's what made the protection of Family so appealing when he was nineteen.

He pushed back his hair—hair long on the top, slicked back, shaved on the sides—and returned to his room. This space was too open. He closed the door behind him. Hit his head on the frame a few times. Put out his cigarette on the wood, huffed the burning lacquer.

He went for another one.

Sedric had never smoked so much. He actually hated smoking. Hell, these girly cigarettes were really Lielyth's. He preferred American Sprits but Lielyth was always buying Camels.[109]

---

[108] The name involved one of the three: "Holy," "Dove," or "Grace."
[109] A man after Odys's own heart.

It also gave him an excuse to chew those lipless lips. He chewed until his lip started to bleed. "Fuck," he cursed when he realized it, dabbing. He stuffed the cigarette back into his mouth to soak the blood.

He was only smoking hers because, well, she wasn't supposed to be smoking anyway. If the Boss found her stash, he'd be pissed. "Do you have to upset your Auntie like this?" Uncle would say. And then Lielyth would make him laugh by saying something like "Says the one who snorts coke twice a day." Sedric had even asked her to stop. He couldn't go into the doctor's office (comfortably) when she had her scheduled visit, let alone be able to do his job right if she had to fight off lung cancer in a hospital. Of course, things could be *arranged* if it ever came to that. But he'd much rather just prevent. THE PREVENTER.

So, he was smoking these for her. Yes, that's the ticket.

He was on his last ones and so went to her main purse, digging through it for her other pack. He went back to his room. Closed the door again as if he'd never left.

He walked back and forth beside his bed. He mumbled several incoherent things to himself, replaying the past week over and over again in his mind—what had he missed? He wondered. He fretted. He stared at a hole in the wall, just there, where a picture once hung.

He hadn't done something wrong, had he? No, just yesterday the Boss had pulled him aside after Lielyth had gotten in the car. "Ibn Sina, I am pleased with you, very pleased. Lielyth sings your praises, I want you to know. Your loyalty has been noted."

And then Lielyth's boss-uncle waved goodbye to her, once again ignoring the bodyguard—as if he wasn't there. He was never "there." That was his job—to be there without being.

But to be acknowledged by her uncle was like being spoken to by a king. The man was so untouchable, it was more than luck that Louis had gotten this far. A divine right of a king. Who was Sedric to question his praise?

Sometimes Sedric would drive Lielyth. Sometimes they had a driver—usually the same old man who pretended not to hear anything. Sedric liked those moments best, when he could sit in the back with her. As an equal. As if she wanted him there.

She would usually talk to him. That's what he liked about her. He didn't have to feel graced with her attention. She always gave it. Eventually.

He only sat in the back on uncle-visit days (though they lived in the same house they hardly saw each other and so met at specific places—"Never bring too much business home," her uncle would say). The rest of the time, Sedric drove. She, in the back.

He smoothed his greased-up hair again. A stiff strand fell out and landed over his eyebrow, causing him to push it back again—again, again, again. When it would not stay, he yanked it out, cursing from the pain and the shock at what he'd just done.

He looked at the clock. He could barely see it on the wall from all the smoke. He realized four hours had passed and it was now eleven o'clock and he was standing in front of his closed door, his foot anxiously tapping, his rolling thoughts chanting *sfumato, sfumato, sfumato.*

SFU-fucking-MATO.

He put out another cigarette on the doorframe, growing angrier with each sizzle. He flicked the hot cigarette down and walked out of the room. What else could he use up or deface?

He wanted to sit down, rest his arms upon his knees, cover his face with his hands. He wanted to be placid and docile. He didn't want to kick the couch. He didn't want to punch the wall. He didn't want to curse. But he did all three.

Three.

Three was his holy number—his trinity. The most beautiful and odd of numbers. The rule in art was three. Two was too symmetrical. Too boring. Too expected. Three throws off the balance. Makes things interesting. Makes art worth staring at.

Destroying three things of hers would keep things interesting, for sure. That was his art.

He looked about for a tchotchke that would give a good smash, deciding on a ceramic cat atop the media cabinet. But he paused as he reached for it. With fake-emerald eyes glinting about, it was too pretty to break. An antique Lielyth had been given from someone whose husband was about to lose a finger. She took this and the finger anyway. She had a penchant for collecting both. It was sitting next to a picture of her and her aunt. He had taken that photo, in Mexico. She had insisted on other photos as well. Ones with him in them.

She hadn't framed those.

Was too risky.

OK, OK, OK. He huffed, smoothing back his hair. He sat down on the couch—a couch that now had a loose arm barely hanging on.

...Lielyth must have gotten a phone call when he'd been tending something else; a note the maid must have delivered when he was taking a piss; a personal e-mail she hadn't read aloud to him. Something that told her not to mention what was going on tonight.

This was not like her, to keep secrets. She wasn't supposed to. She didn't have to. *She didn't have to.*

He would rather think he was getting fired—his services no longer needed—than the other options spreading before him.

What if this was a trap? What if Lielyth had pissed off the Boss? What if the bitch was trying to cover her tracks by keeping him out if it? What if...

Sedric stopped the thought.

The overhead light flickered on. Had he fallen asleep? Three o'clock in the morning. His cloudy eyes searched the entire room for her. He hadn't even heard her come in; only felt the light hit his pupils through his thin lids.

Stanza: Board games and bored games.

"I thought I told you to go out," she said to him, as if she knew he had looked up.

He turned around in his stupor to their kitchenette in the back. "Like Dolly Parton's houses," her aunt had said when she and Lielyth gave him the tour his first day. "All her rooms have kitchens so I wanted them too."

He saw her at the fridge, the top freezer door open and blocking her face. She was wearing a dress she hadn't left in—a very expensive-looking dress.

"Where did you get that dress?" he asked, standing up.

"I bought it on the way there," She answered too quickly as she took something out of the freezer.

"They made you buy a dress? What was wrong with the dress you left in?"

"Wasn't formal enough." She closed the door and walked to the sink, keeping her back to him. Her long hair was falling out of its original styling. It had been twisted back in an elegant, jeweled hairpiece. Her tense shoulder blades—the exposed portion of her bony back—were all he could see. All he could notice.

She placed what she had taken from the freezer to her face as he marched toward her. "What the fuck happened?" he said, trying to get her to turn to him. He took her wrist holding up the frozen peas on her face. He cursed in what little Turkish he knew. "I thought they said I wasn't needed! Where the hell did you go?"

He leaned down to her, trying to get her to react to his presence instead of standing like a fixed statue—a statute curving away from him. She wasn't short, but they still couldn't meet eye to eye so avoiding his gaze proved quite easy. He was talking to her hair.

"This is why you weren't invited," she gestured to her face—a face he was trying desperately to see. She waved him off, her fake nails flashing. She was always fake—fake blonde, fake lashes, fake nails. A Lana del Rey knockoff that didn't suit her and yet made perfect sense. When asked why she wouldn't get her boobs done he once heard her tell a friend, "Because I'm fake but I'm not plastic, honey."

He saw three little red smears on the new dress's otherwise immaculate fabric.

He could stand it no longer and so forced her peas away, grabbed her chin. "What did you do to deserve that?" Though his voice was casual, his hand shook out his building rage—the thing that came after restlessness.

His phone buzzed in his back pocket. He looked at the message. "Says I'm not to let you leave." He showed her, eyes wide. "Why the fuck can't you leave? Who do I work for now?"

She glanced at it half-heartedly, more interested in running her fingers over her stitches above her eyebrow.

"Do they think you're going to run away, is that it?"

"I hope so." And she tried to walk past him.

But he stepped in front of her. There wasn't enough room to squeeze through. He wasn't broad, but almost. He wasn't skinny, but almost. He wasn't much, but almost.

She closed her eyes. She never properly rolled them, just closed them.

"Fuck," he said, noticing her purple ear as she had tried to pass. He wanted to touch it to examine it better, but thought better of it. He had already surpassed his allowance. You only touched Lielyth if there was a good reason to—a reason she approved of. She wouldn't even let him zip up her dress this afternoon when she was getting ready. "I'll give it to whoever taught you this lesson, Lie. They could have done much worse."

"Uncle didn't want them to knock my teeth out. Paid too much to get them the way they are. Braces," she laughed, showing those teeth to him. It was a false smile, but her teeth were the most beautiful thing about her. Usually, her lips were closed and she either looked the part of a stoic bitch or a disapproving sourpuss. She even agreed with the thought—calling herself a "Flannery O'Connor type, minus those twee curls and fucked up teeth." Oh, and the glasses. She didn't have those. LASIK.

Sedric would shake his head when she made comments like that. She only evoked O'Connor because of her unspoken Southern Gothic fetish. No, to him she would always be Parmigianino's *Madonna with the Long Neck*. A towering masterpiece. Tonight she especially looked the part, what with that dress framing her slender throat to perfection—yes, Lielyth had all of *Madonna*'s willowy features, and her face was just as plain and unimpressive. She was nothing remarkable. Not ugly, not beautiful. But there. Distorted in perpetual *figura serpentinata.*

Yes, yes, Sedric loved that neck—but it was when she showed her teeth that Sedric became truly helpless. Imagine the *Madonna* smiling with full teeth—how unnerving it would be, how it would make her long neck look like a cat's looming over its prey; she, about to consume the Christ child in her lap. Lielyth's face would scrunch into proper place when trying to make room for those too-large, too-perfect teeth. She became a disproportionate beauty.

"Tariq stitched you up nicely, though."

"You wouldn't think so, the way Uncle was complaining. Kept reminding Tariq of who he had replaced. 'Odelyn wouldn't have taken this fucking long!' Whoever the fuck Odelyn was. I don't even remember him."[110]

Her eyes slipped to the clock.

Sedric crossed his arms, ready to talk about the real issue. "Why do they think you're going to run away and why do they think I won't help you?"

She put her face in her hands and rubbed her eyes, let her fingers run down to her lips and press into them. "You will find out soon enough, Sed. I'm going to go take a shower. Then, I'm going to go to bed. Wake me up once every two hours." She pointed to her head.

He did not agree to it.

She put a hand on his arm, asking to pass. He turned to the side, not knowing what else to do. She shoved the peas into his chest. *Put these back for me please.*

He watched her close her bathroom door and then threw the peas down in the sink, busting the bag open. He put his palms in his eye sockets, breathing in to calm himself. That's when he noticed her clutch. He went over to it, took out her phone.

---

[110] We do. Must have been a side hustle of Mr. Odi Odelyn. The Lakota must have had something he wanted.

Nothing. No text messages—only his. He was about to put the phone back when he noticed something among her cards and loose change.

A ring.

A fucking expensive ring with a rock big enough to live on. A fucking island.

He stuffed it in his pocket and went to the bathroom door to listen to her. He could hear the water running. But she never took baths, and the shower should have started by now.

Every muscle in his body tensed. *What the hell is she doing?*

He heard her open the medicine cabinet, the rattle of pill bottles. The twist of a lid. The pouring of pills. Her cursing when there weren't as many pills left as she had hoped. The opening of another lid. The pouring of more pills. Too many pills.

"Lie?" he called, tapping on the door with the back of his finger. "Lie?"

He could tell that she froze, caught in her act. He waited for no response, ramming his body into the door repeatedly until it busted the frame. She had already started swallowing some, just to spite his attempts.

"No—," he knocked the water glass out of her hand and grabbed one of her arms with the fist full of pills. "Spit them out," he said, turning her around on the counter and squeezing her cheeks just enough to stuff his fingers into her mouth to check in via the mirror. Nothing.

When she finally got her bearings, she slapped him with her free hand—over and over until he grabbed that one too.

"How many did you take?" He shouted, his face in hers. Though she tried to avoid him, he could tell she had been crying. Rather, attempting to. He had never seen her eyes so much as redden in the past.

She tossed out a number. "Four." She would have kicked him if he hadn't been trapping her legs between his and the sink cabinets.

"And what did Tariq give you before you came home?"

She chuckled into her chest. "Uncle wouldn't let him give me anything. My aunt threatened to divorce him but that still didn't change his heart."

Sedric breathed a sigh of relief, looking at the pill bottles she had opened. She would live.

As his body slackened—thanking Allah—she took advantage, bringing her fist up into her mouth and almost shoving more in. When he caught what she was doing, he pulled her wrist, making her spill some. She tried to crawl away from him—onto the sink counter and against the mirror—trying to leverage her legs to kick him. Her empty hand clawed at his neck.

Knowing he would have to hurt her to get her to stop, he did the thing that would cause the least damage:

He kissed her.

He let go of her wrists and kissed her. A fingers-in-hair, no-room-for-air (or pills) kind of kiss.

She dropped the pills to slap him, the pills scattering like seeds.

"Fine!" she shouted when he let go. "Fine!"

He minded his jaw, turning red from her abuse.

She turned her head from him to stare at the paint, trying her best to fade into the corner of wall and mirror. "It's not fine," he clucked, running his fingertips over her face to test her sensitivity. Their fight caused her forehead to bleed.

Her small brown eyes cut up at him.

He dug in his pocket, pulled out the ring. Put it in her face. "It's not fine if you have to hide this from me."

"Didn't do a good enough job of it." She plucked it from his fingers and examined it. She put it on her finger. "Aren't you going to wish me congratulations?"

"Is that what you disagreed with, then?" he asked, his voice low and hopeful.

"Sure," she shrugged. She smiled, showing no teeth. He hated when she smiled without teeth. Those smiles were meant to hurt him. Meant to tease him. He resisted the urge to force her mouth open again just to see the pearls.

She began to take the pins out of her hair, for they made it hard to fit into the corner comfortably. He watched her do so, unmoving in his *pinning* of her.

When she finished, she leaned back into the corner again, having no other choice. Her hair uncurling in messy angles like hatching meant to contrast her face.

"You going to marry him, then?"

"Guess I'll have to now," she gestured to the pills on the floor. *You dick.*

"Who is he?" He grabbed her chin, shook her until she looked at him. "Who?"

Stanza: The Sports section sucks balls.

"Rodrigo Rodriguez."

"A fucking downtown Chicano?"

"One of *the* Chicanos. Son of the Father who controls the drug mules distributing for the Blah-Blahs. I marry him and have a kid—preferably a boy, apparently—and woosh,"—she waved her hand, the engagement ring sparkling—"they will find it harder to kill family. They'll sever ties with Ghibla."

"That's it? That's all the trade is good for?"

"That's what I said." She leaned forward toward him. "I told Uncle, 'I can find us a better trade.' And he said, 'Go ahead and search. But this one is already found.' Couldn't find a Native for me like he's always gone on about but Mexican is indigenous enough, I guess."

"What?" The move was too desperate—there was something they weren't being told.

Lielyth looked over her shoulder at her reflection in the mirror. "I can divorce him once I have the baby, apparently. The Chicanos are big on babies. That and tequila. Apparently no one wants to marry this fucker and his daddy really wants grandkids. I'm no heir. I was simply a downpayment."

Sedric pulled her chin with a few fingertips and made her look at him, refusing to address her through the mirror. "I know Rodrigo. I know where he's stuck that dick of his. A baby's not worth catching whatever's on the end of it."

"You think I want a baby?" She laughed at him, showing teeth. "That's assuming we can even make one together. You know, I told Uncle that this might be a set up—that Rodrigo might be sterile and nothing will come of it besides an expensive fuck. But he seems to think the trade will start as soon as we tie the knot. 'The Indigenous keep their word!' he said."

"I won't let them force you into this." He put his sweaty forehead on hers.

She closed her eyes, too tired to object. "No one is forcing me into anything. I will willingly marry him."

"And you'll let him fuck you? A *stranger* fuck you?" He was watching her face as if it did not add up—as if Lielyth were a math problem he had calculated before.

"If it buys Uncle a bit of time—for whatever the fuck he's planning—then yes. Rodrigo isn't thrilled either, but he'll accept his punishment for apparently getting his younger brother arrested a few months back. His dad really wants him to settle down. And access to properties held in my name."

"It could get you killed—"

"You should have gone out tonight. Why didn't you? You could have been normal for once. The boys were going to stay in my rooms tonight to make sure I didn't run, but then they saw your car and knew you were still here. Fuck, they knew you'd check up on me when you heard me come in. Jesus, Sedric, you had the night off!"

She tried to push him away.

"Why are they so certain I wouldn't let you run?"

"They think you're loyal to my Uncle more than to me," she stood up, hoping he would make room for her as she did so, but he did not. She was speaking to his chest now. "They don't know otherwise."

"But they didn't invite me. That can't be so."

"But you didn't try and come, did you? You didn't ruin the plans."

"You didn't *want* me to come."

"I didn't," she agreed. "That would have messed up my own plans."

"Plans? What plans?"

She gestured to her face with a flippant air. "I was beaten for a reason. My acting had to be real. I threw my fit—demanded to keep you as a bodyguard even after I got married. Uncle agreed, but still had to show he was in control of me. Ten stiches later…"

"You *acted*, did you?"

"I had to make them think you were fucking me—that you controlled *me*. Oh, don't look at me like that. You know damn well what they all say about us. I simply confirmed it."

"So you control *me*, is it?"

"You control me more than you think, Sedric," she said up to him in disgust. In fact, she had no autonomy over her own space right now.

"And let me guess," he held up a finger before his snarling face. "You begged and begged the Boss to let you keep your lover—which I am not—" (but, would very much like to be, clearly)—"to make yourself look vulnerable. And he loved it. And so did the Chicano clan. They know they can get to you through me now. You fucking made me the target."

"What, did you think I'd actually run away with you? You think this beating was for you? Fuck you, Sedric!" she hissed up at his face.

"Pathetic. I thought you had more authority in this Family than to resort to scheming like this."

"Authority? You think I'm here because of my *authority?* It's by Uncle's grace I'm even alive, Sedric. He should have killed my parents, as I will do once he's dead. He spared me. *Me*. It is my duty to this Family, Sedric, to obey—otherwise, I've no purpose being part of it."

429

"I'm sick of being part of it," he growled down to her. "And by the looks of it, you are too." He pointed behind him, to the pill-spotted tiles. "We *can* leave, Lie."

"I'm not leaving."

"But that's exactly what you just tried to do." He grabbed the sides of her face and bared his teeth. "You can make me the target of your plans, that's fine. That's what I signed up for. But don't you dare leave me with your mess to clean up, understand?"

She refused to meet his eyes. Maybe he had gotten through to her this time. Maybe she would take down this wall.

"Can I take my shower now?"

A hopeful light faded in his face. "If you answer me one question," he replied, a knot forming in his throat. "Why the fuck did you make me get a vasectomy when you hired me, if not because you wanted to fuck me? Why did you pick me—of all the men—to be the one right here, right now, that you are hurting? All these years and I think I deserve an answer."

"Uncle paid you very well to get that vasectomy. I got to pick you so naturally he thought I wanted to fuck you."

"And you didn't let him think *otherwise*."

"I chose you because you had never looked at me before. Some of the men had considered me. But you? Never. I thought I would be safer with you. Even though I was—am—afraid of you. Thought I could buy you off. Why do you constantly ask this of me, as if the answer's changed?"

Indeed, these weren't things Sedric didn't already know, but they were things Lielyth had never stated so clearly, and with so much context.

On outings, Lielyth and Sedric were often mistaken for a couple. She got jealous stares from women much prettier than she. She wanted to tell them she hadn't snagged anything, no. She'd *bought*.

She wanted to be clear, especially to the plain ones like her, that he wasn't hers; that he was paid to be with her; that they shouldn't get their hopes up because he would never actually be hers. She hated the envy and awe in their eyes. She hated herself, sometimes, for being seen with him. For keeping him away from girls who had a chance.

"You got what you paid for, then," Sedric muttered, stepping aside.

She waited for him to leave the bathroom.

He saw that expectant look. "No, I'm not going anywhere after the stunt you just pulled, Lie."

"Need I remind you that I can get rid of you in one phone call?"

"And ruin the charade you've worked so hard for? Go ahead."

She huffed at him and stepped into the shower, clothes still on. Before she pulled the curtain: "If you didn't like it, you should've let me swallow them."

Stanza: The cards were shuffled.

He watched as she tossed her clothes over the curtain rod piece by piece. He had seen her naked at least three times before, but he had never supervised her taking a shower. Sure, he had handed her the phone as she was changing in a dressing room once or twice, but even then, she had prepared herself for his presence, covered her breasts with her arm before he entered so she could "handle" the emergency.

The second time he had seen her naked was when he walked in on her changing in her bedroom, about to ask her which car he should order to pull around. She had not screamed and he had not apologized. He had lingered there, in her doorway. Then he had closed the door. And then, he had opened it right back up to finish watching her. Perhaps I should call that the third time, but I won't. There's one more after this—after she had glared at him as she finished getting dressed. This later prompted an excursion to one of the Lakota's favored whorehouses, where Lielyth had ordered Sedric to pick a girl. When he refused, she picked one for him.

"Fuck you, Lie!" he had shouted at her, storming out of the building. She had tipped the girl saying, "It's not you, you are lovely. This is just how you train them." The girl had just nodded, barely able to say "Thank you" in English.

In the car, he had shouted at her, "What the hell was that? I thought you said you needed to pick up a delivery!"

But she had said nothing, merely waited for him to start driving.

"Why do you keep doing this to me?" he shouted again and again, like he wasn't sure he said it the first time.

"Giving you whores?" she asked him, crossing her legs as if this were the most normal conversation in the world. "I need to know you're fucking something."

"So it doesn't end up being you? Fuck, Lie. I'm Muslim. I can't do that!" He had pointed to the building.

She laughed through her nose. *Can't, but you have.* "You can fuck *me*, though, is that it? You can come into my room whenever you want and stare at my chest and your faith isn't threatened then? That it?"

"You—you are not a whore," he tried to clarify.

"Really? I've felt like one recently." Her countenance finally broke and she hid her mouth behind her fingers. She stared out the car window.

"Lie, we are—we're stuck together. That's why I try."

"No, we're not stuck. You can leave any time you want. I can't."

"I don't understand you."

"Good. I don't want you to."

"You should have told me to get out. Should have screamed," he had mumbled under his breath as he started the car.

"Don't put this on me. Control *yourself.*"

"So it's my fault I was attracted to you? Because I can really control that."

"You can keep a door closed. You can knock."

"You can lock doors."

She had no retort.

At the next stop light he said, "I would fuck all those girls if it would make you jealous. But I know it won't. I don't know what makes you jealous. But I swear to—" No, he wouldn't bring Allah into this. "If I ever find out…"

"You'll what?"

"I don't know. I don't fucking know."

The third time he had seen her naked was right after he had helped The Boss's boys during a rather large raid on a skimming casino that wasn't paying its "Lakota dues." Sedric had bashed a few faces in that were too busy looking outward. The Boss's head loan shark had been impressed and offered to let Sedric tag along more often "for these sorts of things." Lielyth had seen the light brighten in Sedric's eyes that night and it had scared her. Sedric had replied that he'd think about the offer, which Lielyth also overheard. It was that same night that Lielyth had told him she was going to bed, as she normally did, but hadn't gone to her room. She had just stood there as he watched TV. He noticed briefly that she was in her nightclothes in front of him, which she hardly ever allowed without acting embarrassed. But she wasn't embarrassed this time. "I know you normally fall asleep on the couch," she had said. "And I don't know the last time you've used your bed, but tonight you are going to."

"Do you not want me to watch TV or something out here anymore? Is it too loud?"

"You misunderstand me. Go to your room."

When he had not gotten the hint, she had walked across the living space and into his room. Gave him more than a hint.

By the time he made it to his room, she was already slipping off her pants. He had paused in the doorway as she took off her top and turned around.

"Are you—are you serious?" he asked, pushing in that nose and staring at her.

"I want you to stop sleeping on the couch," she had said.

He had taken his shirt off and come to her.

"No," she said, moving back as he tried to touch her. "That's not what this is."

"Then what is it?"

Her eyes cut to the bed, telling him to get in it.

433

Her head followed him as he moved.

"If you don't want to be here then why are you?" He lifted the covers and sat down, manspreading as if blocking her from access to the bed.

"I could ask the same of you. If you'd rather work as Uncle's man, then why don't you?" She had stepped up to the bed, but had not gotten in.

"Oh, I see. You won't fuck me unless you're trying to get something out of me?"

"I'm not going to fuck you."

He had snorted through his nose. Itched that nose. "Then thank you for gracing me with your mere presence." He gestured to her body—naked except for those panties, now.

"Take your pants off."

"Is this some sort of test, then?"

"Take you dick out, now."

"No. Come in the bed with me."

She shook her head. "I want you to agree to go on their next excursion. But only if I can come along."

"Don't you already go along on the safe ones?"

"Yes, but I want you to tell them that."

"Why?"

"So it looks like your loyalty is to me first. That will impress Uncle, especially since they won't believe you. Not after what they saw tonight."

He hadn't paid full attention to her words then. How could he? Her pale breasts were taking up too much of his thoughts, outlined by her summer tan. She had been darker than him then. "You think this is the only way to convince me? Like I'm some pervert? Just get out."

She had turned around, not bothering to pick up her clothes. "Like I said, I want you to stop sleeping on the couch. We bought you a bed for a reason. I can buy you much more." And she had closed his door behind her. The next morning, her cleaning lady had knocked and entered Sedric's room. Speaking Spanish, the old woman greeted him like always and mumbled on and on in what Sedric always called "cursing him out, probably." But she stopped suddenly in her normal conversation-making when she noticed Lielyth's bed clothes on his floor. She smiled and nodded to him, probably saying something like "I knew one day you two would slip up. You have always been so hard to catch!" And she had just picked them up and went on tidying like always, mumbling on in Spanish.

Stanza: And in this corner, we have...

And now Sedric was staring at her clothes on the floor again, the ones in front of the shower (*our* obligatory shower scene). Except this time, there were pills there, too.

He looked up. She had just turned on the shower. "Wait," he said, pulling the curtain back. He reached around her and took her razor. Just for the insult.

She had jumped back, making the water spray directly across his torso. "Fuck, Sedric!" She shouted at him, closing the curtain back.

He sat down on the toilet, shaking off the water on his arm. He looked down at his shirt, soaking wet.

"You can't do shit like that!" she said, finally moving in the shower again.

"I barely saw you!" he griped back at her, unbuttoning his shirt so he could take it off.

He could feel the fumes of her hatred wafting toward him. Or, maybe it was just the steam of the shower. He tossed her razor in the sink beside him and took off his watch, checking it for water damage. The seconds ticked by and she had barely moved, the water hitting the same places behind the curtain. Perhaps those pills were kicking in and she was finding it hard to function. He needed to get her to talk.

"I forgot to mention, Lie. You know when we found that storage unit of the Taylor's full of all that collectable memorabilia and we used it to cover their debt?— we used it in the comic book store?"

"What about it?"

435

"Lucky Hardball said he knew the kid who used to rent the unit—said the kid hadn't checked in for years but had paid off the bill for that decade. And when I say kid, Lie, I mean *kid*. Sammy said he was barely, like, twelve. Where do you think a kid gets money like that?"[111]

She said nothing. He listened for a while, to make sure she was moving about.

"Hardball owed us for a reason, Sedric." He gave them storage space, they gave him plenty of coke to use and sell as he pleased. And he used more than he sold.

"Hardball was *sure* it was a kid, Lie. A black kid. Hardball swears the kid had to be dealing. Hardball only let the under-aged fuck rent it out because of the dirt he had on him. You tell me how a little kid can manipulate Hardball like that, Lie? I *told* you Inky was using kids to distribute. We have to put a stop to that. Little kids with big mouths, manipulating our employees. They're gonna get fucking shot."

"Sounds like this kid did, if he hasn't been around."

He heard the shampoo lid close.

Heartless bitch.

He watched the shower's steam float about him. "But seriously, Lie. Inky's got a black nerd working for him. What's that say about us?"

"That you're jealous a little kid has more dirt on Hardball than you? And I doubt it was Inky. That kid had thousands of dollars worth of shit in that unit. He knew what he was doing. He was more likely working for someone else. Someone's nephew or something."

"This is exactly what you said about Cotton's prostitute—the one who *didn't* blackmail him. You give people too much credit."

(Let me wow you with other made-up criminal nicknames and illegal exploits...)

"Speaking of credit and prostitutes, I got another call from that weirdass grad student who seems to think I have [let's just say John Milton's] personal copy of [maybe Ovid's *Metamorphosis* in Greek, because it sounds fancy]."

"But you do, don't you?"

Yeah, but no one was supposed to *know about it*.

---

[111] An Automaton, that's where.

He itched his neck, scruff irritating him. "What was her name again? Gobbler?"

"*Gabbler*," Lielyth corrected, shouting over the roar of the water. "Anyway, the bitch thinks she can blackmail me into letting her see it. She's writing a paper on it or something. You should hear the voicemail she left me."[112]

"Want me to have the boys look into it?"

"No. She's harmless enough. I think I might even meet her. I mean, anyone with the balls enough to try and blackmail a Lakota—while knowing what that name means—deserves my attention."

His face scrunched. She had just tried to kill herself and yet she was making future plans for a black market book she couldn't even read? This wasn't adding up.

He shook his head, leaning over to pick up a few plastic bottles of product they'd knocked over in their tussle. As he did so, he smelled himself. This had been a rough night for him. He needed a shower...

But that would be hard, with having to watch Lielyth's every goddamn move.

His own smell—a smell of smoke and sweat—made him cringe. He couldn't stand it; he shouldn't allow her to make him suffer it more.

He scowled at the shower curtain.

He stood up, undid his belt, took his shirt—pants—shoes—socks off, pushed back the curtain, stepped in the shower...

She jumped back, under the arch of the falling water. Her wide eyes confessed she hadn't expected him to ever do something like this. She didn't even think to cover herself, so stunned at the naked sight of him.

He put his hands out like a man trying to calm a wild animal who might dash for it. Her eyes darted to her end of the shower curtain, but his hand would catch her first

---

[112] Well, I guess the *other* cat's out of the bag. Surprise? I'm a she/her pronoun. And I really wanted that interview.

and she might slip. Slipping was no certain death, only bruising and pain. The thought still tempted her.

When it was clear she wouldn't run, he pulled his portion of curtain back and stepped into the water.

"The hell are you doing?" she asked, true terror in her voice—a voice almost drowned out by the showerhead.

"Taking a shower. Testing myself."

"I could scream!"

He rolled his eyes as she folded over, trying to hide herself. "I'm not going to touch you. I need a shower too. How the hell you think I'll be able to do so otherwise, with you under a suicide watch, huh? It's nothing I haven't seen before." He snatched up the soap from the rack and mumbled, "Tries to fucking overdose [smh]."

He lathered up vigorously, glaring at her as if this was worse for him.

She started to laugh with her eyes tight, turning her head to the side and showing a sliver of teeth. This made him pause as he rinsed.

"You think it's funny?"

Water spit off her lips as she laughed. "You think you're so clever, don't you? To come up with an excuse to—to flash your dick at me." She gestured to it.

"Excuse my excuse." He gave a stolid shrug and stepped forward to rinse again.

This only made her laugh more—made her chest move in a way that matched how those teeth made him feel. Even if it was the laughter of someone on a bunch of pain pills, he couldn't help but get hard.

"Would you stop? Stop fucking laughing." He grew stern. "Seriously, stop!" he barked. This had not been part of the plan.[113]

She noticed her effect and became dead silent as she stared at *it*. The cold took her. She began to shiver at the sight.

"It will go away," he said, glaring at her, blaming her.

She averted her eyes and attempted to hide her shivering.

---

[113] Yeah, sure it hadn't.

"Would you fucking stand in the water too?" he gestured to the open space beside him in the fancy shower-tub. "Making me feel bad."

"I'm fine here."

But he grabbed her arm, planning to step out of the water when he finally dragged her over.

She lifted her arms as he did so, sliding down the wall as if to escape his advances—pushed herself against the tile.

"I'm not going to fucking rape you," he hissed. "Would you please?" He stepped back from her. "Stand here, damn it."

She stood up, still shaking. "I'm sorry," she said. "I'm sorry." She couldn't look him in the eye, he was so angry. What made it worse was that he wasn't hard anymore. She disgusted him.

She had never seen that expression of hurt on his face before. Perhaps because he had never seen that look of terror in hers.

"I'm finished, really," she told him, still looking down, still cupping and crossing herself.

"Let me wash this fucking grease from my hair and I will be too." He pointed at the shampoo behind her so she might hand it to him. No sudden movements.

She picked up her pink bottle, water bouncing off it as she passed it to him. "I'd never want to put you in danger," she said. She took the bottle back. "You are a target. That comes with the job. But I wouldn't want anything to happen to you."

"You just tried to kill yourself, Lie." He rinsed his hair—what little he had the barber leave—and rubbed his face under the water quickly. He hated closing his eyes in front of her—one less second he had to watch her. "They'd kill me if you ever succeeded. So don't tell me you fucking care."

Her eyes grew red at the thought.

He turned off the water, touching her to lean forward. He pulled back the curtain for her, gesturing for her to leave safely. He handed her a towel and took one for himself. She didn't bother to dry off properly, instead using it to quickly cover up.

"You laugh at my attempt at modesty?" she asked him, coming to the sink. She began to push back her dripping hair and examine her stiches. "I may protect my cunt like the fucking Mona Lisa, but that doesn't mean anyone should wait in line to see it." She began to brush her teeth, squirting out too much toothpaste and cursing.

"We did wait in line to see it, you and I," he said, massaging the towel over his wet hair. He still had not covered himself up. She was trying to ignore the fact— ignore his new confidence. The ice was too broken.

"And I fucking hated the crowd. Nothing you can't see on a postcard." She waved her toothbrush at him.

He had to look away as she inserted the brush, her teeth flashing at him. "Says the woman with a black market manuscript."

"If you owned the Mona Lisa, then you wouldn't need the damn postcards to avoid the lines."

Sedric would have laughed...if it had been Lielyth who said it. It was a casual and unfamiliar voice from the anteroom.

"I've seen it." As an afterthought, "Before it was chopped up."

Before the man finished his sentence, Sedric had shoved Lielyth behind him. Cautiously, he peered around the doorframe he had just busted moments ago. Lielyth dropped her toothbrush.

Sedric reeled himself back in and pushed her back into the bathtub—as if the tile might protect her.

"Who is it?" Lielyth whispered, eyes swelling with fear. *How much had they heard?*

Stanza: Team Sedric.

Sedric shook his head; he didn't recognized the man lounging on their couch, hands behind his **Chullo**-hatted head, bare feet crossed and resting on the sofa's arm, his smug smile too ready to grow wider.

The man had waved to him. *Waved.* Waved in a "hello, neighbor" kind of way.

The reclining man resembled a dandified hobo with his wiry mud-red hair, his chin sprouting stubble like metal does rust, his skin kissed with a shade of grime.

"You can come on out. I'm unarmed. Not here to hurt you." He turned on the TV and muted it. They could hear the buzzing.

"Who are you? How'd you get in here?" Sedric shouted, doing up the towel around his waist. He cursed himself for not bringing in his gun. He searched for the phone in his pants pockets laying on the floor. He handed it to Lielyth.

She thought twice before unlocking it.

"Shh. Not so loud. You, my new friends, can call me Julian. And I let myself in, a-thankyouverymuch."

"Didn't you lock the door?" Sedric scolded Lielyth.

"Of course she locked the door!" the man replied. He must have had bat ears. "I didn't *use* the door."

"You've been here this entire—whole time?" Sedric clamored, trying to force him back on subject. *He heard everything.*

"I suppose so," the man replied. They could hear the shrug in his voice. They heard him sit up, groaning as if some strain. "OK, I admit I've heard your entire conversation. Boy do you guys have some issues to work out." He paused, seeming to recollect. "Actually, I was brought in a bag. I should probably tell you that so you don't think I broke in. Everyone else inside the house is fine. I promise. They don't know I'm here."

"A bag?" Sedric tried to keep him talking while Lielyth texted for help. Not that anyone would be checking their phones this late at night.

"Yes, my partner slipped me into Lielyth's clutch at the party last night. Or, this night, really. Time's so relative."[114]

"What the fuck do you mean?" Sedric demanded.

"Do I have to *mean* anything at all, other than what I say?" the stranger questioned, asking himself as if too tired to be sure. Sedric and Lielyth both looked at one another, to confirm they both heard the same thing.

Lielyth tried to call someone she thought might be up—but of course half of them were drunk and out cold because of the party. No pickup.

"Stop calling for help. It will only make things weird. Then I might *really* have to kill someone. Please don't make me kill someone. That was *not* on the agenda, kiddos."

"Just tell me how the hell you got in here, and we might let *you* live."

They could hear him chuckle, a very gentle sound. "I just told you, kid. Lielyth's purse. Why don't you come on out, so we can have a little chat? I promise you, I'm unarmed. I'm a pacifist."

"And a liar too?" Sedric asked him. The joke got his adrenaline pumping. He gestured for Lielyth to stay put while he stepped out.

"Looking for this?" the man asked him, holding up the nearest gun Sedric was going to shoot for. "Could smell this hunk of metal the minute I came in. Here, take it if it will make you feel better." He tossed it to Sedric.

"Jesus Christ," Sedric cursed as he caught it. "You fucking lunatic!" He checked the lock quickly and pointed it at the man.

The stranger adjusted his **skullcap**—hadn't he been wearing a llama-patterned, poof-topped Chullo before? We all know he had.

With his fingerless-gloved hands, he picked up Sedric's half-used cigarette and reached into his long jacket's breast pocket, ignoring Sedric as Sedric growled, "Watch it, now!"

But all he removed was a matchbook, showing him with raised hands. Oddly enough, Sedric hadn't really worried about a weapon. The man didn't seem the type.

---

[114] Wait. Is this Madus or Fletcher?

Putting the crumpled cigarette in his lips and pulling a match between the rough strips, he stated, "I don't carry weapons around. Don't need them. Well, that all depends on what you call a weapon, I guess. Com'on, sit down." He gave a lazy point to the chair across from him.

Sedric looked from the chair back to the man:

The man was now pushing back a **Rastafarian** hat.

Is he fucking with me? How did he do that? "I'd rather stand." He almost wanted Lielyth to witness this, to prove he wasn't going crazy.

The visitor took out his cigarette and yawned, smoke drifting from his gaping mouth. "Have it your way, then," he tried to say through his silent scream. It was so late—past his bedtime! He scratched his scruffy neck, the movement sounding like someone rubbing sandpaper.

The man studied his cigarette for a brief second—where had his matches disappeared to? Julian had only taken up smoking to be able to follow Joslyn around on her smoking breaks. She smoked as much as Odys. He, however, chewed gum as much as Dorian. But the smoking made him feel like an individual. Made him feel like he was *choosing* his addiction; just has he had chosen a new name to match hers, he was choosing Joslyn.

He popped his neck, thinking about his *choices.* When he lifted his head, his hat was gone—Sedric had seen it vanish! Back into his head.

"Whatthehell are you?" Sedric readied to shoot him.

Lielyth's ears perked up, noticing the panic in Sedric's voice—the oddness of the question.

"Well, I'm an Automaton. Specifically, one sent by the god Vulcan to answer your prayers."

"Automicon?"

"Ah-toe-ma-ton." He mouthed out the syllables as if Sedric didn't speak English. "Well, that's what they used to call me, but really I'm more like a shape shifter these days. I can wind myself up." He snapped his fingers and made his entire body a dark, metallic nickel. "Look like a robot, don't I?" The man flashed his metal grill at him.

His voice shaking, "Lie, get out here."

She peeked around the corner and jumped when she saw the metal-man sitting on her couch, smoking. "Oh my god," she mouthed. *What pills did I take?*

"You see it too?"

The fucking Tin-man from Oz? "Yeah, I see him."

Julian crossed his legs and faded back to his more "normal" coloring. "So, now that's out of the way, I want you to know that you've been Chosen to play a game, Sedric—a game involving gods, beings like myself, and humans. You're the human in this scenario. You don't have a choice whether or not to play. Neither do I, really. But we can make it worth your while."

"We?"

"The other players on 'Team Sedric.'" He used bunny ears to show its titular nature. "Well, once we draft them, anyway." He waved a hand, as if they could get to that part later. "The important thing right now, Sedric, is that I can help you get out. And Lielyth too. No one has to get hurt." He pointed at her and then brought that same finger to his mouth to bite his dirty nail. Mumbling as he bit it, "I can make *you* the one in charge, Sedric."

"In charge of what?"

"This situation? The entire Lakota family? Anything you want? Hell, that's the reason you're so *Chooseable*—your lack of choices in this world; you were throwing a fit in here because you didn't get to be her *servant* for the night. Yeah, kid, we've been watching you."

Their eyes looked around for the cameras.

"This can be *yours,* kid. You can still keep all of this,"—Julian's eyes danced around the room, meaning their lifestyle—"Granted, things will change. But we're not taking it away. You need to make a decision: Willingly play or to be forced. It's no coincidence that your happy little *arrangement* is being disturbed with a marriage proposal. Time is of the essence. Especially since Adimar plans on kidnapping Lielyth very soon, so my sources say."

"Kidnap me?"

"He plans to give your head to the Blahblahblahs or whatever the heck you call 'em as a way of getting close to Genji Ghibla of said Blahblahblahs. Then, he's gonna kill Genji and take over both Indian Mafia clusterfucks."

"There's no possible way that freelancer can pull that off," Sedric said in disbelief (he had heard of Adimar, maybe even technically worked with him before signing on officially with the Lakotas in his previous work experience). "They won't follow him even if he does. You're making that shit up."

"He can," the Automaton said, "Especially if he has ex-gods and people like me working for him." He tapped his chest and then bit his nail again, growing more nervous at his words. He didn't like being mean—giving them an ultimatum—but he knew he had to. "Can you put that gun down, please? I don't need it going off and making everyone downstairs and upstairs shit their pants. It won't work on me anyway."

Sedric lowered his gun, laughing. "I'm hallucinating!" he said to Lielyth. "You've driven me insane and now I think I can see fucking Iron Man over here."

There was a knock on the door. "Ms.? Sedric?" it asked. "Open up!"

And when they looked back, the Automaton was gone. Well, what they *supposed* was "gone." Little did they know he had fallen as a paperclip between the cushions.

"I got your text," Jeff said, coming in as Sedric opened the door.

"It was me," Lielyth said, stepping where he could see. "I thought I heard something. Was a false alarm. Probably an—an owl or something." She pointed to her balcony doors, where birds were known to roost for the night.

The omen made Jeff's superstitious eyes widen. "Owls?" Then, Jeff took a step back and looked from Sedric to Lielyth, both still in towels. A smirk spread across his face. "You get mad at her? That what this is, Sed? You scare her?"

Sedric's nostrils flared at what Jeff implied. "Get the fuck out, man."

Jeff raised his hands, chuckling. "OK, Sed. But keep your phone away from her next time, man. I won't escalate this but you gottah be more discrete if you gonna be all mad about it. You one lucky bastard, man. You got a real good situation. You're lucky the boss lets her keep you. It ain't her fault, man."

Sedric stepped in front of his view so he'd stop ogling her. "She's fine. Get out."

"You better cool it if you want her fiancé to let her keep you, though." Jeff shook his round head, still chuckling as he left them.

"Fucker doesn't respect me," Lielyth hissed at the door, as if she were about to follow Jeff and claw his eyes out. Sedric pushed her back. "I have no power over them, see?"

Sedric locked the door behind him and turned back to stare at the couch. He adjusted the towel slipping down his hips, dragged her away from the door. *We have bigger issues right now.* He pointed to the couch. *Like the djinn granting us wishes.*

"I think I killed myself and this is limbo or something. I don't feel well, Sedric." She put her hand on her stomach.

"It's the pills," he assured her, still staring at the couch. "But the seeing things? I don't think that's their fault."

"What—what was he even saying?" Lielyth asked him. "Why does he want *you?*"

"Now like I was saying," Julian said, appearing once more, making them jump.

"Jesus!" Lielyth cursed, covering her mouth as she clung to the wall.

"If you want me to get you out of here—no marriage, no kidnapping, no more taking shit—then there will be a distraction tomorrow at five in the morning." He looked at a watch that appeared on his wrist. "Well, since it's technically morning already, let me correct myself: in a few, my partner will cause a distraction. When it happens, I'm going to escort you out of here so we can regroup."

"Where?" Lielyth asked as if he were some trickster.

"Not far," Julian said. "The game is coming to us, no doubt. We can't escape it. But we need to be free to talk without so many humans around. They won't understand. And we don't make them safe."

"But why Sedric?" Lielyth asked. *Why is he so special?*

"We're going to make Sedric a Master of gods," Julian said, picking underneath his nails and watching them. "And you, Ms. Lakota, can come along for the fun of it. We'll need you, Lielyth. You're great leverage."

Old language dies hard.

"What did you say your name was?" Lielyth asked.

"Julian."

"Julian what?" Sedric asked.

"Just Julian."

Sometimes Fletcher, when I forget.

Sedric tried to play along, as if he wasn't going mad, "And what if we don't want to go? Why do we have to leave, if the game is going to come to us?"

"Oh, you want to go my friend," Julian stood up. His hand formed into a gun and showed them why.

Sedric raised his own, but felt like his was nothing more than a toy, compared.

Julian walked up to Sedric. "Use it on me. Go ahead. You know it won't work. But I need to show you what will happen." He pushed the gun into his chest, dipping it into his fluid shell. The tip of it pulled out—just a little, but still touching—with a silencer. Julian's body. He made Sedric pull the trigger.

Lielyth flinched when it happened. But the man did not fall. Instead, he opened his mouth and plucked out the bullet that had just pierced his chest. He shook out his tongue and licked his lips. "Blech." *Gunpowder is the worst taste.*

He took Sedric's palm (his own gun and the silencer had disappeared somewhere, willingly surrendered) and dropped the golden ammo.

"I'm Alchemy—Alchemy!—personified, motherfucker. And I'm offering you power and glory and fucking control,"—his eyes darted to Lielyth on that last promise. "It's not going to be clean or pretty, but you should damn well take my advice. You both are in danger. Even if Adimar wasn't in the mix, I'd still say you need some divine intervention right about now. The Chicanos have their own plans with Lielyth. Her Uncle is in a corner right now. He's using it to buy more time."

"What do you mean?" Lielyth dared him to speak ill of her blood.

Sedric held her back.

"I mean he hasn't told you that Adimar has bought off [three random names here that sound important and connote a loss of 50% of Lakota operations in some specific area of crime]. He just found out last week. They turned against him. That's why this sudden marriage."

"Prove it."

"I can't, but why would I lie? You've got enough reasons as it is to believe me. I don't get to choose either, and I'm fucking scared too. But we're going to play this game together. And guess what? We're guaranteed to fucking win. We've got cheat codes. We just have to put on a good show."

Still cupping the golden bullet, Sedric found himself speaking the most ridiculous sentence: "If I'm 'Team Sedric' who's the other team?"

"There's going to be more than two teams, probably. And they'll all want to kill you."

"And so I'm going to have to kill the other teams?"

"No. Just the other Chosens on said teams. Starting with *Adimar*."

SEDRIC IBN SINA:[115] Chosen.

WHY?: Because Julian and Joslyn were told to choose.

WHY?: Because Cestus told them the box was now spitting out prophecies. He called them up and said, "You know, I took the box because you were

---

[115] One of his many names. That I've changed. Obviously.

forgetting to live. You kept waiting for it to tell you what to do. Wanting it to give you an oracle. And it finally has. Vulcan's going to make Himself part of the game, it says. Says that when He comes, you should side with Him and His endorsement."

"An incarnation? But that's cheating," Joslyn had said over speakerphone.

But Cestus had only sighed. "Isn't the box cheating too, by telling us what He's planning? This whole game is rigged. The other gods just play along to find out how."

"What did it say *exactly?* Read it to us," she urged, for she knew it was a poem like scripture.

"I have meditated on the meaning and there is no other interpretation. Don't pretend to doubt my exegesis."

But he read it to them anyway.

WHY?: Because they deserved to know the wretched commandments, so that they might break them.

"Why don't you give the box back to Maurice? You know he wants it, Cestus," Julian had pushed.

"No," Cestus had answered, the cell reception making his voice scratchier than usual. They had leaned in, as not to miss a word. "He will destroy it. You give Maurice the box and there will be one less channel open. Don't you see? Vulcan always meant for Maurice to have the box, to get angry and want to destroy the box—as we all once considered doing. But if that happens, if Maurice destroys the box, then the silence will be worse. Or, He'll just give us another object to venerate and follow. It has to be stuck in limbo. Worthless. Just as Maurice is stuck in limbo. Otherwise we're all going to kill each other like the gods want."

"He sounds like Q, Julian."

449

"If that's your concern, Cestus, then why are you telling us about the tissue that came out of it?"

"Because I'm hoping you'll do the opposite of what the tissue wants you to do. If Vulcan's Avatar is coming to us—going to be an Automaton like us in some fuckedup version of the Nativity—then this is our chance to get even with Him. Don't let Him be Christ."

But, my reader, they would. They did.

Learn more at:

www.circodelherreroseries.com

This book is indie.

Support us by leaving an honest review.